TO KISS A ROGUE

"I should find another place to hide. If William finds us together, there won't be a winner. We both lose."

"Not necessarily." Pulling his hand free, Royce used one finger to tilt up her chin. Before she realized what he intended, his mouth covered hers.

He didn't kiss like a St. Clare. Not that she'd ever been French kissed by any of her relations, but she was sure no St. Clare kissed like this. No stuffy, self-righteous lord could know how to make her shiver with longing with just his mouth. This must be the rogue. Only a rogue would be able to dissolve her bones with his lips. And his wicked tongue. And his hands, one holding her face, the other . . . the other sliding down her neck . . . lower . . .

Winding her arms around his neck, Arden melted into the kiss . . .

BOOK YOUR PLACE ON OUR WEBSITE AND MAKE THE READING CONNECTION!

We've created a customized website just for our very special readers, where you can get the inside scoop on everything that's going on with Zebra, Pinnacle and Kensington books.

When you come online, you'll have the exciting opportunity to:

- View covers of upcoming books
- Read sample chapters
- Learn about our future publishing schedule (listed by publication month *and author*)
- Find out when your favorite authors will be visiting a city near you
- Search for and order backlist books from our online catalog
- Check out author bios and background information
- Send e-mail to your favorite authors
- Meet the Kensington staff online
- Join us in weekly chats with authors, readers and other guests
- Get writing guidelines
- AND MUCH MORE!

Visit our website at
http://www.zebrabooks.com

TO TAME A ROGUE

Linda Kay

ZEBRA BOOKS
Kensington Publishing Corp.
http://www.zebrabooks.com

ZEBRA BOOKS are published by

Kensington Publishing Corp.
850 Third Avenue
New York, NY 10022

All Kensington titles, imprints, and distributed lines are available at special quantity discounts for bulk purchases for sales promotions, premiums, fund raising, educational, or institutional use.

Special book excerpts or customized printings can also be created to fit specific needs. For details, write or phone the office of the Kensington Special Sales Manager: Kensington Publishing Corp., 850 Third Avenue, New York, NY 10022. Attn. Special Sales Department. Phone: 1-800-221-2647.

First Printing: March, 2001
10 9 8 7 6 5 4 3 2 1

Printed in the United States of America

To Brenda L. Lester
for twenty years of friendship.

Prologue

Arden St. Clare saw the shop at the corner of Lafitte's Alley and Royal Street for the first time on Friday. She was positive the storefront had been as vacant on Thursday as it had been for several months before. She might have been slightly euphoric when she'd walked home after the momentous luncheon with Uncle Fred yesterday, but she would have noticed a new shop.

Not that this place looked new. Anyone not familiar with the French Quarter would have thought it had been there forever. The name on the artfully faded wooden sign swinging over the sidewalk was Any Time, Any Place. A travel agency? Moving closer, Arden looked at the posters in the shop windows, recognizing the Roman Coliseum and the Acropolis.

Something about the posters wasn't right. Tilting her head, Arden stared at the art work until she identified the problem. The ruins weren't pictured as they looked today, but as they must have looked when new. "How odd," she murmured. "A new shop that looks old, and old monuments that look new."

Arden peered in the window, trying to see past the posters. No one was in view. Any Time, Any Place was not open for business yet. She felt a stab of disappointment as a familiar restlessness began stirring through her. Now would be a perfect time to leave town. Carnival season was in full swing, and grant applications to the Freret Foundation had fallen off in direct proportion to the number of parades and balls distracting both locals and tourists. She didn't have a thing to do at work.

Nevertheless, Uncle Fred would not like it if she signed up for a tour or a cruise. Travel on business was one thing, but a pleasure trip? She could see him pursing his lips in disapproval. A St. Clare never did anything solely for pleasure, he would remind her. Except make money. The accumulation and preservation of wealth could be extremely pleasurable, according to St. Clare family philosophy.

Frivolity, on the other hand, was frowned upon, unless it contributed to the bottom line. That same bottom line explained why even the stuffy St. Clares would unbend enough to participate in New Orleans's famous festivities. Mardi Gras was good for business.

In moderation.

Moderation meant a St. Clare would never wear a feathered mask and ride on a *papier-mâché* float throwing cheap plastic beads to the crowds lining St. Charles Avenue. Rubbing elbows with movie stars and musicians might appeal to some, but the St. Clares would never consider attending a post-parade party for the unwashed masses—meaning anyone who could afford a ticket—in the Super Dome. That would not be proper.

Uncle Fred, the CEO of St. Clare Spices and Arden's financial guardian, was a stickler for propriety. His wife, Arden's Aunt Marie, was even more obsessed with decency and decorum, possibly because she was only a St. Clare by marriage and not by blood. Therefore, she had to work harder at upholding the family honor. Aunt Marie piously agreed that balls and parades, masking and carousing, were much too pagan for the St. Clares.

They could not completely ignore Fat Tuesday, however. Each carnival season, Uncle Fred and the other family members on the Board of Directors made judicial appearances at the more sedate balls—those sponsored by the old-line krewes—and Arden was allowed to go along. Mardi Gras was a tradition, after all, and the St. Clares were certainly traditionalists. There hadn't been a rebel in the family for years.

Not since 1980.

Arden sighed. The family still blamed her parents' tragic deaths that year on Arden's mother's careless daring. If Jeanne Freret St. Clare, the last of the foolhardy Frerets, hadn't urged her husband to race a freight train to a crossing, they might be alive today. Given her notoriously frivolous Freret blood, it was no wonder that the surviving St. Clares still harbored fears that Arden had inherited her mother's appetite for fun and adventure. It was bad enough that Jeanne had left the Freret fortune to a philanthropic foundation instead of to her daughter, who would, Uncle Fred had no doubt, have invested her mother's bequest in St. Clare Spices.

Therefore, Uncle Fred and the Board of Directors kept her on a very short leash.

They meant well. Her relatives might be stuffy and overprotective, but they were not cruel. They only wanted to make sure she grew up to be a true St. Clare, serious, sedate and nothing at all like her mother, the giddy, fun-loving woman who'd captured the heart of Stephen St. Clare, Arden's father. On the surface, they had succeeded. Arden St. Clare looked and acted every inch the perfect lady, refined and well-mannered.

Arden knew better than to tell her relatives that on occasion she dreamed silly dreams or that, every now and then, she had an almost uncontrollable urge to do something shocking. She was fond of her stodgy guardians and would never intentionally upset them.

With a last wistful look at the travel posters, Arden decided to come back next week, after Mardi Gras. The shop would surely be open then. Before she turned away, a movement inside the window caught her eye.

Shading her eyes with her hands, Arden peered inside the shop. Someone was behind the counter now. Pushing open the door, she walked inside. She could pick up a few brochures, make tentative reservations.

If she felt especially daring, she might even purchase tickets.

Once inside the tiny shop, Arden looked around. Any Time, Any Place was definitely a travel agency. A shiny new computer was sitting on an antique mahogany counter, next to a red plastic telephone. Colorful brochures were piled on a scarred but authentic Sheraton table in front of the window, and the walls were decorated with more posters. There were scenes of a Victorian Christmas, a Civil War battle, and a Viking ship. At the bottom of the posters, instead of the names of airlines or cruise ships, there were dates—1884, 1862, 1309.

Again she noticed that the posters had an immediacy not usual in pictures of historic scenes. The paintings were very realistic. If she didn't know better, she'd swear they were photographs.

The man whose movement had caught her eye stood behind the counter smiling encouragingly. He looked like a Dickens character come to life. Short and pudgy, he had a face a cherub would envy. He sported a glorious ginger mustache which curled under his ruddy cheeks and over his smiling mouth.

"Tobias Thistlewaite, at your service," he said, bowing from the waist.

"Mr. Thistlewaite," Arden murmured, extending her hand. He took her fingertips and brushed his mustache across them. It tickled, making her grin. "I'm Arden St. Clare. I'm thinking about taking a trip."

"Any time, any place. Our name, and our motto. What time did you have in mind? For our purposes, time is of the essence." He beamed at her.

"Soon. This week, if possible. I want to go somewhere far away. Somewhere romantic. Maybe even a little dangerous." She eyed the Viking ship poster. "A cruise, perhaps."

Mr. Thistlewaite followed her gaze, then shook his head regretfully. "That would meet one of your criteria—it would be dangerous. However, we really don't recommend that particular voyage for a young woman traveling alone. Those lusty fellows can't be trusted not to ravish our clients. Rape and pillage was their forte, after all."

Rape and pillage? Startled, Arden began edging toward the door. "I believe I should give this more thought, Mr. Thistlewaite. I'll come back another time."

"No time like the present. And we won't be here for long. A week at the most—depending on whether the solar winds stay calm. Extraordinary solar activity wreaks havoc with the space-time continuum, you know. Now, let's choose the proper trip. But I cannot in good conscience recommend the Viking cruise." He glanced at the poster in the window. "A trip to ancient Rome is a bit risky, too. Especially if one is a Christian. If I might suggest a gentler era?"

Arden moved back to the counter. "Oh, I understand. You arrange historical trips. I've heard of those. People with an interest in a particular time go on tours with historians familiar with the period."

Uncle Fred certainly couldn't object to a trip like that. Educational and boring—just the thing for a staid and stuffy St. Clare. A devilish idea began to tickle the back of her mind. Once away from New Orleans, she could leave a tour and strike out on her own. She could have *fun!*

Arden's heartbeat speeded up. She could have an adventure. A romantic adventure, if she met the right sort of man. Or even the wrong sort. Either way, no one but she would ever know.

"What do you recommend?" she asked, smiling at her daring thoughts. Excitement began to thrum through her veins.

Mr. Thistlewaite pointed to a poster in the corner that she hadn't noticed before. It showed beautiful women dressed in high-waisted gowns being twirled around a candlelit ballroom by handsome men.

"They are waltzing, aren't they?" She frowned. How could the waltz look daring? The St. Clares waltzed.

"Are you interested in the Regency period? It would be a perfect time for an attractive young lady like you, an heiress."

Arden started. "How did you know I was an heiress?"

"I read about it in the society column. Yesterday, you and your financial guardian were observed lunching at Galatoire's. It is assumed he used the occasion of your twenty-fifth birthday to hand over control of the trust fund left you by your parents. A fund whose assets are valued in excess of twenty million dollars."

Arden hadn't read the paper that morning, but she was sure that her lunch with Uncle Fred hadn't been mentioned in the society pages. St. Clares never made the society columns. They paid money—lots of it—not to. Society columns were for the vulgar new rich, not for a family that had been successful and wealthy since the Battle of New Orleans. "The story must be in the business section."

Mr. Thistlewaite took a copy of the *Times-Picayune* from under the counter. "You're right. My mistake. Nevertheless, you are an heiress and a perfect candidate for our Regency tour."

"The Regency? When was that?" Arden frowned, searching her memory. "Oh, I know—the early nineteenth century. Jane Austen. Lord Byron."

"Yes, indeed. Eighteen-eleven to eighteen-twenty. The age of romantics and rebels."

Before Arden could deny she was either of those things, Tobias began rummaging through the brochures on the counter. "Would you prefer to go before or after the Battle of Waterloo?"

"I beg your pardon?" She was having trouble keeping up with Mr. Thistlewaite's odd way of selling his tours. "I'm not sure about an historical tour. Don't you have something more exciting?"

Tobias Thistlewaite's hands stilled. He looked her in the eye. "What could be more exciting than a trip through time?"

Arden's only response was a blank stare.

With a chuckle, Tobias added, "I thought you knew, my dear. Any Time, Any Place is a time-travel agency."

One

Arden hurried along Royal Street, weaving her way through the revelers spilling over from Bourbon. Tobias had insisted she be at the travel agency no later than twelve o'clock. They were scheduled to depart at precisely thirteen minutes after noon on Fat Tuesday. His estimate of their arrival time had not been nearly so exact. When she'd tried to pin him down, he had mumbled gibberish about the space-time continuum and solar flares again.

She, of course, was positive they weren't going anywhere at all. Well, they would surely go to some other place—she had paid handsomely for a trip—but they would not be going to some other time.

Or would they?

Tobias Thistlewaite seemed very sure of his ability to accomplish the impossible. All week long, Arden had vacillated between belief and skepticism. One minute she was convinced a miracle could happen; the next minute she was sure Tobias was nothing but a con man. If it turned out she was not his client but his victim, she would have only herself to blame. She had participated willingly—eagerly—in her fleecing. After giving Tobias a large sum of money, Arden had followed his instructions—most of them anyway—about other things as well.

He had told her how she should dress for the trip,

recommending a traveling costume appropriate to the times. When Tobias had given her a copy of *La Belle Assemblee,* he had predicted she would not have any trouble finding someone to duplicate the Regency era dresses. He'd been right about that. The seamstress Arden had hired hadn't asked any awkward questions. She had assumed Arden was ordering Mardi Gras costumes.

For the trip, Arden had chosen a carriage dress, high-waisted, high-necked, and long-sleeved. She and the seamstress had struggled over the meaningless fabric descriptions—bombazine and kerseymere meant nothing to them—before choosing a heavy silk in Federal blue for the dress. The dress was plain, ornamented only by wide silk braid in a pale yellow color at the hem and around the neckline. The seamstress had used a summer-weight wool in a darker blue for Arden's pelisse.

Nevertheless, her nineteenth-century ensemble was not completely accurate. For one thing, she hadn't been able to find anyone to make her a Regency bonnet. She'd decided to take along a soft wool shawl fringed in yellow silk. The gray shawl, printed with yellow hibiscus, had belonged to her mother. She'd also ordered and packed three other dresses, and she had bought several pairs of satin flats from a bridal shop and had them dyed to match the dresses. All in all, the clothes appeared suitable to the times, at least to Arden's inexpert eye. Even the shawl, which had an added advantage: It would help keep her warm. London was bound to be cold in February.

The shawl was not the only compromise she'd made. No one seemed to know what a Regency belle wore under her gown and pelisse. What exactly was a shift, anyway? Arden was wearing a bra and panties, thank you very much, and she had others in the suitcase. It couldn't matter, romantic adventure or not, no one was going to see her underwear. Her wish for a vacation fling did not go that far.

Tobias hadn't said anything about it being against the rules to take a few necessities not-suitable-to-the-period along on the trip. Arden hadn't asked. She had packed linen slacks and a cashmere twin set for the trip home. The return trip was scheduled for well after Mardi Gras, and she had no intention of arriving home in costume.

Arden had also packed a sexy little black dress for no reason at all. Except that it had hung in her closet since the day she had bought it, and if she did not find an occasion to wear it on her trip, it might hang there, unworn, forever. Uncle Fred and Aunt Marie did not approve of sexy black dresses.

She was convinced that her clothes, the ones that showed, were authentic enough. Her hair was another matter. Arden's blond locks were cut stylishly short. Too short to arrange in any of the elaborate styles she'd seen in the pages of *La Belle Assemblee.*

She shrugged. Her appearance would do until she could hire a lady's maid to arrange her hair and a dressmaker to make her a complete wardrobe. There was no need for her to worry. Her twenty-first-century anachronisms would not matter at all, not on an educational tour. She doubted that anyone else would be wearing truly authentic nineteenth-century garments, not unless they had access to a museum's clothing collection. The antique-clothes shops in the Quarter had few items older than the twenties. She had discovered that when she'd visited several old-clothes shops looking for a Regency bonnet.

She had managed to find old money. The coin shop on the corner of Chartres and Iberville had yielded copper pennies and gold coins from the early nineteenth century. Arden had paid more than face value for the money, of course, but her small hoard gave her a sense of security. It could come in handy if she actually ended up in another time and another place. And she could always resell the coins if, as she suspected, she was not going to any *time* but the present.

Time-travel was impossible, of course, but Arden did not argue with Tobias when he insisted that they were going to another century. He had a convincing air about him, even when he talked about the magicians and sorcerers he claimed were his ancestors, but she knew better than to fall for that kind of nonsense.

Most of the time.

As the departure time drew close, Arden found it more and more difficult to maintain her skepticism. The truth was, she wanted to believe everything Tobias said. She'd been tempted to ask Tobias to tell her even more about time-travel, but she'd held her tongue. Too many facts might spoil the fantasy.

Arden had been dreaming for years about having an adventure, and this was as close as she had ever come to making her dream a reality. She was having *fun!* Frivolous Freret fun, just like her mother. If suspending disbelief was what she had to do to make the dream and the fun last, then that was what she would do.

And what a dream Tobias had given her! Time-travel was perfect. She could be as carefree and reckless as she'd ever imagined being, and no one in the family would ever know. Her antics wouldn't upset New Orleans's upper crust or St. Clare Spices's bottom line. And if it turned out she was only going on a very expensive trip to Europe, she would have as much fun as possible for a prim and proper St. Clare.

Arden had spent part of the week since she'd met the proprietor of Any Time, Any Place reading romance novels set in the Regency period. She had discovered that people in the nineteenth century spent a great deal of time at balls, routs—whatever they were—and house parties. Dreamily, Arden imagined how she'd look dressed in beautiful ball gowns, cunning little bonnets, a velvet riding habit. She shook her head. A riding habit was for riding, and she knew better than to think she could ever get that close to a horse. With a regretful sigh, she let go of the blue velvet habit she'd imagined.

Ball gowns were another matter, however. She'd have one for every day of the week, and she would waltz with handsome dukes and marquises, viscounts and earls, all the various noblemen looking for wives on the Marriage Mart.

Not that she intended to marry a man a hundred years older than she was. But she could pretend to look for a husband—it seemed to be the only way to have an active social life in the nineteenth century. From what she could tell from her brief research, the Regency period had at least one advantage over the present: Ladies were truly honored and appreciated in that time, not looked upon as prudes or—

The shrill scream of a car alarm brought Arden back to reality. What was she thinking of? She wasn't going to need riding habits *or* ball gowns. Not nineteenth-century ones, anyway. At best, if Tobias hadn't already taken her money and run, she was about to embark on a highly unusual tour of England.

Feeling deliciously silly for letting her imagination run away with her, Arden looked around. No one on the street was giving her or her odd attire a second glance. It was Mardi Gras, after all, and Royal Street was crowded with celebrants dressed in costumes stranger than hers. Or undressed. She averted her eyes from a man wearing only a top hat and a shocking-pink jockstrap and quickened her pace to match her heartbeat.

Her pulse had been racing for days, ever since the first time she'd entered Any Time, Any Place. She'd returned the next day with a cashier's check for one million dollars. Time-travel did not come cheap, although Tobias had assured her that half the money would be available to her upon arrival in Regency London. He hadn't bothered to explain the mechanics of transferring money across time.

Arden still marveled at how surprisingly easy it had been for her to accomplish her part of the financial transaction. Her banker hadn't questioned her, and he hadn't informed on her. She'd been sure he would tell Uncle Fred about her sizable withdrawal. Owning assets worth twenty million, including a respectable chunk of the bank's stock, apparently gave her the right to spend money any way she wanted to, including foolishly. That had been a heady discovery.

Uncle Fred and Aunt Marie had not been enthusiastic about her leaving town before Carnival was over—and they thought she was going on a cruise. Still, they hadn't raised any serious objections to her hasty departure. They assumed she was running away from the swindlers and fortune hunters she was sure to attract now that the business reporter for the *Times-Picayune* had painted a bull's-eye on her back, figuratively speaking.

Arden stepped off the sidewalk to avoid a rambunctious gaggle of tourists. She might be making the biggest mistake of her life, but at least she would have tried for once to take a chance on something other than a risky investment. Her parents would approve. Her memories of their short but exciting lives had been the deciding factor in her decision to take Mr. Thistlewaite up on his outrageous offer. Her mother would have jumped at the chance of a trip through time, and she would have convinced Arden's father to go along. Arden remembered her father saying Jeanne had saved him from stuffiness and taught him how to laugh.

Sobersided St. Clares only smiled. No chortles, no laughs, certainly no guffaws ever passed their lips. But Arden's blood was tainted by that frivolous Freret strain inherited from her mother. Even now, she could feel a giggle bubbling up her throat.

Arden swallowed it. Time enough to be silly later.

Now she had to use the business sense she'd inherited from her father's side of the family. She'd gone along with most of Tobias Thistlewaite's suggestions, but she had no intention of making things too easy for him. She had learned something from Uncle Fred's dry lectures on the responsibilities of owning great wealth, after all. She knew enough to insist on a money-back guarantee. And Tobias had promised she would have one. Arden frowned as she ducked around a couple dressed as Antony and Cleopatra.

He had agreed to the guarantee, but he hadn't actually given her anything in writing yet. She tossed her head, oblivious to the admiring glances from a group of college men draped in Mardi Gras beads. She'd just tell him this morning: no guarantee, no trip.

Arden arrived at the corner of Lafitte's Alley and Royal, relieved to see that Any Time, Any Place was still there. She kept expecting to wake up and find the last week had been nothing but a dream. A sign in the door of the travel agency said "CLOSED FOR MARDI GRAS," but she'd expected that. Tobias had his client— her. At his prices he only needed one customer. She knocked on the door.

The door opened. "Come in, come in. We must leave immediately." Tobias took her suitcase and hustled her inside.

"Wait just one minute." Arden glanced at the clock on the wall. "It's not noon yet. And I'm not leaving until I get a guarantee."

"Time waits for no man. Or woman. Please, sit down." He indicated one of the chairs at the table in the corner.

Feeling a sudden lurch, Arden sat. "What was that?"

"We're leaving." Another lurch. "We've left."

"Left? Left where? How are we going? I thought there would be a machine of some kind to travel in." A limousine to the airport was what she'd had in mind.

"The shop *is* the machine, thanks to the cornerstone

I used when I built it. That piece of granite is Merlin's Stone," Tobias explained, pointing to the corner of the shop. He took the seat opposite her. "I inherited the magical artifact from my parents. I believe I've mentioned them before—she was a witch, he was a mage. I'm a sorcerer, myself. Not a very good one, I'm afraid. It took me decades to discover the secret of the stone."

Arden stared at him wide-eyed. He was going too far with his time-travel scam, much too far. "Now, Tobias, enough is enough. What time is the flight to London?"

"We're flying now. Look." He pointed to the window.

She turned and looked out the plate glass windows. The crowded streets of the French Quarter had disappeared. Arden saw only blackness, relieved at times by brief flashes of light. Her stomach turned over. Something was definitely going on, something out of the ordinary. Time-travel, or a trick? If this was a trick, it was very well done.

"How?" she asked. Her voice squeaked.

"Magic," he answered matter-of-factly. "Watch the shop."

She looked around. Everything except the view out the windows seemed to be the same. Then her gaze reached the clock. The hands on the electric clock on the wall were spinning counterclockwise. Mesmerized, she watched as the hands spun faster and faster, until they were nothing but a blur. Then the clock disappeared. She gasped. She turned back to Tobias, her eyes opened wide in shock. He pointed to the counter.

The computer was gone. The telephone was fading. As she stared, the shop grew dim. Heart pounding, Arden looked up at the ceiling. The electric light fixtures had disappeared, too. Wall sconces took their place. She'd seen sconces like that before, at the St. Clare plantation house. They were for gaslight. The sconces lasted only a few minutes, then faded away. Candles appeared on the counter and the table.

Tobias did not light them. The shop was dim, but not completely dark. The flashes of light from outside the windows—which had changed from plate glass to mullioned panes—became more frequent. One particularly bright flash revealed that the Sheraton tabletop was no longer scratched and scarred. The chair seat felt firmer, too, she noticed, as if the horsehair padding had been renewed.

Her throat dry, Arden managed to croak, "We really are traveling through time, aren't we? That's why the computer and the electric lights disappeared."

Tobias nodded, a worried look on his face.

"Why aren't our clothes dissolving, too?"

"Customers and their things stay the same. I fixed it that way. Too much trouble otherwise. I would be required to have a boutique with clothes and so forth for every time period. The overhead would be ruinous."

Relieved to discover that she wouldn't arrive in London in the nude, Arden settled back in the chair. She didn't relax for long. Another flash and a clap of thunder made her jump.

"What was that? Is anything wrong?" She giggled nervously. She was witnessing the laws of time and space bend and break, and she wanted to know if anything was wrong?

"Solar flares. They sometimes throw the shop off course."

Arden gripped the arms of the chair so tightly her knuckles whitened. "Off course?" She didn't like the sound of that. "What does that mean?"

"Wrong time, wrong place. Not to worry. Money back, of course," he mumbled, not meeting her gaze.

Arden ignored his first words. She didn't want to think about ending up in the wrong time. The wrong time sounded dangerous. She would not have a house, servants, or money waiting for her. Any time could be *any* time—there might be dinosaurs, saber-toothed tigers. Vikings. Squelching the panic which threatened to make her faint, she focused on Tobias's promise. "The money-back guarantee. I want it in writing."

He nodded. "You will need the direction of your man of affairs, as well. His name is Hugh Mendlicott." Tobias opened the drawer of the table and took out a piece of paper, an inkwell, and a pen. He scratched a few lines on the paper, folded it, and handed it to Arden. She tucked it in the pocket of her pelisse.

"We're here," he said.

"Where?" she asked, looking out the window. Trees. She could see nothing but trees. "Did we land in Hyde Park?" Standing up, she held on to the edge of the table until she was sure her legs were going to support her.

Tobias stood, too. He took her suitcase from under the table and gave it to her. "Time to go," he told her, opening the door.

"But what time is it?" she asked as he pushed her out the door. "Is it the right time?"

"Right time. Wrong place." He shut the door.

Dropping the suitcase, Arden pounded on the door. "What do you mean, wrong place? I want my money back!" As she hit the door again, it melted beneath her hand. She was knocking on mist.

Arden looked around. She was in a small clearing in the middle of a forest. The trip must have lasted longer than it seemed—she had left New Orleans at noon, but it was nighttime here. Wherever "here" was. She could see nothing but trees. The leafless limbs outlined against the star-filled sky did not belong to cypress trees or loblolly pines. Wrinkling her nose, she took a deep breath. No odors of rotting vegetation, no smells of coffee roasting or crude oil being turned into gasoline filled her nostrils. Arden smelled only crisp, clean air.

"Gee, Toto, I don't think we're in Louisiana anymore," she murmured. She was definitely in another place. The Lord only knew what time it was. "This is not what I had in mind," she muttered. "I want my money back."

Reaching in her pocket, Arden pulled out the guarantee Tobias had given her. She unfolded the paper and read it by the light of the full moon. Tobias had written down the name and address of her man of affairs and the date and address where Any Time, Any Place would appear for her trip home. Underneath, in the same copperplate handwriting he'd added, "Your money will be cheerfully refunded if you do not find your heart's desire."

Arden groaned. "What kind of guarantee is that? My heart's desire? All I wanted was to have a little fun." Raising her voice, she said, "Being abandoned in the middle of a forest is not my idea of a good time, Tobias Thistlewaite."

No one answered. Arden folded the so-called guarantee and put it back in her pocket. It might not be worth the parchment it was written on, but it was the only hope she had of getting home again. She walked around the perimeter of the clearing until she found a path. Hoping it led somewhere, anywhere except deeper into the woods, Arden picked up her suitcase and started on her journey.

TWO

The path was dark, illuminated only by the moon-beams that reached the forest floor through the gnarled branches of the trees. Leaves covered the ground, crunching beneath her feet as Arden walked through them. She heard other sounds, too, coming out of the darkness on either side of the path. "Critters," she said firmly. "Small ones. No lions or tigers or bears here." If "here" was England, where she was supposed to be.

But what if she were somewhere else? Tobias had said, "Right time, wrong place."

How wrong? Where could she be? "It must be England. These woods *feel* English. Maybe this is Sherwood Forest. I could meet Robin Hood." Shifting the valise from one hand to the other, she reconsidered. "No, this would be the wrong time for Robin and Maid Marian. They were around in the Middle Ages, weren't they? This is the nineteenth century, assuming that Tobias told the truth, and we did land in the right time."

Stepping over a log in the middle of the path, Arden continued muttering to herself. "I'm being ridiculous. I'm not in a different time. A different place, yes. And I don't know how he managed that . . . unless I was drugged for the trip. That doesn't seem like a prudent way to run a business—drugging clients and abandoning them in the middle of nowhere. Unless his business isn't travel at all, time or otherwise, but plain old-fashioned robbery. Now that I think about it, robbery makes a lot more sense than traveling through time. How could I have been so gullible, falling for Tobias Thistlewaite and his time-travel agency? Uncle Fred will be appalled when he finds out what I've done—throwing away one million dollars for a trip to . . . wherever I am."

Arden stopped berating herself and walked faster, trying to keep warm. The trees weren't the sole reason to deduce a change in location; the temperature also told her she was not in Louisiana any longer. "It must be close to freezing. I know I am." Why hadn't she insisted on a fur coat for her traveling costume "appropriate to the period"? The wool pelisse with its thin silk lining provided little protection against the chill. "I'm c-cold and hungry and lost," she sniveled. "I'm going to sue you, Tobias Thistlewaite."

No one responded to her whimpering or her threat.

Arden allowed herself one last mournful sigh and resolved to stop whining. She had gotten herself into this predicament, and obviously she was going to have to get herself out. Picking up her pace, she continued her musings. This time she tried being optimistic. "Maybe this is the way the tour starts. A few more steps and there will be a tour bus waiting, complete with a guide knowledgeable about the Regency period. Very clever, Tobias. I may not sue you after all. I hope the driver has the heater on."

Arden continued walking, placing one slippered foot firmly in front of the other. The path had to end somewhere. Why not at a bus stop? She hadn't really traveled through time—that was impossible. A bus, a nice solid metal and plastic bus—now, that was definitely a real possibility. Except she was no longer sure about what was real or possible. Arden could not forget that the time-travel agency had disappeared into the mist. How had that trick been accomplished? "More drugs, Tobias? Or did you hypnotize me?"

Arden clung to her bus tour theory until she'd walked for what seemed like hours. "No legitimate tour operator would expect clients to walk this far." She pushed the button that lit up her watch face, and read the time. Five minutes after one o'clock. But was that A.M. or P.M? Central Standard or Greenwich Mean? She didn't trust time any longer.

No matter what time it was, she had to keep walking. It was either that or curl up in a ball on the forest floor and die. Arden stuck out a stubborn chin and picked up her pace. She was nowhere ready to give up.

Her feet were dragging and her spirits sinking by the time she came upon a house, the first sign that she'd ended up in an age inhabited by homo sapiens. But the tiny cottage had a deserted look about it—the windows were dark, and no smoke came from the stone chimney. If anyone lived there, they were most likely sound asleep. Waking up strangers might not be the wisest course to follow, but she had no choice. She could not wander around in the woods forever. Arden knocked on the door. Loudly.

No one answered. Arden tried peering in the window, but the glass was so dirty and the interior so dark she could see nothing. No one was at home, so there was no one to tell her where she was. And *when* she was. Disappointed, she turned away. An empty cottage could not answer her questions . . . or could it? There was something about the place that was not quite right. Arden turned around and looked again. Something was different, and something was missing.

The roof was covered with hay. That was what was different. The cottage had a thatched roof. She'd never seen a roof like that before, except in pictures. Arden shook her head. That didn't prove anything. Thatched roofs hadn't completely disappeared in the twenty-first century. Slowly Arden walked around the small house. She had to make the circuit twice before she figured out what was missing. There were no wires, telephone or electrical, leading to the cottage. No outside water faucets, either. No meters to measure electricity or water use were attached to the house.

Now the chill she'd been feeling seemed to come from inside her. She was standing in front of a cottage that belonged in a different time.

Swallowing panic, Arden talked to herself again. "So the place doesn't have modern utilities. So what? The place could be like the fishing camps back home. Some of them don't have utilities or indoor plumbing. Besides, look at it. No one has lived in it for years. I am not in a different time."

But what if she were? What would she do? "You didn't tell me the rules, Tobias." In true St. Clare fashion, Arden found she wanted rules, regulations, principles to live by. She needed order, tradition, familiarity. Why had she ever yearned for fun and adventure? If taking risks meant having this hollow feeling inside, she wasn't at all sure she should have listened to the call of her frivolous Freret blood. Her mother's careless search for thrills and excitement had gotten both her parents killed. Why hadn't she remembered that before haring off into the unknown?

Swallowing the lump that had formed in her throat, Arden left the disturbing cottage and continued down the never-ending path. As she trudged on, she couldn't help wishing she had something other than thin-soled slippers on her feet. "I should have gotten fur-lined boots *and* a fur coat. My t-t-toes are frozen."

Voices.

She heard voices ahead. Maybe the people who owned the cottage were coming home for the night. Arden hurried along the path, anxious to meet the speakers. She slowed when she got close enough to register that the voices were angry. Even so, hearing them answered one of her questions: The accents were definitely English. Moving off the path, she slipped through the trees until she reached the edge of another clearing. Two shadowy figures were standing over a bundle on the ground. As soon as they spoke again, she knew they were male. And dangerous.

"I says we kill him now and get it over with." A moonbeam silvered the blade of the wicked-looking knife the speaker waved under the other man's nose.

The second man shoved the knife away. "They want it to look like an accident—like the poor lad wandered off in the night and froze to death. A knife between the ribs ain't going to look accidental."

"Being trussed up like a Christmas goose ain't going to look accidental either."

"We'll shake him out of the bag and untie him before we leave. A good dose of laudanum will keep him still until the cold takes hold and does him in."

"What if he don't die? We won't get the rest of our pay."

"He'll die. He's a sickly little cove, even if he is a high and mighty duke. Come on, shake him out. I want to get well away before morning."

The two men opened the bundle, and out fell a boy. Arden swallowed a gasp. They were going to kill a child! She almost screamed at them to stop, but she held her tongue and waited, knowing she couldn't succeed in an open confrontation with the villains.

The boy lay on the ground, tied hand and foot. His feet were bare. As far as Arden could tell, he was wearing nothing but a nightshirt.

The villain with the knife approached him.

"Don't cut him loose yet," said the other man. "Where's the laudanum? Give him the dose before you untie him."

Arden winced as the villains forced the boy to open his mouth and drink from a battered flask.

"Cut the ropes now. And make sure you don't leave any bits lying about."

The work was quickly done, and the two miscreants slunk away.

Arden made herself wait until she counted to ten before she left the safety of the concealing trees. Then she ran to the boy's side. He stared at her, his eyes huge. "Don't be afraid. Those men are gone." Poor little boy, she thought. He must have heard the men talking about leaving him to die. How awful must that make him feel?

The boy struggled to sit up.

Arden put her hands on his shoulders and held him down. "No. Stay still and let me see if you're hurt." As she ran her hands over the boy's slight frame, a few snowflakes drifted to the ground. Finding no evidence of broken bones, she helped him stand. "Those men were right. You will freeze to death, and so will I if we don't get out of this weather." She took the shawl from her shoulders and wrapped it around the boy.

He swayed toward her, unsteady on his feet. Arden caught him and hugged him close. "Your hands and feet were tied. We need to get the circulation going again." She sat down on the cold ground next to him and pulled him onto her lap. Briskly, Arden rubbed his legs and arms. "You are so cold. Between that and being tied up for who knows how long, no wonder you're having trouble standing."

"I—I can stand now." The boy slipped off her lap and stood.

He still looked shaky to Arden. Kneeling beside him, she took his wrist and felt for a pulse. It seemed too fast, as if his heart were beating in time to a fast tune. "Laudanum. They gave you laudanum. That's opium, isn't it? Or morphine. Some kind of narcotic." Arden wrung her hands and gazed at the boy. "I know we just met, and I'm really sorry, but I have to do this. It's for your own good." With that, Arden stuck her finger down the boy's throat.

When he finished retching, she took a handkerchief from her pocket and wiped his mouth and chin. "There, that's better."

* * *

William Robert Stanley Warrick, the sixth Duke of Wolverton, scowled at the woman hovering over him. "Why did you do that?"

"They gave you poison. We just got it out of your system. You are not going to freeze to death. Not if I can help it."

She sounded very determined, even though her voice was soft and she spoke slowly, letting the words drift lazily from her mouth.

"You are not English."

"No, I'm not. I'm an American. How could you tell?"

"You speak with an accent."

"Oh, of course. How clever of you to figure that out, especially considering what you've been through." The woman rummaged in her suitcase, pulling out a pair of stockings. "Here, put these on."

William did not take the stockings, even though his toes were turning into tiny blocks of ice. The girl—the American—was not giving him the respect due to a peer of the realm. He had never met an American before, but his tutor had told him about the upstart colonials. "I do not dress myself." He lifted his chin and gave her the haughty stare his father had taught him.

His ducal scowl did not have its usual effect. She did not lower her eyes or stammer. She only raised an eyebrow.

"Really? I would have thought you were old enough to have learned how to do that. How old are you, anyway?" She pulled a pair of slippers out of the rather large carpetbag. "Here, try these on."

She held out the shoes to him, but William refused to take them.

"I do not dress m-myself," he repeated, his disdainful tone spoiled by his chattering from the cold. "I am William R-Robert Stanley Warrick, Duke of W-Wolverton. I am twelve years old." Almost. His birthday was only a month away, if he lived to see another birthday. William shuddered as he remembered the rough voices talking about leaving him to die.

"Well, Billy Bob, you're going to be a frozen duke if you don't put more clothes on. Here, I'll help you. I'm Arden St. Clare, by the way. I've just arrived from New Orleans. That's in Louisiana."

She continued talking as she got the stockings and shoes on his feet. "It's been a very strange trip. Meeting you has been the nicest thing that's happened so far. There. The slippers are a little big, but they will be better than going without any shoes at all. We don't have far to go—there's a cottage back in the woods. Unless you think it would be closer to walk to your home?"

"I do not know where my home is." To his extreme mortification, William felt his chin quiver. He would not cry! He squeezed his eyes shut and held back the threatening tears. A duke never cried.

"Of course you don't," she said soothingly. "How silly of me. You were in a bag. You couldn't know which way you came." She patted him on the shoulder.

William wanted to turn into her arms and let her hug him again. He stared at his feet until the unseemly longing passed. "These are girl's shoes," he said, horrified.

"So they are. They're mine. Would you rather go without?"

"No."

"Very sensible, Billy Bob. Now, let's go. The cottage is back this way." She took him by the hand and picked up her valise.

William walked silently by her side. He wanted to talk to her—tell her about his "accidents." Until the two men had invaded his room, stuffed him into a bag and carried him away, William had almost convinced himself that the other attempts really had been accidents. He had hoped he had imagined the hand at his back the night he had tumbled down the stairs. And that Murch had been wrong about the wheel on the carriage having been sawed partway through. He could no longer hide from the truth.

Someone wanted him dead.

Arden matched her pace to that of the boy duke's. He was very quiet, but she didn't try to make him talk. The poor little fellow had been through more than enough without having to deal with a time-traveler. So, even though she wanted to ask him a million questions, starting with "What year is it?" and ending with "Do you know who hired those men to kill you?" she kept quiet. She could wait for answers.

When they reached the cottage, Arden set her suitcase on the ground and pushed against the door. At first it didn't budge, but after a few hard shoves and one swift kick, she got it open. She entered first, and William followed.

The inside was gloomy and smelled musty. "I was right. No one has lived here in a long time."

It was completely empty, as far as she could tell. The corners were hidden in dark shadows, but the clouds had cleared, and moonlight illuminated enough of the room for her to see the fireplace in the wall opposite the door. There was a pile of wood next to it. Taking off her pelisse, Arden handed it to William. "Here, wrap up in this while I start a fire." She stacked the wood in the fireplace, smaller pieces first. When the fire was laid, she looked around for a way to light it. "Why didn't I bring matches?"

"What did you say?" asked William. He was standing in the middle of the room, clutching her coat around him.

"I'm looking for a way to start the fire. Why don't you sit down?"

William looked around. "Where? There are no chairs."

"I was thinking of the floor."

That haughty look appeared again. "The floor is dirty."

"I think it *is* dirt. Sit on my suitcase." Arden ran her hands along the hearth—the crude stone fireplace didn't boast anything so grand as a mantel. Tucked in a corner, she found what she was looking for. "Aha! A tinderbox." She took the flint and steel from the box. "And I know what to do with them, too." Arden had spent her adolescent summers as a hostess at Beau Visage, the St. Clare plantation house. Most of that time she'd spent in the kitchen, demonstrating nineteenth-century cooking methods—using St. Clare Spices, of course. She'd had to learn how to light a fire the old-fashioned way. "Don't worry, Billy Bob. We'll have this place warm and toasty in no time at all."

Arden shredded bark from one of the smaller pieces of wood, then struck the flint against the stone close to the fragments. It took several tries before one of the sparks caught and turned into a tiny fire. Arden coaxed it along, feeding larger and larger pieces of wood to the flame, and soon she had the fire blazing. "Finally. I really should have brought matches. Or a lighter."

William moved closer to the fire, dragging her suitcase with him. Kneeling beside him, she checked his pulse again, and rested her ear on his chest. "Your breathing seems all right. How do you feel, Billy Bob?"

"Why are you calling me that? My name is William. And since I have not given you permission to call me by that name, you ought to address me as Your Grace."

"Three whole sentences. You must be feeling better, Billy—William—oops, sorry. Your Grace. Billy Bob is a nickname. Where I come from, little boys like nicknames."

"I am not a little boy. I am elev—almost twelve

years old. Where did you say you come from? New
Orleans? That is French, is it not? Are you a spy for
Napoleon?"

"No. Napoleon sold New Orleans, all of Louisiana
for that matter, in eighteen. . . ." She trailed off. 1803?
Or 1805? Why hadn't she read a few history books
instead of all those Regency romances? She hadn't
thought about being considered a spy. Neither had Tobias. He should have warned her. ". . . a few years
ago. Louisiana isn't French anymore."

"I remember now. Boney sold you to the United
States. You are an American spy."

"I am not any kind of spy," Arden insisted, gritting
her teeth as one bit of history surfaced in her brain.
The War of 1812. She knew when that ended—in Janu-
ary 1815, after the Battle of New Orleans. But what
year was it now?

"We were at war with France and America last year.
But the wars are over. I suppose there are no spies
now." William yawned. "I'm sleepy. I want to go to
bed."

"So do I. It seems as though I've been awake for
days." Joining the child in a huge yawn, Arden considered what to do. The laudanum might be causing the
boy's sleepiness, and she thought about making him
stay awake until she could be sure any effects of the
drug had worn off. But she had made him vomit up
most if not all of it. And the villains had not intended
a fatal dose, only enough to keep him still until he
froze to death. "I suppose it would be all right for you
to sleep. I'll stay awake and keep the fire going."

William looked around. "Where? There is no bed."

"There is the floor, however, dirty though it may be.
We'll have to make do." Shifting her gaze from the
boy's pale features to the fire, she said, "Give me the
pelisse, please." She spread it on the floor next to the
fire, and arranged her carpetbag suitcase for William
to use as a pillow. "Come lie down."

He obeyed, and soon was sleeping soundly.

Arden eyed the woodpile. There seemed to be enough wood to last until morning, as long as she didn't fall asleep and let the fire go out. Now that she was warm again, sleep beckoned seductively. No matter what time it was, she'd been awake for hours and hours of it. She yawned again, then shook her head. "Can't sleep. I have to watch the fire." Reluctantly, she got up and began pacing the room.

What had she gotten herself into? "I only wanted to have some fun, a little adventure—a lark, an escapade, a frolic—not a full-blown dangerous adventure, with kidnappers and murderers lurking behind every tree." Not to mention the danger of being in another time, and in the wrong place. "This is *not* my heart's desire, Tobias."

Heart's desire. What a vague term—no shrewd St. Clare should have allowed such a weasel word in a contract she was party to. "Right now, my heart's desire is a bed." After a moment's thought, she added, "In a room with central heat. Even a second-rate sorcerer should be able to provide that."

Tobias did not respond to insults any more than he had to her threats. Why should he? He had her money, and he probably was far, far away from the clearing where he had shoved her out of the agency. He could be anywhere. And anytime.

Time.

At least one question had been answered. She was in a different time, and the time seemed to be the Regency, just as Tobias had promised. After the Battle of Waterloo, if William was right and the wars with France and the United States were over. Last year, he'd said. So this must be 1816. Almost two centuries from where she had started.

The hollow feeling returned to her middle.

Arden put another log on the fire. This was not going to be easy. She didn't know enough about life in 1816.

She was bound to make mistakes, referring to things that didn't exist yet—lighters and matches, for example.

Or not knowing enough about Regency etiquette. She should have known how to address a duke—there had been dukes aplenty in the romance novels she'd read. But reading about dukes and actually having to deal with one—even a small one—were altogether different things.

"There are rules to this time-travel trick. And Tobias didn't bother to spell them out. I will have to be very careful. I'll have to think before I speak."

The most important rule had to be to fit in. She could not tell people she came from the future. They would not believe her, and she could not blame them for that. She hadn't believed it was possible to travel through time, not completely, not until she had no choice. If she told people about the time-travel agency, they would think she was crazy. The thought of spending the rest of her life in a nineteenth-century insane asylum made Arden shudder.

Tobias should have given her history books. He should have told her to prepare a story that would be believed. A story about her life. Closing her eyes, Arden tried to think. If this was 1816 and she was twenty-five, then she would have been born in . . . seventeen . . . something. With another yawn, she gave up. She couldn't do the math in her head, not when she was so tired. She would think up a story tomorrow.

For now, she had to concentrate on keeping the fire going. She put another log on the fire, then gazed at William, curled up on her pelisse and covered with her shawl. The dirt floor hadn't kept him awake for long.

She sat down next to him and leaned her back against the wall. Her eyes drifted shut. "I won't sleep. I'll just rest my eyes for a minute or two."

She woke up when William stirred in her arms. The sun had come up, and the cottage, if not filled with light, was at least less gloomy. William stirred again. "Are you awake?"

He mumbled something unintelligible and snuggled closer. She checked his pulse again, pleased to find that it had steadied, no longer racing frantically as it had the night before. When she brushed the hair away from his forehead, he opened his eyes and looked at her. "Where am I?" he asked, sitting up. "What happened?"

"I don't know where we are. I'm Arden St. Clare. We met last night, remember? In the woods."

He shuddered. "I remember. When I first woke up, I thought I had dreamed it. But it was real. Those men—"

"Are gone," she said firmly. "We don't have to worry about them. The fire's almost out. I've got to put more wood on the fire." Arden got up and went to the fireplace. She picked up one of the few remaining logs.

The cottage door burst open.

A man stood in the doorway. A large man.

"Run, Billy Bob! The bad guys are back!" Arden yelled, flinging the wood at the man's head.

His arm blocked it and the log fell to the floor.

Arden moved between him and the boy. "Stay away from him, you . . . you creep."

"William, are you all right?"

The boy stayed behind her, holding on to her skirt. "Uncle Royce. When did you return from the war?"

The man was the boy's uncle? Then why was William clinging to her and shaking? Arden thought quickly. The men who'd brought him into the forest and left him to die had been hired by someone else. They had said "they" wanted it to look like an accident. Was this man one of those responsible?

"Come here, William," the man said, beckoning with his hand.

"Stay where you are, Billy Bob."

William peeked around her. "How did you find me?"

"We have been searching the woods all night, without success until we saw the smoke from the chimney. Move away from that woman, William. You are safe now."

Grasping her hand, William stayed by her side. "Her name is Arden St. Clare. She's an American, recently arrived from Louisiana. She was not with the men who stole me away. She came after they left me in the woods, and she brought me here."

"To be held for ransom, perhaps." The man took a step closer.

Arden backed up a step, pulling William with her. She grabbed his shoulders and held him against her.

"No. They meant for me to die," William said. "I heard them talking about it before . . ."

"Before?"

". . . Miss St. Clare came along and brought me here, out of the cold. She saved me."

"You have remembered enough, William."

"They m-meant for me to die, Uncle Royce," William repeated, his voice quivering, and Arden hugged him close.

The man knelt in front of them, at eye level with William. "We suspected something of the sort. There have been too many accidents involving Your Grace."

"How did you know about the accidents?"

"Murch. Your valet kept us informed. He raised the alarm last night when he discovered you missing from your bed. Unfortunately, the men who stole you away had a good head start."

William let go of Arden's hand and took a step closer to his uncle. "You came to rescue me?" he asked, uncertainty in his voice. "I thought perhaps you. . . ."

"You suspected I might be the instigator of your accidents? Clever lad. I do have a motive. If you die, I become the Duke of Wolverton. However, I have no desire to be a duke. Never did I envy my brother his rank or his duties. I would not take them from you,

William. And I promised Robert I would keep you safe."

Motive. The man had a motive to kill his nephew. Arden could believe the man was a villain. Any man his size, with hair the color of midnight and cold gray eyes, not to mention a wicked scar that ran from his brow to his chin, would not make a person think of guardian angels.

Or aristocrats. He was dressed in leather breeches and leather boots—were those the Hessians mentioned frequently in the novels she'd read? His shirt collar was open—he hadn't bothered with an intricately tied cravat. He was wearing a jacket, a tweedy-looking jacket. His head was bare.

As if he were aware of her scrutiny, he turned his gaze on her.

Flustered by the haughty disapproval she saw in his eyes, Arden said the first thing that popped into her head.

"What time is it?"

Three

Captain Royce Warrick, second son of a duke and late of the Prince of Wales's own Royal Light Dragoons, forced himself to stop gaping at the strange girl he had found with his nephew. Under other circumstances, a face and form such as hers would warrant an extended gaze. But she was addled, obviously, babbling about the time. And no better than she should be, alone in the woods without a chaperon. No matter what William believed, she was most likely one of the people responsible for taking him away from his bed.

Royce took off his coat and wrapped it around William, then picked the boy up and turned for the door. "Giles! We've found him."

"Viscount Stanton is searching for me, too?" asked William.

"Yes, and Murch is looking for you, as well." Royce turned his attention back to the girl. "Where are your companions?"

"I don't have any companions." She picked her pelisse up off the floor and dusted it off. "Oh, you mean the men who snatched William. I don't know where they are, and they certainly were not my companions. I never saw them before. There were two of them——"

He stopped her with a gesture. "What were you doing alone in the forest?"

"Trying to find my way out of the forest. Don't you

think getting William home is more important than questioning me? And if there is any water around, we should put out the fire. How did you get here? Where are we, exactly? How far from London are—"

Royce held up his hand again. "Enough. We will sort this out once we are away from here." Addled, babbling, and bold. She looked him in the eye, her clear blue eyes showing not a hint of fear or embarrassment. Whoever she was, she was not a lady. That fact should have been enough for him to dismiss the girl out of hand, but something about her fascinated him.

Royce scowled. At thirty, burdened with duty to the Prince Regent and responsibility for his family, he should have been well past being fascinated by females of her sort. Impatiently, he called out, "Giles?"

"Here I am, Royce. I've got your clothes, Your Grace." He stopped when he noticed the girl standing behind Royce. "Who is she?"

"She has not told us that, or how she came to be here."

"I beg your pardon. William introduced us." She turned to Giles. "I'm Arden Camille Elizabeth St. Clare, recently arrived from America. Who are you?"

Giles, always gallant in the presence of a woman no matter what her station in life, bowed. "Giles Fairfax, Viscount Stanton, at your service."

"How do you do?" She extended her hand. Giles took it, but before he could raise it to his lips, she shook his hand briskly. "I'm not clear on titles and things. We don't have aristocrats in America, you know. William had to remind me to address him as Your Grace. I'm from New Orleans, Lou—in the Louisiana Territory. What should I call you?"

"Lord Stanton is proper, Miss St. Clare. But under the circumstances, you may call me Giles."

"How nice. Please call me Arden." She gave Giles a winning smile, a smile that disappeared as soon as she turned her gaze to Royce. "What should I call you?"

"Captain Warrick," he answered curtly. Giles appeared to be well on his way to being charmed by the girl. His friend had a bad habit of falling in love with unsuitable females, most recently with the daughter of a coal monger. Having extricated himself from that trap, Giles should have learned his lesson.

"Captain? You're in the army? I thought the war was over."

"It is over," acknowledged Giles. "That being the case, Lord Royce would be the proper way to address him, since he has resigned his commission."

"I don't understand. You are Lord Stanton. Why isn't he Lord Warrick?"

"Lord is merely a courtesy title in my case, since I am the second son of a duke and not the heir," Royce explained. "Now, William, do you need assistance with your boots?"

"No, sir. I am able to dress myself." He shot a triumphant grin at the girl.

"You most certainly are capable of that. And we should tell Giles and Lord Warrick—"

"Lord Royce," William corrected.

"Whatever. We should tell them how very brave you've been." She gave the young duke a quick hug, then turned her gaze toward Royce. "You said you weren't the heir. But you are. You said you would become the duke if William di—if anything happened to William."

"I was not my father's heir; my older brother was. And since I do not intend for anything to happen to William, I will never be the Duke of Wolverton."

"I see. I think. So am I to call you Lord Royce or Captain Warrick?"

"Do not concern yourself about what to call me."

"Oh, I won't. I'm sure I'll think of something appropriate to your station . . . and your manner." Her blue eyes twinkled mischievously.

Royce ignored her, and the tiny voice whispering in his ear, the voice that was telling him his manner had bordered on rudeness. Being rude was as good a way as any to keep the chit at arm's length, he decided. He turned his attention to his nephew, but could not quite keep his gaze from straying to the young woman hovering over William.

There was something very appealing about Miss St. Clare. Royce told himself it was nothing more than the sort of appeal an opera singer or a dancer might hold for a man in search of a woman to offer carte-blanche. And a mistress was one commodity he did not need or want.

As soon as William was dressed, Royce retrieved his jacket and shrugged into it. "You take His Grace, Giles. I will carry the chit. Come along," he told the girl.

"What did you call me? A chit?" She draped a scarf around her shoulders, picked up her carpetbag, and followed him out the door.

"Yes. Forgive me. I should, for politeness' sake, address you as Miss St. Clare." His tone was sarcastic, meant to put the bold little baggage in her place.

Her chin came up. "You don't strike me as the polite sort. What, exactly, is a chit?"

"A chit is a young woman. Do not the Americans use that term?" Royce lifted her onto the saddle, mounting behind her.

She did not answer, grasping his arms tightly instead. "Wait! Wait! Don't move! I'm going to fall off, I know I am. I can't sit sideways like this. Let me get astraddle."

"You will not fall. I have you." He tightened his arms around her. Definitely not a lady. A lady would not attempt to ride astride, and a lady would certainly object to having his arms wound so closely about her.

"Giles, get Miss St. Clare's bag." She had dropped her case when he'd lifted her onto the horse.

"I don't like horses." She turned against him and wrapped her arms around his waist. "Not that I hate horses. I like animals, and horses are animals. B-big animals." The words were muffled by his jacket. Miss St. Clare had her face buried in his chest. "I should have said I don't like to *ride* horses. If you let me down, I could walk. Just tell me which direction."

"You cannot walk and keep up with us." What a strange creature this girl was. Her fear of being on horseback was not feigned—he could feel her trembling. Yet, if what William believed was the truth, she had saved his nephew from two hired assassins. And she had been prepared to defend William against him— his arm would be bruised from the log she had hurled at him.

"Where are we going?" she asked. "Is it far?"

Giles caught up and directed his horse next to Royce. "Where *are* we going? To Wolverton?"

"No. We will return to your hunting box. We will let the villains think they have succeeded. That should keep William safe for a while." William should never have been in danger, and would not have been if Royce had not allowed pride and vanity to keep him away from his family and his betrothed. He had not wanted to face them scarred and weak from his injuries. And any thought that he had recovered completely was banished by the painful ache in his right leg. He and Giles had ridden fast and hard in their search for William, and he was paying the price.

"What about Miss St. Clare? She cannot stay at the lodge with us. No servants there but Dawkes and Murch. Not even a maid or housekeeper."

The chit—Miss St. Clare—spoke up. "I don't need a maid, and you don't have to give me a place to stay. Just direct me to London and I'll be on my way."

"Not just yet." Royce did not intend to allow Miss

St. Clare to get away, not until he was convinced that she had nothing to do with William's latest "accident."

"We need your help. Taking care of William."

"Yes, please," William piped up. "I would like very much for you to stay with me until . . . until I return to London. I will take you there myself, in my traveling coach."

"Thank you, William. That's very kind of you. I accept your invitation. When do you think you might be returning to London?"

Royce answered for his nephew. "That is a question we will answer later, after we have made our plans. For now, we will stay at Stanton's hunting box. All of us."

"I will send to the village for a maid and a housekeeper," said Giles, his tone resigned.

Royce almost allowed himself to grin. Giles, who thought all women were gifts from heaven, was worried about the girl's reputation. He needn't be. She might feel like an angel in his arms, but Miss Arden St. Clare was clearly not an innocent. And she might well be one of those seeking to harm William. He tightened his hold on her. "Not the village. We want servants we can be sure are loyal to the duke."

When they arrived at Giles's hunting box, Royce immediately dispatched William's valet to Wolverton with orders to bring back a lady's maid and a cook. Murch was to tell the staff that the duke had not been found, and that the search continued under the leadership of Viscount Stanton. Giles was well known at Wolverton, being the closest neighbor to the estate and an old friend of the family. The need for the maid would be explained by the fact that Giles was entertaining a distant cousin, recently and unexpectedly arrived from America.

Dawkes, Royce's former sergeant and current valet, fixed a quick meal for the party, then went to make up the beds in two guest rooms, grumbling all the while about being forced to do cook's and maid's duties. Arden shocked Dawkes and surprised Royce by offering to help with the cooking.

"That will not be necessary, Miss St. Clare," Royce told her. "Pay no attention to his ill-mannered mutterings. Dawkes knew when we retired to the country that he would be the only servant. And help is on the way."

After William was fed and tucked up in bed, Royce and Giles ushered Miss St. Clare into the drawing room.

"Now, Miss St. Clare," said Giles as soon as she was seated. "Tell us how you came to be with His Grace."

With a winsome smile for Giles, she began, "I was walking in the woods and—"

Royce interrupted her. "Begin by telling us how you came to be in the woods alone."

Her head swiveled around so that she faced him instead of Giles. "How I came to be in the woods?"

Royce nodded.

She gazed at him, anxiety apparent in her eyes. After a rather lengthy pause, she said, "I—I was abandoned there by the man who was supposed to take me to London."

"Ahh. Deserted by your protector. I thought as much."

"Protector? Tobias? I don't think so. Stranding someone in the middle of a forest is *not* my idea of protection."

"Tobias . . . ?"

"Tobias Thistlewaite. I met him in New Orleans, and I paid him a mill—handsomely to escort me to London."

"But he brought you here, instead?"

"Yes." She paused. "Where is 'here'? Exactly."

"Somerset," said Giles. "At which port did you arrive?"

"What is the closest port?" she asked.

"Barnstaple. But that is not a usual port of call for ships from America."

"Oh. Well. That is not where we docked, then. To tell you the truth, I am not sure where the ship put in to port."

"Never mind that," said Royce. "How did you arrive in the woods?"

Another pause. Her gaze shifted from his eyes to a spot below his chin. "The usual way."

"On horseback? The paths are too narrow for a coach or a wagon."

She nodded, still not meeting his gaze. She also blushed. The girl was lying, he was sure of it. "But you do not like to ride."

"No. I don't." Her stubborn little chin came up, and she looked him in the eyes again. Hers were sending sparks in his direction. "But sometimes we have to do what is necessary whether we like it or not, wouldn't you agree?" She didn't wait for him to respond. "Can we get on to how I met William? I was walking on the path, and I heard voices. I moved off the path and hid in the trees. I saw two men arguing. One of them had a knife. He wanted to use it on William, but the other man said it had to look like an accident, as though William had wandered into the woods and gotten lost. They gave him laudanum, to make him sleep until hypothermia set in."

"Hypo . . . what?" asked Giles.

She stared at him, chewing on her full bottom lip for a moment before she replied. "Hypothesize. From what I heard, I hypothesized that they meant for William to freeze to death. It was certainly cold enough for that to be a possibility. Especially since Billy Bob was wearing nothing but a nightshirt."

"Who?" asked Giles.

"Oh. William Robert. His Grace. Billy Bob is a silly nickname I gave him on the way to the cottage. I was trying to keep his spirits up, poor little thing. Anyway, as soon as the men left, I made William throw up—"

Royce interrupted again. "How did you do that?"

"I stuck my finger down his throat."

"Why did you do that?" Royce asked.

"To get the poison out of his system. Laudanum is opium, isn't it?"

"Of course."

"Well, a child shouldn't be given drugs. And William was not in any position to just say no—not to two men armed with knives and opium and Lord knows what else."

"Did the men mention anyone by name?" asked Giles.

"No. They didn't call each other by name, either. But one of them said '*they* want it to look like an accident.' There must be more than one other person involved, don't you think?"

"Perhaps," agreed Royce, slanting a look at Giles. They had speculated that whoever was behind William's accidents must have accomplices.

"Didn't you say there had been other attempts on his life?" she asked.

"There have been several accidents involving His Grace," said Royce.

"What kind of accidents?"

Giles answered her. "A fall down the stairs. A broken carriage wheel. Fortunately, William was not seriously injured on either occasion. This latest attempt may have succeeded but for you."

"Your arrival on the scene was indeed a development William's kidnappers could never have anticipated," Royce pointed out. "Fortunate, indeed, wouldn't you agree, Miss St. Clare?"

She turned her gaze from Giles to him. "Why was William surprised to see you?"

Royce raised an eyebrow. It seemed that Miss St. Clare had tired of being questioned and had decided to turn the tables. "My nephew was not aware that I had returned from France. None of my family know."

"Why not? How long have you been home?"

"How long have you been in England?"

That stopped her impertinent questions. "N-not long," she finally answered. "Not long at all."

"And you want to go to London?"

"Yes. Mr. Thistlewaite has rented me a house for a few months. I have the address of my man of affairs. His name is Hugh Mendlicott. Do you know him?"

Royce shook his head. "No. Will you be joining your family in London?"

"No. I came alone. Except for Tobias, of course."

"Your parents allowed you to travel from America to England alone?" Giles sounded dismayed.

"My parents are dead. Uncle Fred and Aunt Marie know I'm traveling abroad."

"Uncle Fred?"

"My father's brother, Frederick St. Clare. He's my financial guardian. Or he was, until my last birthday. Now I control my trust . . . my money."

"You have money, then, Miss St. Clare?" Royce inquired.

"Millions." She glared at him.

"Is that so? So you did not come to England to marry a wealthy man?"

"Certainly not."

"Perhaps you are seeking a title. Is your family in trade, perhaps?"

"My family own St. Clare Spices," she said. "And Beau Visage—a sugar plantation."

"Your family raises sugar cane?" Giles sounded enthralled. He was known for his sweet tooth.

"Among other things. We grow peppers—cayenne and chilies—and other herbs and spices. We have a salt mine on our property, too. There are lots of salt domes in south Louisiana. They call them islands because they rise out of the swamps and . . ." She stopped abruptly. "I don't suppose you wanted a geography lesson."

"So you are property owners, not tradesmen, after all," said Giles. "Royce, are you certain Miss St. Clare should stay with us? Even with a maid, her reputation—"

"Will not suffer," said Royce. It could not get worse.

"What is wrong with being in trade? The St. Clares have a store in New Orleans where they sell what they mine and what they grow. They are most definitely in trade. What do you do for a living?" she asked, directing the question at him.

"I serve king and country," Royce responded curtly. Miss Arden St. Clare, late of America, had pride. He could almost admire her. "Giles is a gentleman. A gentleman does nothing."

"Oh. That must be very boring." She looked him in the eye. "Does that mean you are not a gentleman?"

It was Giles's turn to smile. "Not exactly. Royce is the second son of a Duke, and therefore a commoner, but he is a gentleman."

"Could have fooled me," she muttered, covering her mouth to hide a yawn. "It's been a long day. I know the sun has barely set, but I'm ready for bed. Where am I to sleep?" she asked.

"Giles? Is there another room prepared?"

"Yes. Dawkes made up the room across from William's."

Royce and Giles both rose from their chairs.

"I don't need an escort. I know the way."

When she'd left the room, Giles turned to Royce. "Well, what do you think?"

"About William?"

"About the beauteous Miss St. Clare. Intriguing, is she not?" Giles grinned at him, a twinkle in his green eyes.

"She appears capable of intrigue, if by that you mean she is evasive and devious."

"I meant no such thing. Miss St. Clare is brave, beautiful, and bold. Exactly the sort of female, in fact, that you would have found very appealing at one time."

"She is . . . attractive. I will give you that." Giles would not have believed him if he had denied any interest at all in their unexpected guest. Royce was well aware his friend had not accepted that he was a changed man. Giles knew him well enough to guess that Arden was the sort of woman he once would have pursued and caught, to their mutual pleasure.

But Giles did not know he had promised his dying brother never again to do anything to tarnish the name of Warrick. Kidnapper or not, Miss Arden St. Clare was, at the very least, a scandal waiting to happen. "However, we will discuss Miss St. Clare later. First, we must decide what to do about William. We won't be able to conceal his whereabouts for long—not with your hunting box so close to Wolverton."

"What do you suggest? Is it time to take our investigation to London?"

Royce absently rubbed his thigh. "Perhaps."

"Is your leg very bad?"

"It aches some," he admitted.

"I feared it was too soon for you to be riding. You will not be able to ride to London, but we could borrow William's traveling coach."

"And advertise our arrival to all and sundry? No."

"I could go to London alone and begin making inquiries."

"And leave me here with Miss St. Clare?" Royce shuddered.

Giles ignored his feigned horror. "No, you have the right of it there. A maid would not save her reputation if it got about that she spent time alone with you at my hunting box."

"I was concerned with my well-being, not Miss St. Clare's reputation. The woman is maddening."

"Did you find her so? I found her charming."

"You find any attractive female charming. And her family is in trade, if she is to be believed. I thought you'd had enough of tradesmen's daughters."

"Alice was a cheat and a liar. Miss St. Clare is intelligent and resourceful. Only recall how she thwarted two armed villains and rescued William."

"So she would have us believe," muttered Royce, unwilling to give her credit for William's rescue just yet. "We will wait a few more days. Miss St. Clare may give us additional information. Or she may decide to proceed on her journey without our assistance."

"But surely we owe it to her to escort her to safety."

"I suppose so," Royce reluctantly agreed. "Lady or not, we owe her our protection."

"I, for one, intend to treat her as a lady until she proves unworthy of the title. Do you suppose she is as wealthy as she claims?"

Royce shrugged. "If so, I doubt that she inherited her wealth. And her story of being abandoned in the woods does not ring true."

"Why not? What other explanation could there be?"

"She may be an accomplice in William's kidnapping."

"Surely not," objected Giles. "Miss St. Clare is obviously concerned about William's welfare. Why else would she have saved him from the two men who meant to kill him?"

"A falling out among thieves, perhaps? She may have decided William was worth more alive than dead."

Giles shook his head. "No. I cannot believe that of her. Miss St. Clare is—"

"Too pretty to be a villainess?"

"—too good. You saw how she coaxed William to eat, how tenderly she bade him good night."

"William is a duke. Any adventuress worth her salt would be kind to a wealthy and powerful aristocrat."

"She was not only concerned with William. She offered to help Dawkes, as well. Perhaps she is not quite a lady—she is from America, after all—but I refuse to believe her to be a villainess."

Royce raised an eyebrow. "Not quite a lady? Not a lady at all."

Arden undressed and slipped into a pair of cotton pajamas. She shivered violently as she changed clothes. The room was icy cold, but the bed was nicely piled with quilts and blankets, and someone, Dawkes more than likely, had warmed the sheets with a hot brick wrapped in flannel. As she burrowed under the covers, she knew she wouldn't be able to sleep right away, no matter how tired she was.

The strain of trying to behave like a nineteenth-century woman had been exhausting. Exciting, too, in a fight-or-flight kind of way. Having to come up with answers to Royce's questions on the spur of the moment had made her pulse race and her muscles tense.

Not that matching wits with Royce had gone all that well. Tobias really should have told her to come up with a cover story before he landed her in the wrong place. The redoubtable Captain Warrick obviously thought she was no better than she should be. Arden smiled. She was getting better at thinking in Regency terms already. "No better than she should be." What a quaint phrase that was, and one that authors of Regency novels used often. Her reading had been of some use, after all. She would have to concentrate on remembering more about the way Regency ladies behaved.

It might be too late. Arden had read several novels where the heroine had been forced to marry a man simply because they had been discovered alone together. And here she was, alone with two men—four, if she counted Mr. Dawkes and Mr. Murch. Four men and a boy duke. "I can't marry all of them," she giggled.

It couldn't matter. Once she got to London, no one

would know where she'd spent her time on the way there.

"I will have to learn how to ride a horse, I suppose. Side-saddle, no less." She did not look forward to that. The last time she'd tried, when she was ten years old, the horse had run away with her. He'd scraped her off his back by running under a tree with a low-hanging branch. Arden had ended up on the ground, with two broken ribs and a badly sprained wrist.

"Tobias—if you can hear me, I've decided not to sue. I may not be in London, but you landed me in the middle of a fine adventure." One with an intriguing cast of characters—a duke in danger, a charming viscount, and a disapproving captain. Royce had not tried to hide the fact that he suspected she was involved in William's kidnapping. A smile curved Arden's lips. He might think the worst of her, but William's scowling uncle felt something else for her, too.

She might not have all that much experience with men, but she was her mother's daughter, after all. And her Freret intuition was telling her that Captain Warrick was attracted to her.

Heart's desire.

The phrase popped into her head at almost the same moment her thoughts turned to Royce. She shook her head violently. "No way. Not him."

The chance of a romantic adventure might have been one of the reasons she had taken a trip through time, but she had longed for adventure, first and foremost. She could do without romance, especially one with a man who clearly thought the worst of her. As far as adventures went, *The Mystery of the Kidnapped Duke* would do quite nicely. She was not at all interested in starring in *The Seduction of Miss St. Clare,* thank you very much.

Although . . . teaching the stuffy Lord Royce a thing or two about a modern woman might make an interesting subplot in her little adventure.

"Not a good idea," Arden told herself sternly. The very idea of engaging in a flirtation with the captain had her shivering, and not from the cold. "A very, very bad idea, in fact. What do I know about attracting a man only to spurn him? Not one thing."

Punching the feather pillow into submission, Arden drew the covers up to her chin and closed her eyes. Willing her reckless Freret blood to stop its annoying tingling, she gave her subconscious the choice of dreaming of dukes and danger, or villains and viscounts. Lord Royce Warrick, with his scowls and superior airs, was not on this night's fantasy menu.

Four

"My lady? I have brought your chocolate."

The soft voice woke Arden. She opened her eyes and stared at the ceiling. Except there was no ceiling. A gold brocade canopy covered the bed she lay on. She frowned. Her bed didn't have a canopy. "Where am I?" she murmured, momentarily disoriented.

"At Viscount Stanton's hunting box, my lady."

Arden sat straight up. "Good golly! It wasn't a dream. I really am in another place and another—"

"My lady? Are you all right?" A young woman was standing next to the bedroom door holding a tray. She was dressed in a plain black dress and a white apron, and her hair was covered by a white cap.

"Yes. I'm okay—that is, I'm fine. I *am* fine, or I will be as soon as I get used to . . . is that coffee for me?"

The woman dipped her head. "Yes, my lady." She moved closer and set the tray on the table next to the bed. "But it is chocolate, not coffee."

"As long as it has caffeine. And please call me Arden."

"Yes, Lady Arden." The girl—she couldn't be more than sixteen or seventeen—carefully filled the china cup with chocolate.

"Not lady, just plain Arden. What's your name?"

"Jane."

Arden took the cup Jane handed her. "Thank you, Jane. You weren't here yesterday, were you?

Jane shook her head. "No, miss. We arrived late last night, after you were abed."

"We?"

"Murch brought me and Cook from Wolverton."

"Wolverton. That's William's home, isn't it?"

"Yes, miss. Wolverton is the country estate of the Duke of Wolverton."

"How is William? The duke. His Grace. Have you seen him?"

Jane nodded, a sweet smile curving her lips. "His Grace is the one who told me to bring you the chocolate. I believe he is most anxious to see you."

Arden took a sip. The chocolate was lukewarm, probably because the room was freezing. Shivering, she glanced at the fireplace. "Would you mind starting a fire? I've come from a warmer climate, and I'm not used to the cold."

"Right away, miss." As she placed chunks of coal on the grate in the fireplace, Jane said, "Murch said you were from Louisiana. Is it always warm there?"

"Most of the time. It cools off a few weeks in winter."

"Oh, that must be lovely. I do not care much for the cold myself." Once the fire was blazing, Jane picked up Arden's carpetbag. "I will unpack for you now."

Arden threw back the covers and leapt from the bed. "Don't touch that!" Her suitcase contained items she was not prepared to explain.

Startled, Jane dropped the bag and promptly burst into tears.

"Oh, please don't cry. I didn't mean to yell at you. I am so sorry." She put her arm around Jane's shoulders and steered her toward the bed. "Here, sit down. Would you like a sip of chocolate?"

"N-no, miss. Th-thank you, miss." Jane wiped her eyes with the hem of her apron. Her eyes widened as her gaze swept over Arden. "What are you wearing?" she blurted, then covered her mouth with her hand. "S-sorry. I should not have been so . . . so . . ."

"Curious?"

"B-bold." She looked as if she might burst into tears again.

"Nonsense," Arden said briskly. "What's wrong with asking questions? It is the best way to learn. I'm wearing pajamas."

"Pie-ja-mas?"

"Yes. Sleeping trousers." Arden mentally kicked herself. She had made another mistake—one she could not blame on Tobias. She had known from her reading that the "night rails" worn by Regency belles were nightgowns. But she didn't own a nightgown. Arden hated the way a gown always ended up bunched around her waist. She had been so sure no one would see her underwear or her nightclothes. Why hadn't she anticipated a maid? Maids figured prominently in Regency novels.

Eyeing the real-life maid staring at her, she decided to brazen it out. "The latest style in New Orleans. Don't women here wear pajamas?"

"No, miss. Nor trousers, either." A knock sounded, and Jane slipped off the bed. "Murch is bringing hot water for you to wash." She went to the door and brought back a steaming pitcher of water. "Shall I help you dress? Arrange your hair?"

"No, thank you."

"I told Murch I could not be a lady's maid." Jane's bottom lip quivered. "I sometimes help Franny when the duchess is at Wolverton, but I have only ever been a chambermaid."

"Please don't cry. I'm sure you are a very good lady's maid. It's my fault. I've never had a maid before, you see, so I'm not used to someone helping me dress."

"Oh. Are you poor, then?" Jane clapped her hand

over her mouth. "I did it again," she mumbled from behind her hand.

Laughing, Arden pulled Jane's hand away from her face. "Don't worry about it. I don't mind answering questions. I'm sure I'll have some for you later. I'm not poor. But in America, rich or poor, we learn to look after ourselves."

"You have no servants?"

She may have finessed the pajama question, but Arden was not about to get herself entangled in explaining cleaning services and caterers. "A few. A cook and a housekeeper. And my uncle Fred has a chauf—a coachman."

"Oh." Jane's inquisitive gaze moved to Arden's short, curly locks. "Did you have the fever?"

"Excuse me?"

"Your hair. It is very short. I thought it might have fallen out from the fever. My sister's hair did that."

Arden self-consciously patted her curls. "No, I didn't have a fever. I cut it short intentionally. I imagine it is too short for you to be able to do anything with it."

"Oh, no, miss. Dressing hair is one thing I do very well, if I do say so myself. Would you like me to try?"

"Later, perhaps. I will just give it a good brushing for now."

Jane's gaze moved to the chair where Arden had put the clothes she'd worn for her trip to the past. "Shall I take your dress to be brushed and pressed?" She took a step toward the chair.

Almost too late, Arden remembered that her bra and panties were on the chair under the dress. "No!" Racing Jane the short distance to the chair, she picked up the bundle of clothes. "I may decide to wear this dress again today. If I don't, I'll give it to you later."

"Is there nothing I can do for you now?"

"Take the tray downstairs," she said, then winced. Her order sounded curt even to her ears. Arden quickly added, "Please. And tell William I'll be down shortly.

Thank you for the chocolate and the hot water. And for making up the fire. You have been very helpful, Jane. Truly."

"Thank you, miss." With a bewildered expression, Jane picked up the tray and left the room.

As soon as she was alone again, Arden flopped back on the bed and loosed a heavy sigh. "This time-travel business is *not* easy." Landing in the wrong place added to the difficulty. If Tobias had steered their course correctly, she could have remained secluded in her own house in London until she had figured out a few things. "Like maids. And night rails. And shifts."

As it was, she would have to muddle along as best she could. Arden got out of bed, determined to face the day with confidence. She plumped the pillows and smoothed the bedclothes, then unpacked her meager assortment of clothes. Hanging them on pegs in the armoire, she murmured, "I wonder who invented clothes hangers. And when?"

Not finding any place to hide her lingerie, she left it folded in the carpetbag. The carpetbag she shoved into the bottom of the armoire. "Let's hope out of sight is out of mind as far as Jane is concerned. I should have gotten a bag with a lock. Shoulda, coulda, woulda—I have to stop second-guessing everything I've done. After all, I couldn't have known Tobias was telling the truth about traveling through time. Now that I'm here, I may as well enjoy the trip. If I do make a few mistakes, so what? As long as I don't do anything to make people think I'm crazy, I will be okay—I mean all right." She crossed her fingers. "I hope."

Arden dressed quickly in the lemon yellow creation that *La Belle Assemblee* had described as a morning gown. "It is morning, so I suppose this is the correct sort of dress to be wearing."

The dressmaker had trimmed the gown with tea-dyed lace at the neck and the sleeve cuffs. Thankfully, the dress was made of wool and had long sleeves. "My heart's desire is still central heat, Tobias." After one last check in the mirror fronting the armoire, she left the room.

William was waiting at the bottom of the stairs.

"Good morning, Your Grace." Arden bent her knees in a quick curtsy. She was almost sure women curtsied in the presence of a duke.

"Good morning, Arden. Sorry. Miss St. Clare."

"You may call me Arden. I am sure fellow adventurers always call each other by their first names."

"Adventurers? Is that what we are?" William grinned. "I never had an adventure before."

"Neither had I. As a rule, St. Clares do not believe in having adventures. But I really, really wanted one."

"Why?"

"Precisely because I never had one before. I like trying new things, don't you?"

William eyed her, uncertainty in his gaze. "I don't like people trying to kill me," he said.

Arden gave him a quick hug. "Of course you don't. But you're safe now. No one is going to hurt you again, I promise. The adventure will be in finding out who is behind this, and seeing that they are punished."

William brightened. "That would be exciting." He took Arden by the hand. Leading her toward the dining room, he said, "You slept ever so long."

"What time is it?" She had left her battery-operated watch in the carpetbag.

"I am not sure. I have been awake for hours and hours."

"Have you?" She ruffled his hair. "What have you been doing all those hours and hours?"

"I ate breakfast, and talked to Lord Stanton. He is waiting for you in the dining room."

"And your uncle?" Her heart gave a little wobble at the thought of seeing Royce again.

"Not about yet. Lord Stanton said he probably had a bad night—his leg, you know."

"What about his leg?"

"It is one of the injuries he suffered at Waterloo. He was shot. Uncle Royce kept fighting the French, even with a bullet in his leg. He is a hero," William said proudly.

Arden's heart wobbled again. "Is he? Heroes must run in the family. You've behaved quite bravely so far."

"Oh, no. I was very afraid when I was in the woods with those men." William opened the dining room door for her.

"That doesn't mean you're not brave. Truly courageous people do feel fear, but do what they must in spite of being afraid."

"Very true," said Giles, rising from his chair. "Good day to you, Miss St. Clare. Did you sleep well?"

"She must have. She slept ever so long," said William.

"I did sleep well, thank you. But I'm not the only lazybones. Royce—your uncle—is still asleep."

"Lord Stanton said they stayed up late last night." William jumped to the defense of his uncle. "Making plans."

"Plans? What kind of plans?"

"None of your concern, Miss St. Clare." Royce entered the room. His eyes were bloodshot, his complexion gray. He certainly hadn't slept well, and he appeared to be in pain. That might have excused his curt dismissal of her question, if she were in a charitable mood. She wasn't. Even looking like something the cat dragged in, Royce still had her heart pounding, and she did not like that one little bit. It made her feel vulnerable and weak. "Doesn't your plan include what to do with me?" she asked archly.

He eased into a chair, not bothering to look at her. "You are the least of our concerns."

"Royce!" Giles said, obviously shocked. "Pay him no mind, Miss St. Clare. That is not true. We are concerned with your well-being. But I must confess, our discussions last night centered on William and how to keep him safe."

"That is enough, Giles. We do not want to alarm His Grace." Royce jerked his head in William's direction. He slowly lowered himself into a chair, stretching his leg in front of him.

"Sorry," said Giles. "Eggs and sausage on the sideboard. You will have to serve yourselves, I'm afraid. Dawkes cooks and cleans in a pinch, but he draws the line at playing footman."

"I don't mind," said Arden, taking a cover off a steaming dish of scrambled eggs. "What would you like, Captain Warrick?"

He struggled to stand. "You are not a servant."

"No. But that doesn't mean I can't help out. Please don't get up."

"I am not helpless."

"I suppose not. But you don't look well. Bad night?" she asked. "Did your leg keep you awake? William told me about your injuries."

"My leg is none of your concern."

Arden gave up trying to be polite. "It is if your injured leg is keeping me here in the country," she snapped.

"Have you forgotten William?"

"No, of course not." Arden smiled at William, who was sitting at the table next to his uncle. "But he said you had a plan. Do you want anything else to eat, William?"

"Address my nephew as Your Grace."

"She can call me William, Uncle Royce. Fellow adventurers always call each other by their first names." He grinned at her. "No, thank you, Arden."

Royce said something unintelligible under his breath, then asked, "Did she call you an adventurer?"

William nodded. "That makes her an adventuress, does it not? Isn't that what you called her last night when you took me to my room?"

Giles choked on his tea. Royce turned a dull shade of red.

"We're all adventurers together, aren't we?" Arden forced the words through clenched teeth. She filled a plate with eggs and sausages and set it in front of Royce, virtuously resisting the temptation to dump them on his head, then inspected the contents of the two steaming pots on the table. "Tea or chocolate? There doesn't seem to be any coffee."

"Tea."

"Cream? Sugar?"

"Nothing."

Arden filled a cup and put it on the table, then returned to the sideboard for her own breakfast. When she was seated opposite Royce, she asked again, "Well, do you have a plan or not?"

"We do," he answered around a mouthful of sausage.

"What is it?"

Royce swallowed, then scowled at her. "None of your concern."

"Oh, please. Don't start with that again. If getting to London is not my concern, and helping you with your plans is not my concern, and getting your breakfast for you is not my concern, what, exactly, should I concern myself with?"

"Not one bloody—"

Giles interrupted. "It would be a help if you could keep His Grace amused while Royce and I get on with our investigation."

"Investigation? Is that the plan? Then you are trying to discover who is behind William's accidents?"

"We are," said Giles.

"How? Have you called—I mean, have you contacted the pol—the Bow Street Runners?"

"Runners?" said William, bouncing up and down in his seat. "Am I to have a Runner?"

"Perhaps," said Giles. "When we return to London."

"And when will that be?" asked Arden.

"When we can keep William safe there," Royce said. "But first we need to find out who is behind these attempts on his life."

Arden nodded. "I could help you with the investigation, you know. I know quite a lot about murder."

"Do you really?" Royce asked, his tone disdainful.

"Yes, I do." She had read everything Agatha Christie ever wrote, after all. "And about how to find the perpetrator. Motive, means, and opportunity. Find the person who has all three, and you have your villain."

"Where on earth did you learn that?" asked Giles.

"NYPD Blue."

"What?"

Three pairs of eyes gazed at her quizzically.

Arden bit her lip. She really had to concentrate on thinking before speaking. "Books. I've read a lot of mystery novels."

"Novels. I see." Royce turned to his nephew. "William, would you find Sergeant Dawkes and send him to me?"

"But, Uncle Royce—"

"Now, William."

"Yes, sir." William left the room.

"Now, Miss St. Clare, I must ask you not to speak of murder in my nephew's presence. He is prone to nightmares as it is."

"I should think so, with people trying to kill him every time he turns around. That would disturb anyone's sleep. But boys like solving puzzles. If we make a game of it—"

"No. Too much excitement is not good for a boy as delicate as he is."

"Delicate? I wouldn't call him delicate. A little scrawny, maybe, and he looks like he could use more exercise, but you should have seen him in the woods. Once we got rid of the laudanum, he kept up with me every step of—"

"Confound it, Miss St. Clare—"

She threw up her hands. "I know. I am not to concern myself." Arden turned her attention to her breakfast, determined to ignore the infuriating Captain Royce Warrick if it killed her.

Royce forced himself to eat, although the pain in his leg was interfering with his appetite. He needed food to regain his strength—and he would need to have his health completely restored to protect William, not to mention dealing with the hoyden seated across the table from him.

Giles cleared his throat. "Shall we advise Miss St. Clare of our immediate plans?"

"No."

"But, Royce—"

"No."

"Am I allowed to ask a question?" She directed the question to Giles, who merely shrugged and looked to Royce.

"What is it?" asked Royce grudgingly.

"Does William have a mother?"

"Of course."

"Where is she?"

"London."

"Won't she be worried about him?"

"We have discussed that," said Giles. "Her Grace will not be overset by William's disappearance for a few more days. The duchess will not have heard of the kidnapping yet, you see."

"But you will tell her that he's all right as soon as possible, won't you?"

"When the time is right, yes," said Royce, puzzled. Arden seemed genuinely concerned about the feelings of a woman she had never met. That sympathetic attitude did not fit the sort of woman he imagined her to be.

"And that would be . . . when?" she asked him.

"When I am able to protect him." Royce winced as he stood.

"Oh. Your leg. What have you been doing for it?"

"Rest."

"My uncle Fred injured his leg in a boating accident. His doctor prescribed exercise and massage. Have you tried that? I could show you the kind of exercises, and I give a mean massage."

"I expect you do. However, I will follow my own doctor's advice."

"I expect you will. And that means we'll all be stuck here together for Lord knows how long." She rose from her chair. "I'm going to find William . . . to keep him amused."

As soon as she had left the room, Giles said, "I should go to London in a day or two. I can inform Her Grace that William is safe."

"Take her with you, then."

"She does not ride, remember? Why do you dislike her so? She has offered to help at every turn."

Royce raised an eyebrow.

Giles continued his defense of Arden. "She tried to assist Dawkes with the cooking. She wanted to help us in arriving at a solution to the attempts on William's life. She—"

"—wants to massage my leg. Where do you suppose she learned that skill?"

"She told us. Her uncle's doctor."

"And you believe her?"

"I know you think I am easily befuddled by a pretty face, but I have no reason to doubt Miss St. Clare's honesty."

"I do. She did not tell us the truth about how she came to be alone in the forest."

"Perhaps she cannot, without betraying a trust she owes to another."

"Giles, my friend. Let us not argue about Miss St. Clare."

"Very well. Shall we continue with our analysis of the attempts on William? Perhaps we could examine the facts in light of Miss St. Clare's suggestion. Who had motive, means, and—what was the third item?"

"Opportunity."

"Ah, yes. Opportunity. I suppose that means being at the scene of the accidents. The person must have had access to the Wolverton London house and to the stables. According to Murch, the parties present included the duchess, her brother Osbert, your betrothed, and her cousin, Lord Neville."

"And a score of servants," muttered Royce.

"Of course, Dora can be eliminated. No mother would kill her own son," Giles said. "And I cannot see Her Grace sawing through a carriage wheel."

"Nor can I. But I thought we had agreed the villain must have an accomplice. That surmise has proved true: The two men who kidnapped William were in someone's employ."

"But they were not on the premises the night someone pushed His Grace down the stairs. Unless the duchess has innocently employed murderous footmen."

"Murch would know if there were any servants recently hired."

"Shall I call him?" asked Giles.

Royce nodded, rising from his seat. "Please. Tell him to join us in your study where we can be more private."

Giles entered the study a few minutes later, followed by Murch. Royce stood, his shoulder braced against the mantel, and listened as Giles put the question to William's valet.

"No new servants were hired before the accidents began," Murch answered firmly.

"I thought not," said Royce. "The Dukes of Wolverton have always inspired loyalty in their staff. Thank you, Murch. You may go."

"Yes, my lord." He opened his mouth, then closed it.

"Is there something else you wish to tell us?"

Murch took a deep breath. "About the young lady . . ."

"Miss St. Clare?"

Tugging at his collar, Murch nodded.

"What about her?"

"Jane—the maid I brought from Wolverton—mentioned a few odd things about her."

Royce pulled away from the mantel, alerted by Murch's statement. "Odd? In what way?" Perhaps the baggage had done something that would confirm his suspicion that she knew more than she pretended about William's kidnapping.

"I—I—" Murch stammered, seemingly at a loss for words.

"Out with it, man," Giles interjected impatiently. "What oddities are you talking about?"

"Miss St. Clare would not allow Jane to unpack her clothes or help her dress."

"She may be unused to servants."

"Aye. She told Jane she had never had a maid before."

"There, you see? That explains it," said Giles.

"It also makes it unlikely that she is a lady, or wealthy. What else?" asked Royce.

"Jane said she was wearing strange bedclothes. She called them sleeping trousers or some such. Told Jane all the ladies in America wore them."

"Perhaps they do," Giles said faintly, his eyes glazing over.

Royce surmised that his friend was picturing Miss St. Clare in trousers, since he himself was engaged—unwillingly—in the same activity. Clearing his throat, he asked, "Anything more?"

"No, my lord."

"Very well. Thank you, Murch."

The valet left the room.

"Well," said Giles. "What do you make of that?"

"What? That our Miss St. Clare is not used to being waited upon? I suspected as much."

"Not that. Sleeping trousers."

"Miss St. Clare can sleep in nothing, for all I care." As soon as the words left his lip, Royce groaned. Not one to dwell on the female form, he found himself imagining Arden naked. The image was quickly suppressed. "Let us get on with the matter at hand. We know now that there were no new servants about when William was attacked."

"There is always the possibility that an old servant succumbed to bribery."

"True," agreed Royce. "But the villain need not have used an accomplice for the first two attempts. Any one of those present is capable of giving a small boy a shove in the back."

"But surely neither Her Grace nor Lady Christabel could have sawn through the wheel. Or hired the two miscreants who stole William away. Where would they have met such men?"

"I do not suspect either of the ladies. That leaves Osbert and Neville. I admit I am not fond of Christabel's cousin, but Neville de Courcy can have no motive. William's death would not benefit him."

"We are left with Osbert Sharpless," said Giles.

Royce nodded in agreement. "He is the only one who had the opportunity, the means, and the motive."

"And his motive is?"

"Possibly to conceal his handling, or mishandling, of William's estates in my absence. He may have been plundering the duke's coffers. We need a look at the estate's accounts."

"Which are in London." Giles gave him an inquiring look.

"Yes. You are right, of course. We will not be able to confirm our suspicions until one of us has a look at the books. If it turns out the accounts have been fiddled, Osbert is the culprit. If not, then we must look elsewhere." Royce frowned. "But where? There are no other obvious suspects."

"Perhaps to the other heir," suggested Giles. "He may well believe you are dead, and that William is the only obstacle between him and the title."

"The Reverend Mr. Warrick? I find it difficult to imagine that a country parson would stoop to murder."

"So do I. But who else has—"

Giles was interrupted by a loud thud from above.

"What the devil?" asked Royce, heading for the stairs. Giles followed close behind.

Five

Arden lay on her back on the landing next to a pile of pillows, gasping for breath.

"Arden! Miss St. Clare!" William bounced around her, wringing his hands. "Speak to me. Please."

"I . . . I will. Soon as I . . . catch . . . breath." Closing her eyes tightly, she concentrated on filling her lungs with air.

"William! What happened?" Royce's deep voice came from the top of the staircase.

Her eyes popped open. Royce was bending over her, a fierce scowl marring his features more than the scar on his cheek ever would. Giles was behind him, peering over his shoulder and looking worried. Royce was staring at her legs, exposed to her knees. His look implied that no proper woman's dress ever left the neighborhood of her ankles, no matter what the provocation.

If she hadn't been prone and breathless, Arden would have kicked him on his injured leg.

William was still dancing around her. "It is my fault!" wailed the young duke. "I *killed* her!"

"I'm not dead," Arden murmured, still a bit dazed from her fall. "I didn't land on the cushions. My fault."

"Explain yourself." Royce directed the order to the duke. "Why is Miss St. Clare sprawled at our feet?"

"Possibly because no one is helping me up," Arden muttered under her breath.

"Arden—Miss St. Clare—is teaching me how to defend myself, Uncle. She pretended to attack me from behind, and I tossed her over my shoulder." He pointed to the pillows. "She was supposed to land there."

"Nonsense. You could not toss someone larger than you over your shoulder."

Struggling to sit up, Arden snapped, "He most certainly could. He did it, just the way I showed him."

"Are you truly all right?" asked William.

She nodded reassuringly. With a helpful hand from Giles, who shouldered Royce aside and apologized for their belated assistance, Arden got to her feet. "I had the wind knocked out of me." She rubbed her bottom. "And I landed on my tailbone. It smarts a bit."

"Oh. I am sorry." William's bottom lip trembled. "I never meant to hurt you."

Laughing, Arden gave William a quick hug. "I know that. And you did exactly what I wanted you to do. I just didn't expect you to learn the maneuver so quickly. You are a very clever boy."

Beaming, William turned to his uncle. "Shall I show you? It is very simple, really. When Arden grabbed me from behind, I quickly bent at the hip and sent her flying over my head. I used her own momentum against her, do you see?"

"Very clever," echoed Giles. "Where on earth did you learn that trick, Miss St. Clare?"

Arden fussed with her skirt, which persisted in clinging to her calves, refusing to fall to the floor. When she straightened, she smiled at Giles, whose gaze was glued to her ankles, now hidden from view. From his dazed expression, she concluded he must be a leg man, doomed to life in the wrong century.

Her smile widened to a grin as she imagined Giles's reaction to a miniskirt. "I thought we had agreed that you should call me Arden. As to how I learned to defend myself"—she stopped herself before she told them about the self-defense course she had taken—"my uncle taught me."

"The colonials must teach their women to fight off attackers?" Royce seemed appalled at the notion.

The expression of disgust on his face reminded her of Cousin Albert, one of the more pompous St. Clares. She wondered suddenly if the captain might be a distant ancestor of the clan. He certainly would have met with Uncle Fred's approval, related or not.

"Red Indians, Royce. Savages," said Giles with an exaggerated shudder.

"Not Indians. Native Americans," Arden automatically corrected. "They are not the problem."

"Then why?" Royce seemed determined to make her explain.

Arden bit her tongue to keep herself from telling him about the drunken tourists—not to mention the homegrown muggers—that one might encounter on the shadowy streets of the French Quarter. Uncle Fred would never have let her move from the family mansion on St. Charles Avenue to the old Freret townhouse on Royal Street if she hadn't taken the self-defense course.

"Well, we are a young country, not quite as civilized as England," she temporized.

"Tell them about the river rats, Arden," said William, his eyes sparkling with excitement.

"Those are the trappers and hunters who bring their furs down the Mississippi River on rafts. They were—are—a rough breed of men," explained Arden.

"And are those the men you must defend yourself against?" asked Giles.

"Not exactly. To tell the truth, I've never actually met a river rat."

Royce raised a haughty eyebrow. "Then one wonders why your uncle felt the need to instruct you in how to toss men over your shoulder."

She matched his raised eyebrow and, for good measure, tilted up her chin. "Drawing rooms can be as dangerous for a woman as the wharves and jetties, don't you agree?"

"Are you saying you found it necessary to protect yourself from gentlemen?" Giles asked, aghast.

"A time or two," Arden said, recalling the occasional tussle with an overly amorous escort. "Not that I was ever in a situation where I had to throw a man over my shoulder, but you never know when the need may arise. There are men, including men who call themselves gentlemen, who will try to take advantage of a woman."

"It was your uncle's duty to defend you against unwanted attention from men," said Royce, his tone brooking no disagreement.

"Never mind about my uncle." In comparison to Royce, who seemed determined to disapprove of her every word and action, stuffy Uncle Fred was beginning to look downright tolerant. "This discussion is pointless since I have never been attacked by anyone. Nevertheless, I know how to take care of myself. And that is something William needs to learn, what with unknown assailants lurking around every corner."

"The course of William's education is not up to you, Miss St. Clare," Royce decreed imperiously. "Nor is keeping him safe your responsibility. That is my concern. As to your own ability to take care of yourself, you did somehow end up alone in the woods. Are you ready to tell us how?"

"No, I'm not." She could not resist adding, *"That* is none of your concern."

"It is if you are one of the people responsible for William's latest misadventure," Royce insisted.

"You still suspect me?" Her hands went to her hips, and her chin came up again.

"Yes. And I will continue to do so until you have been completely honest with us."

"It's not a matter of honesty. There are some things I simply cannot tell you." Time-travel was definitely not a subject she cared to broach with the redoubtable Captain Warrick. He would have her put in whatever passed for a psychiatric hospital in 1816 before she could blink an eye. "But I assure you my presence in the woods was an accident, totally unconnected with William. As to William's education, you said I should entertain him."

"It was Giles who suggested that activity for you, not I. And entertainment does not mean teaching him useless tricks and filling his head with stories of wild Americans, native or not," Royce countered.

"The tricks are not useless, Uncle Royce," William said anxiously, tugging on Royce's coattail. "Show him, Arden."

"Yes." More than ready to do battle with the haughty lord, Arden shoved up her sleeves. "I believe I will."

"Do not be absurd. I am larger than you are."

She looked him up and down. "I can see that. But your size doesn't intimidate me, since I intend to use it against you." Turning her back to Royce, she said, "Go ahead, big, bad man. Grab me."

"Let us save the demonstration for some other time, shall we?" said Giles. He sounded amused.

"For all time," said Royce, very clearly not at all amused. "I have no intention of grabbing you, Miss St. Clare. Now or ever."

Arden looked over her shoulder. Royce might say he would never assault her, but he certainly looked as if he wanted to strangle her. She spun around to face him, ready to spar verbally if not physically. "Too bad. You might have learned something."

"Unlikely. No upstart American hoyden can teach me anything I care to learn."

"Royce!"

"Uncle!"

Bowing to his friend and his nephew, Royce smiled grimly. "I do beg your pardon, Miss St. Clare," he said mockingly. "I should not have insulted you."

Arden's chin came up. "You didn't. Uppity women are admired in my country. As they should be in yours."

"I disagree. We citizens of the more civilized country reserve our admiration for the fairest product of our long and noble history—a true English lady." He could not have sounded more pompous if he had been a St. Clare.

Eyes flashing, Arden demanded, "Define your terms. What exactly do you mean by 'lady'?" She should have more than qualified for the status if all those lectures from Uncle Fred and lessons from Aunt Marie counted for anything. "From what I've seen so far, being an English lady means being a mindless piece of fluff whose only purpose is to obey and please her lord."

Royce advanced a step toward her. "I cannot conceive of anything a woman like you could do which would please me. But, lady or not, you will obey me as long as you are under my protection."

"Obey? You?" Smarting from the "woman like you" remark, Arden forced a disdainful laugh. "I don't think so."

"Then I suggest you think again." Royce took another step in her direction.

"Oh, now you're going to grab me and beat me into submission, I suppose," she said, stubbornly standing her ground.

"Uncle Royce! You are not going to hit Arden, are you?"

Royce stopped his menacing advance. "No. Of course not. A gentleman does not attack a lady under his protection."

"Aha! So I am a lady, after all."

"I used the term loosely."

"Well, tighten it up. Unlike you, I'm willing to learn from anyone, even a sanctimonious, overbearing lord. So tell me, *Lord* Royce. What is a true lady?"

Giles groaned. "Please do not ask him that. Warrick

has an endless list of ladylike virtues. I had to hear him expound on them for months when he was searching for the paragon he would marry. But on behalf of all other Englishmen, let me assure you that you possess every quality any man could desire in a lady or a bride."

"Bride?" Arden's anger left her as quickly as air from a punctured balloon. She sent a shocked look at Royce. "You're married?"

"Betrothed," he said curtly.

Engaged. Her heart, which had sunk to her toes, returned to the vicinity of her chest, although it insisted on stuttering along instead of beating steadily. "Oh." He did not behave like an engaged man. Or perhaps he did, and those sparks between them had not been caused by mutual attraction after all. She cleared her throat, which was suddenly clogged with an inexplicable lump. "So you are betrothed. Recently?"

"Since shortly before I left for the Continent."

"Royce has been engaged for almost two years," Giles explained.

"Years? You've made your fiancée wait for years to get married?"

Royce looked momentarily uncomfortable, maybe even a little guilty. "I did not think it prudent to marry before going off to war."

Prudence was a quality much admired by St. Clares. Arden was struck again by how well Royce would fit in with her father's family—more than enough reason for her to look elsewhere for a romantic entanglement. What had she been thinking of? A man like Royce could never be her heart's desire. So his betrothal could not matter to her. Not at all. "Why isn't your fiancée here looking after you? Doesn't she know you were hurt?"

"Certainly. I wrote her about my injuries. However, Lady Christabel believes me to be in Paris."

"Why?"

"That is—"

"—I know. None of my concern. This time, I agree with you. Your personal life is none of my business." There was absolutely no reason for her to feel bereft— mildly disappointed—because one infuriating lord was engaged. To a paragon of Regency ladyhood. "Please excuse me for asking. William, would you like to go for a walk?"

"No," said Royce. "You may not venture outside, William. We do not want you seen about the place. And if you have any concern at all for your reputation, you should remain out of sight, as well."

"Who would see us?" asked Arden.

"Tradesmen. Servants from nearby estates. Farmers. Poachers. Spies." Royce ticked off the list on his fingers.

"You've made your point. So we must remain indoors all the time?"

"For now."

William tugged on Royce's coattails. "But, Uncle Royce, we cannot. We must go outside. I promised to teach Arden how to ride."

"Ah." Royce slanted a triumphant look her way. "You admit you do not ride?"

"I never said I did." Before Royce could come up with more unanswerable questions about her method of transportation to the forest where she encountered William, she quickly explained, "I don't ride because I was thrown from a horse when I was ten. That ended my desire for riding lessons."

"Were you badly hurt?" asked Giles, his tone sympathetic.

"Mostly I was badly scared. But it's past time I got over my fear of horses."

"I would have thought you would have found that necessary before now," Royce said.

"Well, I didn't. New Orleans is a small town, and

people walk almost everywhere. Except to Beau Visage, of course. We take the carriage there."

"Beau Visage?"

"The St. Clare sugar cane plantation. It's a few miles out of the city."

"Your plantation has a French name?"

"Beau Visage was named by my great . . . by my mother's family." Justin St. Clare had married the daughter of Pierre Duplantier, a French planter, shortly after the Battle of New Orleans. Arden felt a chill as she realized that the wedding of her great-great-grand-parents could be taking place even as she spoke.

"Miss St. Clare. What was your mother's family name?"

"Freret," she replied absently, still distracted by the notion that her ancestors were now her contemporaries.

"So you are half French." Royce made his deduction an accusation.

"I am all American. And before you ask, I am not a spy. Not for the United States, or for France. Since the wars are over, there is no need for espionage, any-way. We won the American one, if you will recall. You have heard of the Battle of New Orleans? A lot of uppity Americans beat the tar out of your English red-coats." She refrained from mentioning the wounded redcoat who had been nursed back to health by Camille Duplantier. Together they had founded the St. Clare dy-nasty.

Royce responded to her brief history lesson with no more than a raised eyebrow. He turned to his nephew instead. "I am sorry, William, but it would not be wise for you to be seen riding about the countryside with Miss St. Clare. We want to keep your location a secret as long as possible, until Giles and I decide on a course of action."

"I understand. You are trying to keep me safe." The duke turned to Arden and bowed. "I beg your pardon, Arden. I shall not be able to keep my promise to you."

William looked dejected, but resigned. Then he brightened. "But you could keep it for me, Uncle Royce. You could teach Arden how to ride."

"No." Royce must have seen the disappointment in William's expression, for he added, "I am not able to ride just now . . . for pleasure. If it becomes necessary to mount a horse in defense of you or Miss St. Clare, I will do my duty."

"Oh, your leg," said William. "I forgot."

"Exercise might do it good," Arden said. "You know what they say: Use it or lose it." For some unknown reason, the thought of being alone with Royce—even if horses were involved—had a deliciously wicked appeal.

"Use it or lose it? What a quaint phrase," murmured Giles. "What does it mean?"

"It means that if muscles aren't used, they lose the ability to function."

"An interesting theory," said Giles. "Perhaps you should give it a try, Warrick. Inactivity hasn't accomplished much in the way of restoring the strength in your limb."

"She recommended massage, as well, I believe," said Royce, something approaching a grin curving his lips.

The sinful gleam that suddenly appeared in his eyes surprised her. "I did mention massage as a treatment option. But I no longer volunteer for that duty. Someone else can rub your leg—excuse me, your limb for you." There. That did it. The sexy gleam disappeared, replaced by the now familiar disapproving scowl. Arden turned her attention to the viscount. "Perhaps you could teach me to ride, Giles."

Giles sketched a bow. "I would be honored, but I fear I cannot. I will be leaving for London at dawn tomorrow."

"London? You're going to London?" Her gaze returned to Royce. "Are you going, too?"

"No."

"Royce is unable to ride so far. His injuries prevent him from accompanying me. And we cannot wait any longer to inform William's mother that he is safe."

"Is that the only reason you're going? Couldn't Murch or Dawkes take care of that?"

"No." Royce answered for Giles, giving him a sharp look as he did so.

Arden caught the look. "Telling William's mother that he's all right isn't the only reason you're going to London, is it? You're continuing the investigation into William's accidents, aren't you?" She directed her questions to Giles, certain that Royce would not answer her. She was wrong.

"Dawkes and Murch are needed here," said Royce. "To assist me in guarding William."

Giles hastened to add, "I must see my sister, too. Penelope is recently engaged, and I have not met her husband-to-be."

"Oh. How long do you expect to be gone?"

"Not longer than a fortnight."

"A fortnight?" Her jaw dropped. "Two weeks? You expect me to stay here alone with him"—she pointed to Royce—"for two whole weeks?"

Giles nodded. "I am sorry, Miss St. Clare—Arden. I realize it is a great imposition, asking you to risk your reputation by remaining here with Lord Royce—"

Waving her hand, Arden said, "My reputation is not the problem."

"I agree," said Royce. "Any harm to your reputation has already occurred. Therefore, you may walk or ride about the place as you wish."

"I advise against that," Giles said. "Protection of your good name must always be your first concern. We, of course, will do everything in our power to keep this . . . interlude our secret."

"Thank you, Giles. But isn't there any way I could travel with you?"

Royce answered her. "No. Giles rides to London. You

do not ride. And we cannot arrange for a carriage without alerting the people in the neighborhood that His Grace is here."

"You do not wish to stay with me?" asked William, his lower lip threatening to pout.

"That's not it, Billy Bob. I don't mind being here with you, not one little bit." She ruffled his hair and smiled at him, pointedly avoiding Royce's gaze.

Giles smothered a grin. It seemed that the American had the same reaction to being alone with Royce that Royce had voiced at the prospect of being alone with her. He almost wished he could remain and watch the developments between the two. He wondered how long it might take Royce to see that a woman like Arden, lady or not, would be a better life companion for him than Christabel the Perfect.

Giles understood why Royce had chosen Christabel. She had breeding, beauty, and an unblemished reputation. He did not understand why Royce had settled for a loveless marriage, and he did not approve. He had never voiced his disapproval, however. Who was he to give advice on love?

Giles had found his beloved on the date she had wed another. For years after, he had pursued any woman who caught his fancy, but he had never managed to find a woman to supplant his first, and, it seemed, his last love in his heart. His many flirtations made people think he found all women, suitable or not, worthy of his amorous attention, but Giles had never felt the slightest tweak of Cupid's arrow when in the presence of Lady Christabel de Courcy.

Strange, now that he thought about it. Christabel was perfection, a glittering star in the *ton*'s firmament of beauties. Accomplished in all things which identified a lady, she sang with a voice like an angel, she danced with grace and charm, and she certainly knew how to ride a horse.

She had at least one flaw, in his opinion. Lady Christabel seldom laughed. "Seldom" was perhaps a misstatement. In point of fact, Giles had never heard the Exquisite laugh.

When he had remarked on that defect, Royce had merely shrugged. Laughter, it seemed, no longer mattered to him. Royce had buried his enthusiastic enjoyment of life along with his brother and his comrades in arms. Giles had hoped rusticating in the country where they had been boys together would revive Royce's love of laughter and gaiety. So far, neither his body nor his heart had recovered.

Giles still had hopes that Royce's physical wounds would heal, but he feared that marriage to Lady Christabel would doom him to a life without joy. He thought it highly unlikely that Christabel would teach her lord to laugh again. She would not know how to accomplish such a task. The daughter of an earl, Lady Christabel had been trained from birth in the skills needed to manage a gentleman's household, not his temperament.

Therein lay the problem.

Royce was not quite a gentleman.

True, only an old friend would know that. No matter how much it chafed, Royce stoically wore the cloak of respectability which he donned after his brother died. When Royce became the temporary head of the family, he put aside his love of sport, of gaming, of women. He did not resign his commission, however, since he believed duty to country must take precedence over duty to family. As a sop to the latter, before leaving for the Peninsula, Royce had become betrothed to a woman of decorum and propriety, a lady more than suited to be the wife of the heir presumptive of a duke.

With his engagement to Lady Christabel, Royce had abandoned his rakish ways entirely. And since he had returned from the war, it seemed as if there were nothing of the rogue left in him. But occasionally, and more frequently since Miss St. Clare had appeared on the scene, flashes of the old Royce broke through the somber facade he had constructed.

Giles missed his fun-loving, reckless friend.

With any luck, the combination of boredom and an uppity woman would awaken the old Royce.

He slapped Royce on the shoulder. "You all must find a way to pass the time pleasantly until I return."

"That will not be an easy task."

"It certainly won't," Arden agreed. "No walks, no riding lessons . . . no conversation. Bo-ring."

"I will talk to you, Arden," said William. "And we can play games. You can tell me more about America."

"That's true. Now that I think about it, there is no way I will be bored as long as you are around. We have a lot to talk about."

"What?" asked the young duke.

"You can tell me about all the wonderful places to see in London. The museums, the theaters. Vauxhall Gardens. And isn't there a circus?"

William shook his head sorrowfully. "I have never been to those places."

"You haven't? Why not?"

"I am not allowed to go."

"Oh, because of the accidents?"

"Even before that."

"Why, then?"

"Because I am prone to sickness."

"Well, we can take care of that. All you need is good food and exercise to build up your . . . system." Arden bit her lip. She had almost said "immune system," a term she was almost sure hadn't been used in 1816.

"Miss St. Clare has an answer for everything, it seems," said Royce. "Perhaps she should have been a doctor."

"I thought about it, but the sight of blood makes me nauseous."

"A woman cannot be a doctor, Arden," said William, certainty in his voice.

"A woman can be anything she wants to be," said Arden firmly.

"And what do you want to be, Miss St. Clare?" Royce asked, forgetting for once to sound disapproving.

Giles grinned broadly.

He had been right, after all. Royce did find the charming American intriguing, as he had suspected. And curiosity was a quality the old Royce had often displayed, being a man who wanted to know everything and everyone. Arden might not be a doctor, but she was exactly what the doctor ordered. "Yes, Miss St. Clare, do tell us. What do you want?"

"Me?" That entrancing mischievous twinkle lit her big blue eyes as she smiled winningly. "I'm just a girl who wants to have fun."

Six

Early the next morning Arden stood at the window of her bedroom and watched as Giles mounted a horse. Royce was standing at the head of the horse, and the two men were talking. About what, she had no idea, since with the window closed she could not hear what they were saying. Carefully she eased the window open, but only a few disconnected phrases reached her ears.

". . . Osbert . . . careful," said Royce.

Giles nodded. ". . . Christabel?"

Royce shook his head. He pulled a letter from his coat pocket and gave it to Giles. ". . . written . . . do not . . . St. Clare . . . and William . . . Mendli-cott . . ."

Mendlicott? Her man of affairs? Arden strained to hear more, but could not without leaning out the window and exposing herself to Royce's view. Catching her spying on him would only increase his distrust of her. Not that she cared what Royce thought of her, not at all. She only wanted to be included in the search for William's kidnappers, and that would not happen as long as he suspected her of being one of the conspirators.

She moved a step back from the open window, contenting herself with watching the pair below. Eavesdropping hadn't done her much good, in any event. She was left with more questions than answers. Who was

Osbert? Was the letter for him, or for Christabel? Why had Mr. Mendlicott's name come up? Was Giles going to check up on her?

If he did, what would he find? Since Tobias hadn't made good on his promise to take her to London, she couldn't be sure that he had fulfilled the remainder of their bargain. She might not have a bank account waiting for her in London. No house. No servants. No return trip to the twenty-first century.

That disturbing train of thought almost kept her from seeing Giles take up the reins of his mount and ride off. As soon as he disappeared down the lane, an even more unsettling thought popped into her mind.

She was alone with Royce.

"I am not alone with him. William is here, and Jane."

Not to mention Murch and Dawkes and the cook she had yet to meet. There was no need for her to feel like the heroine in a gothic novel, all fluttery and witless at the prospect of having the brooding hero's attention concentrated on her.

"Humph. Royce may be a hero, at least in the military sense, but he's no Heathcliff. Not even Mr. Rochester. And he doesn't brood tragically so much as he scowls disapprovingly. Mostly at me." She sighed. "All I wanted was to have a little fun, and here I am, stuck in the middle of Lord knows where with a clone of Uncle Fred. An *engaged* clone of Uncle Fred."

"Good morning, miss."

She turned away from the window. "Oh, good morning, Jane. Giles—Lord Stanton—is gone, I see."

"Yes." Jane set the tray on the table next to the bed and began fussing with the covers.

"What?" asked Arden. "I can see you are bursting to say something."

Ducking her head, Jane picked up the pot on the tray and poured steaming tea into a china cup. "No. It wouldn't be proper."

"Proper schmoper. Out with it."

"Are you . . . that is . . . is he . . . ?"

"He who?"

"Lord Royce. Is he keeping you here against your will? Are you a prisoner of passion?"

A shiver went swiftly up, then slowly down Arden's spine. "Prisoner of passion? Certainly not. Never. Not a chance. Why do you ask? What have you heard?"

"Cook—Mrs. Brown—thinks it is very strange that you are here. She says you cannot be a lady." Jane's hand flew to her mouth.

"Don't worry about that. The cook is not the only one who thinks I'm not a lady."

Lowering her hand, Jane blurted, "But she thinks you are Lord Royce's ladybird."

"Ladybird?" It took her a moment to remember what that term meant in Regency times. "Lord Royce's mistress? Me?" Arden laughed, a little shakily.

"I knew it was not so," said Jane, obviously relieved.

"No, it is definitely not true." She eyed Jane, who persisted in refusing to meet her gaze. "And? What else?"

"Nothing."

"Yes. You've still got that look about you—you're curious about something else."

"Well, if you are not Lord Royce's ladybird, why are you here? I told Mrs. Brown either you must be His Grace's governess, or you are being held here against your will."

"As a prisoner of passion? Where on earth did you get that term?"

"*The Prisoner of Passion*—the title of a novel I'm reading."

"Oh, you must let me borrow it. The only books I've seen here are musty tomes on farming or hunting and fishing. Not one single novel."

"I brought *The Prisoner of Passion* from Wolverton. I have almost finished it."

"I must say being a prisoner of passion sounds thrilling, but I am not being held against my will. And the only passion I have observed emanating from Lord Royce is his passionate desire to be rid of me. I'm not a governess, though. Not exactly. But because William is in danger . . . you do know that he was kidnapped, don't you?"

Jane nodded.

"Well, until he can safely return to his home, I agreed to help take care of him."

"Are you not worried about your reputation?"

"No. Why is everyone so concerned about my reputation? How can helping someone hurt my reputation?"

"You are living under the same roof with a gentleman, and there is no other woman here to act as chaperon."

"That's not true. You are here. Mrs. Brown is here."

"We are servants."

"That shouldn't mean you don't count. But even if you and Mrs. Brown don't qualify as chaperons, I'm not worried. Once William is safe, I intend to continue on my journey to London. No one there will know where I've been, or with whom I've been staying."

Jane shot her a dubious look. "I suppose not."

"Plus, I can guarantee that Lord Royce does not have wicked designs on me. As you said, he is a gentleman. A gentleman wouldn't do anything to harm a woman's reputation."

It was Jane's turn to laugh.

"What's so funny?"

"Lord Royce, before his brother died, was a notorious rogue. Being alone with him for even a few minutes would have tarnished any girl's reputation beyond repair."

"A rogue? The sanctimonious Captain Warrick? I don't believe it. Who told you that?"

"It is common knowledge below stairs." With a guilty look over her shoulder, Jane lowered her voice to a whisper. "He had mistresses—opera singers, dancers, a widow or two. And that's not all. He bet on anything, and he raced everything—horses, phaetons. Once I heard he even raced the old duke's traveling carriage against another lord's curricle—and won. Lord Royce fought—"

"Duels?"

"No. At least, not that I ever heard. But he engaged in mills."

"Mills? Fistfights?"

"Yes, miss."

"Well. My goodness. I never would have thought . . . Are you telling me Lord Royce is a rake?"

Jane sobered. "Was. But he is a gentleman, as you said. I never heard even a rumor that he had ruined an innocent. And once his brother died and he became head of the family, he left off his wild ways. The last time Her Grace was at Wolverton, I heard her say it only needed his engagement to Lady Christabel to make his reformation complete."

"Good for him." Arden said, disgruntled and strangely disappointed. "And for me. I don't have anything to worry about from that quarter now that he is no longer a rake." What was the matter with her? She certainly could not want to be a prisoner of passion. But honesty forced her to admit to herself that a rogue sounded much more exciting and entertaining than a stuffed shirt.

And she did want to have fun.

Arden had read several books about Regency girls who had undertaken the task of reforming a rake. She had never read one about a woman trying to do the opposite, however. The Freret side of her brain immediately put forth the suggestion that unreforming a reformed rake might be an interesting way to spend the time until Giles returned.

Firmly squelching the thought of doing any such thing, Arden virtuously reminded herself that she had other useful ways to spend her time. "Where is William? He must have been up to see Lord Stanton off."

"Oh, yes, ma'am. But Lord Royce made him watch from the doorway. He didn't want anyone to see His Grace. The duke and Murch are in the billiard room. I believe Murch is teaching him how to play the game."

"That's nice. The exercise will be good for William."

"I should have realized that the young duke's safety was the reason for your presence. Wait until I tell Mrs. Brown."

"Oh, don't spoil it for her. Let her think I am a prisoner of passion if it makes her happy. Now, would you like to try to do something with this mop?" Arden pointed to her unruly curls.

Jane nodded, her eyes sparkling.

As soon as her hair was combed and styled, Arden followed Jane down the stairs.

"Good morning." Arden entered the dining room in a whirl of blue muslin. "Don't get up on my account."

Royce shifted in his chair, stretching his injured leg in front of him. The room seemed suddenly brighter, the day ahead full of promise. Not because Miss St. Clare had suddenly appeared, however. Any person entering the room would have had the same effect. He was bored, and even though Giles had ridden off only minutes ago, he already missed his company. "I did not intend to."

The saucy wench sent a careless smile in his direction, then went to the sideboard and began heaping a plate with food. "I'm starving. It must be the country air. Although I must admit I have always had a healthy appetite. I hope you're not one of those men who think a woman should eat like a bird. Not that your opinion of me matters in the least," she said, fluttering her eyelashes at him. "Can I get you anything else?"

"More tea, if you please." Royce narrowed his eyes

suspiciously. Miss St. Clare was behaving most charmingly this morning.

"My pleasure." Setting down her plate, she walked over to him and picked up his empty cup, brushing his arm with hers.

What was the chit up to? He would swear she was flirting with him. His pulse quickened. Royce put his heightened awareness to the fact that he had not been alone with an attractive female in months. Raising an eyebrow, he said, "That you care nothing for anyone's opinion is quite clear."

"Not true. I would want someone I liked to think well of me. William, for example." She refilled his cup and placed it in front of him. She reclaimed her full plate and sat down, taking the chair next to him.

"And Giles?"

Her mouth full, Arden nodded.

"But not me?"

"No. You don't like me. Therefore, I don't like you." Her words were softened by another brilliant smile.

"You are very direct."

"Honesty is the best policy," she said, lowering her eyes demurely.

"Except when you speak of how you came to be in the neighborhood." Her behavior was making him surer than ever that she had been abandoned by her protector. And, by the looks of things, she had set her sights on him to take up where the unknown man had left off.

She pouted prettily. "I told you as much as I can about that. Why is how I came to be here so important?"

"The how is not as important as the who. Who left you alone in the forest?"

Waving a fork in the air, she said, "Tobias Thistlewaite. I'm quite sure I told you that before. Tobias is the owner of the agency that arranged my trip from New Orleans to London."

"You are not in London."

"I know. There was a problem. We got off course.

That is really all the explanation I can give you." She took a bite of toast and chewed for a moment or two. "You still suspect me of being involved with the people who are trying to hurt William?"

"Yes. I do."

"I'm not. I wouldn't do anything to harm a child. Or an adult, for that matter. But there is no way I can prove my innocence." She fluttered her lashes again. "I don't suppose you could just take my word for it?"

"No."

Sighing, she nodded. "I understand. William's safety must come first."

"Yes."

"Even if you aren't sure about me, couldn't you let me help anyway? If you tell me who the possible suspects are, and why you suspect them, I could offer my opinion. Perhaps I would see something you've missed."

"That could be a clever way for you to find out what we know."

"Oh. You're right. I hadn't thought of that. Isn't there anything I can do?"

"Not at the moment. There is little to be done by any of us until we hear from Giles."

Pushing her empty plate to one side, Arden put her elbows on the table and rested her chin on her folded hands. A speculative gleam lit her large blue eyes. "What shall we do to occupy the time until Giles returns?" Not giving him time to respond, she added, "I know. You can tell me about—"

"Vauxhall Gardens? Astley's Royal Amphitheater?"

"Later, perhaps. Tell me about the Season."

"What do you want to know?"

"Are there balls every week?"

"At least one or two every night."

"With dancing?"

"Naturally. Have you never been to a ball?"

"Oh, yes. But only Mardi—carnival balls. And I was

only allowed to dance with men approved by my uncle. They were usually his peers, not mine. And no one waltzed. I think the waltz is the most romantic dance, don't you?"

"The waltz has not been accepted in Louisiana? With its French heritage, I would have thought the dance would be as popular there as in Paris and London."

"It is. But my uncle Fred does not approve. I can't wait to go to a ball and dance until dawn. Will you waltz with me?"

"Miss St. Clare, have you forgotten that I am betrothed?"

Her lips curved into a rueful smile. "I didn't forget. I was hoping *you* had. I suppose you must save all your waltzes for your fiancée. Tell me about her. What does she look like? Is she beautiful?"

"Lady Christabel is very beautiful," Royce said, his inflection repressive. It did not seem proper to be discussing Christabel with Arden. On the other hand, for some reason, he was loath to end the conversation.

"Is she blonde? Brunette?"

"She has auburn hair."

"And her eyes? What color are they? Green?"

He did not remember. Frowning, Royce tried to conjure up an image of his betrothed, without much success. He knew she was beautiful, but the features that made her so would not come into view. Christabel's eyes might be green. "Her eyes are the color of emeralds," he said decisively.

Arden sighed. "I always wanted green eyes. I don't suppose you think my eyes resemble sapphires?" She opened her eyes wide and gazed at him. "Never mind. Don't answer that. Where did you meet her?"

"Who?"

"Lady Christabel. Where did you meet?"

He could not recall that at the moment, either. "At a ball," he improvised, although it might have been at the opera. Of one thing he was sure. "My sister-in-law introduced us."

"When did you kiss her for the first time?"

"On the occasion of our betrothal." This was outside of enough. Her impertinent questions had to be stopped. "Miss St. Clare—"

"Not before?"

"Certainly not. Lady Christabel is a lady."

"Calling a Lady a lady seems redundant somehow. So. Ladies do not kiss men unless they are engaged?"

Royce's gaze fell to her lips, parted invitingly. As if she were aware of the direction of his stare, she let her tongue slide slowly over her upper lip. "Miss St. Clare—"

She closed his lips with the tip of a finger. "Not Miss St. Clare. Arden."

"Miss St. Clare." She *was* flirting with him. Most outrageously. Royce was tempted to remain and see how far the bold minx would go. But, although he had never promised Christabel that he would be faithful before, or after, their marriage, he could not forget his vow to his brother. No matter how seductive she was, he had no intention of allowing the brazen Miss St. Clare to think she could lure him into a scandal broth.

Shoving away from the table, Royce prepared to retreat from the dining room with his family's honor intact. "I believe I will retire to my room to rest." His attempt at a dignified exit ended when his leg buckled. Royce grabbed the edge of the table to steady himself.

"Oh!" Arden exclaimed as she half rose from her chair. "Are you all right? Is your leg bothering you?"

"No more than usual. I stood up too quickly."

"Are you so anxious to get away from me?"

"Yes. No. That is, I am merely obeying the doctor's orders."

"Rest is not going to restore your strength. You really should exercise. Let me see if I remember . . . Leg raises—that was one of the exercises Uncle Fred did several times a day. He also did squats and lunges, once his muscles could take it."

"Squats? Lunges?"

"I could show you."

"No." He groaned the word.

"What's the matter?"

"Leg. Cramp." Wincing, he sat down again.

Arden left her chair to kneel by his side, her hand going to his thigh. "I can feel the muscle spasm. Lie down."

"I beg your pardon." Royce had noticed when she entered the room that the blue dress had a neckline lower than the dresses she had worn before. Now, as she knelt in front of him, the neckline gaped open, and he could see that her breasts were barely covered by a scrap of satin and lace. Royce had never seen a shift like that.

"Oh, never mind. I can do it with you seated." She began to knead his thigh.

"Take your hands off me."

Giggling, Arden continued with her massage. "You sound like an outraged maiden in a gothic novel. Have you read *The Prisoner of Passion?*"

"Good God, no." Royce would have repeated the hands-off order, but Arden's hands were beginning to work some kind of magic. The poor abused muscles in his injured leg were loosening and relaxing in the most amazing way.

"Neither have I, but it sounds as if it might be entertaining. The book, I mean, not being a prisoner of passion. Although I can imagine that might be exciting, too. How do you feel about passion?"

"Indifferent."

"Really? How sad. How am I doing? Do you feel better?"

"Yes." Royce felt constrained to add, "But it is most improper for you to be touching me."

"Pooh. I'm not exactly caressing you."

She had the right of that. Her fingers dug into his thigh hard enough to make him wince again. But no caress could have brought more pleasure. Perhaps the American doctors knew more about reviving injured muscles than the village bones he had consulted.

Shifting position slightly, Arden said, "This would be easier if you were on a bed, and if you had your trousers off."

"Miss St. Clare!"

"Well, it would. But I suppose there's no chance I could get you on a bed with your pants down."

"No chance at all," he said, giving her a severe look. He might protest, but he could not prevent his body from reacting to her improper suggestion. Royce felt himself growing hard. His semi-aroused condition must be obvious to Arden. But she seemed to be concentrating only on the deep massage she was zealously administering.

"You don't have any relatives who've emigrated to America, do you?"

"No."

"Hmmm. Must be a coincidence, then."

"What?"

"That you're so like the stuffy St. Clares."

His eyebrows shot up. "Your family is stuffy?"

"You needn't look so surprised. My father's family is extremely straightlaced. The St. Clares are stuffy, staid, and proper. Just like you."

"And your mother's family? Freret was her name?"

"The frivolous Frerets. My mother was reckless and bold, and she loved to have fun." She looked up at him, smiling. "I take after her."

"I might have known."

"You sound as if you don't approve of people having fun."

"Duty and responsibility must come before pleasure."

"Why not hand in hand? Couldn't one be dutiful and responsible and have fun, too?"

"No."

"I don't see why not. Unless the duty is unwelcome and the responsibility oppressive. Are we talking about duty to one's family, by chance? If so, I understand. I must admit I do not always enjoy the duties and responsibilities of being the St. Clare heiress."

"You have no brothers?"

"No, and Uncle Fred and Aunt Marie are childless. I've already inherited my father's estate, and I will inherit from my aunt and uncle, too, some day. So I have to learn about the business. Uncle Fred says wealth is a terrible responsibility. So many people depend on you."

"Your uncle sounds like a sensible man."

"Oh, Uncle Fred is nothing if not sensible. And dutiful. And responsible. But I do think he could unbend now and then and have a little fun."

"How is it that you have not married? Would not your uncle prefer to hand over responsibility for his dependents to a man?"

She sat back on her heels and stared at him, eyes widened. "You think Uncle Fred should have arranged a marriage for me just to gain a CEO?"

"CEO?"

"Chief Executive Officer. A manager. Knowing Uncle Fred, I think you may be right. It is very possible he would prefer to have a man running things, but, since I have my own fortune, there is no way he can force me to marry."

"You prefer to remain a spinster?"

"Yes, I do. I don't like the label 'spinster,' however. In Louisiana a single woman is called a *femme seule.* I like that better."

"French again."

"Yes. We were a colony of France for a long time. As to why I remain a *femme seule,* I haven't met a man . . ." She stopped abruptly, frowning. After a moment, she continued, "If I must wed, I want to marry for love."

"Ah. You are a romantic."

"Where marriage is concerned, most definitely. Don't you love Lady Christabel?"

"Lady Christabel has every quality I desire in a wife. I am sure that we will deal very well together."

" 'Dealing together' sounds like a business arrangement. Is that how you think of marriage?"

"A successful marriage is one of the duties and responsibilities owed to one's family."

"Yes, but in the absence of love, what makes a marriage successful?"

"Being of the same class. Valuing the same virtues."

"Oh." The frown reappeared. Royce resisted the impulse to smooth the wrinkles from between Arden's brows. "Yes, I suppose having similar backgrounds would help. But what about opposites attracting? That happens quite frequently, I believe."

"Usually with disastrous results."

"So you would never consider marrying someone from a different class or . . . country?"

"The question is moot, since I have found my bride. Why all the questions about marriage? I believe you denied any interest in seeking a husband. Have you changed your mind?"

"N-no. I am curious about the local customs, that's all. One reason to travel is to learn how other people do things." She stood up and patted him on the knee. "That's enough for now. If I remember correctly, my uncle's masseur massaged his leg twice a day. Shall we make an appointment for another treatment this evening, after dinner?"

"It would be better if you could show Dawkes the technique."

"Would it?"

Royce swallowed a groan. The improper Miss St.

Clare had a way of reminding him of the pleasure to be found with a woman of the world. "Yes, it would." He uttered the words from between clenched teeth.

"Well, it's your leg. But the sooner you can ride, the sooner we can leave here and join Giles in London."

"This evening, then."

"Your room or mine?" she asked, her voice seductively low. The minx winked at him.

Mesmerized, Royce did not answer. Her eyes were like sapphires, and her lips as red and juicy as the tastiest apple.

"Royce?" She waved a hand in front of his face. "The massage. This evening. Your room?"

He shook his head, clearing it. "No. The parlor. You can demonstrate the massage there."

Seven

"Well, that was interesting," Arden murmured as Royce left the room.

Interesting, but inconclusive.

Royce had reacted to her touch, but she had a feeling the reaction was both involuntary and unwelcome. On the other hand, he did not want her touching him again. Perhaps he was afraid he might succumb to her caresses and . . . what? Throw her onto the nearest flat surface and make her his prisoner of passion?

Not likely, no matter how appealing the prospect.

Perhaps he wanted to avoid her because he was being true to his fiancée. Piously, her St. Clare side chided her for attempting to come between a man and his betrothed. "Bite me," Arden responded. Playing the femme fatale had felt deliciously wicked, and her Freret side was cheering her on.

"It's not like I'm doing anything really terrible, like wrecking a home. There isn't a home to wreck, yet. He's only engaged, not married."

And Royce had seemed a little vague about the details of his courtship. All in all, his enthusiasm for the wedded state—at least with Lady Christabel—had been encouragingly underwhelming.

" 'Deal very well together' doesn't sound like a sound basis for lasting happiness to me. I certainly wouldn't settle for that. If it were me, I would want to marry my—"

Heart's desire. That odd phrase of Tobias's slipped into her consciousness again.

Knees trembling, Arden sat down in the nearest chair.

Could Royce be what she had traveled through time to find?

With a violent shake of her head, she said, "No!" After a moment, she said, "All right, so he is honorable and brave and responsible. Not to mention handsome and sexy as all get out. But . . . Royce Warrick is no *fun.* Therefore, he cannot be the man of my dreams." Frowning, she tapped her nails on the table. "All right, so he is dream worthy. Is he worth being stuck in the past forever? I don't think so."

She had begun her experiment in flirtation with the vague idea of a brief fling. After all, this might be the first and last chance she ever had to have an affair. She could almost guarantee that Uncle Fred and Aunt Marie would keep her on an even shorter leash once she got home again. Royce had been right about one thing: Uncle Fred would like nothing better than to arrange a marriage for her. And if she knew her uncle Fred, his choice of a husband for her would be a stodgy businessman without a chuckle in him.

Someone exactly like Royce was pretending to be, in fact. Unless he wasn't pretending, and fun really was not important to him. Now that she thought about it, having a good time couldn't matter to him, not if he'd gotten himself engaged to someone he did not love.

Arden pressed a hand to her chest. Her heart hurt at the thought of Royce spending a lifetime of "dealing well together" with his perfect English lady.

But it was not her job to save Royce from his future, no matter how gloomy it looked to her. Even if she wanted to save him from himself, she didn't have a lifetime to dedicate to making him happy. She had her own future to return to, and their two futures were centuries apart.

The wedded bliss, or lack thereof, between Lord Royce and Lady Christabel should be 'none of her concern,' to use the reformed rake's favorite admonition.

Placing both hands on the table, she pushed herself up and out of the chair. This was not the time to be sitting around wasting time mooning about affairs of the heart, neither hers nor Royce's. She needed to find Tobias, expose William's assailants, and get to London, not necessarily in that order. Worrying about Royce's chances for happiness was not going to help her reach any of those goals.

Firmly repressing all thoughts of love and marriage, Arden considered what to do next. William might be able to answer some of her questions about the people Giles had mentioned, but pumping a child for information seemed tacky. If she had been thinking like a St. Clare and not like a frivolous Freret, she might have used her time with Royce to wheedle the information out of him. As it was, she still didn't know who Osbert was, or why Hugh Mendlicott's name had come up.

Jane might know, at least about Osbert, and her maid seemed more than willing to talk. Arden rang the bell hanging next to the sideboard. A moment later, Jane entered the room.

"Jane, do you know anyone named Osbert?"

"Would that be Osbert Sharpless, Her Grace's brother?"

"I suppose so. How many Osberts can there be? What do you know about him?"

Jane wrinkled her nose. "Mr. Sharpless is not well liked by the servants. Especially the female servants. He pinches."

"Good grief. Did he ever pinch you?"

"No. But he is not often at Wolverton. He prefers London. Isabel, Lady Christabel's maid, warned me about him the last time he was at Wolverton."

"I see. So you have met Lady Christabel?"

"Yes, miss. She has been a frequent visitor since her betrothal to Lord Royce. She almost always accompanies the duchess on her trips to Wolverton."

Feeling as if she were worrying a sore tooth, Arden asked, "Tell me about her. Is she beautiful?"

"She looks like an angel, and she behaves charmingly when in company, but . . ."

"Go on."

"She is not very nice."

"No? Why do you say that?"

"Not just because of what I've heard from other servants. I know about Lady Christabel from personal experience. She has her own maid, but she demands one or two others to serve her whenever she visits Wolverton."

"High maintenance," muttered Arden.

"Excuse me?"

"I meant it sounds as if she requires a lot of attention." Who had provided it while Royce was away?

"Oh. Yes. The last time she was a guest, her maid told her that I was good at dressing hair, so she asked for me. She slapped me because I pulled her hair."

"She *slapped* you?" Arden straightened her spine in outrage. "That is terrible! I hope you hit her back."

"Oh, no, miss. I couldn't do that. I would have lost my position."

"Did you tell the duchess what she did?"

"No. You are the first person I have told. Please do not tell the duchess. She and Lady Christabel are good friends. Her Grace would not believe that she is mean and hateful to the servants."

"Don't worry. I won't tell anyone. But if she ever asks you to fix her hair again, please tell her you are my maid now, and I don't share."

"Yes, miss." Grinning broadly, Jane asked, "Is there anything else you wish to know?"

"Not at the moment. Thank you, Jane. You've been very informative."

Jane curtsied and turned to go.

"No, wait. Do you know where William is?"

"His Grace is in the parlor with Lord Royce, having his lessons. Murch said Lord Royce has taken on the task of tutor."

Arden did not see William and Royce until dinner. Royce was his old somber self, and William appeared subdued as well. He left the room as soon as he finished picking at his food, pleading a headache from so much studying. Royce went with him to tuck him in.

After the meal, Dawkes asked her to show him how to massage his master's leg, which she did by demonstrating on a pillow. The valet refused to allow her to put her hands on him. She also told Dawkes how to do leg raises and squats, and she contented herself with drawing stick figures doing the exercises, rather than shocking the poor man by doing them herself.

For several days, Arden saw William only at breakfast and at dinner. He spent his days closeted with his uncle, and they took the noon meal together in the parlor or the study. Royce she saw hardly at all. Instead of being hurt because he ignored her, or angry because he avoided her, Arden took Royce's retreat as an encouraging sign.

The man was obviously scared to death to be alone with her.

His knees quaked, his heart beat faster, and his palms grew moist. Giles had faced danger a few times in his life, and he recognized the signs. He was afraid.

And the cause of his fear was one small woman, Dora Sharpless Warrick, the fifth Duchess of Wolverton and the woman he had loved for thirteen long years.

The duchess was small in stature, with brown hair and hazel eyes. She dressed simply and seldom wore jewels. Today she wore a round dress in gray muslin trimmed in white lace. A white cap topped her brown curls. Giles knew she thought herself plain, but she never saw herself smile, as she was smiling at him now. Joy transformed her pleasant but unremarkable face into a thing of beauty. She also had a keen mind and a sharp tongue. He had felt its edge the last time they had met when he had attempted to press his suit.

"Giles, how kind of you to call." She held out both hands to him, and he took them in his own. "Do you have news from Wolverton?"

"Yes. Good news. Royce is returned from France." He omitted telling her that Royce's return had occurred several months earlier. She would find out in due time.

"Oh, that *is* good news. Is he well? He wrote that he was injured, but provided few details. You may tell him for me that stoicism can be carried too far."

Giles grinned at her, still holding her hands. "I will. His wounds were serious, but I assure you he is almost fully recovered. He intends to join you here as soon as he is able to travel. Now, I have other news. Your son—"

"William?" Dora pulled her hands free, and one hand went to her breast. "What has happened? Another accident? Tell me he is well."

"He is well and safe. For now. But he is in danger, even more than we suspected." Giles quickly ran down the events of the past week, beginning with William's kidnapping and ending with Arden's part in the duke's rescue.

After shedding a few tears, which she assured him were of happiness, Dora said, "How fortunate that Miss St. Clare was in the woods that night. Did she say how she came to be there?"

"Yes." Giles recited the tale he and Royce had agreed upon. "Her carriage broke an axle, and the coachman left her and her maid with the coach while he went for help. When, after some hours, no help arrived, Miss St.

Clare set out on her own to find assistance. That is when she came upon William."

"What a brave and resourceful young woman! I cannot wait to meet her. She is staying at Wolverton, I presume?"

"Yes." Giles kept his answer brief to the point of curtness. He did not enjoy lying to Dora even though he understood the need to protect Arden's reputation. "Royce and William are at the Stanton hunting box. Royce thought it best to keep William's whereabouts secret as long as possible."

"My poor little boy. Are you sure he is all right?"

"Quite all right. To tell the truth, I think he is enjoying himself. Arden tells him stories of Indians and fur trappers, and Royce is acting as tutor."

"Good. But, Giles, how long will this nightmare go on? Who can be behind these dreadful acts?" Her eyes filled with tears.

"We will do our best to find out." Giles wanted to take her in his arms and comfort her with kisses, but he dared not. Neither could he tell Dora about their suspicions of Osbert. Royce had insisted they keep their own counsel until they had more proof.

"Does Lady Christabel know Royce is returned from the wars?" asked Dora, dabbing at her damp cheeks with a linen handkerchief. "It would be very bad of Royce not to tell her."

"I have a letter from him for her. I will deliver it as soon as I take my leave."

"He has not done well by her," said Dora with a sniff. "Leaving her alone for almost two years—he is fortunate she has not cried off."

"I suppose so."

"She has waited patiently for him. And I can attest to her faithfulness. She never allows anyone to escort her about town except her cousin, Lord Neville. Some women in her position, betrothed and abandoned, might have sought solace in another's arms."

"Abandoned? Surely that is too harsh. Royce had to do his part to defeat Napoleon."

"Nevertheless. He could have written more often. And why did he not return home immediately after Waterloo?"

"You will have to ask him, but I believe he was loath to face you or Lady Christabel in his scarred and weakened condition."

"Scarred? Weakened? Oh, dear. You must think me heartless. How could I have forgotten that Royce could have died? I should not have criticized him. He is a hero, a wounded hero who deserves better from his sister-in-law. Please do not tell him what I said. And do not think that Christabel complained about his treatment of her. It was I, not she, who found his attentions lacking. I am a shrew, just as Robert always said."

"Robert was a pompous ass," Giles blurted.

Dora looked startled. Then she smiled at him. "Well, yes. He was. But he was my husband. As his widow, I must respect his memory."

"Forever? Will you never—"

"Never." Her smile faded. "Is there anything else, Lord Stanton?"

"Now I am out of favor—you called me Giles earlier." Her obvious distress made him hurry to add, "Never mind. I abused our friendship and deserved your set-down. Please forgive me for bringing up a subject distasteful to you."

"Oh, Giles . . ." She bit her lip and looked away.

"On to other matters, then. Royce had a request. He wants Osbert to turn the estate's books over to me so that I may take them to Royce's steward."

"W-why?"

"Royce will, of course, take over the management of the Wolverton estates now that he is back in England."

After a brief pause, Dora nodded. "Of course. I will pass along the request to Osbert."

Giles had a fleeting impression that his request had

annoyed Dora. His presence was the more likely cause, and he had other calls to make. Lady Christabel next, and then Hugh Mendlicott. "Is Osbert not at home?"

"Osbert has removed to his club."

"Recently?"

"Months ago."

"I understand that he dismissed your steward. Has he employed a new man?"

"No. And Osbert did not dismiss Mr. Wells. I did. The man was paying tradesmen only a portion of what they were owed and pocketing the rest."

"Ah. I see. The estate was being bilked, and you thought the steward was to blame."

"Who else? Certainly not Osbert."

He wanted to ask why not Osbert, but Dora seemed even more annoyed. And he was not prepared to accuse her brother. "I will take my leave now. Please send word when I may pick up the books."

Giles bowed and left.

Dora went to her office and pulled out the account books. She spent the remainder of the day checking and double checking the neat rows of numbers, bringing the list of investments she had made up to date, making absolutely sure that Royce's steward could not find fault with her management of her son's estates.

Satisfied that she had done very well by her son, Dora closed the books. The estate could not be in better shape, if she did say so herself.

Of course, Osbert would get all the credit.

Eight

A week after Giles's departure for London, a letter arrived for Royce. Arden happened to be descending the stairs when the messenger arrived. She assumed the letter came from the viscount, since presumably no one else knew where Royce was. She watched as Royce opened the letter, scanned it, and called for William. When the boy arrived in the entryway, her assumption proved true. Royce said, "I have news from Lord Stanton. Miss St. Clare, please excuse us."

With that, Royce and William disappeared into the parlor, leaving Arden standing on the stairs. She had been left to her own devices more often than not since Giles's departure. Time spent with William was devoted to teaching him more self-defense tricks, and she had started him on an exercise routine. Apart from that, Arden had passed the time pleasantly enough talking to Jane and Mrs. Brown. She had won over the cook by sharing recipes with her.

As soon as Jane finished the book, Arden kept boredom at bay by reading *The Prisoner of Passion,* which she enjoyed tremendously in spite of, or perhaps because of, the convoluted plot and florid prose.

Later that afternoon, when his lessons were completed, Arden was invited to join the young duke in the parlor for tea. Lord Royce was nowhere to be seen. Not that she cared. The presence or absence of Royce

Warrick made no difference to her, none at all. *Liar,* said a tiny voice in the back of her head. Arden ignored it and focused her attention on William.

"Is your mother well?"

"Yes. And Lord Stanton says she was very glad to hear that I am safe." He took a dainty sandwich from the tray and bit into it.

"I'm sure she's been very worried about you."

His mouth full, William nodded. Swallowing, he added, "But there was no reason for her to worry. She did not know I was kidnapped."

"Even so. You've been away from her for some weeks. She must miss you. And you must miss her, and your other uncle . . . Osbert, is it?"

"Yes. But I do not miss Uncle Osbert. I had much rather be here with Uncle Royce. He reminds me of my father, or he used to, before he got hurt."

"Has he changed, then?"

"He doesn't smile as much now. I suppose that is because of the war and his injuries. But as soon as he is recovered, he will be his jolly old self again, don't you think?"

"Jolly? Your Uncle Royce was jolly?" She found herself entranced by the image of Royce laughing and having fun. That appealed even more than the idea of a roguish Royce. He was entirely too somber.

"Ever so. He laughed all the time, and he made my father laugh, too, even when he scolded him." William lowered his voice to a whisper. "Uncle Royce sometimes did things my father disapproved of, you see."

"Did he, really?" She almost asked what things, before she remembered her vow not to pump William for information. "Older brothers do that, I suppose— lecture their younger siblings, I mean."

"My mother says that my father would be very proud of him now that he has left off his irresponsible ways and embraced his duty to the family honor."

The singsong way William quoted the duchess made

Arden suppose he had heard the words more than once. "Poor Royce."

"Uncle Royce isn't poor. He has his own estates."

"I didn't mean 'poor' in the monetary sense. I was referring to his not being jolly any longer. What about your uncle Osbert. Is he jolly?"

William shook his head. "Uncle Osbert is bo-ring."

"Does your uncle Osbert live with you?"

"Sometimes. Usually he stays at his club. But he moved to our house for several months when Uncle Royce left for France. He is looking after my estates, you see."

"Oh." Arden drew her brows together. So Osbert had control—at least temporarily—of William's money. That could be reason to suspect him. Giles must be investigating the state of the dukedom's finances. And his findings must be in the letter. Where could Royce have put it? There was an escritoire in the corner of the parlor. She sat her teacup down and began an aimless sort of amble about the room.

"Tell me, William. Do you have any other relatives?"

"Oh, yes. I have a grandmother, a great-aunt, two aunts, my mother's sisters, and their husbands, and"— he paused to count on his fingers—"seven cousins. Plus a distant cousin of my father's. He has the living on one of the Warrick estates in the north."

"A living? He's a minister?" She opened the drawer of the escritoire. Nothing there but blank stationery.

"Yes."

"You don't have any brothers or sisters, do you?"

He shook his head.

"Neither do I. It's lonely sometimes, isn't it?"

"Yes." William lowered his gaze, but not before Arden detected a sheen of tears.

She returned to her seat next to William and patted him on the shoulder. "But now you have me and your uncle Royce to keep you company. How old were you when your father died?"

"Nine."

"I was six when my parents were killed. It's very hard to lose the ones you love, isn't it?"

William nodded, his expression solemn. "I was afraid I had lost Uncle Royce, too. We heard nothing from him for ever so long."

"Humph. That doesn't sound very responsible. He should have written to let you know he was okay."

"O-kay. I like that word. What does it mean?"

"All correct. All right. It's American slang."

"Tell me more about America."

"What do you want to know?"

"Is it true that you do not have a king?"

"Yes. No kings or dukes or earls."

"But who rules?"

"We all do. We vote for men to represent us. We have a president, and senators and congressmen."

"Who is your president?"

That stopped her. Who was president in 1816? Arden quickly ran through the list she'd memorized in grade school. Washington, Adams, Jefferson, Madison, Monroe. Madison's or Monroe's terms would have been in the early nineteenth century, if she remembered correctly. But which one? She hazarded a guess. "James Monroe."

"Have you been presented to him at court?"

"No, I haven't met the president. And he doesn't have a court. He has a cabinet. Men who assist him in running the country."

"You said 'we vote,' but surely women do not vote."

"Yes, we do." she answered absently, still distracted by the notion of Royce as a fun-loving young man. "I mean, no, of course not. Women are not allowed to vote."

"I thought not. It is an outrageous notion."

"For now, I suppose it is. But women will vote some-day, in America and in England."

William gave her a disbelieving look, but politely refrained from contradicting her.

"Now, what shall we do this afternoon? Would you like to play a game?"

"What sort of game? Cards?" He gave her a sly look. "Billiards?"

"No, something else that will have us moving around more. We need exercise, and since we can't go for walks or ride horses . . . I know. How about hide-and-seek? Do you know that game?"

"Yes. But there are only two of us. One of us will always be it, and no one will ever win a game."

"You're right." Arden snapped her fingers. "I know. We'll get Murch and Dawkes to play, too. And Jane."

"We cannot play with servants."

"Is that a rule?"

"Yes."

"Good. Breaking rules is fun. Let's go find them."

"Breaking rules is something a duke may not do," Royce said, standing in the doorway to the parlor. "He must remember his position and set a good example for others."

"But a second son may bend a few rules?" Arden asked, feigning innocence.

Before Royce could respond, William ran to him. "Will you play with us, Uncle Royce? We need a third."

"What game are you playing?"

"Hide-and-seek."

Royce surprised her by agreeing to join in.

"Fine," said Arden. "You're it. Hide your eyes and count to one hundred by fives, and then come look for us."

"I know how to play the game, Miss St. Clare. The first one I find will be it next, and the last one I find wins the game. Correct?"

"Yes." Arden stared at him for a few seconds, not quite able to gauge his mood. Playful or resigned?

"I want to be it," said William. "I am better at finding than at hiding."

"Very well," said Royce. "Begin counting, nephew."

Royce immediately headed for the kitchen at the back of the house. Not wanting to follow him, Arden climbed the stairs, taking them two at a time. She could hear William counting slowly and loudly.

"Twenty, twenty-five, thirty . . ."

When she reached the landing, Arden looked down the hallway. Where to hide? Her room seemed too obvious. Giles's room was next to hers, and William's was opposite. She couldn't hide there—she would feel uncomfortable invading their privacy. She started toward the stairs to the next floor, where Jane and the other servants had rooms. She stopped before she reached the stairs. It didn't seem right to hide in their rooms, either.

"Eighty-five, ninety . . ."

She opened the last door in the hallway, the door to Royce's room, and stepped inside, closing the door softly behind her.

The room was not much different from her own. A bed, an armoire, a chair, and a writing table were the only furniture. She forgot about the game the moment she saw the letter on the table. She headed straight for it.

My dear Warrick:

The Wolverton accounts are in the hands of your steward. At first glance, everything seems to be in order, but he said a thorough examination may turn something up. Osbert did seem a bit nervous when he delivered the books to me, however.

Her Grace is well and sends her love to you and her son. She wept a bit when I told her of William's latest adventure, but she is most gratified to hear the heir is safe, thanks to Miss St. Clare. The duchess wishes to meet William's rescuer as soon as possible so that she may express her gratitude in person. Dora claims she was responsible for dismissing William's steward. She says the man was stealing.

Hugh Mendlicott has not responded to my written inquiry. I will visit his offices later this week.

I delivered your letter to Lady Christabel. Her reply is enclosed.

> Yrs,
> Giles Fairfax, Viscount Stanton

Arden dropped the letter from Giles and quickly searched the table for Christabel's letter. It was not there. "He must have it with him," she murmured. In a pocket next to his heart?

The banging of a door downstairs reminded her that she was supposed to be finding somewhere to hide, not searching for love letters addressed to someone else. Arden looked around the room again. The armoire was the only possible hiding place. She opened the door.

Royce was seated in the back of the armoire, his legs stretched out in front of him. "Find another hiding place, Miss St. Clare. This one is taken."

Clambering into the armoire, Arden pulled the door shut. "Too late. William is on the stairs."

"I do not hear him."

"Don't you?" she whispered, squirming around until she was sprawled across his thighs.

When he attempted to push her away, she wrapped her arms around his waist and held on. "I love playing games, don't you?" she whispered, resting her head on his broad chest. His heartbeat seemed to speed up, encouraging her to press her body closer to his. "This is *fun.*"

"This is a child's game, Miss St. Clare. One we both agreed to play for William's sake."

"True. But we could play an adult game while we

wait to be found." She slid one hand slowly up his chest, feeling his muscles under the fine lawn of his shirt.

He put his hand on top of hers, stopping her exploration.

"Miss St. Clare. I must insist that you find another place to hide." His voice sounded strained.

"I don't want to find another place. I like it here, with you. Cozy, isn't it?"

"I find it crowded." He hissed the words. "You had better leave."

She ignored his order. She wasn't about to leave now that she had him where she wanted him. "How did you get here before me? You went toward the kitchen."

"Back stairs," whispered Royce, his breath tickling her ear. "Be still. You're making my leg cramp."

"Oh, sorry." Forcing herself to remain motionless, she held her breath and listened. She heard nothing except Royce's breathing and their separate heartbeats. His seemed a little faster than hers. Taking a deep breath, she snuggled closer.

Reaching across her, Royce pushed on the armoire door. It did not open, much to Arden's delight.

"The door must be stuck," she said. "We're trapped in here. Together."

Groaning, Royce drew his arm back from the door. "It is not stuck. I cannot get leverage to open it with you in my lap." His hand came to rest under her breast, against the underwire of her bra. Tracing the wire with his finger, Royce asked, "What are you wearing? Stays? I thought they went out of fashion."

"Not in New Orleans," she squeaked. His hand so close to her breast was causing her nipples to pebble. "Stays are all the rage in New Orleans," she gasped, not prepared for her reaction to his touch. She was supposed to be seducing him, not the other way around, she reminded herself severely.

"I never felt stays quite like these," he whispered, continuing his exploration.

"Oh, no? Are you so familiar with women's undergarments, then?" She tried to match his cool sophistication, but her voice sounded embarrassingly shrill.

"I used to be something of an expert. My brother's death and the war interrupted my studies, however."

"And your engagement should have put an end to them altogether," she said, deciding to put off his seduction for another day. She tried to pull his hand away from her midriff.

"Do you think so? I am sure Lady Christabel would be interested in any novel colonial undergarments. She is something of a trendsetter. Are you not wearing a shift?"

"That is most definitely none of your concern. And Louisiana is not a colony, but a state—territory—in an independent country."

"With independent misses as its chief export." Now his hand moved to her waist, and lower. His questing fingers found the elastic waistband to her bikini panties. "What have we here?"

"P-panties. In lieu of a shift."

"Aha! So you are shiftless." He made a noise that could have been a chuckle. "Pants. Sleeping trousers. Why do American women give their garments masculine names?"

"Not pants. Panties." She grabbed his hand and held it. "On second thought, I believe you're right. I should find another place to hide. If William finds us together, there won't be a winner. We both lose."

"Not necessarily." Pulling his hand free, Royce used one finger to tilt up her chin. Before she realized what he intended, his mouth covered hers.

He didn't kiss like a St. Clare. Not that she'd ever been French kissed by any of her relations, but she was sure no St. Clare kissed like this. No stuffy, self-righteous lord could know how to make her shiver with longing with just his mouth. This must be the rogue. Only a rogue would be able to dissolve her bones with his lips. And his wicked tongue. And his hands, one holding her face, the other . . . the other sliding down her neck . . . lower . . . not low enough. Arching her back, Arden offered him her breast, aching with need for his caress.

He complied. His hand closed on her breast, his thumb finding her nipple and coaxing it even more erect. Someone moaned. She thought it might be herself. Winding her arms around his neck, Arden melted into the kiss.

The armoire door was flung open. Almost simultaneously, Arden was flung from Royce's embrace and out of their hiding place, landing in a heap at William's feet.

"Arden! Uncle Royce! What are you doing? Were you *kissing?"*

"No, of course not," Royce said, following Arden out of the armoire with considerably more grace.

As she self-consciously straightened her clothes, Arden avoided meeting William's eyes, which she suspected held the disgust only an eleven-year-old boy would feel for such adult activities as *kissing.*

"Yes, you were. You were kissing her. You lied to me."

"We will discuss this later, William." Royce straightened up with a grimace.

Arden held out a hand to him, which he did not take. "Is your leg cramping?"

"No. My leg is much improved. But it fell asleep while you were sitting on it."

"You *sat* on my uncle?" William, obviously outraged, turned his glare toward Arden. "I don't want to play games with you anymore." He stormed out of the room.

"Well. Now look what you've done," said Arden. "I told you I should find another place to hide."

"I beg your pardon. I told you first. You were the

one who wanted to stay in the armoire and play adult games."

"I didn't notice you trying too hard to escape. You are the one who started fondling my underwear, and you are the one who kissed me. If you didn't want to play my game, why did you do that?"

He looked down his aristocratic nose at her. The stuffed shirt was back, in spades. "To prove to myself the kind of woman you are."

"Not a lady."

"Definitely not."

"Well, then, you're no gentleman. What kind of gentleman kisses one woman when he's engaged to another?"

"Most gentlemen, as a matter of fact, would take advantage of the opportunity you offered in the armoire."

"Oh, I see. Well, let me tell you a thing or two, Lord Royce—"

A door slammed from below.

Royce pushed her away. "That was the front door. William has gone outside." He headed down the stairs.

Arden followed close behind.

"Dawkes! Murch!" Royce called from the stairs. "William has run away. We must find him immediately."

"I'm coming, too," Arden said, rushing past Royce to the cloakroom. Quickly donning her pelisse, she followed the three men out the door.

Once outside, Royce directed Dawkes and Murch to the stables for horses. "I will search on foot . . . there." He pointed to the woods north of the house.

"I'll go the other way," said Arden. She ran, as fast as her long skirt would allow, toward a small lake. Willow trees lined the shore, and William might be hiding beneath their weeping branches. When she reached the lake, she began a slow tour around its perimeter, peering up into the leafless branches of the trees.

"William? Are you here? Please come out. You mustn't be angry with your uncle. It wasn't his fault. He did not kiss me. I kissed him."

She heard a noise, a soft rustle of the fallen leaves. Looking around, she saw no one, but the tiny hairs on the back of her neck were standing at attention. Shivering, and not from the cold, she hissed, "Is that you, William?"

Someone sniffled. The sound came from in front of her, and the other noise had come from behind. Slowly, Arden moved toward the sniffle. "You aren't crying, are you? I am so sorry I upset you, William. I—"

She saw him. William was sitting at the foot of a willow tree, his legs hugged to his chest, his forehead resting on his knees. As she approached, he looked up at her. His face was flushed and wet with angry tears.

"You are lying. A lady *never* kisses a gentleman. A gentleman kisses her." He glared at her. "And a gentleman does not kiss a lady unless they are engaged. Uncle Royce is not a gentleman. He is a rake, just as my father always said. He has not changed at all, even though my mother said he *promised* my father he would."

"William Robert Warrick! Your uncle is not a rake. He most certainly is a gentleman. And I did so kiss him. Where did you ever get the idea that women don't kiss men?"

"My mother told me that a lady may not kiss a gentleman until they are engaged. *She* would not lie to me."

"No one lied to you. Your uncle did not kiss me, and your mother told you the exact truth when she said a lady never kisses a gentleman. However, I'm afraid I'm not as ladylike as I should be sometimes."

William scrunched his brows together, obviously deep in thought. After a moment, his brow cleared and he nodded. "I heard Uncle Royce tell Giles something of the sort about you. I believe you did kiss my uncle in the armoire."

"I'm glad we got that settled. Are you ready to go home now?" She held out a hand.

He did not take it. *"Why* did you kiss him? You do not like my uncle. You are always arguing with him, and you wanted to throw him over your shoulder."

"Yes. Well. It's a little hard to explain. Come on, William. We need to get back to the house."

"Not yet." William wiggled closer to the trunk of the tree and leaned his back against it. "I wish you would explain. Were you trying to compromise him? It would not have done you any good. He could not marry you. Uncle Royce is betrothed, and he may not honorably break his engagement, even if he is seen kissing another girl." Narrowing his eyes, he looked up at her. "Although, if Lady Christabel knew about the kiss, she could cry off."

"Trust me, William. Lady Christabel will never know about what went on in the armoire. And I was not trying to compromise Lord Royce. I have no desire to marry your uncle." *Liar,* said a tiny voice in the back of her head. Shock made Arden stammer. "I-it was only a k-kiss, for heaven's sake. There is no need to be talking of compromising positions and breaking engagements."

"But why *do* men and women kiss? I would like to know more about kissing . . . and things. No one wants to tell me anything."

"Billy Bob! Are you asking me about the birds and bees?"

He shook his head. "No. I want to know about men and women."

"Oh. Men and women. What exactly do you want to know about them?"

William's cheeks turned bright red. "What they do together when they are alone. I asked my tutor, but he said I was too young to be concerned with such matters."

"I don't think you're too young. But I am not the person to tell you." Arden was almost positive she knew more about sex than any unmarried nineteenth-century girl would or should know. And, while she was all in favor of sex education, she did not want to overwhelm an eleven-year-old boy with more than he wanted or needed to know. "I will ask your uncle to answer your questions as soon as we get back to the house. Come on—"

She heard the noise again—a faint rustle of leaves, as if someone were creeping up on them. "William." She whispered his name. "Do you see anyone behind me?"

"N-no. But I heard something."

"So did I. I think someone is watching us. I want you to stand up slowly, then get behind the tree as fast as you can. This is important, Billy Bob. Okay?"

"Okay."

In a louder voice, Arden said, "All right, William. Enough of your nonsense. You get up and come with me this minute."

William followed her instructions, getting up slowly as if he were reluctant to obey her order, then moving quickly to put the tree between him and whoever was stalking them.

A loud crunch of leaves made Arden look over her shoulder. A masked man came out of the trees holding a gun. "Run, William!" she cried.

"Who the devil are you?" the man muttered as he raised his weapon and aimed it straight at her.

William chose that moment to peek from behind the tree. "Arden! Look out!"

The barrel of the gun swiveled in William's direction. Arden could see the masked man's finger begin to squeeze the trigger. She threw herself at him, pushing his arm up as the gun went off.

With a snarled curse, the man backhanded Arden, hitting her on the side of her face and sending her sprawling to the ground.

Arden saw stars. William was yelling, and she could hear shouts and the sound of people running.

Everything went black.

Nine

Royce raced toward the sound of the shot. He heard William shouting, and then he saw him. William was kneeling next to Arden, who lay on the ground. She was very still. Too still. His heart stopped beating. "Arden," he called, using her name for the first time. He prayed it would not be the last.

Kneeling next to her, he began running his hands over her, searching for a wound. William knelt next to him, his eyes wide with anxiety. "William, are you all right?"

"Y-yes. I am sorry I ran away. This is all my fault. She is bleeding. Do not let her die, Uncle Royce. Please don't let her die. He was pointing the gun at me and she hit his arm and then the gun went off." William began crying noisily.

Her face was bloody from a small cut just below her left eye, and she was unconscious. But she was breathing. "Hush, William. Miss St. Clare is not dead. Not shot, either. The bloody bastard must have hit her. We must get her back to the house."

As Royce took Arden into his arms, Dawkes rode up, followed closely by Murch. "We heard a shot. What happened?" asked Murch, dismounting.

"Someone tried to shoot William. Arden stopped him, but the villain hit her hard enough to knock her out. Murch, take William up and return to the house.

Dawkes, see if you can find any trace of the gunman. Be careful. He has had time to reload."

With a nod, Dawkes rode off. Murch tossed William onto the saddle and mounted behind him.

Royce held Arden close and began walking toward the house. After only a few steps, she moaned and opened her eyes. "William?"

"William is fine. Murch has him safe. How do you feel?"

"Like someone hit me. It hurts." She closed her eyes and rested her head on Royce's shoulder.

"I know it hurts, my brave girl." He placed his lips on the top of her golden head. "But you are alive, and so is William. No one will ever hurt either of you again. I promise."

Mrs. Brown and Jane were waiting for them with hot water and bandages, alerted by Murch and William. Royce carried Arden up the stairs and placed her on her bed. Jane covered her with a soft blanket. Mrs. Brown held the basin of water, while Jane carefully washed the blood from Arden's cheek.

"I'm going to have a shiner, aren't I?" she said, wincing.

"A shiner?" asked William, who had been ordered to bed but had insisted on staying with Arden. "What is that?"

"A black eye."

"Oh. Yes, I believe you have the right of it. Your eye is already beginning to swell. But, Arden, he could have *killed* you. The gun was pointed right at me, and you . . ." His face crumpled, and he threw himself against her.

Arden hugged him close and kissed the top of his head. "I'm all right. A little cut on the cheek is nothing to get excited about."

"In this case, I would call it a badge of honor," said Royce, struggling with the most appalling desire to push his nephew aside and let Arden shower her affection on him instead.

"I've brought you a nice cup of tea, miss," said Murch, bustling into the bedroom with a tray. "Whenever you feel up to a sip, let me know."

Dawkes crowded into the room, too. He reported to Royce, then joined the others surrounding the bed. Moving closer to the door, Royce watched as his nephew and his servants cosseted and cuddled Arden.

She had charmed them all.

Including him.

Damn. Damn. Damn. Royce began pacing from one side of the room to the other. He could not allow Arden to add him to her list of conquests. But how to stop her? He could no longer use suspicion as an antidote to her allure. She had saved William twice, and the second rescue left no room for doubt: Arden was not involved in the attempts on William's life.

If she were inexperienced and naive—in other words, a virgin—continuing to treat her with the respect and deference due her status would be easier, no matter how tempting he found her. But while Arden had always proclaimed herself innocent of harming William, she had never claimed to be an innocent where men were concerned. The interlude in the armoire would have put an end to any such claims, in any event. She had deliberately set out to tempt him.

Royce found himself wishing he had met Arden years ago, before the hunting accident that ended Robert's life. He would not have hesitated to offer the bold temptress carte-blanche, an invitation Arden surely would have accepted. Then he would have kept her tucked away in a cozy love nest until he had cured himself of his desire for her. With a disgusted snort, Royce abruptly ended that line of thought. He was acting like a lovesick schoolboy, weaving silly dreams about, when one came down to it, nothing more than scratching an itch.

A damned inconvenient itch.

For a damnably appealing woman.

Royce stopped pacing. As soon as William was safe, and Royce intended that to be very soon, he would wed Christabel and find release in the marriage bed. This was not the time to allow his lust for another woman to overcome the respectability he had worked so hard to achieve.

"All right. Miss St. Clare has had more than enough attention from all of you. Leave her now, and let her rest."

As her admirers filed out of the room, Arden looked at him and grinned, her cheek marred by a jagged cut, her eye beginning to swell shut. No woman had ever been more beautiful to him. Royce forced himself to look away from her. One more moment gazing at her poor bruised face and he might not be able to resist her.

As he stared out the window, an insidious voice whispered that it was possible for him to have Arden and to keep his promise to Robert, too. Many men of the *ton* kept mistresses after they wed, without bringing dishonor to themselves or their families.

Royce tried to quiet the voice, telling himself that Arden, lady or not, experienced or not, deserved a chance to find a man who would marry her. He could not selfishly take that opportunity from her. The wicked voice sneered that she was already beyond the pale. Had she not spent a week under the same roof with him? If that became a matter of public knowledge, no gentleman would offer for her.

But no one would know. He had instructed Giles to tell the duchess that Arden was staying at Wolverton. Her reputation would be safe, her future as a woman eligible to wed secure.

Arden married.

Perversely, he did not want to think of that possibility.

But was marriage for her truly a possibility? No matter what steps he and Giles took to protect Arden from gossip, they could not guarantee that no one would talk. Outspoken and recklessly unconcerned with what others might think of her, Arden herself could not be trusted to conceal where she had spent her first weeks in England. There was also the matter of her fortuitous arrival in the woods—she had never explained to his satisfaction how she came to be there.

Royce suppressed an emotion somewhere between hope and regret. Seeing Miss St. Clare safely wed to a gentleman worthy of her might prove to be an impossible task.

In which case she might be better off under a gentleman's protection, his wicked voice whispered gleefully.

Not so, his virtuous self countered. Balance her tarnished reputation against her other admirable qualities—her intelligence, her courage, her enthusiastic joy of living—and some decent man might be coaxed into coming up to scratch. Yes, sneered his alter ego, and if she is in fact an heiress, some scalawag under the hatches might consent to make her his bride. But what kind of life would she have with such a man?

Royce continued staring out the window as he pondered that question. Would Arden willingly marry a man who despised her behavior and sought to reform her? Or a man who wanted her only for her money? He had never considered such a match from a woman's point of view before, but he was certain that Arden would hate being reformed. Nor could he see her happily giving over control of her wealth, supposing it existed, or her future to a fortune hunter.

Marriages such as he envisioned for her would not be fun. And Arden wanted above all else to have fun.

Fun. Empathy made him grin, albeit reluctantly. Fun had been his goal for much of his life, until death and war had forced him to give up his youthful quest for excitement and pleasure. He had forsworn that enjoyable search, reformed by age and responsibility, and it was too late—

"Why are you scowling? What do you see out the window?" Arden's questions interrupted his musings. "Have they found the man who tried to kill William?"

Royce looked over his shoulder. "No. He apparently had a horse waiting. Dawkes found only hoofprints in the dirt, close to where you were attacked." Moving to stand next to the bed, he gently traced her cheek below the cut with his finger. "We may have matching scars. I owe you an apology."

"For what?"

"Suspecting you of wanting to harm William."

"Oh. That. You really had no choice. William's safety had to be your first priority, and you knew nothing about me."

"I know that you are brave and beautiful."

"Beautiful? Even with a shiner?" The eye that was not swollen shut twinkled happily.

"Even so."

Her cheeks turned pink. "Thank you. I'm glad you don't suspect me any longer."

"Miss St. Clare—"

"You called me Arden earlier."

"I thought you were unconscious."

"No, I heard you. You called me your brave girl, too. That was nice." She closed her eyes, and a sweet smile curved her lips.

"You are tired. Rest, and we will discuss what happened later."

"No." Opening her eyes, Arden struggled into a sitting position and leaned back against the headboard. "I'm not tired, just feeling the aftermath of all that excitement. We should talk about it now, while the details are fresh in my mind."

"Perhaps you are right." Royce sat on the bed next to her, his hip touching hers. She did not object or try to move away. *Not a lady,* hissed the insidious voice. "Did you recognize the man? Was it one of the men you saw in the forest with William?"

"No. He wore a mask. But I'm sure it wasn't one of the two men who kidnapped William. His voice was different—more cultured."

"What did he say?"

"Something like 'Who in blazes are you?' He was pointing the gun at me when he asked. Then William peeked from behind the tree, and he aimed the gun at him. He was squeezing the trigger, Royce! He was going to k-kill a little boy." Covering her face with her hands, she burst into tears.

With a muttered oath, Royce pulled her into his arms. "Arden, my brave girl. Don't cry. William is safe, thanks to you." He held her until the sobs subsided, regretting her need for tears but not the opportunity to hold her in his arms. When she stopped crying, he took a handkerchief from his pocket and carefully blotted the tears from her face. "All right now?"

She nodded, hiccuping softly. "I'm sorry. I don't usually fall apart like that. But I do not understand how anyone could want to kill a child."

"Nor do I. But we must accept that someone wants William dead. What else do you remember about the man?"

"He was tall—not as tall as you, but taller than Giles. His hair was brown. I couldn't see the color of his eyes because of the mask. His clothing was dark, except for his cravat. That was white and tied differently—more elaborately—than the way you and Giles tie yours."

"Did he say anything when you rushed at him?"

"No. The gun went off, and he hit me with the back of his hand. That's all I remember. No, one more thing. He is left-handed. I think he is, anyway. He held the gun in his left hand. But he hit me with his right hand."

Gently, he touched her cheek below the cut. "We know something else about this villain. He was wearing a ring. His knuckle alone could not have cut your cheek."

Arden placed her hand on top of his and nestled her cheek in his palm. "How did he know where to find William?"

"A good question." He dropped his hand from her face and stood. Touching her was not wise, especially not when she was reminding him of her bravery at the same time as she was showing her vulnerability. Royce feared that his admiration for her courage coupled with a fierce desire to keep her safe, would weaken his resolve to remain respectable. "The kidnappers must have wondered what became of William. It has been a week since he was left in the woods to die. Perhaps they remained in the neighborhood, waiting for a death announcement, and when none was forthcoming they began searching for him. Giles's hunting box would have been a logical place to keep watch on. Many people in the county know that we are friends."

"And they found him, because of me and that stupid game I played. If I hadn't gotten in the armoire with you, none of this would have happened."

"You must not blame yourself. If the villains are still in the neighborhood, they would have come across William sooner or later. This time, thanks to you, no harm was done. Except to your poor face." He resisted the impulse to stroke her cheek again.

"But what about the next time?"

"There must not be a next time. We must find whoever is behind these attempts, and put a stop to them once and for all."

Arden eyed him thoughtfully. "Did you notice? This time they didn't try to make it look like an accident. The murderer must be getting desperate." Her brows drew together in a frown. "But why? What has changed?"

"Three failed attempts at an 'accidental' death may have forced them to take a more direct approach. As to what has changed—they must know I have returned from the Peninsular Wars. Perhaps they now intend for William's death to be laid at my feet. As William noted, I do have a motive."

"Is being a duke such a prize?"

"Not to me. But others might not agree."

"Others. You suspect Osbert, don't you?"

"Clever as well as brave. How did you reason that out?"

"William told me his uncle Osbert is in control of his estates until you return. If he has been helping himself to William's money, that would give him a motive."

Royce nodded. "Greed."

"Yes. But I don't understand how he planned to continue with his thievery after William's death. Wouldn't you manage the estates yourself if you inherited?"

"I would. Perhaps Sharpless thought I was dead when he began his attacks on William. The first attempts came before I notified the family that I was only wounded, not deceased. The fact that I am alive and have William with me may explain the change in tactics—Osbert plans for me to go to the gallows for William's death. Then the Warrick estates would be inherited by an unworldly man of the cloth. He and Dora—the duchess—would most likely rely on Osbert to continue to manage the Wolverton estate."

"I don't know. If William dies . . . if you are tried and convicted of his murder . . . if the duchess doesn't realize what her brother is up to . . . if the reverend keeps Osbert as his manager . . . That's a lot of ifs. Is Osbert not too bright?"

"He is cunning. And fear of discovery may be his motivation now, as well as greed."

"I suppose he could be trying to avoid prison. But . . . isn't there anyone else who might benefit from William's death?"

"No. Giles and I have gone over and over the possibilities. No one benefits from William's death except me and, indirectly, Osbert."

"I would like to meet Osbert."

"You will have the opportunity soon. William is no longer safe here, and Osbert is in London. We leave for Town tomorrow morning."

"We're going to London?" Her pulse began racing in anticipation of reaching her destination. At last. Arden wondered suddenly if Tobias had planned the detour. If Royce was her heart's desire—

"Yes. And that brings up another matter we need to discuss. When we arrive at the Wolverton townhouse together, there will be questions about you. Giles has told the duchess that you stayed at Wolverton while Giles and I remained at his hunting box."

"But William knows I've been here. We can't ask a child to lie to his mother."

"We must. We will tell the duchess that you visited here every day, accompanied by your maid."

"Is this really necessary?" She supposed it was not surprising that, as a reformed rake, he would be overly concerned with appearances. When he had touched her cheek, she had felt a strong connection between them. There was no sign of that mutual attraction now. Royce did not act anything like a man who had fallen hopelessly in love with *his* heart's desire. She sighed. She would have to be content knowing he no longer suspected her.

"Yes. For your reputation—"

"I don't care about that."

"—and mine."

"Oh." Arden drew her brows together. She hadn't considered that she could be a threat to his good name. "Are reputations so fragile?"

"Yes. And once lost, almost impossible to regain."

"I can see that. But why would it be so awful if

people knew we stayed here together? It is not as if we did anything illegal or immoral."

"You have forgotten our rendezvous in the armoire so soon?"

"That wasn't immoral. It was . . . impulsive and unwise, maybe." Her gaze lowered to his mouth. She could not bring herself to regret the kiss. Far from it. She wanted his mouth on hers again.

"Definitely unwise. If William hadn't interrupted us, it might have led to—"

"—more?"

"Exactly."

"Would 'more' be so terrible?"

"Yes. Honor—"

"—forbids it. I know. You are engaged to another, and, of course, you cannot betray your fiancée."

"My honor is not the issue. A man is expected to have . . . liaisons before marriage. You must think of yourself. A young lady caught in an embrace such as ours would find herself in a scandal broth, compromised beyond redemption."

"Because of one kiss?"

"Yes. But, if you recall, we did more than kiss. I touched you."

His gaze fell to her breasts, and her nipples tightened in response. Arden crossed her arms over her chest. "What exactly does 'compromised beyond redemption' mean?"

"A young lady of the *haute ton* would be refused vouchers to Almack's. She would be denied invitations to the balls and routs where she might snare a husband. If the man who compromised her was unwilling or unable to marry her, she would be doomed to remain unwed forever."

"I'm not at all sure I want to marry."

"The point is, that choice would be taken from you if you were compromised."

She could not want to marry Royce, no matter what

that silly little voice had said when William accused her of trying to compromise his uncle. Especially not when Royce was in his stuffiest mode. After his brief loss of control in the armoire, he seemed determined to remain reformed. "Is that why you don't want people to know we stayed in the same house for several days? They will assume that we . . . that you and I . . . were intimate?"

"Assuredly. And that will keep you from making an advantageous marriage."

She wrinkled her nose. "I am sure I do not want an *advantageous* marriage, whatever that is. It sounds calculating and practical and awful. If I marry at all, it will be for—"

"Love?"

"Don't sneer. Yes. And passion. And mutual respect. And because I cannot imagine a happy life without . . . him. I want much more than 'dealing well together.' "

"Now who is sneering?"

"Well. Will you really be satisfied with that kind of marriage? Will Lady Christabel?"

"Lady Christabel will be content. As will I."

"Will you be faithful to her?"

He gave her a severe look. "That is none of your concern."

"I have the impression from reading about the Season, and the aristocracy, that fidelity in marriage is the exception rather than the rule. Why are reputations so carefully guarded before marriage if people are going to . . . fool around after they're married?"

Royce frowned. "It is true that many men of my acquaintance keep mistresses after they are wed, without bringing shame on themselves or their families . . ." He trailed off and looked at her, his intent gaze suddenly making her very warm.

"They have mistresses because their 'advantageous' marriages are not based on love, I suppose." Arden wanted to ask if he intended to have that sort of marriage, but she wasn't sure she wanted to hear his answer. "What about their wives? Don't they mind?"

"As long as the affair is handled discreetly, there is no reason for the wife to be concerned. And I believe some wives are grateful to be relieved of that particular wifely duty."

"They think making love is a duty?"

"Some do. An onerous duty."

"Their husbands must be rotten lovers."

"That is a possibility. Some married women do take lovers, perhaps for that very reason."

"Only married women? That seems unfair, and hypocritical as well. I would think it would be better for both men and women to . . . to sow their wild oats while single, then remain true to their spouses after marriage."

"Perhaps it would, but that is not the way of the world."

"Your world." A lover. Was that really what she wanted? She looked at Royce. She was very much afraid that she wanted more than a brief affair with . . . her heart's desire. There. She had admitted it. She had found her heart's desire, just as Tobias had promised.

But what was she supposed to do with him?

"What are you thinking?"

"That I don't know what I want from you," she answered truthfully.

"Kisses?"

There was a gleam in his dark eyes—a roguish gleam? Arden's heart beat faster. "Yes. No. I don't know. Do you?"

He surprised her by nodding. "I know I want kisses and . . . more. But, as we said at the beginning of this most improper conversation, that would not be wise."

"I suppose not." Sighing, she closed her eyes. She could end up with a broken heart. She *would* end up with a broken heart. Even if she turned out to be his heart's desire, there was no way they could have a future together. Their futures were centuries apart.

"You must rest now, and then prepare for our journey."

"How long will it take to get to London?"

"Three days." He pressed his lips to her forehead. "Two nights."

Ten

A magnificent carriage, its mahogany doors emblazoned with the crest of the Duke of Wolverton, arrived at the door promptly at eight o'clock the next morning. A less imposing carriage followed, and four armed men on horseback completed the entourage. The impressive procession caught and held Arden's attention, a welcome diversion from her own tumbled thoughts.

The coachmen and outriders waited patiently while the baggage was loaded. Dawkes climbed up and took a seat next to the coachman on the duke's carriage, while Murch and Jane took their places in the second carriage.

Three days. Two nights.

Not much time to decide what she should do about Royce. During the long, sleepless night she had narrowed her options to two. One, she could attempt to engage him in a fun-filled, Freret-approved affair, an affair that would last until it was time for her to return to the twenty-first century. Or, two, she could forget all about Royce and spend her trip to the past in St. Clare fashion, sedately visiting museums and cathedrals and other nineteenth-century tourist attractions.

Option number three, that she and Royce would fall in love, marry, and spend their lives together, had been firmly eliminated from the list of choices. He might be her heart's desire, and she might be a closet romantic, but she was not a fool. Arden was positive it would be very foolish to fall in love with a man who would be 216 years old in 2001.

In other words, dead.

Even if the age difference could be overlooked, even her Freret side ought to be realistic enough to recognize that, to be within her reach, a goal had to be within her control. She could not make Royce love her by wishing, and she had no desire to suffer the pangs of unrequited love. Arden refused to listen when her stuffiest St. Clare voice pointed out that she might not be able to control with whom she fell in love. Her frivolous Freret genes agreed.

She was left with the unanimous opinion that option three was still on the table, within her reach or not.

A hand on her elbow made her jump. Royce assisted her into the coach, then lifted William onto the seat opposite her, the seat facing the rear of the coach.

"You'll be riding backwards," she said inanely, her mind still busily juggling her options.

"I like to ride backwards." William yawned. "Pardon me. I could not sleep last night."

"Nightmares?"

"No. I could not stop thinking about today. I am going home." He grinned at her. "When we get to London, I will escort you to all those places you asked about. And the first place we will go is Astley's Circus. We may have to wait a day or two, until Uncle Royce finds the man who is trying to kill me."

Royce gave final instructions to the coachmen and the armed escort, and entered the carriage. He sat down next to her and stretched his injured leg out, resting his booted foot on the seat opposite.

"It may take longer than a day or two," said Royce. "But never fear. We will see to it that you are safe. And your mother will see to it that Miss St. Clare does not lack for escorts."

"I promise not to accept any escort to the circus but you," Arden told William. "But I would like to visit the British Museum. And Westminster Abbey."

Royce raised an eyebrow at her remark, but said nothing.

"How is your leg, Uncle?" William asked.

"Much improved, thanks to Miss St. Clare's recommended treatment."

William grinned at Arden. "Arden has helped us both enormously, has she not?"

"Enormously."

"Arden? Did you tell Uncle Royce what I asked you about before that masked man appeared?"

"Oh. No. I forgot all about it." She turned to Royce. "Hmm. William wants to know about what happens between a man and a woman when they are alone."

He eyed his nephew. "Do you?"

"Yes. And I am not too young. I will be twelve next month. I am old enough to know about . . . kissing and so forth. Will you explain?"

"Yes, but not today. It would not be proper to discuss such matters in the presence of a lady."

"You won't mind, will you? She won't mind, Uncle Royce. Arden isn't always a lady."

"William! Apologize at once."

"No apology necessary," said Arden. "I know I do not always behave in a ladylike manner." She slanted a look at Royce. "You have pointed that out on several occasions."

"Yes," said William, nodding. "And she told me herself that she was not very ladylike when she kissed you. I thought you had kissed her, you see. And that would not have been the proper thing."

"I see. Did you happen to ask Miss St. Clare why she kissed me?"

"Oh, yes. She said it was complicated. And then the man with the gun appeared, and we didn't talk about kissing anymore." William yawned again, his hand over his mouth. "Pardon me. I cannot keep my eyes open."

"There are blankets and pillows under the seat," said Royce. "You may nap if you wish."

William stood and raised the seat, pulling out a soft woolen blanket and a pillow. "Are you cold, Arden? Do you want a blanket?"

"No. I feel rather warm, actually." She shrugged out of her pelisse. She was wearing her blue muslin, with the modest addition of a chemisette in the neckline. Jane had assured her that made the dress appropriate for travel. The way Royce was staring at her chest made her wonder if her maid had been right about that.

"I will have one, if you please," said Royce, snagging a blanket and placing it in the corner of the carriage.

Arden helped William arrange his pillow, and she covered him with the blanket. "There you are, all nice and cozy."

"Thank you," said William with a huge yawn. His eyes fluttered shut, and within a few minutes he appeared to be sound asleep.

In a low voice, Royce asked, "Why did you tell William that you initiated the kiss?"

"He was angry with you for kissing me. And I did start the . . . activity that led to the kiss."

"Why was he angry? Was he jealous?"

"No, of course not. Why would he be jealous? He's only a boy."

"A boy beginning to be curious about girls. And a boy who appears to have a *tendre* for you."

"*Tendre?* A crush? He doesn't have a crush on me. That's not why he was angry. William thought you were behaving like a rake."

"Did he? And that upset him?"

"He seemed to think it was something his father

would not have approved of—your kissing one woman while engaged to another."

"No. Robert would not have approved of that. My brother did not approve of many things which I found pleasing."

"And the things that brought you pleasure—were they so bad?"

"I did not think so at the time. But I was young, and in my brother's view, hotheaded and irresponsible."

The idea of a reckless and bold Royce took Arden's breath away. As soon as she could breathe again, she asked, "Are you so very old now?"

"I am thirty."

"I'm twenty-five."

"That old?" He appeared shocked. "And still unmarried?"

"Not because I haven't been asked," she answered sharply. "Twenty-five isn't *that* old." Or maybe it was, considering that the life expectancy in the nineteenth century had to be decades shorter than what she took for granted. What had they called unmarried women in those Regency novels she had read? Not over the hill. On the shelf. Royce obviously thought she was on the shelf.

But he was the one who was a century or two older than she. Smiling, Arden changed the subject. "Tell me about your brother. Were you close?"

"No. Robert was twelve years older than I. And he was the heir. His days were filled with instruction in the duties and responsibilities of the title. He had little time for a younger brother."

"Were you jealous? Lonely?"

"Never. I was free to indulge in any activity that interested me. Sport, betting . . . women. And, no, I was not lonely. I had friends, chief among them Giles, willing to join me in any escapade that caught my interest."

"Did you have fun?"

"Yes."

"And Robert objected to that?"

"Robert objected to almost everything I did. He accused me daily of blackening the good name of Warrick. My brother was mightily concerned with the family honor."

"He sounds a lot like my uncle Fred, stuffy and self-righteous and no fun at all." The way she had once thought of Royce. "And unfair, if he thought you were anything but a gentleman. Do you think he resented your freedom? Maybe that was why he was so hard on you—he was the one who was jealous."

"You may have the right of it. And he may have been lonely, as well. His responsibilities left him little time for the fun and camaraderie I was free to enjoy."

"I'm sure that's why he was so disapproving of you. If I had a little sister who was allowed to do all the things forbidden to me, I would resent the heck out of her. And while I can see you and Giles getting into scrapes, I cannot imagine you doing anything bad enough to be called dishonorable."

"Your belief in me is flattering, but undeserved. I was careless of my honor at times." Glancing at his sleeping nephew, Royce lowered his voice. "And I am tempted to be that way again."

"Tempted? Here? Now? By what?"

"You, of course. If we were alone, I would kiss you again."

Arden's brows rose in surprise. "You w-would? Yesterday you said that would be unwise."

"Definitely unwise."

"Isn't it fortunate that we are not alone?" Arden turned away from him to stare out the window. She wished she had a fan. She was definitely warm and getting warmer. She wanted Royce to kiss her more than anything she had ever wanted in her life. But he was right. It would be foolish to follow her heart—if it was her heart, and not her hormones, urging her to forget about museums and cathedrals and live for the moment.

"Very fortunate." He did not sound happy about it. When she looked at him, he had a familiar expression on his face. His scowl was not directed at her, for once, but at his sleeping nephew. "Especially since a kiss would not be enough."

"It wouldn't?" Now the heat was definitely turned up.

"No. One kiss would lead to another, and then kisses would not be enough. Kisses would only be a prelude to the other enjoyable things we would do together."

Someone had sucked all the air out of the carriage. "What . . . things?" Arden gasped breathlessly.

"I believe you know exactly what things."

Arden opened her mouth, but she did not speak. The way Royce was devouring her with his eyes so unnerved her that she could barely manage a nod.

"I thought as much. That being the case, there is nothing to stop us from . . . having fun. You do want to have fun, do you not?"

"Fun. Oh. Yes." She fanned herself with her hand. "So. Are you going to kiss me?"

"I believe I am."

"When?"

"Soon."

"Where?"

"There is a pulse beating on the side of your neck, beneath your earlobe. Perhaps I will kiss you there. First."

"And then?"

"Lower. The hollow where your neck meets your shoulder."

"Next?"

"Lower still. On the swell of your breast. Then, if we were alone, I would undo the tapes of your dress and your American stays so that I could kiss your bare breasts."

"Oh. My."

The rogue was back.

She suddenly understood why all those Regency maids had struggled to reform their rakes. The riot of feelings generated by Royce's verbal foreplay included a large portion of jealousy. If this once-reformed rogue became her lover, she would not want to share him with anyone else, including first and foremost Lady Christabel de Courcy. She would re-reform him so fast—

Royce took her hand and raised it to his mouth. Turning her trembling hand, he kissed her palm—a long, lingering kiss.

Arden could scarcely breathe. "Are you . . . what are you doing?"

With a glance toward the sleeping duke, Royce whispered, "Tasting you."

"How . . . do . . . I . . . taste?" Arden gasped.

"Spicy. Hot. Delicious." He punctuated each word with another touch of his mouth to her palm.

"William—"

"—is asleep."

"He may wake up at any moment."

"That only adds to the excitement. You want excitement." It was not a question.

"Not right this minute." Royce's unexpected assault on her senses was wreaking havoc with her ability to calmly choose between her two options. "Have you ever been to the British Museum?" she asked desperately.

"Yes." He kissed her wrist, placing his warm mouth where a pulse beat frantically. "Where would you kiss me first?"

"I—I don't know. What is your favorite exhibit there?"

"The mummies. My favorite place to be kissed is on the mouth. But if you want to start somewhere else, I have no objection. In point of fact, I would not object if you prefer to start with touching instead of kisses. Like this." His hand covered her breast, and he began gently kneading.

Arden bit her lip to keep from moaning, but made a noise deep in her throat anyway. Royce tugged the lace chemisette free, exposing the swell of her breasts. His long, wicked fingers touched her bare skin, tracing the neckline of her dress. He lowered his head and kissed the tops of her breasts, first one, then the other.

"Captain Warrick. Lord Royce." Her voice squeaked, spoiling her attempt to begin a stern lecture about inappropriate behavior.

"Yes, Arden?" He kept his mouth against her breast as he spoke. "Have you decided?"

"W-what?" For a moment she thought he referred to the choice she had to make. An affair, even if it meant a broken heart, was more and more appealing with each caress. *No pain, no gain,* she told herself, feeling reckless and bold.

But scared.

"Will you kiss me or touch me first?" Royce prodded.

"Kiss. Mouth," she said, surrendering. She took his face in her hands and touched her parted lips to his. His mouth was closed. Using her tongue to trace his lips, she coaxed them to part. Tongue met tongue, and the first kiss deepened. A second kiss followed, then a third. Hearts pounded, pulses raced, breaths came quick and shallow.

Royce groaned and pulled Arden onto his lap, wrapping his arms around her waist. Beneath her bottom, Arden could feel his arousal. He wanted her. She wanted him. She made her choice: option number one. They would be together for a few moments out of time. That would have to be enough.

"This is torture," she gasped.

"Indeed. But fun?"

"That, too," she had to admit. "But I don't know how much more I can stand without screaming. That would wake William." She could feel his mouth widen into a grin, even as his hand cupped her breast once again. Arden was melting, her bones liquefying from the heat generated by his touch.

"You will survive, my brave girl. You have faced down kidnappers and murderers."

But he might not. He had to stop before he forgot himself entirely and took her on the carriage seat, with his nephew for an audience. Reluctantly, Royce took his hand from Arden's breast. He found the lace fichu and carefully replaced it, tucking the edges into the cleft between her breasts.

"Are you stopping?" She sighed the words against his throat.

"For now." For always, if he regained his senses.

Royce put her away from him and leaned back against the squabs. He closed his eyes to block out the confusion and distress he saw in Arden's gaze.

She had bewitched him. Nothing less than sorcery could explain his inability to resist her. If not a witch, a practiced temptress. Arden was no young chit fresh from the schoolroom. No innocent young girl would have allowed him to take such liberties or kissed him with such abandon. And definitely not a lady. Arden was a grown woman, experienced in the way of the world.

If he were not engaged . . . if he had not promised Robert . . . if William were finally safe, the villain exposed. . . .

Too many ifs.

He was engaged. He had promised Robert. And William was still in danger.

Eleven

Neville de Courcy handed over his gloves and hat to the Duchess of Wolverton's butler. "Where is Lady Christabel?"

"Lady Christabel is with Her Grace in the duchess's small parlor."

"Announce me."

A few minutes later, Neville entered the parlor. "Good afternoon, Your Grace. Cousin." He sketched a bow. "I have come to take you both for a drive in the park. Now that we know that the duke is safe, there is no reason for you to hide from society."

The duchess rose from her chair and held out both hands in greeting. "Thank you, kind sir. Your thoughtful attentions to two lonely ladies are welcome, as always, but I fear I cannot join you today. I am waiting for Lord Stanton to pay a call."

"See that he escorts you somewhere away from here," Neville said, wagging his finger. "You need to forget your troubles for a while."

"I cannot forget my poor boy's ordeal. And it will not be over until the villains responsible for these attacks have been unmasked."

"But the duke is safe for now, Dora," said Lady Christabel. "He is with my beloved Royce. Royce will not allow His Grace to be harmed."

"No. The brave captain will surely guard his nephew

with his life," said Neville, adjusting the fall of his cravat. "Will they join you soon, Your Grace?"

"I hope so. Giles—Lord Stanton—brings news of that very thing. He has received a letter from Royce announcing his plans to return to London."

"Ah, then, you must await his arrival. And you, Cousin, do you wish to forgo our jaunt in the park? Perhaps Lord Stanton has a message for you from your betrothed."

Lady Christabel lowered her lashes demurely, but not before Neville detected a flash of anger. He smiled. It was very bad of him to tease her. He knew how anxious she must be to hear his report. "I hope he has not forgotten all about me," she said with a charming catch in her throat.

"No man could forget you, Cousin," Neville drawled. "Will you take the air with me?"

Christabel glanced at the duchess. "Your Grace? Shall I go?"

"By all means. A ride through the park is just what you need to bring the bloom to your cheeks. You do not want Royce to see you pale and mournful."

Lady Christabel murmured her farewell to the duchess, and allowed Neville to take her from the parlor, down the stairs to his waiting curricle. Neville expertly guided his matched pair of chestnuts to the park, then down a secluded path.

As soon as they were alone, Christabel turned her glittering gaze on Neville. "Well? What news?"

"William was at the hunting box, under close guard by your betrothed."

"As Giles told Dora. Go on," Lady Christabel hissed impatiently. "Did you—"

"I tried, but I fared no better than your hired henchmen."

"The duke lives?"

Neville nodded. "Regrettably. I almost had him. Only a day after I arrived at Stanton's hunting box, William ran from the house and headed straight for my hiding place."

"And you could not kill him?"

"Alas, no, my bloodthirsty love. Fate, in the form of a pretty girl, saved him once again. The Duke of Wolverton bears a charmed life, it seems."

Disgust and disappointment twisted Christabel's beautiful features into something almost ugly. "He should have died years ago."

"The poor lad was on his deathbed when you accepted Lord Royce's offer, I believe."

"You know I would not have accepted Royce's offer had I not thought he would be the Duke of Wolverton within a fortnight. But no sooner was the betrothal ring on my finger than the brat recovered."

Neville made a sympathetic sound. "Bad luck."

"You said a girl saved him this time. The same one the duchess told us about? The one who kept him from dying in the forest?"

"I assume so, unless your betrothed has accumulated a harem."

"Royce? After his solemn pledge to his dying brother? I think not. He is too respectable by half."

"Think again. I fear you have a rival, my dear. It seems that William ran from the house because he saw your faithless fiancé kissing the girl. I believe the embrace took place in an armoire."

"An armoire? That is beyond belief."

"Nevertheless. I heard what I heard. William accused the chit of trying to compromise your lord. Rather clever of her, in my opinion—pushing a man into an armoire and kissing him." Neville eyed his beauteous cousin. "We might try it sometime. When can we be alone again?"

"Do not be ridiculous. Now, of all times, we must be discreet. And I refuse to do anything so crude as tumbling about in an armoire. Ever."

Neville sighed. "You are becoming more and more

like your betrothed each day. Staid and proper and high in the instep. I vow, I miss my wild and wanton . . . cousin."

"I am behaving as becomes a future duchess," she said primly. "When can you try again? The sooner William is dead, the sooner I will have everything I want. I will be a duchess, married to the richest and most powerful duke in the kingdom." Christabel placed a hand on his thigh. "And you need not worry. You know I will be generous with you. Never forget that I gave you the most precious gift a woman may give a man." She purred the words.

"Yes, my darling duchess-in-waiting." Neville knew full well that Christabel had bestowed her "precious gift" on a sweaty groom. He had watched the proceedings from the hayloft where he had gone to indulge in solitary pleasure. They had both been fifteen. Once her sexual appetite had been awakened, it had not taken Christabel long to look for another male to seduce.

Neville had made sure he was the one she found. As a boy, he had thought himself in love with her. He had never seen a girl as beautiful, as seductive as she. He had long since learned that she was as wicked as she was beautiful. He loved her even more because of that. Christabel was far from the prim and proper miss she pretended to be. It excited him to know that he was the only man who knew her darkest secrets. Secrets that even she did not realize he had unmasked.

Neville smiled. He still found it amusing that they had both pretended to be virgins at their first sexual encounter.

"Do not fret, my pet. Another opportunity may soon arise. I stayed in Somerset long enough to see preparations being made for travel. The duke and your betrothed should be arriving in London in a day or two."

"Good. When the child is close at hand, we will find a way to rid ourselves of the impediment once and for all." She paused. "And the girl? Is she traveling with them?"

"I did not witness their departure. I thought it prudent to leave the vicinity. Why do you ask? Are you jealous?"

"Of a light skirt?" She laughed prettily. Christabel did everything prettily, including cold-bloodedly planning a murder. Neville admired her tremendously, but he trusted her not a whit. "Of course not. I do not care if Royce has a mistress. I hope he does. It will lessen the burden of the marriage bed."

"Will you find it a burden, my insatiable love? Royce was once deemed a skilled and generous lover."

"But not skilled in the ways you know to please me."

"Perhaps not. But you could always teach him the pleasure of pain. He might make an apt pupil. As apt as you were." Smiling, Neville noted the way the rise and fall of her creamy breasts quickened at his suggestion. He might yet convince Christabel that a visit to his apartments would not be amiss. Placing his hand on top of hers, he rubbed their joined hands against his swelling manhood. "Remember how you enjoyed my lessons?"

Her eyes dilated, and she leaned her shoulder against his. "I remember. But I dare not take on the role of instructor. Royce would want to know how I learned . . ."

"How to drive a man mad with desire?"

A greedy gleam appeared in her eyes. "I would like to control him that way."

The way she thought she controlled him. "You shall, dearest. Never doubt it. After only one night in your arms, he will be your slave." He wondered idly if he might witness the wedding night. It would be amusing to see if Christabel could convince Royce she was a virgin at the same time as she used her expertise to ensnare him.

"Flatterer," she simpered, squeezing his erection.

Glancing around, she said, "There are very few people about this morning."

"No one of importance is in Town yet."

"Perhaps a brief visit to your chambers would not be noticed."

"Leave everything to me. You know I am the soul of discretion."

Twelve

On the afternoon of the third day, Arden finally found herself in London, feeling as if she had not only traveled through time but down the rabbit hole. "Maybe this is all a dream, a very bad dream. If it is, I hope I wake up soon," she muttered. She had all but given up trying to make sense of the last two days.

After their first day on the road, Royce had hardly spoken to her, much less renewed his amorous attentions. He had seen to it that they were never alone, so she had not had an opportunity to ask him why he had gone from hot to cold overnight. On her own, she had come up with several answers, none of which were satisfactory, and all of which made her angry, either at him for reverting to his reformed personage, or at herself for being stupid enough to fall for Tobias's "heart's desire" nonsense.

After surreptitiously shedding a few tears, Arden had convinced herself that being a tourist was much preferable to being the heartbroken victim of a man who could turn his passion on and off at will. The sooner she saw the last of Lord Royce Warrick, the better. For him, as well as for her. If he tried his tricks on her one more time, her simmering temper would boil over and he would be the one wishing they had never met.

Upon their arrival at the Duke of Wolverton's London

mansion, Royce dismounted from the horse he had ridden for most of the past two days—he obviously could not bear to be confined in the coach with her for more than minutes at a time—and opened the carriage door. William leaped from the carriage and ran up the stairs, where a butler and a footman resplendent in Wolverton livery waited.

Royce assisted Arden from the coach. The unbidden and unwelcome thought came that his hand on her arm might be the very last time she would feel his touch. Appalled that she had fallen into some kind of victim mode, Arden jerked her arm free with more force than necessary.

"Is anything wrong?" Royce asked, cool and unperturbed.

"Why, no, nothing is wrong, sir. Nothing at all. I am fine, perfectly fine," gushed Arden in her best imitation Southern belle drawl. "Why ever would you think anything was the matter with little ol' me?" She changed her tone from sugar to vinegar and snarled, "I'm not the one who's acting like Dr. Jekyll and Mr. Hyde."

"Who?" He took her arm again, sounding more bored than curious.

When had Robert Louis Stevenson written that book? How annoying to have her put-down not understood because of bad timing. She glared at him. "Jekyll and Hyde are the names an author gave to the good and evil sides of the same person in a novel. You keep going back and forth, first one way, then the other. One minute the good Dr. Jekyll, the next you're the evil Mr. Hyde."

"Ah. Novels again. Perhaps you should read something more enlightening." He took her arm again and nudged her up the stairs.

"Are you calling me stupid?"

"No."

"Uneducated, then?" She dug in her heels, refusing to take one more step.

"No. Calm down, Miss St. Clare. You are about to meet a duchess."

"Duchess smuchess. You know what?" Using only her forefinger and thumb, she took hold of his wrist and removed his hand from her arm. Then she used the same forefinger to poke him in the chest. "Titles do not impress me. Neither do people who behave one way one day and a completely opposite way the next day. Or two."

"Ah. Now I understand. You are angry with me because I kissed you in the carriage."

"Angry? Me? Don't be ridiculous. I never lose my temper." She stuck out her chin and smiled, proving she was not in the least belligerent. "Certainly not over something as silly as a kiss."

"I apologize," he said, a suspicious twitch in the corner of his mouth. "I can see I was wrong about that. You—"

"Very wrong!"

"—are angry because I *stopped* kissing you."

"Oh. Oh!" Arden made a fist and swung at him. Royce grabbed her hand before she made contact and held on, grinning openly. "You are a cad. And a rake. And a rogue. I hope I never, ever see you again."

"Ahem." The butler cleared his throat.

They had reached the top of the stairs leading from the carriageway, and the butler was holding the door open.

"Good afternoon, Jeffers." Royce dropped her hand.

Arden looked at her toes, peeking at the butler through her lashes. Titles might not impress her, but butlers who looked like this one—all pomp and starch—did. Jeffers had witnessed her temper tantrum. Both he and the footman had heard Royce talking about kissing her. And about *not* kissing her. How humiliating was that?

Jeffers inclined his head, managing to make the gesture polite even though she was sure he was seething with disapproval. The footman was not as adept at hiding his true feelings. He gaped at her, openly fascinated. Jeffers spoke. "Lord Royce. May I escort you and your . . . guest to Her Grace?"

"In a moment. I wish to have a few words with Miss St. Clare in private. Is the small parlor free?"

"Yes, my lord."

His hand at the small of her back, Royce pushed her down the wide hallway and through a door into a room only a duke or his uncle would call small. Arden heard the door close behind them, but she kept her spine straight and stared at the wall opposite the door. She would not look at him. "I have nothing to say to you," she said frostily.

"Arden. Miss St. Clare. I have something to say to you. I behaved badly toward you, and I wish to apologize. You deserved better treatment from William's family—from me in particular. I promise that from now on you will receive the honor and respect due to William's friend and rescuer. If I have caused you any distress, and I do not doubt that I have, I am truly sorry." He delivered the speech in a manner that suggested it had been rehearsed. Spontaneity must have gone the way of the rogue—smothered out of existence.

"Oh. Well." Arden felt her anger seep away, leaving behind an absurd desire to weep. She blinked rapidly, then turned to face him. "Does that mean you won't be kissing me anymore?" She bit her lip, wincing at the pitiful sound of her voice.

Royce, who had solemnly resolved to keep his hands and mouth off Arden, realized immediately that he had made a tactical error. He had followed too closely behind her when he ushered her into the small parlor. When she turned around, she was very near to him. Near enough for him to see the shimmer of unshed tears in her sapphire blue eyes, to hear the tremor in her voice, to feel her breath sighing out of her adorable mouth.

What could he do but kiss her again?

Lowering his head, Royce captured her mouth. He tried to keep the kiss soft and gentle, a kiss between friends, a good-bye kiss. But her lips parted beneath his, and he could not resist her bold invitation. He drew her body against his, and deepened the kiss, plunging his tongue into the sweetness of her mouth.

When he finally ended the kiss, his breathing was uneven, his heart was pounding, and she was clinging to him. "Oh. My. The other you is back."

Royce unwound her arms from around his neck and took a step back. What was it about this woman that made him forget all his good intentions? He should never have allowed himself to be alone with her, even for the purpose of offering an apology. "Tell me, Miss St. Clare, which side of me kisses you? The good side or the bad side?"

"The good side, of course."

"So you believe it is good of me to break a promise I made to my brother when he was dying?"

Her eyes widened in surprise. "You promised your brother you would never kiss anyone?"

"Not exactly. I promised not to bring dishonor to the name of Warrick."

"As if," she snorted. "I mean, as if you ever would."

"I had done so before."

"How? By gambling?" Hands on hips, she glared at him. "Did you ever lose more than you could afford to pay?"

He shook his head. "I seldom lost at all, but—"

"Did you ever lie, cheat or steal?"

"Of course not. However—"

"And I suppose you fooled around with women?"

"Yes, if by 'fooling around' you mean—"

"Did you ever force yourself on a woman?"

"Assuredly not. Arden——"

"Did you ever make those women promises you didn't keep?"

"Never. But I sometimes told them——"

"Fibs? To get them where you wanted them? That's nothing. Most men—especially young ones—lie to get into a woman's . . . pantaloons. Tell me what you ever did that was so bad."

He opened his mouth, then closed it. What *had* he done to incur his brother's contempt? Nothing more or less than most of the young men of the *ton*. He had accepted Robert's opinion of his character out of guilt and sorrow. Arden's questions forced him to acknowledge the truth. The fifth Duke of Wolverton had been a prig.

"You have nothing to say? Then I must be right. You don't have an evil side, or even a very bad side, except when you're trying to be someone else's idea of 'good.' That's when you get all stuffy and self-important and unkissable. Why don't you forget about living up to other people's expectations? Do what you want to do." Taking a step closer, Arden tilted her face up again and closed her eyes.

Royce almost accepted her blatant invitation, before he remembered his duty to the family, if not to Robert. "Open your eyes, minx. I am not going to kiss you again." He could not allow Arden, no matter how charming and appealing he found her, to undo his resolution to avoid embroiling the Wolverton clan in scandal. His obligation to his own and the family honor had never depended on his promise to Robert. He always had known the right thing to do, no matter what his brother had thought.

Her eyes opened to narrow slits. "You're not? Why not? And if you say it wouldn't be proper, I'm going to kick you on your bad leg."

He allowed himself to touch her cheek, still bruised

from her latest defense of the Wolverton clan. "Arden. You forget I am engaged to another."

"Oh. That."

"Yes. That. It would be very bad of me to end the engagement. Such an act would humiliate my betrothed and bring dishonor to the name of Warrick."

"Oh."

"So I must apologize once again, and I must not kiss you ever again."

"Oh. Could I . . . ?" She seemed dazed, her eyes filled with confusion. "Would you . . . ? I think I'd like to go to my room now."

"Of course." He had an uncomfortable feeling that he had hurt Arden—yet another reason for him to keep his distance from her in the future. Lady or not, she was a brave and gallant girl who deserved better than the clandestine affair he could offer her.

Royce handed Arden over to a footman who escorted her to a suite of rooms. Jane joined her a few minutes later, directing yet another footman to place Arden's carpetbag on the bench at the foot of the four-poster bed.

"Shall I unpack?" asked Jane.

"What? Oh, yes, please. But just my poor dresses. They're right on top." After almost two weeks, Arden was thoroughly sick of her limited wardrobe. She concentrated on that annoyance rather than her latest encounter with Royce. Coward that she was, she wanted to avoid replaying that scene in her mind and heart for as long as possible. "Leave the rest." She had tucked her lingerie and other items out of sight under her pajamas.

"Which gown will you wear to dinner?" Jane asked as she shook out the dresses and hung them in the armoire.

"I don't care," she said listlessly. Maybe she would ask for a tray in her room. Facing Royce again, seeing him with his fiancée, had absolutely no appeal.

A knock sounded on the door and Jane hastened to open it. She curtsied, and William entered the room, followed by a petite young woman dressed in a yellow muslin gown. Her round face was framed with brown corkscrew curls that bounced when she moved. Golden brown eyes gazed at her, a twinkle in their depths.

"Arden, I would like to present my mother, Her Grace Dora Warrick, the Duchess of Wolverton. Mother, this is Miss Arden St. Clare, of America."

"Hello," said Arden, surprised. This little brown house wren was not her idea of a duchess. She had thought the woman must be his governess, or the housekeeper. Flustered, she said, "I'm pleased to meet you, Mrs. Warrick."

Smiling, the duchess shook Arden's hand, then with a rueful laugh dropped her hand and enveloped her in a fierce hug. "Please call me Dora. I am sorry to disturb you before you have had a chance to rest, but I could not wait to meet you and thank you. William has told me all about your adventures, and how you courageously saved his life not once but twice. And he showed me how you taught him to defend himself."

"Billy Bob!" Arden blurted. "You didn't throw your mother over your shoulder!"

The duchess laughed delightedly. "No, he only told me how he would, if I happened to grab hold of him from behind. It sounds most effective." She raised an inquisitive brow. "Billy Bob?"

"That is the nickname Arden gave me when we first met. Boys in America have nicknames, you see, and she thought I might like one. I forgot to tell you about that."

"I didn't realize he was a duke at the time," said Arden, hoping that might excuse her impertinence.

"Americans do not know much about titles and such, Mother. They don't have dukes or earls or viscounts. Not even a king. Only a president. So you must not mind if Arden forgets to curtsy or call you Your Grace."

"I see," Dora said, a dimple appearing in her cheek. "I will keep that in mind."

Arden dropped a belated curtsy. "I am so sorry. I do know better than to call a duchess Mrs. Warrick. I'm afraid I was distracted, Your Grace."

"Dora. Distracted and no doubt exhausted from your travels. We should not have disturbed you, but this rascal son of mine insisted. And I was more than eager to grant him his wish to see you as soon as possible. I wanted the same thing. William is well and safe, and with me once again. For that, I had to thank you at the very first opportunity."

"You're welcome. And I am glad you both came to see me. You've made me feel very much at home."

"You will always be welcome at our home, Miss Arden St. Clare of America." Arden found herself wrapped in another hug. The duchess released her and looked about the room. Her gaze stopped at Jane, who was holding Arden's carpetbag. "I see you chose my favorite chambermaid at Wolverton as your lady's maid. I trust Jane is performing her new duties satisfactorily?"

"Oh, yes. Jane and I make a good team."

"Is there anything you need? Giles—Lord Stanton told me most of your luggage was lost. May I lend you a gown?" She eyed Arden's figure. "You are an inch or two taller than I, but I believe one of my dresses might be made to fit you without too much trouble. I will send a gown and a seamstress to make any necessary alterations."

"How thoughtful of you. I must confess, I hope I never again see the dresses I've been wearing for days."

William looked from Arden to his mother and back again, a resigned expression on his face. "Are you going to talk about clothes now?"

The duchess's eyes gleamed. "I believe we are. You

may be excused, William. Jane, would you take him to Murch, please?"

Nodding, Jane took William by the hand. With a relieved sigh, William bade them good day and left them alone.

"Your coach broke an axle, I understand," said Dora.

"Yes. The coachman took a wrong turn and ended up on a road through the woods that was little more than a cowpath." Arden had memorized the tale Royce and Giles had come up with, but lying to the duchess made her uncomfortable. This delightful female might not look like a duchess, but she behaved the way a true lady should. She was a woman Arden would be pleased to call friend.

"Giles—Lord Stanton said the coachman and your escort left you alone with the carriage and went for help."

Arden noticed that for the second time the duchess had stumbled over Giles's name. "They did. I grew tired of waiting for them to return, and went looking for a way out of the woods. That was when I came upon William."

"Your misfortune saved my little boy's life." The duchess took a handkerchief out of her pocket and blew her nose. "But we won't dwell on what might have happened if your coach hadn't taken the wrong turn. You never heard from your traveling companion again?"

"No. I don't know what happened to Tobias Thistlewaite, or the coach he hired to bring me to London. I am sure Tobias is all right, though. He is nothing if not resourceful."

"Then we have only your missing luggage to concern ourselves with. What a wonderful excuse to buy a complete new wardrobe. I wish something of the sort had happened to me. My late husband was rather strict when it came to my quarterly allowance, you see. I know I should not have minded, but I had to sometimes resort to tears and other stratagems to persuade him I needed additional funds for a ball gown or two."

"My uncle Fred is the very same way. He was my financial guardian until my twenty-fifth birthday, and he kept me on a very strict budget. It wasn't as if it were his money I was spending, and I am not silly enough to waste money. Well, not too much, anyway. But I could never make Uncle Fred understand how much fun it was to shop."

"Men seldom do."

"Thank goodness I no longer need to beg Uncle Fred to give me more of my own money. I have control of my funds now."

"As do I. Not that I would have wished Robert dead, but being his widow is in some ways more agreeable than being his wife ever was." She put her hand over her mouth. "Now you will think I am a horrible person."

"Hardly. I do believe women are perfectly capable of handling their money."

"Oh, so do I. Unfortunately, my brother Osbert does not agree. He is forever telling me how I should go about investing my money, and William's. I, however, have a much better business sense than he ever will. But I am female, and I must be taken care of."

"As though we are too silly to take care of ourselves."

"Exactly." Lowering her voice to a conspiratorial whisper, Dora said, "But we must be careful to whom we express such sentiments. We will be labeled followers of Mary Wollstonecraft."

Arden grinned at the duchess. "I can keep a secret."

"So can I. Oh, Arden! May I call you Arden?" Arden nodded, delighted to find a kindred spirit. "I know we are going to be great friends."

"I feel the same way." She also felt a sharp pang of regret that the friendship would be of short duration.

The few weeks remaining before she had to return to the future suddenly did not seem enough time.

"Now I will leave you so that you can rest. We dine at eight. A footman will escort you to the anteroom at seven-thirty. We will be a small number tonight—Lady Christabel and her cousin Lord Neville, Lord Royce, Viscount Stanton, and you and I. I invited your aunt, but she prefers to meet you for the first time without company."

Arden had that down-the-rabbit-hole feeling again. "M-my aunt?"

"Miss Lavinia St. Clare. I called on her as soon as Giles found out your direction from your man of affairs. She has written you a letter. Did you find it? It is on the escritoire, along with the message from your man of affairs. Giles—Lord Stanton delivered that. Is anything wrong, Arden? You appear dazed."

"N-no. I'm okay—all right."

"But tired from your travels, no doubt. I have prattled for too long." The duchess enveloped Arden in another quick hug. "Now rest. We will meet again at dinner."

"Thank you. I believe I will take a short nap." She definitely needed time alone to consider everything that had happened. And to read her correspondence.

The two letters the duchess had mentioned waited on the escritoire. One was written on lavender paper, and the handwriting appeared feminine. Arden opened that letter first.

My dear 'niece,'—I hope you will forgive my audacity in claiming such a close relationship, but third cousin twice-removed seemed so awkward. Mr. Mendlicott's letter informing me of our connection and your arrival in England came as quite a surprise. I had no idea a branch of the family had emigrated to America several decades ago.

It was so kind of you to seek me out. Ever since my brother's regiment left for America, I have longed to meet someone from the country where he lost his life. And Mr. Mendlicott tells me you are from the very same area where Justin must be buried!

I have many questions for you about New Orleans and the surrounding countryside. I long to be able to picture my brother's final resting place. But enough about my loss.

Your offer of a home, at least temporarily, came at the perfect time. You may label me ungrateful, but I did not enjoy being a paid companion to Lady Whitehurst, not in the least. After making such a rash confession, let me hasten to add that I look forward with delight to being your companion, my dear niece.

The Duchess of Wolverton tells me you have had several exciting adventures since your arrival in our country. I am eagerly awaiting to hear all about them.

Yours sincerely,
Miss Lavinia St. Clare

Clutching the letter, Arden sat down on the bed.

Lavinia St. Clare. Justin St. Clare's sister. Lavinia *was* her aunt, but several "greats" ought to precede the title. She could not quite get her mind around the idea that she was about to meet one of her ancestors face-to-face. How was she going to reassure Lavinia that her brother was alive and well without revealing that her own branch of the St. Clare family did not yet exist?

Arden put off the problem by reaching for the other letter. It was much shorter. Hugh Mendlicott gave directions to her new address, and told her about Lavinia: "a gentlewoman fallen on hard times since her brother's death, but good *ton* and a suitable chaperon." Mendlicott offered to call upon her as soon as she was settled to explain how he had invested her capital and how she might draw on her account.

Well. Tobias had come through, after all.

She ought to be relieved. Excited, even. Here she was, in a different time, a different place, with money, family, and a delightful duchess ready to sponsor her introduction to high society. She should be on the verge of having more fun than she could imagine. Instead, she felt disgruntled and out of sorts.

All because Royce, after kissing her senseless one last time, had stopped his rakish behavior. He would not unreform himself, not as long as he was engaged to Lady Christabel. And he would not break the engagement.

Engaged or not, he had kissed her again.

Royce could not love Lady Christabel, not if all he expected from marriage was that they would deal well enough together and be content. He had never said he loved Christabel. A man should not marry a woman he did not love. Wasn't it her duty to convince Royce of that?

That might be a hard sell. This was the golden age of arranged marriages, after all. And once arranged, not easily or honorably disarranged.

Why couldn't she have met him, or someone exactly like him, in 2001? She knew what she would do in her own time. She would go all out to get him, whether he was engaged or not. After all, engagements in the twenty-first century weren't nearly as binding as betrothal contracts appeared to be during the Regency.

More than one of her friends had been engaged two or three or even more times before they finally settled on the one man they would marry. No one in her time believed a broken engagement or two reflected on a person's honor.

Honor. Now, that was a subject not often openly discussed in her time. Even the word was seldom used except during political campaigns, and then only by rascally politicians who tended to define the term to mean whatever value concept currently led in the opinion polls.

She rather preferred this century's concept of honor, even if it was interfering with her desires at the moment. How could she find fault with a society that believed promises should be kept? Royce had promised to marry Christabel. It would be very bad of her to try to convince him to break that promise, even if it was for his own good.

But what if Christabel changed her mind? Apparently, a woman could break an engagement and not be thought dishonorable. Might Christabel cry off? She hadn't seen Royce for two years. Both of them must have changed—they might have grown apart. Arden sighed. How would they know that? They hadn't known each other all that well before Royce left for the war. She couldn't pin her hopes on something as unlikely as Christabel suddenly realizing she did not want to marry a stranger.

Arden found herself wishing she really had been born in 1791—she had finally done the math—so that she and Royce would share the same future. But if she were a daughter of the Regency, would she even be thinking about how to break up Royce and Christabel's betrothal? A true Regency miss would never have such wicked thoughts.

As it was, she had nothing to offer Royce except a few weeks of fun—hardly enough to expect him to do something so drastic as breaking his engagement—before she went back to the future. And she had to go back.

Didn't she?

Why? Because she had paid for a round trip? Could she stay in this time? How would that work? Would that mean that in the future she would never be born? Or would she live her first twenty-five years in the future, and the rest of her life in the past? How exactly did time work? And could magic change it forever, or only for the time she had agreed to spend in the past?

Arden grabbed her head with both hands, afraid it might fly off if she continued trying to make sense out of time-travel. She couldn't worry about things like that. She would have to wait and ask Tobias.

But if she could stay in the past . . .

Would anyone miss her? Uncle Fred and Aunt Marie cared about her, but would they *miss* her? She wasn't sure they would notice she was gone. They wouldn't have to worry ever again about her doing some shocking Freret thing and embarrassing the family.

She had friends, but most of them were married, busily establishing careers and families. They would barely notice her absence. Her affairs were in order, as befitted a prudent St. Clare. Her will left her shares of St. Clare Spices to Uncle Fred and Aunt Marie. Beau Visage and the Freret French Quarter house were bequeathed to the Freret Foundation.

Arden shook her head. Even if Tobias could arrange it, she could not stay in the past. She would miss . . . someone. Something.

Even if she couldn't think who or what that might be at the moment.

Thirteen

Lady Christabel de Courcy sat at her dressing table while her maid Isabel arranged her thick, glossy tresses into an elaborate and flattering style. "Well? What have you learned? Have you seen her?"

"Yes, my lady. I was in the main hall when the duke and his party arrived."

"What does she look like?"

"She has blond hair cut very short. Her eyes are blue. She is taller than you and slender. Her face is bruised."

Neville had told her he had hit the girl. Too bad the blow had done no more than bruise the chit. "Is she pretty?"

Isabel shrugged. "I suppose she might be, if her hair were longer and the bruise was gone. And if she dressed well. Her pelisse, besides being wrinkled and dusty, was far from the latest fashion. After they entered the foyer, Lord Royce took her into the small parlor and shut the door."

Christabel arched an eyebrow. "Did he? Why, I wonder?"

"I heard him tell Jeffers that he wanted to speak with Miss St. Clare in private. Jeffers remained outside the door, so I was unable to eavesdrop. I could not even remain in the hall waiting for them to reappear. But . . ."

"What?"

"The footman—his name is Percy—told me he saw them on the front steps, arguing. He said the girl was berating Royce for kissing her, or for not kissing her. He could not be sure."

"Kissing again," murmured Christabel. "What else?"

"Percy saw them when they emerged from the small parlor. He said the lady's lips were pink and swollen, as if she had been kissed."

"Kissing once again. And did this person comment on Lord Royce's appearance?"

"Yes, ma'am. 'Grim' was the word he used."

"Grim. How very odd. I wonder . . ." She trailed off, not wishing to give Isabel information which she would surely share with the other servants. Perhaps Neville was right and Royce had dallied with the American chit while she was at Wolverton. This girl might have more to answer for than interfering with her plans to become the next Duchess of Wolverton.

Christabel surprised herself by feeling jealous, an emotion she usually reserved for those people who thought themselves better than her because of their superior rank or greater wealth.

The oldest of three daughters, Christabel was the only one still unwed. Even her little brother, heir to the earldom, had married last year. Even more galling, she was the only daughter who had accepted an offer unaccompanied by a title. Her middle and younger sisters were married to an earl and a viscount, respectively. Her father had not objected to Royce's status as second son when Royce expressed his intentions to him. The marriage settlements, as well as the connection to the Duke of Wolverton, had satisfied the earl.

But not her. Christabel had accepted Royce's offer because he was the heir presumptive to a title older and more impressive than most, a title she had been sure would be his before they made their vows. But the boy Duke of Wolverton had not died, and he was proving damnably hard to kill.

Thanks in large part to this meddlesome miss.

She would deal with Miss St. Clare soon enough, and not because Royce might have paid the chit some improper attention when they were in the country. One glance at her reflection in the mirror reassured her. No little nobody from nowhere could compete with her. Christabel had been anointed a diamond of the first water by her peers, a beauty deserving of rank and fortune.

The possibility that Royce had seduced the American girl did nothing but send vicarious thrills down her spine. Imagining her fiancé with another woman titillated her senses. Perhaps she might coax Royce to tell her about it, once they were married. Or perhaps, if they continued their affair in the city, she might catch them unawares and witness their lovemaking firsthand. Neville had told her how exciting it could be to watch other people make love.

She wondered suddenly if Neville had ever watched Royce. Christabel had heard it whispered that there were brothels where certain rooms were equipped with peepholes. She would have asked Neville to take her to such a place, but had not wanted to jeopardize her reputation as a virtuous and virginal lady, worthy of being a duchess. She was taking enough of a risk by continuing her affair with Neville. She dared not attempt to visit a brothel.

Moreover, Royce was too fastidious to patronize such establishments. As far as she knew, he limited his sexual appetites to a better class of courtesan. His mistresses had been actresses and dancers, among the most sought-after members of the demimonde. Those women must be the source of Neville's description of Royce as a skilled and generous lover.

Christabel felt a rush of heat pooling in her most secret place. Neville was skilled enough, but not generous. He had left her unsatisfied on more than one occasion. And he was beginning to bore her. Once he had gotten rid of the brat for her, she would have to think of a way to rid herself of him. Royce would be all the man she needed, at least until she had provided him with an heir. Then she could afford to indulge her more . . . exotic needs.

Royce would have his mistresses, and she would have her lovers. They would have a perfect *ton* marriage. Nothing Miss St. Clare had done or would do could change that. Royce might lust after the girl, but he would never do anything so wicked as breaking off his engagement to her.

Arden did not threaten her betrothal, but Christabel could not quite suppress the superstitious fear that the American might somehow discover her role in the attacks on William. She needed to find a way to discredit her, so that any accusations the girl might make would fall on deaf ears.

She studied her reflection in the mirror again. No one would believe that someone who looked like her could be a murderess. Still, if the girl had engaged in an affair with Royce, she ought to be exposed. Dora would be embarrassed if it turned out she introduced to society a girl who was no better than an actress or an opera singer. "Have you met this girl's maid?"

"Yes, my lady. Jane, one of the chambermaids from Wolverton, is her lady's maid. You may remember her. Jane was the girl you slapped for pulling your hair."

Christabel gave her a blank stare. She had slapped many servants, Isabel included. Servants were like dogs, needing constant discipline to keep them in their places. "Miss St. Clare did not bring a maid from America?"

"I suppose not. Or perhaps her maid was lost along with her luggage."

"Oh, yes. Lord Stanton did have some story about how she came to be in the forest where she found the duke." Something about a wrong turn and a broken wheel. She had gotten the tale secondhand from the duchess, who had interspersed the telling with thanks to God and praise for Miss St. Clare. Christabel wished now that she had listened more closely. She had the nagging thought that something about the story did not ring true.

Narrowing her eyes, she turned her gaze on Isabel. "Befriend this Jane and find out what you can about her mistress."

"Yes, my lady."

Christabel smiled, showing her tiny, perfect teeth. She had no reason to worry. Royce would not risk a scandal by crying off. She would be the Duchess of Wolverton before the Season was over.

Giles arrived early for dinner, in response to Royce's urgent summons. As instructed, he brought with him his luggage and his matched pair of dueling pistols. After his baggage was deposited in the bedroom assigned to him, he joined Royce in the study. "How did you explain my need to stay here? Did Dora—Her Grace—raise any objection?"

"Why would she object? I told her that you are needed to assist in William's protection. I have arranged to have William moved from the third-floor nursery to the rooms opposite mine and next to yours. Either Dawkes or Murch will stay in the room with him at night, and the two of us will keep watch on him every minute of the day."

"Does Her Grace know we suspect her brother?"

"No. I cannot accuse Lord Sharpless without proof, and that has not yet turned up. My steward is still going over the books, but so far nothing appears to be missing. It is enough for her to know that William may still be in danger."

"I thought it interesting that Osbert removed himself

to his club shortly after you departed for the Continent. One would think he would have remained close to his intended victim."

"He may have wanted to remove himself from the scene of the crime. And perhaps he found it easier to direct his minions from there." Royce rose from his chair and began pacing the room. "I have decided to hire a Bow Street Runner to keep an eye on Osbert. Sooner or later he must do something that will give him away."

"Sooner, I hope. This continued threat cannot be easy for William or his mother to bear." Giles let his gaze follow Royce as he walked back and forth. His friend seemed worried by more than the threat—now tempered by a twenty-four-hour guard—to his nephew. "Your leg is much improved, I see. Your limp is hardly noticeable. I take it the carriage ride from Somerset did not tax your injured leg too much."

"No. I only traveled in the coach the first day. After that, I rode."

"Ah. You followed Miss St. Clare's advice and used your leg."

"Yes." After a brief pause, Royce added, "She showed Dawkes the massage technique she spoke of, and that seemed to hasten my recovery as well."

"Hmmm," said Giles. A slight flush had tinged Royce's cheeks when he mentioned massage. "Your scar has faded, too. You might say you are your old self again. Did you and Arden have fun together?"

Royce stopped pacing and directed a scowl at Giles. "Another attempt was made on William's life. That was hardly conducive to 'fun.' "

"Oh. Of course not." His friend still suppressed his true personality, Giles thought with regret. But . . . something had happened between Arden and Royce. He would wager his next quarter's income on it. "And seeing her hurt in William's defense would not have been amusing in the slightest. Forgive me."

Royce dismissed his apology with a wave of his hand. "What have you learned about Arden—Miss St. Clare? Did you meet with her man of affairs?"

"Yes." Giles found it revealing that Royce inquired first about Arden and not about his betrothed. "How is Lady Christabel?"

"I have not seen her. I have spent my time since our arrival this afternoon reassuring Dora and consulting with the steward. I will meet Lady Christabel at dinner. What about Miss St. Clare? Is she an heiress as she claims?"

"Yes. According to Mendlicott, she has a sizable fortune at her disposal. He would not give me the exact amount of her account, but he did tell me she has rented a house for the Season not far from here. Her closeness will make it convenient—"

Royce gave a start. A guilty start. "Convenient? For what?"

"—for the duchess to take her about." What *had* gone on between Royce and Arden in the few days since he had parted from them? "Her Grace has expressed the wish to sponsor Miss St. Clare's introduction to society, out of gratitude for what she did for William. She has an aunt, you know."

"I am aware of my sister-in-law's relations."

"I referred to Miss St. Clare's relation. Her name is Lavinia St. Clare, and she is already in residence at the house Arden rented for the Season."

"Arden has an aunt in England?"

"Yes. According to Mendlicott, the St. Clares are an old and respected family in Hereford. Lavinia's brother, Justin St. Clare, was a lieutenant in the army. He was killed in the Battle of New Orleans."

"Strange Arden never mentioned that."

"She may not have known. Mendlicott said the American and English branches of the family were not acquainted, until he tracked down the aunt. So Arden is a lady, after all, and one with English roots. And she is an heiress, just as she told us. What do you make of that?"

"Why should I make anything of it?"

"You were certain she was not a lady. You will have to apologize to her."

"I have apologized." A flush tinged Royce's cheeks.

"Have you? For what?"

"You presume upon our friendship. But I will tell you this much. Arden St. Clare is to be treated with the respect and honor she is due."

"Hmmm. You have gone from accuser to champion in a very short time."

"As I wrote you, Arden saved William a second time. Her brave act established her innocence of any involvement in the plot against my nephew."

Giles grinned. Royce could not conceal the admiration he felt for Arden. There was hope for his friend yet.

Fourteen

Arden was making an alphabetical list of twenty-first century items she ought to miss when the footman arrived to take her to dinner. She'd gotten up to the M's. "Malls, microwave ovens, McDonalds," she muttered as she followed the footman to the drawing room next to the formal dining room. It wasn't working. She had often been told she was an old-fashioned girl, usually by men who thought that was a flaw. They had been more right than they knew. Arden could think of very little—save modern plumbing—that she would truly miss if she missed her return trip to the future.

This elegant era would appeal to her even if it had not been the time of Royce Warrick. The clothes were delightful. She felt very sophisticated in her borrowed finery. The duchess had sent her a cream-colored taffeta—Jane called it sarcenet—dress, embroidered in gold thread around the low-cut neckline and hem. A man might view her pretty dress as nothing more than a frivolous feminine extravagance, but she felt armed and ready to do battle.

Her armor included more than a new dress. She had used her twenty-first-century cosmetics—foundation, concealer, and powder—much to Jane's fascination. She did not know how many more times she could get away with the "that's the way we do it in Louisiana" explanation. She blamed vanity for taking the risk this time.

She did not want to meet Lady Christabel with the ugly green and yellow remnants of her bruise visible.

The duchess and the other guests were already assembled when she arrived. Arden paused in the doorway, taking in the scene. Her gaze went immediately to Royce, standing next to the fireplace. He acknowledged her presence with a curt nod. Giles was standing next to him. He winked at her, provoking a second glance. What was that about?

Another man stood behind a sofa where Dora and another woman—she had to be Christabel—were seated side by side. Christabel had gorgeous auburn hair, dressed in a style that called attention to her aristocratic cheekbones and . . . brown eyes? A tiny, very tiny seed of hope planted itself in Arden's heart. Royce had not remembered what color his fiancée's eyes were.

A wide smile on her face, Arden walked into the room.

William waited just inside the door.

"Arden, you look very pretty," said William, sounding awed. He bowed and offered her his arm.

"Thank you, Your Grace," she said, remembering to curtsy before she placed her hand on his arm. "Are you joining us for dinner?"

"No, but Mother said I could remain downstairs long enough to introduce you to everyone."

He led Arden around the room, stopping first at the pair of Regency gentlemen lounging in front of a marble fireplace. "You know Uncle Royce and Giles."

"Good evening, Miss St. Clare," said Royce.

She nodded, not letting her eyes meet his.

"Arden," said Giles, taking her hand and kissing it. "It is good to see you again. Royce told me about your second rescue of William. Are you quite recovered from that villain's blow?" He used a finger to tilt up her chin. "I see no evidence of it."

Royce took a step toward them, scowling. "You need

not examine her so closely, Giles. She is quite all right. See how her bruise has faded almost completely."

"Yes, I am quite all right." She directed her remark to Giles, who winked at her again. Did he have something in his eye, or was he flirting with her? Why would he be flirting with her? "It's nice to see you again, too," Arden murmured, not a little confused.

Oblivious to the byplay, William led her to the sofa. The duchess and Christabel stood up as they approached.

"This is Lady Christabel de Courcy. I told you about her, remember? She is betrothed to my uncle."

"Yes, I know. How do you do?" said Arden. Christabel's eyes were definitely brown, dark brown. Not even hazel, a color that might contain a hint of green. Arden smiled at Christabel and extended her hand.

Lady Christabel stared at her hand, her expression blank. "Do you expect me to kiss your hand?"

"Oh, no. Sorry." Arden quickly snatched her hand back and dropped a curtsy.

"Americans shake hands, Lady Christabel," William explained.

"How quaint." Lady Christabel expertly opened her fan and held it in front of her mouth. Arden was sure she was hiding a superior smirk.

The remaining gentleman stepped forward, holding out his hand. "I am Lord Neville de Courcy, Christabel's cousin. I would be pleased to take your hand."

Arden held out her hand. Lord Neville grasped it, but instead of shaking it, he raised her hand to his lips. She thought she felt his tongue graze her knuckles, but he released her hand before she could be sure. She barely controlled the urge to wipe the back of her hand on her skirt.

"All right, William," said the duchess. "Arden has met everyone now. Wish our guests good night and take your leave."

"Yes, Mother. As soon as I explain something to Arden." He looked at her, his brows drawn together. "Arden, I am sorry, but I will not be allowed to teach you to ride just yet. Uncle Royce says I must stay inside awhile longer."

"You do not ride?" asked Dora, surprise evident in her voice.

"No."

"How odd," said Christabel.

"She was thrown off a horse when she was a girl." Giles gallantly came to her defense. "That put her off riding."

"But she wants to learn, Mother. And I promised to teach her, but so far . . ." William stopped and rushed to his uncle. "Uncle Royce! You could teach her now. Your leg is much better. You rode on the way to London almost every day. Will you, please?"

Royce shook his head. "I regret that I cannot keep your promise for you. I will not have time."

"Royce!" said the duchess. "I am ashamed of you. After all Miss St. Clare has done for William, twice coming to his rescue. As for you—you yourself told me how she assisted in your recovery from your war wounds. How can you refuse my son's request?"

Looking uncomfortable, Royce replied, "Dora, William's safety must be my first concern."

"He will have guards enough," said Giles. "I am sure we could spare you for an hour or two a day."

"If not, I would be happy to instruct Miss St. Clare," said Neville.

Arden did not imagine the leer he directed at her. The thought of being alone with Neville de Courcy made her skin crawl. Something about the man was . . . creepy. And Royce's refusal felt like another rejection. "Thank you, but that won't be necessary. I'm sure I can hire someone to teach me."

"Nonsense. Royce is a superb horseman. And a wonderful instructor. He taught William how to ride, and he will be pleased to teach you. Won't you, Royce?" asked the duchess.

With an exasperated look at his sister-in-law, Royce capitulated. "Very well. As long as it doesn't interfere with my other duties."

"There. It is settled. Now, William, off to bed with you, young man," said the duchess, kissing him on the cheek. "Murch is waiting for you by the stairs."

"Yes, Mother. Good night, Arden. Good night, everyone."

Jeffers opened the pocket doors at the opposite side of the room. "Dinner is served, Your Grace."

Royce escorted Dora into the dining room, followed by Lady Christabel and Lord Neville. Giles held out his arm to Arden. "That went well, I think," he said.

"What?"

"The next step in your courtship, and perhaps in mine. A little jealousy always stirs the pot. Do you think Dora noticed? I could not see her from where I was standing. Royce definitely noticed. You must have noticed how quickly he removed my hand from your face."

"Courtship? What are you talking about, Giles? Are you and the duchess—"

"Not yet. She will not hear of it. However, hope springs eternal. Royce will . . ."

They reached the dining table before he finished his statement, leaving Arden to wonder what on earth he was talking about. Dora and Royce were sitting at opposite ends of the table. Giles seated Arden at Dora's right, and took the chair opposite her. Lady Christabel was sitting next to Giles and across from her cousin.

Conversation lagged while footmen brought dishes from a sideboard and offered the contents to the duchess and her guests. Arden used the time to dissect Giles's remarks. Giles wanted to court the duchess. That part seemed clear enough. Why wouldn't Dora hear of it? The duchess stuttered every time she said Giles's name. That had to mean something.

But Giles had referred to two courtships. The second one had to be between herself and Royce. Giles must be playing matchmaker. That was the only thing that made sense. But it was not sensible of him. He must know that Royce would not break off his engagement to Lady Christabel. Arden let her gaze stray to her rival.

Rival. No. That implied a contest, and she had decided not to play. The stakes were too high. Giles might think Christabel was the only obstacle keeping her and Royce apart, but there was much more. Different times, different values. She might be perfectly respectable in her own time, but she was something other than a lady in 1816. Her modern behavior seemed to alternately intrigue and repulse Royce. She could never tell him she acted the way she did because she had traveled from a different time. Giles's matchmaking was doomed to failure.

Even so, the tiny seedling of hope growing in her heart sprouted two new leaves. Giles was right, it seemed. Hope did grow in the most unlikely places.

After dinner, the three women adjourned to the adjoining parlor, leaving the gentlemen to their brandy.

"Arden and I are visiting the warehouses and my dressmaker tomorrow. She needs a complete new wardrobe. Would you care to join us, Christabel?" The duchess turned to Arden. "Lady Christabel has exquisite taste, and she always knows the very latest fashion before anyone else. Especially me. I am not much concerned with fashion."

"Thank you, Dora. I will join you. Arden—may I call you Arden?"

Arden nodded warily.

"How is it that you need a complete wardrobe? Are the fashions in New Orleans so out of date? The French are usually the ones setting the styles for the rest of

the world, and your colony lately belonged to France,
I believe."

"I am not familiar with the current fashions here, so
I can't say. I need clothes because I don't have any,
not because what I have is out of style."

"Oh, yes. I forgot. Dora told me your luggage
was . . . what? Stolen?"

"We assume so," said Dora, saving Arden from the
necessity of lying again. "Giles—Lord Stanton told me
that neither her coach nor her trunks were ever found."

"How strange. I suppose your jewels and money
were stolen, too. What happened to your maid?"

Puzzled, Arden said, "Jane? She is here."

"You and your maid traveled all the way from America alone?"

"Oh. No. Jane was not my maid then. I had another.
And I had a travel companion. Tobias Thistlewaite."

"An old . . . friend?"

"Not exactly. A travel agent. He arranged the trip for
me, and was to escort me to London. I haven't seen
him since he went with the coachman to find help."

"How fortunate that you had a maid with you. Imagine being quite alone in the woods. I would have been
terrified." Christabel shuddered delicately.

"I was alone in the woods. My maid stayed with the
carriage when I set off through the woods. I never saw
her again, either."

"I am sure Arden is tired of reliving her adventures,"
said Dora. "Let us discuss where to go first tomorrow."

"Dennings has a new shipment of silks, I am told,"
said Christabel.

"Now, Christabel, let us consider how to dress Arden.
With her coloring, pastels I think."

"Pastels are so wimpy," said Arden, protesting. People always wanted to put blondes in bland colors. She
had a closet full of beiges and pinks and pale yellows
in New Orleans. "I want bold colors—scarlet, emerald,
gold."

"But unmarried girls do not wear those colors. It is not proper," said Christabel, looking horrified. "You would not want people to think you were as bold as the colors you prefer. Pastels it must be."

"She is right, Arden. Although I must admit I was happy to leave my white and pink dresses behind when I married. I prefer brighter shades, myself. Shall we invite your aunt to accompany us? When I called on her, she was still wearing black, although I believe her brother died well over a year ago. I fear Miss Lavinia did not have funds to replace her mourning wardrobe."

"Oh, Aunt Lavinia must go with us. I want to meet her the very first thing tomorrow morning."

"You must be eager to see your new house, as well."

The chatter about shops and warehouses continued until Royce and Giles entered the room. "Where is Lord Neville?"

"He took his leave."

Royce went to Christabel's side.

"Giles, would you please escort me and Arden to the portrait gallery?" Dora asked. "I want to show Arden the paintings, especially the one of Robert and William when he was seven."

As soon as the three were out of the room, Dora explained, "Royce and Christabel have not had a moment alone together since his arrival. They must have much to discuss."

"How thoughtful of you," said Giles, sounding disgruntled.

Christabel felt a familiar excitement as soon as she was alone with Royce, an excitement she had only ever felt when Neville was doing something wicked to her. Frowning, she turned away so that Royce would not see her desire. She discovered that she wanted him, and she was not sure that was a good thing. She preferred to be the object of a man's desire. That gave her power, the only power a woman could wield. Still, having a husband who caused chills to run up and down her spine would not be all bad. Smoothing her brow, she turned to face her betrothed. "How thoughtful of Dora to arrange for us to be alone."

"Yes." He did not bother to hide his scowl. Royce was not pleased to be alone with her, it seemed. She would have to take steps to remedy that. "How have you been, Christabel?"

She let her eyelids flutter shut briefly. "Lonely. It has been two long years since last we met. And we had only a few short weeks to enjoy our engagement before you left me."

"I had to go."

"I know. And now you are returned to me a hero. I am very proud of you. But I did miss you so." She patted the seat next to her. She would have to make sure that he wanted her more than she wanted him. "Come sit by me and tell me how much you missed me."

He sat down. She reached out and traced the scar on his cheek with her finger. Tears welled up in her eyes. "Oh, Royce. How you must have suffered."

He looked uncomfortable. "My wounds have healed. There is no need for you to weep, my dear."

"I have shed many tears for you," she said, resting her hand on his forearm. "And for poor little William. Who can be behind these dastardly attacks? What reason could anyone have to harm a child?"

"I do not know." He placed his hand on top of hers. Royce was pleased that she was concerned about the brat. She could build on that. "But I intend to find out."

"That must be your first concern, of course. And mine. You must give me orders, Captain Warrick. I am yours to command. How can I help solve this mystery?"

"The man behind this plot is dangerous, Christabel. I will not ask you to place yourself in harm's way."

"Very well. There is probably little I could do, being a woman and weak." She sighed deeply, hoping to draw Royce's attention to her décolletage. Her dress was cut fashionably low. So low, in fact, that a possessive man might have objected. She all but gnashed her teeth when his gaze remained fixed on her face. "I hope you may find some time for us. That is why I asked Dora to allow me to stay here for a few days, so that I would be close to you. We must make plans for our wedding. And our wedding night." She blushed prettily.

"I will make every effort to spend time with you, my dear, but as you said, William's safety comes first."

"And you are obligated to take Miss St. Clare riding," she said, allowing only the slightest hint of reproach to sound in her voice.

"Yes. But we will soon expose the villain. Then you and I may proceed—"

Christabel heard footsteps echo on the marble hallway. The others were returning. "I cannot bear to wait a moment longer. I know it is bad of me, but I have longed for your kiss." She pulled his head down and pressed her lips to his, just as the door opened.

"Oh!" said Arden.

"Ah," said the duchess, smiling.

"Damn," muttered Giles.

Christabel and Royce sprang apart, with identical guilty expressions on their faces. Royce's was real. Hers was not. She blushed prettily again as she simpered, "Oh, there you are. Royce and I were . . . discussing our wedding date. We agree that we must wait until any danger to William is past." She sighed again, and cast a longing look at Royce.

"Yes," Royce said. "And now, my dear, if you will excuse me. Giles and I have plans to make."

"Of course. Good night. Are you coming, Dora?"

"No. The plans involve my son. I intend to stay."

Her round chin came up, and she dared Royce and Giles to disagree.

Christabel turned to Arden. "This day has been so exciting. I find I am exhausted. I believe our rooms are next to one another. Will you walk with me?" She placed her arm around Arden's waist, giving the girl no choice but to go with her, however reluctantly.

"I did not realize you were staying here," said Arden.

"Oh, yes. Dora graciously invited me so that I would be close at hand when Royce returned."

"I see. It must have been difficult for you—waiting for him."

"Very difficult. For both of us. Royce missed me terribly, he said. But the wait is over, and soon we will be wed."

Arden did not respond.

Outside Arden's door, Christabel waited until she had opened the door to her bedroom. "This is a charming room. The duchess has such good taste in furnishings, don't you agree? Which room did you have at Wolverton? I swear I cannot decide on a favorite. The Gold Room is the most elegant, but the view is not so pleasing as the one from the Blue Room. I wager you were given the Blue Room, to match your eyes."

"Yes. The Blue Room. The view was most pleasing. Good night, Lady Christabel."

She smiled. "A *very* good-night."

Fifteen

Jealousy made a person wake up cranky.

Cranky, mean-spirited, and suspicious. Suspicion led Arden to question Jane about the naming of rooms at Wolverton before she took one sip of chocolate. It turned out that the rooms there were named after counties where the Dukes of Wolverton owned property. There was no Blue Room. That, of course, explained the "gotcha" look on Christabel's face the night before.

Christabel de Courcy might be a Lady with a capital L, but she was also a witch with a capital B. That kiss between Lady C and Royce had been timed for her benefit, Arden was sure. A clever witch, Arden conceded; clever enough to pick up on the attraction between her and Royce. Christabel was going to fight for her man, it seemed.

Arden really, really wanted to fight back.

Royce deserved better than Christabel's kind of Lady.

Giles must agree with her. But he seemed to be the only one who saw through Christabel, except for Jane and the other servants unlucky enough to have to wait on her.

Arden had to have a long talk with Giles before too much time passed. Then she had to examine her own motives very carefully, no matter how scary that prospect was. Before she interfered with Royce's engagement, she had to be certain she would do no lasting damage to his future.

Or to her heart.

Her St. Clarish self reminded her that there were practical matters to take care of before she could worry about her heart's desire. She needed a wardrobe, for one thing, especially a riding habit or two. First and foremost, she had to meet her aunt Lavinia.

When Arden went down to breakfast, only the duchess and Christabel were at the table. Royce and Giles had risen early and gone out, leaving William in the care of Dawkes and Murch. Dora explained that they were going to hire a Bow Street Runner to assist in their search for the criminals who had attacked William.

Christabel begged to be excused from the shopping trip, implying that she and Royce had a rendezvous arranged for later that morning. She also said she would be removing to her father's house that afternoon, as she had imposed on Dora's hospitality too long. "You must concentrate on keeping the duke safe without the distraction of guests," she said, slanting a pious look at Arden.

With the sweetest smile she could manage, Arden said, "I agree with you, Lady Christabel. I decided last night that I must move to my new house this very morning. I want to meet my aunt as soon as possible." Turning to Dora, she asked, "Would it be all right if we postponed the shopping trip until this afternoon?"

"Of course. I shall be sorry to lose your company. But both you and Lady Christabel are near at hand, and I expect you both to visit often."

After breakfast, Arden set off, accompanied by Jane, two footmen, and the coachman. One square over, the barouche stopped in front of a house. Unlike the Duke of Wolverton's mansion, which, with its gardens and stables, took up one complete side of a square, this house was part of a terrace of similar houses. Her house faced a park in the middle of the square, smaller than the fenced and gated private park in front of William's home.

"We could have walked here," said Arden as she and Jane started up the stairs. "Dora was right. It's not far from the Duke of Wolverton's residence at all."

One of the footmen—Percy he said his name was—followed along carrying Arden's carpetbag and Jane's small trunk. Lifting the heavy brass knocker, Arden let it fall against the carved mahogany door. The door opened immediately, as if the person had been waiting for the knock. Not a butler, but a woman not much older than Arden stood in the doorway. Dressed in black, her blond hair twisted into an uncomfortable-looking knot on the top of her head, she had eyes of the same St. Clare blue as Arden's. Feeling a bit light-headed, Arden murmured, "Aunt Lavinia?"

"Arden?"

"Yes." Arden opened her arms and Lavinia walked into them, hugging her fiercely. When they stepped apart, Arden saw tears in Lavinia's eyes through her own blurred vision. "Aunt Lavinia, I am so glad Mr. Mendlicott found you. And that Tobias asked him to seek out any relatives I might have in England. I never would have thought to do that."

"You cannot be more happy than I am. Who is Tobias?"

"Tobias Thistlewaite, a travel agent. He arranged for my trip to London. Oh, Aunt Lavinia, you are the best thing that has happened to me so far." Almost the best thing. She had found her heart's desire, even if she didn't know what to do with him. But that discovery had come with a downside. Arden hugged her again.

"I am not really your aunt, you know. Our connection is not quite so close." Lavinia tilted her head to one side. "Although we do resemble each other, don't we?"

"Yes. Yes, we do. But you are much too young to be my aunt. We could be sisters."

Percy cleared his throat. "Where shall I put the luggage, Miss St. Clare?"

"Oh, my," said Lavinia, obviously flustered. She pulled on a bellpull and a butler appeared. "Pierson, please take charge of the luggage. And show Miss St. Clare's maid to her room."

When the servants had departed, Arden asked, "Where can we go for a nice long talk?"

"The parlor. Would you prefer to see the house first? I think Mr. Mendlicott made an excellent choice, but you may not agree."

"I am sure the house is fine. I would rather get to know you."

With a delightful smile, Lavinia opened a door opening off the foyer. "In here. Shall I ring for tea?"

"Only if you want some." Her mouth was dry, but that was nerves, not thirst. She was about to tell her aunt some whopping big lies, necessary lies, to relieve Lavinia's sorrow over the supposed loss of her brother. Arden sat down on a sofa and looked about the room, searching for a way to begin her tale.

Lavinia sat down in a chair opposite her. "I was not aware that a St. Clare had ventured to the New World in the last century. But your looks and mine are the proof. There can be no doubt that we are related. If only my dear brother had lived to meet the American St. Clares."

"He is not dead," Arden blurted, too anxious for tact.

"What?" Lavinia's hand went to her heart. "W-who?"

"Justin St. Clare. He is alive."

Lavinia bit her bottom lip. "How can you possibly know that?"

Taking a deep breath, Arden began the story she had worked out, reminding herself that the important parts were true. "Before I left New Orleans, my uncle Fred received a message from a French planter named Duplantier. It seems that last year, after the Battle of New Orleans, his daughter Camille found an unconscious and wounded redcoat—English officer—in the swamp. She managed to get him home, and he soon recovered from his injuries. But he had no memory of who he was until shortly before Monsieur Duplantier wrote my uncle. He wrote because the young man had remembered his name was St. Clare, and Duplantier thought he might be related to our branch of the family."

"Did you meet Justin?"

"No. As I said, I left New Orleans only a day or two after the letter arrived. But I am sure the man's name was Justin St. Clare. You must write him immediately in care of Pierre Duplantier at his Chalmette plantation."

Hiding her face in her hands, Lavinia burst into tears. Arden got up and rang the bell. Jane appeared in the doorway. "Jane, please bring tea for my aunt. She has had happy news, and it's made her cry."

"You must think me a dreadful watering p-pot," Lavinia said with a sniffle.

"I do. Dreadful." Arden grinned at Lavinia, coaxing a watery smile from her aunt.

Jane reappeared with the tea tray.

"Thank you, Jane. I'll pour." Arden prepared a cup for Lavinia and handed it to her. "Drink up, then go wash your face. The Duchess of Wolverton will be here shortly to take us shopping for new clothes." Casting a critical eye on her aunt's black dress, Arden added, "We both are in need of complete wardrobes, it seems."

"Oh, but I have no need for finery."

"You most certainly do. You can't go around in black all the time. It's depressing. And totally unnecessary, since you have no need to mourn. Plus, you are my chaperon. You will be accompanying me to the various routs and balls, the opera, the theater and so on. Of course you will need a new wardrobe."

"Well, perhaps a dress or two, but I do not need a complete wardrobe. The cost—"

"Goodness, Aunt. Didn't Mr. Mendlicott tell you I'm loaded . . . down with money? Hang the expense. We're going to shop 'til we drop."

"You have a droll way of speaking, Niece. 'Shop 'til we drop' indeed." Lavinia giggled.

"Yes. Well. It's an American expression. Now. You must go and write that letter to Justin right away."

"I will, but first I must show you the house."

"Not necessary. Pierson can do that. Do we have any other servants? Never mind. Pierson can answer that question, too. Go wash your face and write your letter." With a gentle shove, Arden sent Lavinia on her way.

She rang for the butler. When he appeared, she asked him to give her a tour of the house. The kitchen and servants' hall, along with separate bedrooms for the cook and the butler, were in the half-basement. On the ground floor, where Arden and Jane had entered, were the parlor and dining room. A drawing room and library occupied the first floor, and there were two bedrooms on the second and three on the third floor.

Lavinia had chosen the smaller of the bedrooms on the third floor for herself. She was seated at a writing desk, busily scribbling when Arden peeked in the door.

Four small bedrooms in the attic provided rooms for maids and footmen. Pierson, with what Arden was beginning to recognize as typical butler starchiness, explained that her staff consisted of himself, the cook, a chambermaid, a scullery maid, and two footmen, in addition to her lady's maid. He had not yet employed a housekeeper, but several women had applied for the position.

"Pierson, I would like my aunt's things moved to the

bedroom on the second floor. And Jane shall have one of the bedrooms on the third floor. You or the house-keeper may take one of the other bedrooms on that floor. I leave that up to you. We could convert the third bedroom to a sitting room, or leave it as it is for guests. We can decide that later." Seeing the shocked expression on her butler's face, Arden asked, "Is anything wrong with that plan? Unless my math is off, all four rooms in the attic are already occupied."

"The scullery maid sleeps in the kitchen, Miss St. Clare. And the housekeeper would normally share the cook's room."

"Oh. Where does the scullery maid sleep?"

"A cot in the corner of the scullery."

"That can't give her much privacy. Would she prefer a room to herself, do you think?"

"I cannot say."

"Ask her, please, if she would prefer a room on the fourth floor. Make sure she knows the choice is hers. And I'm sure the cook would like to keep her room to herself, don't you agree?"

"Yes, miss."

"Pierson, how much do I pay you and the other servants?"

Pierson ticked off amounts that sounded pitifully inadequate to Arden's ears.

"Is that weekly or monthly?" she asked.

"Quarterly, miss."

"You must think I'm very uninformed, but this is the first household I've been in charge of. In this country, I mean. Are quarterly payments usual?"

"Yes, miss."

"I would prefer to make the payments monthly. And double everyone's wages, please. What about benefits?"

Pierson seemed to be having trouble maintaining his butlerish stiffness. "Benefits?"

"Days off, holidays, sick days, retirement plans—that sort of thing."

"We each get a half day off each week."

"And?"

"That is all."

"Good grief. Don't you have a union? Never mind. I can see that you don't. Well, everyone will have all day Sunday off, in addition to another full day during the week. You work out a schedule."

"But, but," Pierson sputtered. "Who will serve you on Sunday?"

"I expect my aunt and I will be able to take care of ourselves one day a week. I'll work out a benefits package later, after I talk to Mr. Mendlicott. Now I must get ready to go shopping with the duchess. Is there anything I can get for you while I'm out?"

"No, miss. Thank you, miss." Pierson unbent enough to give her a broad smile.

"You're welcome." Arden grinned at him. "I'm not crazy, you know. I'm an American."

The Duchess of Wolverton arrived promptly at one o'clock, Arden and Lavinia climbed into her carriage, and they set off for the warehouses and arcades. After visiting only a few of the shops, Arden knew she would never miss shopping malls. She marveled at the variety of goods available, most of them skillfully made by hand. Following Dora's lead, she and Lavinia chose lengths of beautiful fabrics, some of them in the bright jewel colors Arden had lusted after. Next they proceeded to the dressmakers.

Arden had a bad moment there when she was asked to remove her dress so that she could be measured. She asked for a shift, claiming to be embarrassed to be seen in a shift that had been washed so many times it had holes in it. She removed her bra and bikini panties, stuffing them in her reticule, and put on the shift provided to her before the seamstress reentered the dressing room. A shift turned out to be something like a slip. Arden was measured this way and that, and the modiste promised several dresses within the week, along with a riding habit to be made up in dark blue velvet.

When it was Lavinia's turn to be measured, Arden used the opportunity to question Dora about Giles. As they looked through pattern books, Arden asked, "Is Giles an old friend of yours?"

"Lord Stanton? Y-yes. He and Royce have been friends since they were boys together. I met him when I became engaged to Robert."

"He likes you."

"I hope so. I like him, too. He has been a good friend to Royce, and to me. That blue silk you bought would be perfect for this ball gown." She directed Arden's gaze to the sketch.

"No. I mean he *likes* you. Romantically speaking."

"Arden. Giles—Lord Stanton is a boy. Younger than I by several—"

"Years?"

"Months."

"And that's a problem?"

"Of course. I am thirty-one years old, a widow with a child who is almost twelve. Giles—Lord Stanton must look for a young woman when he is ready to set up his nursery."

"I don't see why. Giles isn't a boy. He is a man. I would think a man would prefer a grown woman over a silly young girl. Has Giles ever indicated that he wants you to have his children?"

Dora turned scarlet. "Arden! You are too bold by half."

"So I have been told. I see that Giles has expressed his feelings. What happened?"

"Two years ago, after I had come out of mourning, h-he proposed. I told him no, of course."

"I don't see why. The way he looks at you . . . it must be love."

"Arden. Stop. I may like Giles, but I have no interest in marrying again."

"Oh. Well. I can understand that. Although my instincts tell me Giles is the sort of man who would be a partner to his wife, not a lord and master."

"A partner?" Dora stared at her, obviously intrigued by the notion.

"I believe marriage should be a partnership of equals, don't you? Otherwise, what's the point of giving up one's independence?"

The duchess shook her head, making her brown curls bounce. "That is not possible. No man would accept such an arrangement."

"You're probably right. Not as long as most women have no choice but to marry—men definitely have the upper hand here. But if you are one of the few independent women, then you might use your position to strike a bargain with a potential husband."

"Bargain?"

"Not romantic, I know, but marriages in this age—in this country, I mean—do seem to be more business than romance. A woman might as well use what she's got to get what she wants. Do you want Giles?"

"Giles would never agree to a partnership. Why should he? He will have his choice of girls—and women—eager to be his viscountess."

"It might take a little persuasion, but I think you could do it. If Giles loves you . . ." Arden eyed Dora. "He did tell you he loves you, didn't he?"

The duchess turned even pinker. "Yes, but what does he know of love? A young man's infatuation, that is what he feels. And because I refused him, he persists in paying me attention." She showed her dimple and lowered her voice to a whisper. "I have actually considered . . . taking him as a lover. That would end his *tendre* for me soon enough."

"Dora! You thought about having an affair with Giles?"

Her round chin came up. "Yes, I did. That is one of the advantages of being a widow, you know. Of course, I won't do it. If it became known that I threw myself at a younger man, I would be laughed at, or worse. Pitied. And Royce would never forgive me for causing a scandal."

"Would it cause a scandal?"

"Without a doubt. The Duchess of Wolverton must be like Caesar's wife, above suspicion."

"But Royce must want you to be happy."

"Royce wants me to be proper, just as Robert did."

"Your Robert sounds a lot like my uncle Fred and aunt Marie. I wish I knew why so many people think you can't be proper without being miserable."

"I will admit to being a trifle lonely at times, but I am far from miserable."

"But you might be even happier. With Giles."

"Arden—"

"All right, I'll change the subject. For now. How is William?"

"Bored. Poor boy. His birthday is the end of the month, and he wants very much to go to Astley's Royal Amphitheater. Royce absolutely forbids it. He is right, I know. It would be difficult to guard William in such a place, with so many people around. So William will only have a small party, with some of his cousins invited."

"You could bring a circus to him. Not elephants or horses, of course, but a juggler, an acrobat or two. And clowns. They do have clowns, don't they?"

"What a wonderful idea! I am sure that could be arranged."

Lavinia rejoined them and they continued on to other shops for gloves, bonnets, fans, and other accessories. Arden discovered that she adored hats, a mostly forgotten accessory in the twenty-first century. By the time the duchess called a halt and ordered the carriage to head for home, the footmen were loaded down with packages, many of them hat boxes, and Arden was happily exhausted.

As the carriage passed by Hatchard's bookstore, Arden noted the location for a future visit. Then she saw a familiar face in the shop's bay window. Two faces, in fact. Lady Christabel and her cousin Lord Neville were huddled together. "Oh, look. There are Lady Christabel and Lord Neville. I met them yesterday at Dora's, Aunt Lavinia."

"I have met them, too, on several occasions."

"How odd," said Dora. "I understood Christabel to say she had an appointment with Royce."

"Perhaps Lord Royce is in the bookstore as well," said Lavinia.

"Perhaps," said Dora. "If anyone chose Hatchard's as a meeting place, it would have been Royce. I have never seen Christabel or Lord Neville with a book. Still, I wonder why they did not meet at my home or at the de Courcy house."

The carriage arrived at Arden's townhouse, and she and Lavinia bade farewell to Dora. As they entered the house, Pierson informed them that they'd had a caller. Viscount Stanton had left his card, and a promise to return later.

"Shopping with a duchess, and a caller who is a viscount," Lavinia said. "You are well on your way to a successful Season. Invitations are sure to arrive as soon as the news of your association with the Duchess of Wolverton spreads."

Arden gave her a blank look. "How will that happen? Dora only introduced us to one or two of her friends."

"They will tell their friends, and the merchants and dressmakers will tell their other clients. Is Lord Stanton a particular favorite of yours?" asked Lavinia as they followed the footman and Jane up the stairs.

"He and I are friends, that's all." Arden directed the footman to place Lavinia's packages in the room opposite hers. "I had your things moved to this floor. Should

I have asked you first? I hope you don't mind. I thought it would be nice for us to be closer."

"Very nice. Thank you."

After their purchases were unwrapped, admired, and put away, Lavinia said, "So you and Lord Stanton are . . . friends?"

"Really. Lord Stanton is in love with Dora. And she with him. But she thinks she is too old for him. Can you imagine?"

"Yes. Most gentlemen look for girls just out of the schoolroom when they seek a wife."

"Get 'em young and train 'em right," muttered Arden. "Some men must prefer more mature women."

"I suppose so. But such men are rare."

"Not in America. There are more men than women, you see. They can't afford to be picky. Choosy, I mean. What about you? How is it you are not married?"

"No dowry," Lavinia answered succinctly. "After our father died, the estate yielded only enough to buy Justin's commission. I had to take a position as companion to Lady Whitehurst."

"Companion. I'm not sure I know what that means. What were your duties? To keep her company?"

Lavinia nodded. "And to keep her informed. She prided herself on knowing the latest *on-dits*. Lady Whitehurst entertained frequently, and I also went with her to the routs, balls, and other entertainments to which she was invited. She expected me to eavesdrop on those conversations she was not party to, and report what I heard to her. I am afraid I was often derelict in that particular duty. Gossip can be so cruel."

"Yes. But it can be interesting sometimes. I confess to being fascinated by the odd things people do to themselves and others."

"Oh, yes. I agree. I did not mind passing on tidbits about the foibles of the foolish, but I could never bring myself to repeat the kind of vicious rumors designed to damage a person's reputation."

Reputation again, thought Arden. "Was Lady White-hurst a kind employer?"

"She was not deliberately cruel, only thoughtless at times."

"Well. You do not have to put up with her any longer. As for your lack of a dowry, I can provide you with one. Do you want to get married?"

"I am twenty-eight years old. It is highly unlikely that anyone would offer for me, dowry or not. But it is very kind of you to offer."

"You evaded my question. Do you want to get married?"

"Oh, Arden. Of course I do. I would adore having my very own home and family. But that is not likely to happen, dowry or not. I have you, and my brother. Family enough for me."

Arden grinned, wishing that she could tell Lavinia about her future husband, the wild Louisiana river rat tamed by an English lady. But she did not want to spoil the surprise. And she was not sure how much intermingling of the past and future was allowed. Another question Tobias had failed to answer. She would definitely suggest that in the future—or the past—he provide time-travelers with a handbook, or at least a list of do'es and don'ts. "Well. You never know. You may have your own family someday. In the meantime, I think we should forget about finding husbands and concentrate on having fun."

"As I said, you soon will receive invitations to every amusement now that your connection with the Duchess of Wolverton is known."

"What sort of amusements?"

"Dinners, balls, routs."

"That sounds like fun. People-watching is one of my favorite pastimes. What do you like to do?"

"I must confess a guilty pleasure in reading the latest novels."

"Me, too. Have you read *The Prisoner of Passion?*"

"No."

"Well, we must buy a copy. I read it while I was at Lord Stanton's—that is, at Wolverton. Shall we plan a trip to Hatchard's?"

Lavinia nodded, her eyes glowing with pleasure. "My favorite shop."

Drawing her brows together, Arden mused, "I wonder why Lady Christabel was there with Lord Neville. No matter what Dora thought, I don't believe Royce was there. He would not leave William alone. And Giles was here while we were out. Of course, that still leaves Murch and Dawkes, but I thought they were to watch over William at night."

"Her Grace told me about the attacks on her son, and about how you saved him. Who can be behind such evil?"

"Osbert—Lord Sharpless, William's uncle, is the chief suspect. But I'm not at all sure he is the one. His motive seems weak to me. Lord Royce thinks he may have been stealing from the Wolverton estate."

"But if he has misappropriated the estate's funds, would not the death of the duke only hasten the discovery of his crime?"

"That's exactly what I thought. And now that I have met Dora, I am sure she would know if anything hinky was going on with William's patrimony."

"Hinky? I am not familiar with that term."

"Funny, crooked, larcenous. But Royce and Giles could think of no one else who had a motive to murder William. No one profits from his death, and he is much too young to have enemies."

"Lord Royce would become the duke."

"I know. He is not guilty."

"How can you be sure?"

"He was not in London when the first attempts occurred."

"He might have hired someone to carry out the attacks."

"Royce is too honorable to do any such thing. I am absolutely sure he is innocent," Arden said firmly.

"Absolutely sure. I see." Narrowing her gaze, Lavinia studied her. "Lord Royce is betrothed to Lady Christabel."

"Yes." Arden could not hold in a shuddering sigh.

Lavinia's blue eyes widened in sympathy. "Oh, dear. So that is the way it is? Do you want to talk about it?"

"There is nothing to say. He is engaged, and he is too honorable to break off his engagement."

"Niece. Did that man take advantage of you when you were without a chaperon?"

"Unfortunately, no. I wanted him to, but he didn't."

A startled laugh burst from Lavinia's mouth. "My goodness. You are outspoken."

"I know. I am trying to be more discreet, at least in public, but you are family. I see no reason to keep my true thoughts from you."

"I admire your frankness. It must be wonderful to say what you think. I always had to watch my tongue when I was with Lady Whitehurst."

"You said you had met Lady Christabel and her cousin. I wonder why Christabel didn't mention that she knows you."

"I am sure she did not remember me. A companion stays in the background, you see."

"Are they always together? She and her cousin?"

"Lord Neville is Lady Christabel's constant escort."

"I suppose that is not unusual. For an engaged woman to be taken about by a relative?"

"No. Not unusual at all. No matter what some people may say."

Arden's eyes widened, and she opened her mouth to ask what people said. Before she got her question out, Lavinia shook her head. "Please do not ask me to repeat hurtful rumors spread by jealous misses and envious matrons like Lady Whitehurst."

"I won't. Of course, I won't." Biting her tongue, Arden managed to keep from begging her aunt to tell her the worst. She really wanted to hear what some people, jealous or not, said about Christabel. With a sigh, Arden acknowledged that there were some things it was better not to know, for Christabel's sake and her own. What kind of person would she be if she relied on rumor and innuendo to discredit Christabel in Royce's eyes?

Sixteen

Giles called again a few days later, and Arden greeted him warmly. She and Lavinia had spent the intervening time on domestic matters, rearranging the furniture, deciding on menus, settling into their residence. Arden had given the cook recipes for gumbo and jambalaya, along with the St. Clare spices she had brought with her from the future. She did not think cayenne pepper and filé powder would throw the space-time continuum into a snit. If she was wrong about that, Tobias was to blame.

"Have you been busy?" asked Giles as Pierson took his hat and gloves.

"Very. There is much to do, setting up a household." Arden had filled almost three days with fittings, discussions with Lavinia and the servants, more shopping, and still it seemed as if Royce had been in her thoughts every waking moment. Out of sight did not keep him out of her mind. Whatever she chose to do about him, she had to do soon. Her time in the past was growing shorter every day.

She had received her man of affairs, gone over her financial situation, and approved his investment strategy. Of course, if Tobias was giving him tips, then his investments had to be sure things. But she could not be sure if Mr. Mendlicott knew about the time-travel aspects of Tobias's business. Nothing he said revealed such knowledge, and she hesitated to bring it up.

Her request for a meeting with Tobias had been firmly refused. It seemed that Mr. Thistlewaite would not be available for a conference before her departure date. Whether that was because he was in another time or merely uncooperative, Arden could not discern. Mr. Mendlicott did not know whether or not she could cancel or postpone her return trip. She would have to discuss that with Tobias.

"Your man of affairs chose an elegant residence for you," said Giles, looking around. "This is charming."

"Thank you. We are very comfortable here."

Arden took Giles into the parlor, where Lavinia waited. After introducing Giles to her aunt, she rang for tea. The tea tray appeared promptly, with cakes and scones in addition to the steaming hot pot of tea. "I will pour, shall I?" Lavinia asked, taking the chair next to the tea table.

"Yes, thank you." Arden sank to the sofa, patting the cushion next to her. "Sit here, Giles."

Giles took his seat, shifting his gaze from her to Lavinia and back again, an admiring gleam in his eyes. Lavinia looked particularly attractive, Arden thought. She had been persuaded to give up the unattractive bun, and Jane had arranged her hair in a fashionable style that framed her face with curls.

Both Lavinia and Arden were wearing new dresses delivered only that morning. Arden's dress was deep rose muslin, and Lavinia wore a blue gown that matched her eyes.

"I can see that your shopping trip was successful," Giles said. "You are both turned out in the first stare of fashion. Has your riding habit arrived?" Giles directed the last question to Arden.

"Not yet. I am to have another fitting tomorrow, however. It should be ready a day or two after that." The speed and skill with which the seamstress and her assistants completed their tasks amazed Arden. Except for the riding habit and a ball gown or two, all the clothes they ordered had been delivered.

"You must tell me when it is ready. I will be sure to inform your riding instructor." He grinned at her over the lip of his cup.

Her heart stuttered. "How is . . . William?" Arden asked, when she really wanted news of Royce.

"His Grace is bored. Remaining always under guard is beginning to wear on the young duke. Royce is restless, as well. We can be grateful that there have been no other attempts to harm His Grace, but waiting for a conclusion to this matter grows tedious."

Making a sympathetic noise, Lavinia said, "I am sure all involved want to find who is behind these dastardly attacks as soon as possible. There is a wedding being postponed because of this evil plot, I believe."

"More than one," muttered Giles. In a louder voice, he said, "You refer to the wedding between Lord Royce and Lady Christabel, I presume."

"Yes. It must be difficult for Lady Christabel. Her engagement has lasted longer than most, and now she must wait even longer."

"I believe she is holding up under the strain," Giles said, his tone dry. "Although I must admit I have not seen her for several days. My duties now include visiting my clubs and listening to the talk. Royce wants to know if the duke is the subject of any rumors."

"Is he?"

"I have heard nothing. Most of the talk involving the Warricks centers on Royce's return. Nothing about the duke or the financial activity of the estate manager."

"Then the search for the scoundrel behind these attacks is not progressing swiftly?" asked Lavinia.

"Not progressing at all," said Giles. "One almost wishes for another attempt, if only to move the investigation forward."

"Has Royce gone out at all?" Arden blurted. "That

is, we thought we saw him and Lady Christabel at Hatchard's earlier this week."

"To my knowledge, Royce has not left the house since you and Lady Christabel departed. She has visited each day, however, and is a frequent dinner guest."

Lavinia looked at him over the rim of her tea cup. "You said something about another wedding. Is the duchess planning to wed again?"

"If I can persuade her," said Giles.

"Ah. I wish you success." Lavinia filled Giles's empty cup. "Please try one of the scones. Our cook is from Edinburgh, and her scones are the best I have ever tasted."

"How is Dora?" Arden passed the plate of scones to Giles.

Giles reached for a scone and took a bite. "She is well. Anxious about William, of course. Whoever is behind this affair has much to answer for. Dora sends greetings to you and your aunt, by the way. She has been interviewing the most extraordinary people the past few days—acrobats and the like—for William's birthday party." Giles turned to Lavinia. "I must say, you were right about these scones. Delicious."

"Why is Royce staying so close to home?" Arden asked. "You are out and about."

"All the strangers popping in and out of the house cause him concern even though Dora only sees one or two at a time, and they are kept well away from William. Not only because they may be potential kidnappers or assassins, but because Dora wants the entertainment to be a surprise."

Before Arden could prod Giles to give her more news about Royce, he again focused his attention on Lavinia. "Were you surprised to learn you had an American niece?"

"Delightfully surprised. And she brought me such wonderful news. My brother, whom I had been told was a casualty of war, is alive and well. I have written to him and hope to have a response within a month or so."

"That seems a long time." A very long time, compared to e-mail, faxes, and long-distance telephone calls, Arden mused. Still, the slower pace had its advantages. Long, newsy letters were much more satisfying than the abrupt messages received via the internet. Arden found it surprising how little she missed about the twenty-first century.

"Perhaps sooner, now that shipping is more or less back to normal since the wars with America and Napoleon are finished," said Giles. "Miss St. Clare. Lavinia. Will you think me hopelessly rude if I ask to speak with Arden alone for a few minutes?"

"Of course not." Lavinia rose gracefully and extended her hand. Giles raised it to his lips. "Please call again, Lord Stanton."

"Thank you. I will."

Lavinia left the room.

"More tea?" asked Arden. She had a good idea what—or rather who—Giles wanted to discuss in private. And now, at last, she could ask him about Royce.

"No, thank you." Giles did not resume his seat but began pacing back and forth in front of the fireplace. "You and Dora have become good friends in a short time."

"Yes. As it happens, we have several interests in common. And Dora is full of warmth and charm."

"I am well aware of that, believe me. Did she . . . has she talked to you about me?"

Arden nodded. "Yes, but please don't ask me what she said. I would not feel comfortable telling you. I'm sorry."

"I understand. You cannot betray her confidence and remain a true friend." Stopping in front of her, he asked, "Can you tell me this? Is there hope for my suit?"

"Oh, I think so," Arden said. "Provided you see marriage a certain way."

"What way?" He sat down beside her.

"No, I can't tell you that. You might agree with whatever I say. Not that you would lie, exactly. But you might be tempted to tell me what you suppose Dora wants to hear. *You* tell *me* how you would treat a wife."

"With honor, of course."

"I know that. Be more specific."

"I would cherish her."

"I would not expect you to beat her, for heaven's sake. You are too good for that sort of nonsense. How do you see decisions being made in marriage?"

"What kind of decisions?"

"All kinds. Where to live, whether to have children, what to have for dinner."

"I would expect a husband and wife to make those decisions together."

"But what would you do if you could not agree with your wife on a particular question?"

"Try to persuade her to my point of view, I suppose."

"Would you? How?"

"With reason and logic, and if that failed, kisses. I would never impose my will on hers. And if her arguments were more persuasive than mine—or her kisses more passionate—I would accede to her view."

"Oh, Giles." Arden threw her arms around his neck and hugged him. "You are perfect for Dora."

Grinning broadly, Giles hugged her back. "I think so, even though it may be conceited of me. How can I persuade my dear Dora to agree with you?"

"I recommend you use reason and logic. If they fail . . ."

He winked at her. "Kisses."

"Exactly."

"What about you? Will you follow your own advice with Royce?"

"I have tried, but logic and reason are not proof against honor and duty."

"Have you tried kisses?"

She felt her face grow warm, but she saw no reason to lie to Giles. "Yes. They did not sway him either, or at least, not for long. As soon as he recalls his duties and responsibilities—and his engagement—he stops the kisses. Giles, it may be that Royce does not care for me the way Dora . . . oh, darn. You tricked me into telling you that."

"So she does care for me!" Giles beamed at her. "I am sure Royce feels something more than friendship for you. In my humble opinion, you are perfect for him. He has become much too somber, and you remind him that life can be joyous."

"He may find happiness with Lady Christabel."

"How could he? She never laughs."

"She never laughs?" Arden frowned. Now that he pointed it out, she realized that she had never heard even a small laugh pass those perfect lips. "She smiles."

"Rarely. And I find her smile rather insincere, do you?"

"Well. Yes. The smiles she directs at me are definitely on the smug side. But I thought that was because she doesn't like me."

"I find her dislike for you encouraging. She must have sensed that Royce is attracted to you." He became serious. "You must save Royce from this ill-conceived alliance, Arden. He cannot want to spend the rest of his life being more respectable than his priggish brother ever was."

"Are you sure? The family honor seems very important to him. And he did promise his brother not to cause a scandal."

"His honor and the Warrick name will survive a broken engagement. If Robert had not died, if Napoleon had not become such a nuisance, Royce never would

have acted so precipitously. He asked Lady Christabel
to marry him when he was still grieving for his brother,
and only a few weeks before his regiment left for the
Peninsula. He always planned to marry for love, you
know."

"No, I didn't know that." Arden sighed. If only he
had waited to fall in love with her.

"A second son has that luxury, even the second son
of the Duke of Wolverton."

"But Royce did get himself engaged. Perhaps he does
love her, after all." Arden had taken comfort from the
fact that Royce had never told her he loved Lady Christabel, until she had figured out there was no reason for
him to share his most intimate secrets with her. Knowing Royce, he probably thought his feelings toward his
fiancée were none of her concern. That business about
dealing well together could have been his way of keeping his private life private.

"How could he love her? He does not know her.
They were introduced only a few days before he proposed."

"Love at first sight?"

"Royce was not eager to return to her side after he
resigned his commission."

"He was injured. He did not want her to see him
when he was weak and scarred."

"He has spent very little time with her since his return to London."

"He is busy solving the William problem."

"He has time to teach you how to ride a horse."

"Dora made him agree to do that. And it hasn't happened yet."

"It will happen. Royce asks Dora daily if you are
ready for a lesson."

"He does?" Arden's heart beat a little faster. She was
ever ready to hang her heart on the smallest branchlet
of hope, it seemed. Sternly, she continued to resist

Giles's arguments. "That doesn't prove anything. He probably wants to get the chore over and done with."

"Arden." Giles shook his head, obviously disappointed in her. "You were so brave when you saved William. Where is your courage now? Are you afraid to rescue Royce?"

"Not afraid. Cautious. I am not convinced he needs to be rescued. Interfering with his engagement does not seem right, not unless I know for sure that he . . . how he feels about me. And her. And how I feel about him. What if I succeeded in breaking up their engagement, only to find I do not want him?"

"Ah. Well. It is unfair of me to ask so much of you." Giles sank back against the cushions, a glum look on his face. After some moments in silent thought, his features lightened. He sat up straight and took her hands in his. "There is another way. The engagement can be honorably ended if Lady Christabel agrees to release him from his promise."

"Why would she do that?"

"She does not love Royce. It is possible that she regrets accepting his proposal. It is not at all clear why she did. According to my sister Penelope—she and Christabel came out together—Lady Christabel wanted to marry a peer, one with a title equal or superior to her sisters' husbands. And any woman must prefer to marry for love, do you agree?" He did not wait for her answer. "Perhaps I can find an earl or marquis to steal her heart."

"Where? Titles R Us?" At Giles's puzzled look, Arden said, "Never mind. Where would you find someone to woo Christabel?"

"This is the Season. Titled lords looking for wives abound in London in the Season. Christabel, even without laughter, has much to recommend her. She is the daughter of an earl, the sister to another earl and a viscount."

"Well bred and well connected. Not to mention drop-dead gorgeous. Does she have a dowry?"

"Not a large one, but adequate."

"Even so, wouldn't it be improper for another man to court her now that she is engaged?"

"Improper, but not impossible. If we—I—started a rumor that she was not satisfied with her betrothal, she might attract suitors."

"I don't know. Tell me again, Giles. Why are we plotting to sabotage Royce's engagement?"

"Because he is my friend and yours and we want him to be happy."

"And so we're saving him from marrying a beautiful, well-bred, well-connected woman. Right. Royce is sure to be grateful for that."

"If he marries Lady Christabel, he will be forever miserable."

"You can't know that. Perhaps they will grow to love each other after marriage. That happens sometimes, doesn't it?"

"If you love Royce—"

"If I was sure I loved him, and I am not at all sure, that would still not be enough." *Yes, it would,* said her Freret side, urging her to throw caution aside and *live!* But her unadventurous St. Clare side told her to wait. "I need to know how he feels about me. What if it's no more than lust?"

"But if he did love you?"

"Then I would fight for him. With logic, reason, and more than kisses."

Giles did not say anything, but he could not hide the disappointment in his eyes. He obviously had expected her to take some bold step that would force Royce to choose between Christabel and her. He took his leave, promising to call again in a day or two.

Arden remained alone in the parlor, trying to decide what to do about Royce. She did want him. She might even be falling in love with him. And she agreed that

Lady Christabel was all wrong for him. But when it came to taking action, she felt paralyzed.

Giles was right to be disappointed in her. She was a coward.

"Are you all right? Did Lord Stanton say something to overset you?" Lavinia asked as she entered the room.

"No. Giles wanted to talk about his love, the Duchess of Wolverton. If I am upset, it is my own doing." She rolled her head on her neck, easing the tension knot there. "I'll get over it. What is that you have?" Arden pointed to the papers Lavinia held.

"Invitations. While you were closeted with the viscount, I gathered the invitations we have received. Shall we go over them?"

"We have invitations? Already? Who are they from?"

Lavinia rattled off a list of names. Arden recognized some of them—Dora's sisters and Giles's parents—but others were complete strangers.

"Most of the invitations graciously include me," said Lavinia, obviously pleased. "There is a sweet note from the duchess, inviting us to tea any afternoon of our choice."

"Good. I would like to see Dora. And William." She felt left out of the investigation now that she was not with her fellow adventurers on a daily basis.

"For my part, Lady Whitehurst has sent an invitation to her box at the opera Saturday, with strict instructions to bring you along."

"I would like to meet her," said Arden. Lady Whitehurst was up on the latest gossip, according to Lavinia. She might have heard something about Osbert's handling of the duke's affairs.

Arden made a solemn promise not to ask about Christabel. Rumors about Royce's fiancée were none of her concern. Of course, if Lady Whitehurst volunteered information about her rival, it would be rude to tell the woman to shut up. "Which opera?" she asked.

"Lady Whitehurst did not say. It does not matter. The show is in the boxes."

Arden and Lavinia spent the week being entertained at dinners, card parties, musicales, and a rout. The latter turned out to be a large evening party, similar to a ball but without dancing. Arden did not see any of her friends. Royce, Giles, and Dora were not accepting invitations, it seemed. They could not leave William unguarded.

After they returned home from a soiree at the Marquis of Eldonberry's early one morning, Lavinia exclaimed, "I vow you are well on your way to being the success of the Season. Only recall how many gentlemen sought your attention. Have any of them proposed?"

"No! I certainly do not want to encourage that sort of thing. Actually, I think they hang about waiting for me to say something outrageous."

"Ah, yes. You are becoming known for being outspoken."

Tongue firmly in cheek, Arden said, "Oh, dear. And I was trying so hard to be sedate."

"You may practice decorum tomorrow night, at the opera," Lavinia responded with a smile. "Although Lady Whitehurst is not the best example of ladylike behavior."

Aunt Lavinia proved to be right about the opera. When they joined Lady Whitehurst in her box at the Royal Opera House, she had her quizzing glass trained not on the stage but on the boxes opposite. She was far from the only one so employed. It seemed that hardly anyone, in the pit or in the boxes, paid attention to what was happening on stage.

After her perusal of the crowd, Lady Whitehurst subjected Arden to an exhaustive examination concerning her family, her fortune, her trip from America, and her acquaintance with the Duchess of Wolverton. Arden found she did not in the least mind telling this woman the most outrageous lies. "You remained in the country for some time after your arrival in England, did you not?"

"For a week or two. The Duke of Wolverton asked me to be his guest."

"How did you meet the young duke?"

Arden knew that Royce wanted to keep the attacks on the duke as much a secret as possible. "My carriage suffered a broken axle and I applied to the duke for assistance, which he graciously offered. He promised to escort me to London as soon as his uncle was able to travel. Lord Royce was injured at Waterloo, you see, and he had not quite recovered from his wounds."

"Ah, yes. Lord Royce. A fine figure of a man, as I recall. Broad shoulders that owe nothing to his tailor. I do like large men." Lady Whitehurst shuddered delicately. "They make one feel so deliciously helpless. Did you find him attractive?"

Arden leaned closer and whispered conspiratorially, "To tell you the truth, Lady Whitehurst, I found him boring. He is dull."

"Is he? That was not always the case, I believe. I know I have heard several juicy tidbits in connection with Lord Royce. Several years ago he was quite the rogue, if memory serves. Lavinia, do you recall the particulars?"

"No, my lady," Lavinia said repressively, disapproval apparent in her narrowed eyes and pursed lips.

"Ah, well." Lady Whitehurst turned back to Arden. "Lord Stanton was with you as well, I believe. He is a charmer, is he not?"

"Giles is very charming. However, he left for London soon after I met him. I actually spent the majority of my time at Wolverton."

"But His Grace remained with his uncle at Stanton's hunting box?"

"Yes."

"Why? They surely would have been more comfortable at Wolverton."

"I believe they were concerned with my reputation. No female relative was in residence at Wolverton at the time."

"I see." Lady Whitehurst trained her eyeglass at a woman in the box opposite.

"Who is that?" asked Arden. There was something familiar about the woman, although she was sure she had not met her.

"Countess Argent. She is Lady Christabel's youngest sister. The family resemblance is very noticeable, although, of course, Christabel is acknowledged to be the most beautiful of the de Courcy girls." Lady Whitehurst opened her fan and in a loud stage whisper said, "Something of a scandal there, you know. She married first, instead of waiting for her two older sisters to wed."

"Is that what she should have done?" asked Arden.

"Yes. But her father did not want to risk the Earl of Argent changing his mind, and so he accepted the suit. And Argent would not agree to a long engagement. Poor Christabel." Lady Whitehurst tapped her fan against her gloved hand. "Last to be engaged and last to marry. Well. There she is."

"Where?" asked Arden.

Lady Whitehurst pointed with the fan. "There. She is with Lord Neville, as usual. Now, that I find strange."

Lavinia's gaze went to a box opposite. "That Lady Christabel would allow her cousin to escort her now that Lord Royce has returned?"

"No. I have it on good authority that Lord Royce is still recuperating from his war wounds and is not accepting invitations. The duchess remains by his side, and is also not participating in the Season. What I find strange is that Lord Neville would escort no one but Lady Christabel. He should be searching for a wife, but he never shows an interest in anyone but her. He must still love her, after all these years. That is sad. Tragic, even. To fall in love with someone you can never have. Do you find that sad, Miss St. Clare?"

"Yes. Very." Arden did not meet Lady Whitehurst's gaze.

Lady Whitehurst leaned closer and lowered her voice. "There are stories about him, you know. He frequents brothels that cater to rather exotic tastes."

"Lady Whitehurst!" Lavinia sounded shocked.

Her former employer was not deterred. "Voyeurism. Bondage."

"No wonder he gives me the creeps," Arden muttered. She could almost accept Neville as a tragic figure, but something about him had made her skin crawl. Perhaps his taste for sexual perversions was the cause.

"Creeps? An interesting term. You have met Lord Neville, then."

"Yes. At the Duchess of Wolverton's. He was there with Lady Christabel when we arrived from the country."

"That must have been a touching scene—the lovers reunited after so long a time apart." She slanted an inquisitive look at Arden.

"I can't say. I did not witness their reunion."

"Poor Christabel, abandoned by her affianced almost on the eve of their betrothal, then forced to wait for him for two long years. I can almost understand why she allows her cousin to take her about, no matter how painful that must be for her."

"Why do you say that? Doesn't she like Lord Neville?"

"Oh, she likes him well enough. More than she ought, I should not wonder. One would think she would want to avoid him for the sake of her heart. And his."

"I don't understand."

"Some people claim that Lord Neville and Lady Christabel are closer than cousins should be. It is said that he offered for her when they were very young—

before Lady Christabel had come out. Of course, his suit was refused. There could be no question of their marrying, since they are first cousins."

Arden felt a tug of sympathy for Lady Christabel. She had fallen in love with the wrong man, and look what happened to her.

She never laughed.

Seventeen

Lady Christabel de Courcy opened the invitation
bearing the crest of the Duke of Wolverton. After reading it, she made a disgusted noise and tossed it to the
floor. "The duke is having a birthday party."

"And you are invited." Neville leaned his shoulder
against the mantel in Christabel's boudoir, letting his
gaze slide over his mistress. Seated on the chaise lon-
gue, she looked lovely, as usual. Wearing a peach gown
cut much too low for morning, she made his mouth
water when he ought to be angry with her. She had
donned the gown before he arrived, when she knew he
liked to play maid and help her dress.

Picking up a brush from her dressing table, he stood
behind her and began brushing her thick auburn tresses.
"Since you dismissed Isabel before she dressed your
hair, I will not scold you for allowing her to dress you."
He glanced at the invitation which lay crumpled on the
floor. "You are invited to the young duke's birthday
party. Will you go?"

"I wish I knew if it will be the last birthday he will
ever celebrate," she said, sulking. "If I had that guarantee, I would go and enjoy wishing him happy. As it
is, I do not see why I should attend a children's party.
Royce will be occupied with guarding his nephew. He
will have no time for me."

Neville set the hairbrush down, pushed her hair to

one side, and nipped her nape with his teeth. "And you will have no opportunity for mischief. With the duke or with Royce. Have you decided that the duke may never again be vulnerable to attack?"

Tossing her head, she wriggled from under his hands. "Never say that! I *will* be Duchess of Wolverton. But when?"

"There, there, my dear. Do not scowl so. You will make wrinkles."

Effortlessly, Christabel smoothed her features. "It must be only a matter of time. They cannot keep close watch over the boy forever. Dora tells me he complains ceaselessly about his imprisonment. Sooner or later he will run away again. Or they will tire of keeping watch. We have only to wait for the right moment."

He sat down beside her. "Patience is one of the many virtues I cannot admire. This waiting is becoming a bore. Perhaps you should consider another route to your goal. I hear that the Duke of Birchwood is seeking a new wife. His duchess died in childbirth only last month. He is anxious to wed—anxious enough to ignore the proprieties of mourning. But then, he cannot have much time left to sire an heir."

"Birchwood? That disgusting old lecher? I could not bear to have him touch me."

"Ah. But you will not shrink from Lord Royce's caress, will you? With such an eager bride, I wonder that he delays the marriage. Has he made no attempt to anticipate the wedding night?"

She bared her teeth in a frustrated snarl. "He has not had the opportunity. We are never alone."

"Christabel. You know such opportunities abound if one is clever . . . and eager. Perhaps Royce is immune to your charms. Birchwood would be much easier to control. His eyesight is so poor we could make love in his presence, and he would never know. Would not that be stimulating?"

Raising her shoulders in a negligent shrug, Christabel

said, "His fortune is no match for Warrick's. And Royce is not immune to my charms." She sounded a trifle unsure of herself, unusual for a woman as vain as Christabel.

Neville could not resist teasing her. "I believe you are wrong. I think he prefers the little American. He has had his way with her, has he not?"

"What do you think? She stayed with him for weeks at Lord Stanton's hunting box, with only the boy duke for chaperon."

"Then they must be lovers. Does not that worry you?"

"Their affair is over. He has not seen her since his return to London."

"I suppose you have the right of it. Miss St. Clare would not risk having her liaison with Lord Royce exposed, now that she is on the Marriage Mart. She is quite the success, you know. Word has it that she has garnered several proposals already."

"She may have Birchwood," Christabel said magnanimously.

"Although . . . some of the old hens are scandalized by her. They deem her American ways too bold by half. But others come to her defense and name her an Original. Thus far, her fortune has weighed the balance in her favor, and she remains popular with the gentlemen of the *ton.*"

"Is she very rich?"

"Very. Are you convinced the affair is over? Her residence is very close to Wolverton House. Royce may pay her nightly visits."

"No. He never leaves the duke's side." She was frowning again now, and her cheeks were flushed.

"You told me he is teaching her to ride."

"The lessons have not begun."

"If not Birchwood, perhaps Lynch. I know he is older than Birchwood and only a marquis, but—"

"Stop this ridiculous matchmaking! I am betrothed.

To a man who will be duke. I am not interested in
another man."

"Not even me? I thought as much. You have kept
me at bay for days now. Waiting eagerly for your wedding night?"

She arched an eyebrow. "Are you jealous?"

"I believe I am. Strange. I had not known that jealousy could be so arousing." He shrugged out of his
coat and reached for her.

She drew back and pushed at his chest with her
palms. "Neville. Not here. You have access to my boudoir only because you are my dear cousin. If you abuse
the privilege, I will withdraw it."

"I have access to your chamber because you need
me. Who else will do murder for you? You had best
keep me happy, or I am the one who will withdraw
from this scheme. When we succeed, you will become
a duchess, a very wealthy duchess. What will I gain?"

"Me." She lowered her eyes demurely, the picture of
innocence to a stranger. But he knew she was looking
at his arousal. She wanted confirmation of her power
over him.

"I would have you now." He reached for her again.
This time she let him slide his arms around her waist,
but she kept her hands between them, resting on his
chest. "You are all I want, Christabel. All I have ever
wanted since I was fifteen." That was a lie, of course.
He wanted many things. But it was true that he still
wanted Christabel. She was the only woman who
shared his taste for certain forbidden pleasures.

Neville jerked down the bodice of her dress, exposing
her lush breasts. Lowering his head, he took one brown
nipple in his mouth and sucked hard.

With a gasp, Christabel let her head fall back. "I am
yours. I will always be yours. Now, and after I marry.
You know that," she purred, arching her back, allowing
him to suckle at her breast. When he used his teeth on

the tender flesh, she cried out but did not push him away.

He had taught her to enjoy pain.

She raised her hands to his cravat. "Did you lock the door?" Her voice was husky, her eyes glittering.

"No." He kissed her, grinding her mouth with his, plundering her open mouth with his tongue. As he expected, she began to struggle. He gloried in the feel of her bucking against him, twisting her head from side to side.

"Get off me, you fool," she hissed. "Someone will see us."

He released her hands and sat up. "Fool? You dare to call me a fool?"

She immediately stilled. "I spoke hastily. You are not a fool. You are the cleverest man I know."

"You persist in refusing me." He placed his palm on her still naked breast.

She placed her hand over his. "For now. Only for now. I will satisfy you. You know I will. But not here. This is not the time or place. The door is unlocked. Anyone may come in at any moment. Have you forgotten my father is in residence?"

"The risk of discovery heightens excitement." He squeezed. Gently. Her back arched. The involuntary response pleased him. He could arouse her anytime he wanted.

"So you have told me. But discovery now would ruin everything. I must appear virginal and pure to my betrothed."

"I have confidence in your ability to deceive your husband, my dear." He bent his head down and kissed her tenderly on the forehead at the same time as he stroked her breast, her throat, her cheek. She relaxed beneath his gentle caresses. "And do you really think your father would expose you to censure if he did discover us together?"

"Perhaps not. But the servants would delight in it.

Neville, dearest, only recall how anticipation increases pleasure. Think of all the exciting things we can do together after I am safely married. Imagine making love in the Duchess of Wolverton's chambers when the duke is in residence."

"You would risk that? It could be dangerous. Your husband-to-be may not enjoy the role of cuckold."

"Royce may have been dangerous at one time, but he is tamed. Even if he is not, it will not matter. He cannot divorce me. And he must get his heir on my body. I will do as I please."

He took her nipple between his thumb and forefinger. She pressed against his hand expectantly. He pinched, hard enough to make tears wet her brandy-colored eyes. "And does it please you to attend the duke's birthday party?"

"Yes. Oh, yes." Her words were forced between teeth gritted against the pain.

He released her. "Remember, your rival is sure to be there. She is a favorite of the duchess."

Panting a little, she lay back on the chaise and closed her eyes. "We must do something about that. Poor Dora will be mortified when she learns she has befriended Royce's latest demi-rep." She opened her eyes. "Are you going out tonight?"

"I thought I might drop by the Widow Morrisy's musicale. I believe the Misses St. Clare will be there."

"Perhaps you could whisper in a few ears . . . ?"

"Consider it done, my dear. Now let me help you arrange your dress."

Eighteen

Royce and Giles formed an unconventional receiving line for the birthday party guests. Even though the guest list had been limited to family and close friends, Christabel, Arden, and Lavinia, they were vetting all who entered. Lord Sharpless was one of the first to arrive. Osbert was family and had been invited as a matter of course. They had been somewhat surprised when he accepted. William's uncle had been noticeably absent from family gatherings since Royce's return.

Dora had insisted on inviting Arden and her aunt. Royce's token protest—they were not family—had been met with a stern reminder of what they owed William's rescuer. He had not argued further. How could he? If not for Arden, William would not be celebrating his twelfth birthday.

The truth was, he wanted to see her again. The independent Miss St. Clare had been out of his sight but not out of his thoughts for days. He had not seen her since she moved to her own house. Giles had called on her several times. His old friend was ever eager to tell him the latest about Arden and her conquests. She was the success of the Season, according to Giles.

He ought not to be looking forward to seeing Arden. He felt no such anticipation for Christabel. He tried to put it down to the fact that his intended had been a frequent visitor, but not even the guilt he felt could make the lie believable. Arden was an obsession, Christabel a duty. More and more, the duty seemed too onerous to bear, but he could see no way out.

Royce had avoided being alone with his fiancée. He could not face Christabel until he rid himself of his unseemly craving for another woman. Arden filled his thoughts, almost to the point of causing him to neglect his duty to William. On more than one occasion Giles had been forced to raise his voice, to rouse him from his libidinous daydreams of Arden.

She appeared in the doorway with her aunt.

"Good afternoon, Misses St. Clare," said Giles, bowing. "Royce, see who is here."

Arden and Lavinia were assisted out of their pelisses by a footman. "Are we late?" asked Arden, avoiding Royce's gaze.

"Not at all. Nor are you the last to arrive. Lady Christabel is not arrived," said Royce, willing Arden to look at him.

She flicked a look in his direction, and he was relieved to see her blue eyes were sparkling with excitement. For a moment, he had sensed an aura of sadness about her. "Hello, my lord." She curtsied.

"Arden. It is good to see you."

She nodded. "Yes. I feel the same."

Other guests arrived, ending the brief exchange. When their duties as doormen were finished, Royce and Giles made their way up the stairs to the ballroom, transformed into a miniature amphitheater for the day. While most of the guests watched jugglers juggle and clowns clown, several pairs of eyes were trained on William. Dawkes and Murch were in attendance. The Runner, dressed in footman's livery for the occasion, had been ordered to keep close watch on Osbert.

Royce found his gaze straying to Arden. She was seated between Dora and William, and her frequent smiles and laughter made him grin in response. A guilty glance at Christabel, seated on Dora's left, found that exquisite staring into space, a blank look on her face. He could not tell if she was bored or merely daydreaming.

When the performers had finished, and all the presents had been opened and admired, Dora's sisters and their children took their leave. Osbert remained, along with Christabel, Arden, and Lavinia.

"I want to play a game," said William in an obvious attempt to make the party last longer.

"What game, dearest?" asked Dora.

"Hide-and-seek."

Arden blushed bright pink. Royce felt his own face grow warm as they shared the memory of that last game.

"Not now, William. It is well past your bedtime. And hide-and-seek is an outdoor game for children. All your cousins have gone."

"Some grown-ups play hide-and-seek. Uncle Royce and Arden and I played it indoors at Lord Stanton's hunting box. Remember, Arden? You and Uncle Royce both hid in the same place, in the—"

"We remember, William," Royce said, his gaze shifting to Arden. Her face was frozen. He could not tell whether she found the memory pleasant or disagreeable. He had mixed feelings, and perhaps it was the same with her.

Royce could not regret their tryst in the armoire, or their time together in William's traveling coach. Or the kisses they had shared in the small parlor. He had long since faced the fact that Arden was a fever in his blood, one that would not break until he tasted all of her. Which meant never.

He could seduce Arden and make her his mistress. Or he could end his engagement to Christabel. A choice between two dishonorable acts was no choice at all.

"No more games tonight." Dora held out her hand to William, "Come along with me, and I will tuck you in."

When Dora returned, she asked if the remaining guests would care to play a rubber or two of whist. Osbert accepted immediately, and Giles followed his lead. Arden confessed that she did not know how to play the game, but said she would like to watch and learn. Lavinia agreed to make up the table.

Lady Christabel pleaded a megrim and asked Royce to escort her home. He had no choice but to grant her reasonable request.

Royce escorted Christabel to the door of the de Courcy house, waited until the door was opened by a servant, and turned to leave. She put her hand on his arm, gently restraining him. "My lord. Please come in."

"Your headache—"

"Is miraculously gone. The carriage ride in darkness must have cured it."

When he would have refused again, she pleaded, "Please, Royce. We have had so little time together."

Unable to gainsay that remark, Royce followed her into the wide hallway, down the hall to a small drawing room. A fire burning in the fireplace gave off the only light in the room. Royce looked for candles.

"Do not light a candle. Brighter light will make my megrim return." She did not sit down but walked aimlessly about the room, shedding her pelisse as she moved.

"Firelight becomes you." He said nothing but the truth. The flickering light alternately lit and shadowed her perfect features, and made her auburn hair glow with streaks of fire.

"Thank you. Do you know, that is the first compliment you have paid me since your return?"

He frowned at her. "Surely not."

She smiled wistfully. "Surely yes. I do not complain, Royce. I am not one of those women who constantly need flattering words. I know you have been preoccupied with other things, but I would have you spend a few moments with me."

"Christabel . . ." He stopped, not knowing what to say. He had treated his betrothed with indifference for years now, and this gentle reminder was the first reproach that had passed her lips. The thought came to him that if he had treated Arden in such fashion, she would have voiced her displeasure loudly and long. He ought to be grateful his future wife was not of a shrewish nature. "Please forgive me, my lady."

She sat down on a sofa. "There is nothing to forgive. A woman's silly needs must always wait on honor and duty. I admire you tremendously, my lord."

"Do you? Why?" He sat in a chair opposite her.

"Your bravery in war. Your concern for your nephew." She lowered her lashes. "The responsible way you honor your commitments to your family. And to me."

Resisting the urge to squirm, Royce bowed his head. Every word Christabel spoke sent him sinking ever deeper into a spiral of shame. "You are more generous with your compliments than I deserve."

"Now that we are alone, I could be even more generous. With more than words."

He jerked his head up. Was she offering herself to him? He immediately rejected the idea. Lady Christabel was too much a lady. At the most, she was giving him permission to press a chaste kiss or two to her virginal lips. "Thank you, my dear. I am content to wait."

A flash of something that might have been anger shone in her dark eyes. He must be mistaken. The firelight reflecting in her eyes had made what was probably relief appear to be anger.

She smiled at him—a gentle smile, banishing any thought that he had annoyed her. "His Grace seemed to enjoy his birthday party. It was ingenious of Dora to hire jugglers and acrobats to entertain the children."

"I believe it was Arden—Miss St. Clare—who suggested that Dora employ the circus performers."

"How clever of her. Miss St. Clare is very clever.

As clever as she is beautiful." Her voice had a brittle edge, and her smile seemed forced.

It occurred to Royce that she might be jealous, and he sought to reassure her. "Qualities you also possess, my dear."

Her stiff smile slipped into something resembling a simper. "Now you must think I am fishing for compliments. Will you sit by me, Royce?" She patted the cushion beside her.

He moved from the chair to the sofa. "Did you enjoy the party?" he asked.

"Oh, yes. Very much. It was kind of Dora to include me. I vow, I feel a part of the family already. William—His Grace—is such a pleasant boy. I hope that our children will be as sweet." Lady Christabel put a hand to her mouth. "Oh, dear. Now you must think me bold, to speak of our children when we are not yet wed."

"Not at all." To his chagrin, he found that "bold" no longer seemed a vice, but a virtue. Arden had made him appreciate a woman of spirit, a woman who knew her own mind and did not shrink from speaking it.

"Is anything wrong? You seem distracted."

"I should take my leave." It troubled him that his thoughts kept returning to Arden. He tried once again to focus on the lovely woman next to him. "Your father cannot approve of his daughter being closeted alone with a man for so long."

"Lord Royce. You are my promised husband. Father would expect us to spend time getting to know one another." She raised her hand and traced the scar on his face with her finger. "My poor Royce. Wounded and alone. Why did you stay in the country? I could have cared for you."

"At the time, I thought it best to recover my strength before facing you and my family again. I confess, Christabel, I wish now that I had returned home immediately."

She gave him a brilliant smile. "Would you care for

a brandy? Father keeps a bottle in the cabinet next to the window."

"Yes, thank you. I believe I would." Liquor could not cloud his thoughts any more than the confusion caused by his betrothal to one woman and his desire for another. Christabel had the right of it—he should get to know her better. If they became better acquainted, Arden might fade from his thoughts.

"Allow me to serve you." Rising gracefully, Christabel crossed to the cabinet. She stopped in front of the fire, obviously unaware that the flames behind her thin muslin gown illuminated her form in a most provocative way. "Brandy or port?"

"Brandy." He said, beginning to feel a trifle warm. "Please."

She opened the cabinet and removed a crystal decanter. After pouring a generous measure into a goblet, she returned to his side. He reached for the glass. "Not yet. Let me warm it with my hands."

Christabel wrapped her hands around the bowl of the goblet and held it for a few seconds before giving it to him. "There. My father taught me how to do that," she explained, resuming her seat next to him.

He took a sip of the fiery liquid. "Your father? Or your cousin?" He did not know why he asked the question. Something about the way she had handled the goblet made him think it too intimate a gesture for a daughter. But that did not make sense. Neville was not her lover.

"Neville? Why do you say that? Have you heard those awful rumors?" Her voice broke, and she turned her face away from him.

"Rumors? What rumors?"

"Some say Neville and I are more . . . attached than cousins should be. Merely because when we were little more than children, he developed a *tendre* for me and asked my father for my hand in marriage. I swear to you, my lord, Neville is my friend and relation, nothing more. He would never—"

"Do no overset yourself, my dear. You are a true lady. I have no doubts about your character. No one could question your virtue." He had questioned Arden's virtue at every turn, questioned her status as a lady, and she had done nothing but laugh at him. She thought he was pompous—

"You are distracted again. What are you thinking?"

He took a large swallow of brandy. "Nothing of importance."

She took the empty glass from his hand. "Another?"

"No. It grows late. I should be—"

She flung herself against his chest and wrapped her arms around his neck. "Oh, do not leave, Royce. I cannot bear it if you leave me again."

His arms went automatically around her waist. "Christabel . . . you have been very patient. I wonder that you still hold to our betrothal. Have you ever considered crying off?"

"Never. Oh, Royce, have you never asked yourself why I accepted your offer? Why I chose you over all my other suitors?"

"We realized we would deal well enough together. I was, of course, honored by your acceptance."

"We will do more than deal well enough together. Royce. Dare I call you my darling Royce? Oh, you must see my weakness for you. I love you, Royce, with all my heart. Only true love could have seen me through the past two years. Alone. Miserable without you. I cried myself to sleep every night since you left me."

"Christabel—"

"Kiss me, Royce. I am not ashamed to beg." She moved against him, pressing her breasts against his chest. Tilting her head back, she closed her eyes.

"You do not have to beg." He felt ashamed that he had more or less ignored Christabel since he had placed the betrothal ring on her finger. She deserved better than he had given her so far. Lowering his head, he touched her lips gently with his.

Her virginal lips did not part beneath his. Unlike Arden, whose every response was eager and passionate, Christabel seemed intent on not reacting at all. With a groan, Royce ended the kiss.

"What is wrong?" asked Christabel. "Do I not please you? I know I am not . . . experienced like Arden—"

"Why do you mention her?"

"I thought . . . it seemed as if you and she . . ."

"Miss St. Clare is a friend. Nothing more."

"She wants to be more than a friend to you." Christabel pouted. She pouted adorably, pursing her lips and drawing her brows together in a delicate frown.

"Christabel—"

She stopped him by placing her fingertips on his mouth. "I may be an innocent, but I am not completely ignorant of men and their desires. I know you had mistresses before we were betrothed. I will not complain if you keep a mistress after we are wed." Her voice caught, and he could see her lips tremble. "Only . . . I could learn to please you. I know I could. Teach me, Royce. Please." She pressed her lips against his throat, his jaw, his mouth. This time, she parted her lips in sensual invitation.

Royce did not deepen the kiss. Grasping her hands, he set her away from him. "My dear. This is not necessary. I care for you." He must have felt some sort of attraction for her, since he had asked her to marry him. At the moment he felt nothing except guilt. Guilt and regret.

"I have shocked you, behaving like a wanton."

"No. But this is not the time. After we are wed—"

"Soon. Let us marry soon. I burn for you."

"As soon as William is safe."

"William. Yes. I almost forgot. But he is the only

impediment, is he not? Nothing else stands in the way of . . . our marriage?"

"What else could there be?" Royce temporized.

"Your mistress? Perhaps you do not want to give her up. I will not complain if you continue your affair after we marry. It is the way of the *ton,* is it not?"

"I have no mistress. I have not had since my brother's death. And now I really must go."

Royce left Christabel and returned to the Duke of Wolverton's house. He was appalled at his treatment of Christabel, and not a little shocked at her behavior. After confessing her love for him, Christabel had all but offered herself to him. She was not to blame for her behavior—behavior that Robert and his ilk would have found shameful.

The shame was his. His negligence toward her had compelled her to throw herself at him. She had even given him permission to take a mistress. No, he could not blame Christabel. Even a lady must tire of waiting to become a bride.

But he was not eager to be a groom.

Arden paid close attention to the card game, trying to dispel the envy she had felt when Royce left with Christabel. Seeking a way to keep from imagining what the two of them were doing, she contrived to sit next to Osbert at the card table. While Dora dealt a hand, she engaged him in conversation. "I understand that you had the responsibility of looking after William's affairs while Lord Royce was away." Out of the corner of her eye, she saw Giles's head jerk up.

Osbert nodded. "Yes."

"You must be relieved to be finished with that chore."

Dora sent a playing card sailing off the table. Giles retrieved it from the floor. Lavinia slanted a quizzical look at her.

Osbert, seemingly oblivious to the byplay, pulled a large handkerchief out of his pocket and wiped his face with it. "By Jove, I must confess I am most relieved. Don't care much for that sort of thing. Much prefer to spend my time breeding horses. I have a fine stable, you know. Must come by and see my beauties some day."

"You breed horses in the city?" asked Arden.

"No. I have a small estate not far from London. I spend most of my time there. Or I did, before Robert died. I have spent more time at my club since then. Have to be close to my sister. And my nephew. I dote on the boy, don't you know?"

"I am sure Her Grace is grateful for your assistance." Arden grinned at Dora, who smiled weakly in response.

Osbert arranged the cards he had been dealt. "Don't know about that. Dora thinks she can take care of . . ." He stopped, cleared his throat, and eyed his sister sheepishly. "Sorry. Didn't mean to complain."

Giles spoke up. "The duke's finances are Lord Royce's problem now."

Nodding vigorously, Osbert said, "Just so. Handed over the books to his man of affairs only last week." He eyed Giles. "Nothing wrong there, I trust."

"Not a thing, according to Royce's steward. Tip-top, in fact. He was very impressed with some of the riskier investments you made. They all turned out to be sound in the end, and you turned a tidy profit for the estate. That canal project was particularly chancy. How did you happen to choose that investment?"

"Canal?" Osbert gave Giles a blank look. "Let me see now—believe a friend recommended it. Can't think who at the moment."

Dora played a card but kept her eyes on the table. Arden could sense the tension building, and she didn't think the cards were the cause.

"Still, you knew enough to take that friend's recommendation. Was that luck or skill?" Giles inquired.

"Wouldn't like to say I depended on luck, not with another man's money. But if I say 'skill,' you might accuse me of bragging."

Arden smiled at Osbert. "Perhaps you would be so kind as to advise me on an investment or two. Mr. Mendlicott seems rather conservative to me. Personally, I like taking risks."

"Happy to oblige. Next time I hear of a good thing, I will let you know."

Arden saw the desperate look Osbert gave his sister. Dora smiled reassuringly. "I am very grateful to Osbert," she said. "He handled the estate just as I wanted."

Not at all, in other words. Using her fan to hide a grin, Arden knew in that instant that Dora was the one who had managed William's estate so skillfully. Why didn't Giles see that? He was still eyeing Osbert suspiciously. But with a hint of confusion.

Osbert was guilty, but not of fleecing his nephew. He had done the unthinkable—allowed a woman to take over his duties and responsibilities. "I intend to manage my own investments," said Arden. "With helpful hints from my friends."

"Do you? That would be most unusual," said Lavinia.

"Most improper, in fact," said Dora, clearly trying hard to keep a straight face.

"Improper? Why?" asked Arden, all innocence. "If a woman is good at that sort of thing, why shouldn't she manage her own affairs?"

"Might be all right in that case. Don't you agree, Stanton?" asked Osbert, dealing the next hand. "More than all right if she knew what she was about."

"I suppose so," said Giles cautiously.

"I am so glad you feel that way," said Dora, dimpling.

Giles looked from Osbert to Dora. "Oh."

Arden and Dora smiled at him.

The card game ended soon after, and Osbert was

leaving as Royce entered the parlor. "Evening, Warrick. Must not blame me. Nothing I could do about it. Woman has a stubborn streak." He rushed past Royce and out the door.

"What was that all about?" asked Royce, raising an eyebrow.

Giles placed a hand on his heart and declaimed dramatically, "Dora has confessed all."

Obviously startled, Royce looked at the smug faces. "All what? You cannot expect me to believe Dora is trying to murder her son."

"Of course not," said Giles. "Dora confessed to managing his estate. She is the one who kept the books and made the investments, not Sharpless. Dora handled everything. Osbert never had a chance to embezzle anything, even if he had been so inclined."

"Dora managed the estate?" Royce could not hide his shock.

"Just so." Giles smiled at him. "And very well, too, as your steward informed us."

"Well. So Osbert is innocent. Where does that leave us?"

Dora let out her breath in a huff. "You and Giles thought Osbert was behind the attacks on William? How could you? Osbert is my brother. He may be something of a fool, but he is not a bad man. He would never harm a hair on the head of my son."

"Now, Dora," said Royce soothingly. "We were merely exploring all possibilities. And he could have had a motive if he had been stealing from William."

"Did you suspect me, too?"

"Never." Royce and Giles spoke in unison.

"Well. That is something, I suppose."

"But if not Lord Sharpless, who?" asked Lavinia.

After a moment's stunned silence, Dora said, "It must be a madman."

"Or someone bent on punishing the son for the sins of his father," said Giles.

"Robert did not sin." Dora was emphatic.

"He may have offended someone," Giles suggested.

"It would have to have been a grievous offense to warrant such retribution," said Royce.

Looking from one to another, Arden asked, "Are you sure no one else gains from William's death?"

"The parson," said Royce, shoving a hand through his hair. "I suppose we could question him."

"I will send for him," said Dora. "I want to be involved in this. William is my son, after all. I am still angry that the three of you did not include me in your discussions."

"Spare Arden your disgust. She never agreed with our suspicions of Osbert," Giles pointed out.

"His motive seemed weak, that's all," Arden explained. "And none of us wanted to make accusations in the absence of proof." She turned to Royce, ignoring his crumpled cravat. "What does the parson look like?" asked Arden. "Could he have been the man who shot at William?"

"Not if he was as you described. The Reverend Mr. Warrick is an elderly gentleman, a bit rotund."

"Not the man who hit me, then," said Arden.

"No," said Royce. "He could have paid an accomplice."

Giles said, "Three accomplices, counting the two who left William in the forest."

"Where would he get the funds?" asked Dora, obviously distressed. "He spends most of his allowance on the poor. Oh, I cannot believe he is behind this."

"Nor can I," said Royce. "But we must be sure."

Arden said she and her aunt must take their leave. She could not keep from looking expectantly at Royce. After it became clear he was not going to offer, Giles filled the embarrassing silence.

"Allow me to escort you home, ladies." He offered each of them an arm. Before they reached the door,

Dora asked, "Arden, have your riding habits been delivered?"

Looking over her shoulder at the duchess, Arden replied, "Why, yes. The blue velvet one arrived only this morning."

"Royce? Will you begin her riding lessons soon? I long for a companion while riding in the park."

"I would be happy to ride with you whenever you wish, Dora," said Giles, making her blush.

After a pause, Royce asked, "Are you free tomorrow morning?"

Arden's heart rose and her lips curved into a delighted smile. Royce might be reluctant, but he was going to do his duty as he saw it. "Yes. Yes, I am."

"Good," said Dora. "I am pleased that you are fulfilling our promise to Arden. William has been feeling that he disgraced the family somehow by making a promise he could not keep. He is perhaps too young to understand that some promises are better broken. When one has an honorable reason to do so, I mean." Dora took Arden by the arm and walked with her to the door. "You may ride my Dolly," said Dora. "She is a very gentle mare, Arden. She will give you no trouble at all."

"No trouble," murmured Arden, her spirits falling. The Warrick men and their sense of honor—would either of them ever break a promise? "Thank you for a lovely party. Good evening." She managed a shadow of a smile for Dora as Giles led her and Lavinia out the door.

Nineteen

The next morning Royce mounted his stallion and, with the assistance of a groom, led Dora's mare to the house rented by Arden for the Season. He left both mounts in the charge of the groom, mounted the stairs, and lifted the door knocker. Anger made him knock louder than strictly necessary. He should have refused to instruct Arden in horseback riding. His anger did not arise from his failure to refuse, however. He was angry with himself because he looked forward to the task.

Why could he not banish Arden from his thoughts? Christabel possessed every quality a man could want in a wife, and it appeared that she cared more for him than he had any right to expect. He ought to be satisfied—more than satisfied—with a fiancée such as she. Instead, images of Arden St. Clare filled his dreams at night and his fantasies in the daytime. He must be mad. Only madness could explain why he should prefer an American hoyden, no doubt no better than she should be, over his betrothed.

A butler with a countenance more cheerful than typical for the breed allowed him in and showed him to the parlor. Arden's aunt was seated on the sofa, embroidering a pillow cover. She rose when he entered and dropped a curtsy. "Good morning, Lord Royce."

"Miss St. Clare." Royce bowed. "Is Arden ready for her lesson?"

"I believe so. Her maid has gone to fetch her." Lavinia resumed her seat and picked up her embroidery. "Please be seated."

Royce sat in a chair opposite the sofa. "How is your niece?"

"A bit nervous, I believe. She told me about the unfortunate incident when she was ten."

"She fell from a horse."

"She was thrown. The poor child suffered two broken ribs and a sprained wrist. It is no wonder she gave up horseback riding. I think she is very brave to attempt it again."

"Arden is one of the bravest women I have ever met." And more modest than he would have given her credit for—she had said only her pride had been injured when she fell from the horse. He ground his teeth together. One more quality for him to admire. Royce slapped his gloves against his thigh. "Confound it!"

His over-the-top response startled Lavinia. "I beg your pardon. I was thinking of something else."

"I see. You must have much on your mind. Her Grace told me the story of the attacks on the Duke of Wolverton. To think that my niece saved him. Twice. She is brave and resourceful, is she not?"

"Yes. Arden has many admirable qualities."

"And a flaw or two, chief among them her lamentable tendency to say exactly what she thinks. But then, she would not be human if she were perfect, would she?"

"I suppose not." He had thought he wanted perfection when he'd set about looking for a bride. Giles had poked fun at his stringent list of requirements, but he had spouted some lofty nonsense about having standards to uphold. And he had found a girl who lived up to those impossible standards, a perfect English lady. The thought popped into his head that perfection might be difficult to live with. That thought—whether because it was true or because it demonstrated his disloyalty toward Christabel—made him frown.

He was frowning still when Arden entered the room. She was dressed in a stylish blue velvet riding habit, holding a matching blue bonnet jauntily trimmed with a white ostrich feather. She looked adorable, damn her eyes. He scowled even more fiercely.

Tilting her head, she grinned at him. "My goodness. Now, that is an expression I remember with fondness. What have I done to incur your scorn?"

"Nothing," he said, gritting his teeth. "I was thinking of something else."

"About how much you do not want to be my riding instructor?"

"Not at all." What would she say if he told her he had been thinking about how much he *did* want to be her instructor, and how wrong it was of him to feel that way? He jerked his chin down in an abbreviated bow. "It is my pleasure to fulfill William's promise to you."

"Then that scowl can only mean you are thinking about William, and the reason he cannot keep his own promises." Arden's grin faded. She moved to the mirror over the fireplace and donned her bonnet, arranging the feather so that it curved down her cheek and under her chin. "I am sorry I teased you."

Arden would tease the devil, he thought. It was part of her charm. "It is true that the attacks on my nephew are never far from my thoughts. While I am relieved to know that Osbert is not the culprit, his acquittal has left us without an obvious suspect."

"There must be a way to draw the villain out, whoever he is," said Lavinia.

"Giles and I have a plan to do just that, Miss St. Clare. We have yet to convince Her Grace that our idea is sound, however."

"What plan?" asked Arden. "I miss being part of the team protecting William."

"Do you? Giles tells me you have been very busy, attending several parties every night."

"We are inundated with invitations daily," said Lavinia, smiling at her niece. "I believe Society is attempting to determine if Arden is an Original or an Exquisite."

"I am a novelty, that's all."

"American heiresses who speak their minds are extremely rare," Royce agreed, keeping his face solemn.

Arden looked at him suspiciously. "Was that a complaint or a compliment?"

"Merely an observation. Your bonnet is fetching, and before you ask, that was a compliment. Are you ready to go?"

She nodded. Royce bowed to Lavinia and offered Arden his arm. He escorted Arden out the door and introduced her to Dolly, standing patiently next to the groom.

"Nice horsey," said Arden, patting the mare on the neck. Her voice quavered only a little.

Royce assisted Arden into the saddle and sent the groom back to Wolverton House.

Clinging to the saddle, Arden said, "Who thought up side-saddles? It must have been a man. What do you call this silly protuberance? It's something like a horn on a Western saddle, but not quite the same. And whatever is the point of this stirrup? I can't be supposed to control the horse with my legs perched up here like a bump on a log."

"You control the horse with the reins." Royce could barely suppress a grin. His worries lessened and his heart lightened with every word Arden babbled. Lord, he had missed her. She was obviously very nervous, but determined to go through with the lesson. "In order to do that, you have to release the saddle and take up the reins."

"Oh, right. Like that's going to work. You use your legs, don't you? I wanted the modiste to make my habit with a split skirt so I could ride astride. I thought the woman was going to faint when I made that suggestion. I might have been able to convince her—money talks, you know—but Aunt Lavinia wouldn't hear of it. I do not understand this ridiculous need to pretend that women don't have legs."

He started to chastise her for mentioning legs, but she would only call him stuffy if he did. Royce did not feel like being stuffy or critical with Arden. Not today. It might be his last opportunity to be himself with her. His true self, not the imitation of Robert that he had made himself into. Royce wanted to be reckless. Bold. Silly, even. It seemed a long time since he had laughed and cavorted like a carefree child. "I know you have legs. I have seen them."

"You have not!"

"On the landing. After William had practiced your defensive trick on you."

"Oh. Then." She turned her head away, but not before he saw pink blossom in her cheeks. "I didn't think you noticed."

"I noticed. But you will not find it necessary to use your legs to control Dolly. She is very well trained, and you will not be riding far or hard. We will attempt nothing faster than a walk today." When Arden still appeared nervous, he added, "Dolly is very gentle."

"She may be gentle, but she's tall." Arden looked at the ground. "It's a long way from up here to down there. Are you sure this is necessary? I really do not see why I need to learn how to ride at this stage of my life. Why can't I just have a little one-horse carriage? I'm sure I could manage that."

"A pony cart? Not fashionable."

"I'm interested in transportation, not fashion."

"Are you going to grumble all morning?"

"Probably." With a sigh, she let go of her death grip on the saddle and picked up the reins. "Where are we going?"

"Hyde Park. It is not far."

They rode on for a few minutes with Royce instructing Arden on how to handle the reins. When they arrived at Hyde Park, Royce was relieved to see that there were few people about. He did not want to expose Arden to crowds of people on horseback and in carriages while she was still a novice. For that reason, and not because he had any intention of using their time alone together for anything but equestrian instruction, he chose one of the less traveled paths.

Dolly responded exactly as a well-trained horse should until the path they followed through the park reached an open field. Then the mare, obviously sensing that her rider was inexperienced and nervous, left the path and headed for the tender new shoots of grass.

"Rein her in, Arden. Keep her head up," Royce instructed.

She pulled on the reins, but too late. Dolly's nose went down. With a shriek, Arden tumbled head over heels over the mare's neck, landing flat on her back in the grass.

Dismounting quickly, Royce hurried to her side. Her fall had knocked her bonnet sideways, and the ostrich plume covered her face. She was shaking. "Do not cry, Arden. Please, darling, talk to me. Are you hurt?" He began running his hands over her body.

Arden pushed the feather off her face. She was laughing. Her face was pink, and her blue eyes sparkled with glee. She looked adorable. "Did you see that?" she gasped. "I did a somersault off Dolly. How graceful was that?" She wiped her mouth with her hand. "And I think I swallowed most of the feather."

Royce was holding her very tight and raining kisses on her eyes, her cheeks, her nose. "Royce?" she murmured as his mouth found hers. "Did you call me darling?"

He did not answer, his mouth being fully occupied with kissing hers. She parted her lips and allowed—

urged—him to deepen the caress. Only the sound of approaching hoofbeats brought him to his senses.

Pulling her to her feet, he began straightening her clothes. He looked around for her bonnet, picked it up, and put it on her head. "I am afraid the feather did not survive your fall." He snapped off the broken shaft.

"Royce. Why do you do that?"

He met her gaze. "What?"

"Kiss me and then stop kissing me? This is at least the third time you have done that. I am not counting the first time, when William interrupted us."

"Arden. Dearest. You know why. Your reputation—"

"Hang my reputation!" She looked around. "I don't see any other people about. There must be some sort of a lovers' lane around here somewhere. Or don't Englishmen make love in the open air?"

"Lovers' lane?"

"A place where a man and woman go to be alone. That reminds me—did you ever tell William what men and women do together when they are alone?" She brushed the dirt from her skirt, then turned her gaze to his. Narrowing her eyes, she asked, "Or don't you know?"

"I have yet to have that talk with William. And do not try tricks to make me prove I know what men and women do together. Trust me. I know. And I know exactly what you and I would do together if we were alone. I have imagined it a thousand times."

She shivered. "Tell me."

"No." He placed his hands on her shoulders. "We cannot be together, not in that way. Arden, tell me you do not want me. That my kisses disgust you."

Her eyes opened wide. "Why on earth should I lie to you?"

He swallowed a groan. "Even lies would protect you from me. If you do not tell me to leave you alone, I cannot guarantee I will not take what I want from you."

His saucy wench grinned at him. "And that would be?"

"Your sweet body, nothing more."

"Is that so?" She stepped out of his embrace, eyes flashing. "You only want my body? Not my heart?"

"No. I cannot take more than I can give. And my heart is pledged to another."

Her hands went to her hips. "Actually, I think that particular pledge covers everything: body and heart. Isn't there something about forsaking all others? I certainly expect to promise everything to the man I marry. And vice versa. Most definitely vice versa. In case I am not making myself clear, if you were mine, I would not willingly share you with another woman. Not your body or your heart."

"Are you angry?"

"Yes. I believe I am. You are a tease, Lord Royce. Every time we are alone together, we end up in each other's arms. Have you given any thought at all to what that might mean?"

"Of course I have. I cannot stop thinking about you."

"Really?" Her expression softened. "I have the same problem. I don't think we're going to solve our problem by pretending this is only lust. I think we may be in love, only we're both too cowardly to admit it."

"That cannot be true. It is lust, nothing more."

"How can you be sure?"

"Because I do not love you."

"Oh. Well."

"You are not going to cry, are you?"

"Because you do not love me? No. I don't love you, either. I only said that so you would . . . so we could . . . Oh, darn." Two large tears slipped from her blue eyes and slid down her cheeks.

He pulled her into his arms again. "Do not weep, sweetheart. I cannot bear to hurt you."

She stiffened. "Well, I have news for you, Royce

Warrick. You *are* hurting me. And yourself. And Lady Christabel, too, for that matter."

"I know. I am being unfair to you and to Christabel."

"You certainly are. You must choose between us."

"I have chosen."

"That choice doesn't count. It was made before you met me. Choose now. Who do you want to spend your life with? Me or Christabel?"

He could not answer her. If he confessed what was in his heart, it would only make things more difficult for both of them. It would be better if she thought he felt no more than lust for her. Lust could not break a heart like love lost. "I intend to spend my life with my betrothed. But you are correct. I have not honored my pledge to her. I have lusted after another woman's body. I must apologize to Christabel, and to you for once again treating you as less than a lady. I will escort you home, and then it will be best if we are not alone together again."

The ride home was accomplished in silence. When they arrived at her door, Royce helped her from the saddle and said, "I think you must agree that there can be no more riding lessons."

She nodded but did not speak. He had finally learned what would still her sharp tongue: cruelty. Her chin was trembling, and her eyes were filled with tears. He had hurt her, as he had intended. Then and there Royce made a solemn vow never to hurt her again.

Arden went directly to her room, flung herself on the bed, and burst into noisy weeping. She had all but confessed her love for him, and Royce still intended to go through with his marriage to Christabel.

There was no hope, none at all.

If she knew how to contact Tobias, she would ask for a return trip to the twenty-first century this very minute. She cried until she had used up all her tears;

then she stripped off her riding habit, leaving it crumpled on the floor. She would never wear it again. Or the rose-colored one hanging in the armoire. She did not need to know how to ride a horse. In a few weeks—sooner if she had her way—she would have cars, trains, planes, and buses to take her about. The only reason she had even pretended to need riding lessons was to be close to Royce, and he didn't want her.

One last tear trickled down her cheek. "No. That isn't true. He wants my sweet body." She hiccupped softly and drew her brows together. "He wants more than that, but he won't admit it. I do not understand why he cannot see that he has already violated his pledge to Christabel. I don't care what he thinks. It cannot be honorable to pretend that a promise has not been broken. He l-loves me. Not her."

There must be a way to convince him of that. Wasn't love supposed to conquer all? That must include excessive notions of honor. She had to make Royce see that it could not be honorable to marry one woman while loving another.

Had she really been thinking about running away? Giving up? Letting Christabel win the day? Clenching her fists, she shook her head violently. "No! St. Clares may be stuffy, but they are not quitters. Neither are Frerets."

She had to seduce Royce.

He deserved it.

The man was too stubborn to see the possibility of a true and lasting love right under his nose. Lust, indeed! If all he wanted was her body, why hadn't he taken it? She certainly hadn't put up any kind of a struggle. His concern for her reputation was nothing more than an excuse, and a feeble one at that. What kind of rogue gave a fig about his victim's reputation?

One that did not want to hurt her heart.

She knew for absolutely, positively sure that he was her heart's desire, and she would prove to him that she was his. Arden recalled reading something, whether in a psychology textbook or in *Cosmopolitan* she could not remember, that explained his reluctance. A woman needed to be in love before having sex, but a man needed sex before falling in love.

On some level, Royce must know that, too. His avoidance of intimacy was telling—everyone knew that men were afraid of becoming intimate with a woman they knew they could love.

So. All she had to do was to supply the missing element. If Royce, once thoroughly seduced, admitted he loved her, he would surely see that it was better to break an engagement than to spend a lifetime in a loveless marriage.

Seducing Royce should not be too difficult. The man could not keep his hands, or his mouth, off her. How dare he apologize for treating her as less than a lady? He should know by now that being a lady, at least the wimpy kind, was not her goal in life. She would show him what a woman could do. She was her mother's daughter, and she was going after her man.

Smiling, Arden fell back on the bed and hugged a pillow to her chest. Royce had called her his darling. Her insides turned warm and mushy at the memory of his voice, husky and oh so sexy. She squirmed at the memory of how he had looked at her, his eyes hot with desire.

No question about it. Seduction was the only way.

Her St. Clare side tried one last stratagem, inquiring what she intended to do if after she'd had her way with him, no love bloomed in Royce's heart. After only a moment's hesitation, she repeated the Freret family motto: "Nothing ventured, nothing gained." Risk taking was in her blood, and what better time to risk everything than now?

She was not worried—yet—about how she would accomplish her goal. She had read all those sex manuals when she was a teenager. Since then she had read romance novels and seen R-rated films. If she hadn't resorted to books and movies, she never would have known what went on between a man and a woman. Uncle Fred and Aunt Marie would not have told her, and sex education in her conservative private school had stopped at the bedroom door. Which more or less made the whole course useless.

She could handle *how*. *When* was the problem. The whole of Regency etiquette seemed designed to keep men and women—unmarried ones, anyway—from ever being alone together. Royce had said they would never be alone again, but she could get around that. He wouldn't have to know they were alone until it was too late.

She could give all the servants the day off, send Aunt Lavinia on an errand, and invite Royce for tea.

He would refuse, not wanting to leave William alone.

She could visit Dora, lure Royce into a vacant bedroom, strip naked, and see what happened next.

What if Dora—or worse, William—walked in on them?

Were there Regency equivalents of no-tell motels? If so, she did not know what they were, and she could not ask Aunt Lavinia.

This was not going to be easy. But she would find a way.

Arden looked at the calendar. Only a few more weeks before she had to go home. She said a quick and fervent prayer that Tobias would tell her she could stay in the past.

If by that time she had a reason to stay. A knock on the door interrupted her scheming. "Come in."

Lavinia opened the door and entered holding a letter.

"Another invitation?" asked Arden, smiling. Then she saw the moisture clouding Lavinia's eyes. She got out of bed and reached for her lawn wrapper. Shrugging into it, she hurried to Lavinia's side. "What's wrong?"

"This letter is from Justin. He invites me to join him

and his new wife in New Orleans. My little brother, married." She burst into tears.

Arden put her arm around Lavinia's shoulders and steered her toward a chair. "That is wonderful news. Of course you will go." Once Lavinia was seated, she found a handkerchief and handed it to her.

"Thank you." Lavinia wiped her eyes with the hanky. "I cannot leave you alone, unchaperoned."

"Yes, you can. I will be perfectly fine alone—" At Lavinia's shocked expression, Arden hastily added, "Or I can hire a companion. How is it that you received an answer to your letter so soon?"

"This letter was written before I wrote mine. It is addressed to me in care of Lady Whitehurst." Lavinia scanned the letter again. "Strange. He makes no mention of your uncle."

"Well, he was probably most concerned with telling you about Camille."

"How did you know her name?"

"Uh. I assumed he married Monsieur Duplantier's daughter. Am I wrong?"

"No. She is the one who found him in the swamp, suffering from a head wound. Camille nursed him back to health, and in the process they fell in love. He would not offer for her until he regained his memory—he tells me he feared he might have a wife and children in England. But he prayed it was not so, and that he would soon remember he was a bachelor. As soon as his prayers were answered, he proposed. Is that not romantic?"

"Very romantic. So Justin has decided to remain in Louisiana?"

"Yes. Monsieur Duplantier has no sons. He has persuaded Justin to assist him in managing the sugar plantation. Justin has written to his commander, resigning his commission."

"And he wants his sister to join him."

"I cannot."

"Oh, yes, you can. We will have Pierson send for the sailing news right away. You are going to be on the next ship to New Orleans."

"I am not leaving you. I can wait until you are ready to return to your home in America. We can travel together."

"No. We can't." Arden chewed on her bottom lip. She had to reveal her secret. She could see no way out. Lavinia wanted to travel with her, and that was not possible. And once she reached Louisiana, Lavinia would learn there was not a Frederick St. Clare in New Orleans. Yet. Praying that her aunt would believe her, she cleared her throat. "Lavinia, it's time I told you about exactly how I arrived in England."

Taking Lavinia's hands in hers, Arden led her to the sofa. "Sit. First of all, we are not distant cousins as Mr. Mendlicott told you. You are my aunt. My great-great-great-aunt. You and Justin St. Clare are my ancestors. I was born in 1976, you see."

Lavinia stared at her, wide-eyed, as Arden explained about Any Time, Any Place, the time-travel agency, and its proprietor, Tobias Thistlewaite. She told Lavinia everything, including how she arrived in the forest where she had stumbled upon William and his kidnappers. So absorbed were both women that neither of them noticed Jane standing outside the partially opened door.

"Niece. I cannot take this in. You are truly from the future?"

"Truly. Look. I'll show you." Arden pulled her carpetbag from under the bed and opened it. She took out her sweater set and slacks and showed Lavinia the zipper. She took the penny out of her penny loafers and pointed to the year: 2000.

The makeup bag revealed more of the future. While Lavinia twisted the lipstick in and out of its tube, sniffed the perfume, and stared at herself in Arden's compact, Arden began a quick overview of the intervening centuries, emphasizing the wonders that lay ahead and dropping in a few tips on what investments to make. It pleased her to think that she might have a small part in ensuring the financial success of the St. Clares.

Grabbing her head with both hands, Lavinia said, "Stop. I believe you. No one could imagine such a variety of marvels. You have actually flown like a bird?"

"Not like a bird, exactly. More like a traveling coach with wings." Arden took her aunt's hands in hers. "Dear Aunt Lavinia. I must return to my own time very soon. You must see now that you cannot travel with me. Nor can I travel with you. I'm not sure, but I think if I returned to my birthplace centuries before I am born . . . well, I don't know what would happen. But it doesn't seem like a good idea."

"No. I suppose not. Oh, Arden, I will miss you."

"I will miss you, too. I am very glad I was allowed to spend this time with you."

"Do you know about my future?" asked Lavinia, her eyes bright with curiosity. "Am I buried in a family plot? You must know the date of my death."

"We don't have plots in Louisiana. People are not buried underground because of the high water table. The cemeteries have aboveground tombs and mausoleums—the locals call them little houses of the dead. The St. Clare mausoleum is particularly impressive, built all of marble. It even has stained glass windows and—"

"Arden. When will I die?"

"Do you really want to know?"

"Yes. No. No. Of course not."

Breathing a sigh of relief, Arden said, "Oh, good. I was afraid you would say yes."

"I do not die en route to America, do I? No, do not answer that. I must live my life without foreknowledge, as does everyone else."

"Except Tobias. He must know his own life span." Unless magicians lived forever. Arden kept that thought to herself. She had been deliberately vague on the mechanics of time-travel. Arden had not mentioned magic or Merlin's Stone, implying instead that time-travel was one of the scientific wonders of future centuries, on a par with horseless carriages and rocket flights to the moon.

"If you do not mind, dear niece, I believe I will retire to my room. You have given me much to think about."

"Of course." Before Lavinia left the room, she added, "You won't tell anyone else what I told you, will you?"

"Never. We would both end up in Bedlam if the story got out."

Twenty

After dinner, Royce shut himself up in the Wolverton library with a bottle of port. He and Dora had dined alone, since Giles was at his club listening to the latest *on-dits,* attempting to find a clue that would lead them to the duke's enemy. Dora had spent the greater part of the meal talking about Arden. She had questioned him closely about the riding lesson, undeterred by his monosyllabic answers. When she had finally given up and changed the subject, she had asked him about his wedding plans.

He had repeated his intention not to marry until William was safe. Dora had been blessedly silent after that, obviously in deep thought about he knew not what.

He did not want to think at all. Hence the port. Enough of the rich liquor would banish all thought of Arden, of Christabel, of William. Of vows made in haste.

Royce was on his second bottle, but still far from the oblivion he sought, when Giles burst into the library without so much as a knock. "I heard the most appalling tale—"

"About William?"

"No. About Arden. They are saying she spent a week alone with you at my hunting box."

Setting his glass down with enough force to splash the liquid onto the table, Royce stood and faced Giles.

"What? How is that possible? No one knew except the three of us."

"And the duke. And the servants. One of them must have talked. I do not know who—I could not trace the rumor to its source."

Dora hurried into the library. "I saw Giles return. Is there news of William's attacker?"

"No." Giles quickly repeated the gossip about Arden.

"A servant must have talked," said Dora, echoing Giles's supposition. "It is possible that one of the maids or footmen overheard William when he told me Arden stayed with him at the hunting box."

"William told you? When?" asked Royce.

"The day he arrived home. He did not mean to betray Arden, but he was so excited about their adventures together that it slipped out. It was bad of you to ask a boy to lie to his mother."

Royce and Giles exchanged sheepish looks.

"I understand why you did it—to protect Arden. That is why I have not tasked you with it before now. I thought the fewer people who knew, the better. I told William not to speak of it to anyone else."

Giles drew his brows together. "I do not think a servant spread the tale."

"Nor do I. Not Dawkes or Murch," Royce agreed. "And I doubt that Jane or Mrs. Brown would do anything to harm Arden. They adore her."

"No one who knows Arden would intentionally say such poisonous things about her. They are calling her a demi-rep and speculating that she earned her fortune on her back," said Giles.

Dora gasped.

Giles rushed to her side. "Please forgive me. I should not have said that in your presence."

"And why not? Arden is my friend. I know about the demimonde, shocking as you may find that. I am one and thirty." Dora glared at Giles. "I told you, a partnership of equals. Have you forgotten so soon?"

"I have never forgotten anything that passed between us. But I am accustomed to protecting ladies from—"

"Words? I assure you I have heard them before. That means you are to tell me everything to do with this, scandalous or not." Giles held up his hands, signaling surrender. Mollified, Dora asked, "What are we going to do about this? Is there any way to counteract these rumors?"

Royce nodded. "The truth. We will tell Society that we stayed together for William's sake, and that there were chaperons present, Jane and Mrs. Brown. We need not mention that Mrs. Brown was the cook. We will deny that anything dishonorable has occurred between Arden and me, and make it clear that anyone insinuating that it did will answer to me."

Giles cleared his throat. "That will not work, I fear. Lord Graystone was exercising a new gelding in the park this morning. He saw you and Arden locked in an embrace."

"Damn and blast." Royce began pacing the room.

Dora gasped again. "Oh, my goodness. You and Arden?" Instead of looking shocked, she showed him her dimples. "But that is wonderful."

He stopped pacing and stared at her. "How can you think that? I am engaged."

"Oh. Yes. So you are. But if you love another—"

"I do not love Arden." The emphatic statement sounded shockingly unconvincing to his own ears.

And to Dora's, too, apparently. Her dimples disappeared, and she gave him a dubious look. "But you kissed her in the park."

Royce did the unthinkable. He lost his temper in the presence of a duchess. "So I did. I also kissed her in an armoire, *and* in the duke's traveling coach, *and* in the small parlor under this very roof." Struggling to regain his equanimity, he added in a rather surly tone, "But I do not love her. And kissing is all we have done."

"Oh, my," said Dora. "You have kissed Arden more than once—and in such odd places—but you do not love her? That is very bad of you, Lord Royce."

"I am well aware of that. I have besmirched the family name once again, and harmed another in the process. Robert must be turning in his grave."

"Robert was a prig." Giles and Dora spoke in unison.

"And, as he is no longer with us, his opinion cannot matter," said Dora. "But what about Christabel? She will hear these horrible tales sooner or later. Royce, you must go to her and explain." Dora paused and looked at Royce, concern evident in her expression. "Oh, my. But what will you tell her about Arden? Will you confess you kissed her?"

"I will tell her that Arden is a friend. Nothing more." He uttered the lie between clenched teeth.

"But, Royce, dear. That cannot be true. You must feel something for Arden."

"If you tell her the truth about Arden, Lady Christabel may end the engagement," said Giles. He sounded almost hopeful.

"Oh, I doubt that she would go that far," said Dora. "Christabel wants very much to be a part of this family." Looking Royce up and down, she added, "Even without a title, you are a fine catch, you know. Handsome, intelligent, wealthy. And a hero to boot. She would have a difficult time finding a better prospect."

"You make her sound very calculating," said Giles. "Do you really believe she would insist on holding Royce to his promise once she knows the truth about him and Arden?"

"I do not know what to believe," said Dora. "It seems to me that Royce has not yet decided what *is* the truth about him and Arden."

"The truth is," Royce said through clenched teeth, "Arden is my friend. Christabel is my betrothed. Those are the only truths that need concern you, Dora."

"I beg your pardon, Royce. Your feelings for Arden

are your business, not mine. But Arden is my friend, too. I hate to see either of them hurt, but Christabel would recover from a broken engagement. Broken hearts require a longer recuperation."

"I have not broken anyone's heart," Royce said, hoping against hope that his denial was true. "And I have no intention of breaking my engagement."

"But, Royce, if you love another woman, you cannot—"

"Dora. This is the last time I will tell you. I do not love Arden." The denial sounded even more lame this time. Before Dora could question his sincerity, Royce seized on another of Dora's unexpected remarks. "Why do you think Christabel would recover from a broken engagement? You said I am a catch, difficult to replace."

"And so you are," Dora said soothingly. "What I meant was, Christabel is . . . rather shallow. I do not think she feels deeply about anything. I may be wrong—perhaps she saves her passion for you, Royce. But I have only ever seen her show excitement over clothes and jewelry. And the possibility of outshining her sisters."

"And she never laughs," Giles said, repeating a criticism Royce had heard before. "But Arden is anything but shallow. She feels deeply about"—he slanted a look at Royce—"any number of things. She will be hurt by the gossip."

"She will put on a brave front," said Dora.

"We must do something to help her," insisted Giles.

"A ball in her honor?" Dora suggested. "If the *ton* see all of us together, Christabel included—"

"And if we let it be known that Arden stayed with Royce only to help him with William—"

Royce interrupted Giles with a gesture. His sister-in-law and his best friend were fast taking control of a problem that he had created and that should be his to solve. "Dora, you do understand that this course of ac-

tion will require us to make the attacks on William
public knowledge."

"Keeping them a secret has not brought results.
Maybe if the world knows that someone is trying to
kill my son, someone will have information to share
with us. And the knowledge that Arden saved his life
twice cannot help but dispel the awful rumors about
her."

"A ball it is, then. Shall we make it an engagement
ball?" asked Giles.

Royce shook his head. "Christabel and I had a ball
on the occasion of our betrothal. There is no need for
a second announcement."

Giles slid his arm around Dora's waist. "I was not
speaking of your engagement, but mine own. I have
asked Dora to marry me, and she has accepted."

"What? You and Dora?"

"Do you not approve, brother?" Dora asked. "I may
as well tell you—I do not need your approval. But I
hope you will wish me happy."

Royce grabbed Dora from Giles's arms and whirled
her about the room. "My best friend and my favorite
duchess—why would I disapprove?"

Laughing breathlessly, Dora said, "Put me down,
Royce. You are making me dizzy."

He restored her to Giles's protective embrace. "I
wish you both very happy. This is the best news I have
had since my return from Paris." His glance slid to
Giles, whose self-satisfied expression made Royce wish
for things he could not have. "How did you convince
her?"

"I told her she could manage my estate."

Royce laughed out loud. Clapping Giles on the shoulder, he said, "I approve of an engagement ball."

Giles slanted a look at Dora. "But . . . we had decided to wait to announce our engagement until after
William is safe."

"No," said Royce. "We must have the ball as soon

as possible, before the rumors become even more vicious. Consider this, Giles. The ball can serve two purposes: to restore Arden's reputation as quickly as possible, and to allow the villain an opportunity for another attempt on William. Only recall that our plan was to catch him in the act. This will be the perfect opportunity to put our plan into action."

"No," said Dora. "I see that a ball could help Arden, but there must be another way to find out who is behind the attacks on my son. I never agreed to make William a target. I cannot intentionally place him in danger."

Giles hugged her to his side. "He will not be in danger, Dora. We will keep him safe."

Royce nodded in agreement. "We will make it appear that we have withdrawn his protection. The Bow Street Runner will be dismissed. Giles will remove to his own house. We will all go out more. They will assume we are becoming lax, or indifferent, since no attack has been mounted recently."

"Dora, you must agree to have the ball," Giles said. "Let it be known that the Duke of Wolverton will act as host, to announce the betrothal of his mother."

With a shuddering sigh, Dora surrendered. "You are right. This must end. William cannot be kept a prisoner in his own house forever. A ball it is. And it must be a masquerade ball. A mask will make the villain feel invisible."

"An excellent suggestion," said Giles. "I promise you that William will not be in any real danger. Murch and Dawkes and the Runner will all be close at hand."

"But we must make it appear that he is vulnerable, to bait the trap," said Royce. "We can also tell the world that Arden St. Clare will be an honored guest. She and Lady Christabel can appear as friends together. That will prove to Society that there is nothing scandalous between me and her."

"We must tell Arden what is happening," said Dora.

"What if she goes out and hears these rumors? Someone may go so far as to give her the cut direct."

"I will visit her first thing tomorrow," said Royce.

"No. I will go. If you are seen on her doorstep at the crack of dawn, it will only add spice to the scandal broth."

The next morning Pierson knocked on Lavinia's bedroom door and announced the arrival of the Duchess of Wolverton.

"It is rather early for a call, isn't it? I hope nothing bad has happened. Show her up here, if you please." Arden and Lavinia were busily packing Lavinia's trunks.

"Good morning, Your Grace," said Lavinia, pausing long enough to curtsy when Dora entered the room. "Please excuse us for greeting you in our private chambers, but as you can see, we are hastily preparing for a trip."

Dora took in the open trunks, and gasped. "Are you leaving? You cannot do that, Arden. Flight will make you appear to be guilty."

Arden dropped the stack of folded shifts she had been holding. "Guilty? Of what? I'm not the one who is leaving. Lavinia is going to join her brother in New Orleans. He has married, and plans to stay in Louisiana. The ship sails early tomorrow."

"Oh. You have not heard then." Dora allowed Pierson to take her pelisse. When he had left the room, she added, "I fear I bring you bad news."

"What news?" said Arden, her hand going to her throat.

"Heard what?" asked Lavinia.

"The rumors flying about Arden and Royce." Dora looked at Arden. "They are saying you and he are . . . that you stayed with him in the country, without a chaperon."

"I did. But nothing happened." The fib made her face hot. But surely Royce had not told Dora about the armoire incident. He would never admit to being such a . . . a . . . rogue. Not to the wife of his uptight, upright brother. And nothing really scandalous had happened between them. Yet.

"I know that. But Society delights in believing the worst about people."

"I am sorry I lied to you, Dora, but Royce and Giles were determined to protect my reputation."

"They failed. You are being called a . . . a . . ."

Arden smiled. "A ladybird?"

"Worse. But you are not to worry. We have a plan to restore you to respectability—"

"I don't care about being respectable." Arden was surprised to realize that that was a lie, too. She did care. No one would enjoy being the subject of scurrilous gossip, and after years of being too prim and proper to be anything but a wallflower, she had enjoyed being the darling of the *ton*.

But she did not regret her lost popularity enough to give up her plan to become even more notorious.

"Arden!" said Lavinia, shocked. She began taking things out of the trunk.

"What are you doing?"

"I cannot leave you unchaperoned. Not now. You are too reckless and bold by half. Left to your own devices, you will thumb your nose at Society and do exactly as you please."

"No, I won't." She planned to do exactly what would please Royce. "And you must leave. Justin is waiting for you."

"He can wait a little longer. I am not leaving you alone."

"I will not be alone. Dora will stand by me. And Giles."

"Royce, too," added Dora. "He is threatening to call out anyone who repeats the slander in his presence."

"There. You see? There will be duels." Lavinia crossed her arms in front of her chest and glared at Arden. "This is what comes of flaunting Society's rules."

"Oh." Arden had a sudden insight into the source of the St. Clare stuffiness. "Are you and your brother very much alike?"

"We are. What has that to do with this?"

"Nothing." She turned to Dora. "There will not be any duels. Did he really offer to fight for me?"

"He did. Royce also wanted to come here this morning to tell you what was happening, but Giles and I dissuaded him. Under the circumstances, we did not think it would be wise for him to be seen on your doorstep at the crack of dawn."

Lavinia rolled her eyes. "This is terrible."

Arden felt immensely better once she heard that Royce had wanted to come to her side. She almost laughed out loud. But that would make Lavinia, and Dora, too, think she was completely without good sense. "This is a lot of talk, nothing more. Sticks and stones . . . It will pass. Keep packing, Aunt Lavinia."

"Arden, I cannot go."

"Of course you can." She gave her aunt a severe look. "Remember what we discussed? What people now—here and now—think about me today will not matter tomorrow. I will be returning home soon. My family and friends will not think the worse of me because of some silly rumor. They probably will never hear it." She took the items Lavinia was holding and put them back in the trunk.

"Your aunt is right, Arden. You must care about what people think of you. And your family may very well hear of these rumors. Travel between England and America is becoming very common once again. If these rumors go unchallenged, you will be ostracized on both sides of the Atlantic."

"Being snubbed is not much of a punishment, even if I did not commit the sin."

"A greater punishment than you know," said Dora. "You will not receive any offers."

"I did not come to London to find a husband." Or her heart's desire. But she had found him, and she was going to do everything in her power to keep him.

"What about Royce? You must care about him. Or did he force his kisses on you?"

Arden's mouth dropped open. "He told you he kissed me?"

"He had to. You were observed kissing in the park yesterday morning. Lord Graystone saw you."

"Oh. Well. He did not force me. I was never a prisoner of passion."

"If you kissed him willingly, you must care about him."

"Well, of course I do. I don't kiss people I don't like."

"Then you must care about his reputation, too. Only listen to the plan we have come up with. The Duke of Wolverton is giving his first ball, on the occasion of his mother's engagement to Giles Fairfax, Viscount Stanton. Miss Arden St. Clare of America will be an honored guest."

"A ball? A betrothal ball, for you and Giles? Oh, that is wonderful. He loves you so much. It is true, isn't it? Your engagement is for real, isn't it?"

"Very real." Dora smiled, flashing her dimples at Arden. "And the ball has another purpose. We hope the man behind the attacks on William will try again. Royce and Giles will catch him in the act, and that nightmare will be over once and for all. Is that not an excellent plan?"

"Excellent," Arden agreed.

"Before the ball, we must go on as if nothing is wrong. Since your aunt is leaving, perhaps it would be better if you returned to Wolverton House. I will invite

Christabel, too. If the world sees the two of you as friends, it may help cast doubt on the rumors."

"Or add to them. What if they decide Royce is enough of a rogue to keep his mistress and his fiancée under the same roof?"

"Oh. I hadn't thought of that. Royce did have a reputation for boldness at one time, but he changed. At least, I thought he had."

"He tried. I had hoped to change him back."

"Arden. You do care about him."

"Well, of course I do. We are friends."

Dora frowned. "That is what he said. Friends, nothing more."

Friends who were about to become lovers. But Royce did not know that, so she would overlook his "nothing more" statement. "I think I prefer to stay in my own house, if you don't mind, Dora. But I thank you for the invitation."

"Invitations. You will not receive any invitations. Not now that this foul rumor is abroad," said Lavinia.

"Or you will receive them only from people who want to witness you being shamed and humiliated," added Dora.

"Really? I suppose you know your peers better than I do. All right, then. I will not accept invitations, should any arrive. I will spend my time visiting museums and seeing the sights."

"I will go with you," said Dora. "Of course, if we visit too many educational sights, the *ton* will call us bluestockings. That approbation is almost as deadly as being called a demi-rep."

"Your Grace!" Lavinia put her hand to her mouth.

"Well, it is. However, I prefer to flaunt my intelligence rather than pretending to be a . . . a . . ."

"Fluff-head?" asked Arden.

"Yes. But we need not spend all our time on educational matters. We can shop." Dora's eyes glowed in anticipation. "We will both need costumes for the ball—I did tell you that it is to be a masquerade, did I not?"

"I don't believe you did. A costume ball? What fun!"

"Fun with serious consequences," said Lavinia sternly. "Your reputation and the young duke's safety are at stake."

Sobering, Arden said, "You are absolutely right, Aunt Lavinia. I am sorry, Dora. I did not mean to make light of the danger to William."

"I know that. And it will be fun—I always enjoyed dressing in costume. We will have even more fun when it is over and we are celebrating our success. Now, when shall we make our first excursion together? Tomorrow?"

"Oh, I don't think it is necessary for us to be seen together before the ball. I would not want you to be shunned because of me."

"Do not worry. No one of importance will dare shun the Duchess of Wolverton. Besides, you will be doing me a favor. Part of the plan to make William's attacker reveal himself is for us—Royce and me—to be seen out and about. The villain may think we are relaxing our watch on William. Now, can I assist with the packing? What time does the ship sail?"

"Tomorrow morning, but the captain wants all passengers on board tonight."

"Giles and I will accompany you to the docks. You must spend the night at Wolverton House tonight, Arden. You cannot stay here alone. Tomorrow, if you insist on returning here, you can hire a companion."

That order from the duchess seemed to satisfy Lavinia. She nodded brusquely and resumed packing.

Later that evening, Arden waved good-bye to her aunt, standing on the deck of a ship bound for New Orleans. A part of her wanted to go with her aunt. The cowardly part. Running away from the rumors and gossip had an almost irresistible appeal. She was appalled to learn that words could hurt—even spiteful, lying words out of the mouths of people she did not know well, or know at all.

But she would not run. She had things to do in this time and place. Important things. She had to know once and for all if she belonged in this time, with Royce, or in her own time.

After seeing Lavinia off, Arden returned to Wolverton House with Dora and Giles. Royce greeted them at the door. "Is your aunt safely on board?" he asked.

"Yes. But I am sure she will not sleep a wink tonight. She is very excited about her voyage to the New World."

"Why are you here?" asked Dora, removing her gloves. "I thought we agreed that you should remove to your club tonight. You and Arden should not be under the same roof."

"I concluded that we should behave as we would had these rumors not surfaced."

"That seems rather risky to me," said Dora. "People will think the worst, I fear."

"If Arden wants me to go, I will."

The intense look Royce gave Arden made her shiver. And gave her the opening she had been waiting for. "No. Please stay. I happen to agree with you. I hate making decisions based on what other people think—especially when they are wrong." She took a deep breath. "That being the case, I think we should continue with my riding lessons."

"Oh, good show," said Giles. "If you are seen in the park, not locked in an embrace, Lord Graystone's story may lose credence."

"No," said Royce.

"Why not? I think I was getting the hang of it."

He shot her an incredulous look. "You fell off the gentlest mare in London."

"Yes. Well. That is why I need another lesson. From you. I believe you said we should go on as if the rumors were false."

"They *are* false," said Royce.

"Not the one Lord Graystone started."

"He exaggerated. We were not locked in an embrace. was assisting you after your fall."

"Oh. Is that what you were doing?"

"Yes." He would not meet her eyes. Arden took that s a good sign.

"You could take a groom with you," said Dora, smil-ng at Royce. "That would satisfy propriety."

"Oh, is that really necessary?" asked Arden, contriv-ng to look disappointed.

"It most certainly is," said Royce in his most pom-ous voice. "We *will* take a groom."

"Whatever you say," said Arden, smiling brilliantly. Royce had agreed to take her riding, with hardly any rouble at all.

The trap was set.

Twenty-one

Arden waited on the front steps for Royce, wearing her rose-colored habit and a gray bonnet trimmed with a ribbon in the same rose color. She had sent all the servants away early that morning, and the house was empty.

All she had to do now was untame a tamed rogue.

Her heart beat steadily. She was not breathless. Her palms were a trifle damp, but her gray gloves would conceal that small sign of nervousness. Even if Royce noticed, he would assume she was nervous about getting on a horse again. He would not suspect that he was about to be seduced.

She heard hoofbeats on the cobblestones and stepped from beneath the portico. Royce and the groom appeared, the groom leading Dolly. "Good morning, Lord Royce."

He gave her a curt nod before dismounting. "Why are you out here alone?"

"It is such a beautiful day, I could not wait to be out of doors."

Royce looked at the cloud-filled sky. "Beautiful day?"

Startled, Arden looked up at the leaden sky. She would have sworn the sun had to shine on a momentous day like today. If she believed in omens, she might be forced to conclude that Mother Nature did

not approve of her plan. Crossing her fingers, she told
herself she was not at all superstitious. Another quick
glance at the sky, and she improvised. "I like cloudy
days. They remind me of home. It rains a lot in Lou-
siana."

He gave her a severe look. "If it rains, the lesson
will be over."

"Then let's get started." She allowed the groom to
help her onto the saddle.

Royce watched until she was settled, then remounted.
They rode three abreast until they reached Hyde Park.
Then the groom reined his horse in and stayed a few
feet behind them.

"How is Dora this morning?" Arden asked.

"Busily planning the ball. She has decided on cos-
umes for Giles and me. We are to be buccaneers."

"Like Jean Lafitte. He's our local pirate back home
in New Orleans. I am sure you will look very dashing.
What will Dora wear?"

"Something classical, I believe. She mentioned Cae-
ar's wife."

Arden waited, but Royce made no effort to continue
he conversation. "Aren't you going to ask me about
my costume?"

Royce ignored her question. "You are holding the
reins too tight. Dolly will not know what you want her
o do."

Arden loosened the reins. "I will tell you even if
you aren't interested. I plan to go as a woman from
he twentieth century. Or perhaps the twenty-first."

That got his attention. His gaze shifted from Dolly
o her. "That is not possible. You cannot know what
women will be wearing one hundred days from today,
much less one hundred years."

"Yes, I can. I have a vivid imagination."

They reached the spot where Dolly had stopped for
a snack. Arden tightened the reins again, letting Royce
go ahead of her. Just before the groom drew even with

her, Arden kicked the mare in the side and let the reins fall from her hands. Dolly danced sideways, and Arden tumbled from the saddle, landing on the soft grass with a satisfactory thud. Dolly trotted away. Arden closed her eyes and waited.

"Billy, go after Dolly." She could feel Royce kneeling beside her. "Miss St. Clare. Arden. Are you all right?"

She kept quiet. Royce took her in his arms and lifted her onto his saddle. Mounting behind her, he wrapped his arms around her waist. Arden let her body sag against his chest, her head lolling against his shoulder.

When they reached her house, Royce cradled her in his arms and dismounted. He strode up the stairs and knocked on the door. The door swung open. She had intentionally left it unlocked and slightly ajar.

"Pierson! Jane! Your mistress needs assistance."

When no one responded, Royce carried her up the stairs. He pushed open the door to her bedroom and placed her on the bed. Arden allowed her eyelids to flutter open. "W-where am I?" She moaned the words softly.

"In your bedroom." What was she up to? His cursory examination of her had found no obvious injuries, not even a bump on her head. He assumed she had fainted, overcome by her fear of horses. But her eyes were clear, and her breathing was normal. He would suspect her of trying to compromise him but for the lack of witnesses. "Where are your servants? Pierson did not answer the door, and Jane has not responded to my call."

"Brighton. Holiday."

"You sent your servants away? All of them? And your Aunt Lavinia has departed."

"Yes. All. Gone."

"So. We are alone."

"Alone." She closed her eyes and moaned again.

"Are you hurt?"

"Yes. No. Can't breathe. Perhaps . . . you . . . should loosen . . . clothing."

Royce pulled her into a sitting position. She fell against him, her body limp. He had suspected her moans were fake. Now that she wanted him to remove her clothing, he was certain she was up to something shocking. He forced his lips, which wanted to curl into a grin, into a straight line. He knew he should leave, but he wanted very much to stay. Only because he was curious to see exactly what she had in mind, he told himself. After telling himself that outrageous lie, he could no longer suppress the grin.

He helped Arden remove the jacket of her riding habit, turning his face away so she would not see his smile. Once the jacket was dispensed with, he discovered that the minx was wearing nothing beneath her jacket but the strange garment he had glimpsed when they were in William's coach. Two scraps of silk and lace barely covered her breasts. "Are these your American stays?"

She nodded, her eyes half closed. "Still . . . can't breathe. The skirt . . . heavy." She moaned again.

"I suppose you want me to remove your skirt as well."

"If you think it would be a good idea," she said demurely, her voice surprisingly strong for one unable to breathe only moments ago.

"I think it would be a very bad idea." He found the tapes and made short work of stripping the heavy velvet from her. "And I suppose those are the pantaloons you mentioned." Another strip of lace and silk rode low on her hips.

"Panties. Not pantaloons. Panties." She fell back on the bed, arching her back and drawing one shapely leg up in what she must suppose to be a seductive pose.

It might have been if she hadn't looked as if she would swoon if he touched her. As a seductress, Arden was remarkably amateurish, and not at all subtle. "That is a pretty pose." He looked her over from head to toe, smiling when his gaze alone made her shiver. He stood.

"You're not leaving!" She shrieked the words as she quickly sat up. "Can't you see I—"

"I can see very well." He looked her over once again, causing her to blush in several interesting places. "Very nice."

Arden gasped, obviously outraged. "Nice? You call this nice? What are you, blind? You have never seen underwear as sexy as this. Never. It hasn't been . . . never mind. Here I am, almost naked, ready for you to . . . to . . . have your way with me, and all you can say is *nice?*"

He felt the laughter bubbling up from inside him, true joyous laughter that he had not felt since his brother's death almost three years ago. The laughter burst from his lips.

Grabbing a pillow, Arden held it in front of her. Her eyes filled with tears. "It isn't *nice* to laugh at a person."

Sitting on the bed, Royce drew her and the pillow into his arms. "Oh, Arden. I am not laughing at you. I am laughing because you make me happy. Happier than I have been in years."

"Happy? I make you happy?" She beamed at him through her tears. "Now, that *is* nice." Brushing away her tears, she slanted a sultry look at him. "Is there anything, anything at all, that I can do to make you happier?"

Royce did not answer her. Erotic images clogged his brain, overwhelming speech. But not reason. Not yet. He pushed her out of his arms and stood up.

"W-what are you doing? You are leaving, aren't you? Royce, I have to tell you. I do not handle rejection well, especially when I'm naked."

"I am not leaving. I should leave. But I cannot seem to move."

"Oh. Good. I think." She waited for a heartbeat or

two while he stood next to the bed staring at her. "Should I move? Would that help?" Not waiting for an answer, Arden slipped off the bed and stood before him.

Royce eyed her strange undergarments. They left little to the imagination, but that did not stop him from wanting to see what lay beneath the silk. "You are not naked. Not completely."

"Well, no. Not yet. Do you like my American stays? They are quite attractive, if I do say so myself." She looked down at her favorite blue lace and satin bra, then traced the edge of the bra with her finger. "This is called a brassiere."

"That sounds French."

She cupped her satin-covered breasts with her hands. "Call it a bra if the French name offends you."

"I am not offended." He mimicked her actions, tracing the lace edge of the bra with his finger, then resting his hands on her breasts. He could feel her heartbeat beneath his palm. It quickened in response to his touch.

Her pupils grew large, turning her blue eyes almost completely black. Arden's physical responses to him made Royce feel powerful, invincible. Bold. "Bra," he repeated, stroking her breasts.

"Th-that's right. You said y-you were something of an expert on women's underthings. Would you like to see how this works?"

Royce nodded, rendered speechless again by the moves in Arden's seductive game.

"Okay. Well." She took a steadying breath and pressed her breasts into Royce's palms. That felt good. It would feel better once her breasts were bare. "All right. Lesson number one. See this little hook? You twist it like so, and voila, it opens. Some bras hook in the back, but the principle is the same."

Royce reached for the tiny clasp between her breasts

and twisted it. "Voila." The cups of the garment parted, exposing her creamy, pink-tipped breasts to his view. His gaze alone made her nipples harden into pebbles.

Arden shrugged out of the bra, letting it fall to the floor. She stood before Royce, naked except for her bikini panties. He seemed frozen in place, whether from shock or disgust she couldn't tell. "I'm running out of nerve here. Are you going to do anything, or not?"

He nodded his head. "Yes. I am definitely going to do something."

"What? When? You're not going to stop now, are you? You do have a habit of stopping at the most inconvenient—"

"I am not stopping this time. Not a chance. Take it off."

"Them. Not it. Panties are plural. I don't know why." She shimmied her panties to her ankles, then stepped out of them. She was completely naked, and he hadn't removed a stitch. He hadn't moved, either. Arden took the baby step necessary to reach him, then pressed her naked body against his clothed one. "That feels . . . better than good. This is exciting, wearing nothing while you are still completely dressed. Kinky, but exciting."

"Kinky?"

"Sexually deviant. In the nicest possible sense." She moved back a step.

He reached for her. "No. Don't move. Not yet. I want to do that again." She moved closer, pressing her body against his again, rubbing her breasts against his jacket, pushing one bare leg between his trousered legs.

"Arden—"

She touched her fingertips to his lips, silencing him. His swelling manhood poked her tummy. She rubbed against that, purring like a cat. He felt remarkably like a statue. Hard. Unmoving. But warm. Royce was alive. Why wasn't he doing something? Anything? "Royce?"

He grabbed her waist and pushed her away. Her heart sank precipitously, until he moved his hands from her waist to her breasts. She leaned into him, glorying in the feel of his hands. "I like that. What do you like?"

"Undress me."

He was going to allow her to seduce him. Relief made her confident enough to take control. "Please? This is my game, Royce. I make the rules. Rule number one is you are not allowed to give orders. You may, however, make reasonable requests. Maybe even an unreasonable one. Or two."

"Please, Arden." His voice was husky. "Undress me."

"Well. Since you asked so politely . . ." She reached for his cravat and untied it.

He used the time to stroke her breasts, teasing each nipple upright, then gently pinching it between his thumb and forefinger. She trembled beneath his touch.

She pushed the jacket off his shoulders and began working on the buttons to his shirt, frowning as she concentrated on her task.

Royce slid his hands from her breasts to her waist. He wanted to laugh again, at Arden's fumbling attempts with his buttons. Not wanting to embarrass her, or distract her from her fierce determination to do away with his clothes, he held in the laughter, letting it bubble refreshingly in his blood. To encourage her, he pulled her against his arousal. "See what you do to me?"

"Wouldn't any naked lady have the same effect?" she gasped.

"No. Only you." He took her face in his hands and kissed her. Thoroughly. Only Arden could make seduction so sweet.

When he finally released her mouth, they were both

panting. "You're not helping here. I'm naked, but you're still wearing way too many clothes."

"Take them off. Please."

"My fingers have all turned into thumbs. You did that to me."

"Two more buttons. You can do it," he coaxed.

"I suppose I should thank you for that vote of confidence. However, I think, Lord Royce, that you may be a tease." While he encouraged her with kisses on her brow, her eyes, and her cheekbones, she fumbled with the remaining shirt buttons. "I can't do this," she complained. "You're distracting me."

He laughed again.

Laughter was an aphrodisiac. None of the movies she had seen or the books she had read had mentioned that fact. "Are you snickering? I mean, laughing at a girl is one thing, but snickering?" Giggling, she gave up on the remaining buttons, pulling the shirt from his breeches, and shoving it up over his head. "There," she said, panting only a little. "That was harder than it should have been."

"Touch me."

"That sounded suspiciously like an order, but I will treat it as a request." Her hands went to his chest, and his hands found her naked buttocks.

She rubbed.

He kneaded.

"Royce. I really cannot stand up much longer."

He picked her up and tossed her lightly onto the bed.

"You still have clothes on. Shouldn't you be naked? Your boots—"

He came down on top of her, breeches, boots, and all.

"Oh, well. Maybe not." She wiggled a little, making him groan. That was very satisfying. He levered himself onto his elbows.

"I am crushing you."

"That's all right. Crush away. But first . . ." Arden

pushed his shoulders. Her gentle touch was enough to make him roll onto his back. Leaning over him, she smiled. "You said once that I would never get you on your back on a bed with your pants down. Well, look at you now. On your back. On *my* bed. With your pants down. Or almost down. Would you like me to help you with your boots?"

"I would, yes. Very much. If it would not be too much trouble. Please."

"No trouble at all." She moved to the end of the bed, grabbed the first boot, and pulled it off. "Stockings, too?"

He nodded. Lying on his back, arms crossed behind his head, he watched her as she removed a stocking and garter. She kissed his instep. Then his ankle. He swallowed a groan. "Arden. One more boot."

"Oh. Right." She removed the second boot and stocking, then slithered up to his waist. "Now your breeches."

"Allow me." He raised his hips and shoved the breeches to his ankles, releasing his aroused body.

"Oh. Wow." She tugged the breeches from around his ankles and knelt beside him. "You're quite . . . large, aren't you?"

"At the moment. It will pass. Soon."

"Not too soon, I hope." She touched him, stroking his shaft gently. "Shall I use my mouth?" Not waiting for him to answer, she touched her lips to the tip of his penis, then opened her mouth and used her tongue.

"Stop, or it will be too soon."

"Oops. Sorry. I didn't mean to . . . to rush you."

"Quite all right."

"May I kiss you here?" She pressed her lips against his abdomen. "Here?" He felt her mouth on his chest. "Or here?" She found the pulse beating in his throat.

"Anywhere you like. Come here, Arden." He opened his arms and she fell across his chest. He hugged her close, glorying in the feel of her soft body draped across his.

"This is nice. Skin to skin, I mean." She moved experimentally, letting her body mold itself to his. "Better than nice. There isn't a word—"

"No words are needed. Hush, Arden."

Royce rolled on top of her again, using a knee to push her legs apart. He settled himself between her legs, then lowered his head and kissed her until she was breathless.

And hot.

Heat spread in waves from her head to her toes and back again, finally coalescing low in her abdomen.

Hot and wet.

Arden could feel dampness between her thighs. She moved, arching her back, urging Royce to . . . to . . . "Do something."

"No words, remember."

"I don't like that rule. How will you know—"

His hand slipped between her thighs, feeling the wetness there. "Your body speaks for you." He slowly inserted one finger into her damp heat. Her hips lifted of their own accord, pressing closer, seeking . . . more. He was right. Her body would tell him what she wanted. Lucky for her. She could not say another word now, the power of speech lost in sensation. She writhed beneath his hand, pleading silently for his touch.

Royce answered her plea, withdrawing his finger, finding the tiny bud of desire nestled beneath the tight blond curls. He grasped her hips and lifted them, spreading her legs wide as he moved against her. Arden felt his erect penis at the mouth of her vagina. She held her breath, and her body tensed against his penetration.

Sensing her hesitation, Royce dropped reassuring kisses on her face, her throat, the tops of her breast. He found the secret place between her legs again, stroking it with his thumb while he inserted two fingers into her hot, wet sheath. Her legs parted without his help, and she arched against him.

He entered her slowly, carefully, until he reached the barrier he expected. Then with one quick thrust, he completed their union. She cried out, but she did not push him away. She wound her arms around his shoulders and arched her back, signaling silently that she wanted more. He thrust into her tight sheath again and again, until she dug her nails into his back, urging, demanding her release. When she trembled convulsively in his embrace, her climax shattered his control and his body joined hers in release.

They lay entwined in each other's arms for minutes or hours, Arden could not have said which. Finally, she stirred.

"Oh. My. That was . . . fun."

"Fun?"

"Not just fun. The most fun I have ever had."

"Good." He had not hurt her, and he had not disappointed her. That *was* good. At the moment nothing else appeared anything but very bad. He had seduced a virgin. He had betrayed Christabel. He had broken his promise to Robert. He had allowed his reckless self to reemerge, thinking only of pleasure, of today, forgetting about duty and responsibility and tomorrow.

Royce forced himself to untangle their arms and legs. He stood and reached for his breeches and pulled them on.

"What are you doing? Getting dressed?" She sat up, dragging a pillow in front of her, covering her nakedness. "You're leaving? Shouldn't we talk about what happened here?"

"No." He found his shirt and quickly donned that, and his jacket.

"Oh, good grief. You're going to *think* about what happened, aren't you? No—I know you, Lord Royce Warrick. You're going to *brood*. Well, brood about this.

I love you. And I do not regret one thing I've—we've done."

"Thank you." He found his boots but did not stop to put them on in her presence. Royce had to get away before he said things he had no right to say to her. "I will leave by the back gate. Your reputation—"

She threw a pillow at his back.

Twenty-two

Dora was waiting for him when Royce returned to Wolverton House. "How is Arden? The groom returned with both your horses. He said Arden fell off Dolly again. I do not understand that. Dolly is so well trained and gentle—"

"Arden is quite all right. Excuse me, Your Grace, I must change. I have a call to make."

On the short walk from Arden's house, Royce had engaged in an internal debate. On one side were the arguments in favor of making Arden his mistress. The rumors about them, now true, had made it highly unlikely that anyone worthy would offer for her. She was most assuredly not a lady. No lady would have set out to seduce a man betrothed to another. Arden did not care about her reputation. Why should he? Why shouldn't he make her his mistress?

Because she deserved better from him.

Because he loved her.

There was really no debate at all. He had to do the honorable thing and offer for her. A broken engagement would be scandalous, but the alternative would bring unhappiness to him, to Arden, and to Christabel, dooming them all to live their lives without love. Why had he ever thought that honor required him to hurt others?

With that decision, Royce felt a great weight lifted off his shoulders. Now that he had resolved to be true to himself, he felt at peace. And optimistic. Surely, when he explained that he loved another, Christabel would be gracious and release him from his promise.

She was a lady, after all.

Lady Christabel entered the drawing room where Royce waited. She curtsied. "You wanted to see me, my lord?"

"Yes. There is something I must tell you."

"My. You look so grim." She smiled coquettishly. "You need not worry. I know that you and Miss St. Clare spent time together at Lord Stanton's hunting box."

"The rumors—"

"I heard no rumors. She told me."

"What? When?" Arden had not seen Christabel since the ugly talk about them had surfaced.

"The night you arrived at Wolverton House. She told me you were lovers. She wanted me to know you had been unfaithful."

Christabel was lying. But why? "Arden and I were not lovers in Somerset. She stayed at Stanton's hunting box for William's sake, not mine."

Lowering her eyes, Christabel nodded. "Very well. I believe you."

"Do you? That is very generous of you."

"I will always be generous with you, my lord. And I will always believe whatever you want me to believe."

"Interesting. But you did believe Arden when she told you we were lovers."

"Yes. I was distraught. I had been true to you all those months and years of our separation, and when you returned you seemed so distant. And she was with you. Then, that evening on the way to our rooms, she told me you were her lover—"

"Not true." Not then. But Christabel had decided, for whatever reason, that he had taken Arden as his mistress. She saw Arden as a rival. Christabel was the source of the rumors about him and Arden. Royce was sure of it. "But you believed it to be true. You told others, no doubt."

Wringing her hands, she said, "I may have done so. Yes. Yes. I did. I told Neville. He is a man, and I needed a man's advice. He told me to forget what she said. He said all men take lovers from time to time, to satisfy their basic needs. It means nothing. She could mean nothing to you. To us. Neville told me to forgive you. And I did. I do. I told you before. I know that men have mistresses."

"Arden is not my mistress. I intend to make her my wife."

"What?" Her eyes grew huge, and she took a step back. "You cannot. You are betrothed to me."

"Christabel. I am sorry. But I cannot—"

Her beautiful face twisted into ugliness. "No! You cannot humiliate me, make me a laughingstock. How can you even suggest such a thing, after all those years I waited for you?"

"No one will laugh at you. You may allow them to think you are the one who ended the engagement."

"And be labeled a jilt? No. I will not give you up, not after all I have done for you."

"I do understand. You waited patiently for me—"

"For two long years. I gave up countless other opportunities to make a favorable match because of that long wait. You do not realize what I have done . . ." She stopped abruptly. "I love you."

The words were spoken too fast, with too little inflection. She was lying. To think he had believed her the first time she had professed to love him—but that time she had been much more convincing.

Royce had not relished the meeting with Christabel, but he had not expected her reaction to be so . . . frantic. Or that she would profess an emotion she did not feel. That led him to question why she had accepted

his proposal in the first place. No matter what Dora
said, he had not been much of a catch two years ago.
A younger son, untitled, about to go off to war.

Untitled.

That Season, everyone had said Christabel wanted to
marry a title. At the time, he had been pleased to prove
everyone wrong. But had he? William had been ill,
very ill. What if—

No.

He could not bring himself to think that. Shaking his
head to clear it, he tried once more to do what he had
come to do: win his release.

"Christabel. You do not love me. I do not love you."

"Very well. Refuse to believe me. What has love to
do with it, anyway? You made a solemn vow. To me.
To my father. And to your brother. Honor requires you
to fulfill your promises to me and to them."

"I cannot. No matter how dishonorable it is for me
to break my promises, it would be more dishonorable
for me to marry you when I love Arden."

"No! My lord, I beg you. If you want to keep the
American in your bed, I will not complain. But you
must marry me. Me!" Her voice rose to a shriek. "I
will never release you! Never. I will see you dead first.
You and her!"

"My lady! You cannot mean that." Royce feared that
she meant exactly what she said. She would harm Arden if she got the chance.

"No. No. I do not mean it. I could not mean it. I
do love you. I swear I do. How could I harm you? You
are my promised husband. Do not turn away from me."
She threw herself into his arms. Clinging to him, she
began to weep softly. "Royce. I can make you forget
her. I know how to please a man." Leaning against him,
she backed him up against the sofa. Off balance, Royce
sat down heavily, and she fell into his lap. She took
his hand in hers and placed it on her breast. "You may

do anything to me. Anything you want. I live only to please you, my lord."

Her threats rang more true than her professions of love. If what he was beginning to believe was really true, then Christabel was capable of murder. Royce needed to calm her down, to make her believe he had acted impulsively. He needed time, time to prove what he suspected was true. He stroked her back, muttering soothing words.

Slowly she relaxed in his arms. Tilting her head up, she smiled at him, but a feral gleam lit her eyes. Christabel *was* capable of harming those he loved. He was sure of it.

"Kiss me, Royce. Tell me you forgive me as I have forgiven you.

"I forgive you." He could not bring himself to touch her lips with his. He kissed her forehead.

"And you will keep your promise to me?"

"Yes. And you need not fear Arden. I will not see her again. I must have been mad, to think I preferred her over you." Would she accept his abrupt about-face?

"I understand. She is a witch, skilled in the ways of the Cyprians. But you can teach me how to make love to you. I am yours to mold into the woman of your dreams." Again she took his hand and placed it on her breast.

His nightmares, more likely. Since she expected it, Royce fondled her breast briefly and kissed her on the lips. He ignored the invitation of her open mouth. Promising to meet her at the duchess's ball, he made his escape.

Royce immediately returned to Wolverton House and sent for Giles. He wasted no time in sharing his suspicions. "I believe Lady Christabel and her cousin are behind the attacks on William."

"What? I cannot credit that. Why?"

"She wants to be a duchess."

"But you are not a duke," said Giles. Then his eyes widened. "You will be a duke if William dies."

"Exactly. When I asked her to marry me, William was a very sick boy. Some thought he might die. Christabel must have thought he would die, and that I would be the Duke of Wolverton before we wed."

"Yes, I remember. There was also talk that Season about how Lady Christabel resented the fact that her sisters outranked her. Most people thought those rumors were slander, started by jealous rivals. But even if they were true, surely—"

"When I asked her to release me, she threatened my life and Arden's."

"Wait a moment. Let me take this in. You asked Christabel for your freedom?"

"I did. I intend to marry Arden."

"Hurray! I knew you two belonged together, almost from the first. She will make you a much better wife. Have you asked her?"

"Not yet. I could not propose to one woman while I was still betrothed to another. That is why I went to Christabel today and asked for my release. But now I must wait."

"Why?"

"I withdrew my request. I allowed Christabel to convince me that my infatuation with Arden is not reason to end our engagement. Until we have proof that Lady Christabel is the villainess I believe her to be, the engagement must stand. If I cry off now, I have no doubt she will attempt to harm Arden. She said she would, and her eyes were wild with hate when she uttered the threat."

"Lady Christabel? She is beginning to sound more like Lady Macbeth. It is fortunate you discovered her true character before you wed."

"It is unfortunate I was so dazzled by her outer beauty that I did not see the ugliness inside. I might have saved William from harm."

"True. But you would not have met Arden. I can see why it would be unwise for you to go to her now. With you and Arden under such close scrutiny, someone might very well tell Christabel. I will pay a call on her and—"

"No. And I must ask you not to share my suspicions with Dora, either. I am almost sure that what I believe is the truth, but as long as there is the slightest chance I am wrong, I must keep these terrible suspicions private."

"I understand. I hope Dora will. She is adamant that we must share everything."

"I will explain that I told you so that we might guarantee William's safety. You and I will watch Christabel and her cousin closely at the ball. The others—Dawkes, Murch, and the Runners we have hired—will watch William. That way, if I am wrong, William will still be guarded."

"And if you are right, you will have your proof when she and Neville make their final attempt," Giles said, nodding. After a moment he added, "Neville is left-handed and wears a signet ring on his right hand."

"I know. That had occurred to me, as well."

"He is the one who struck Arden."

"Yes. And he will pay for it."

Lord Neville opened the door to his lodgings in response to a frantic tap, tap, tap on the door. A woman dressed in black with a heavy veil covering her face stood in the hall. The disguise did not conceal her identity from him.

"Christabel. What a pleasant surprise—"

She shoved past him.

"Is anything wrong?"

Pulling the veil away from her face, she said, "Everything is wrong. Royce visited me this morning. He intended to cry off, and wanted me to agree to end our engagement."

"What?"

"He thinks he is in love with that . . . that . . . American."

"His mistress? But that does not explain why he asked for his release. He surely cannot intend to marry her."

"He actually said he would marry her."

"He is mad!"

"Yes. Mad with lust for that whore. However, he changed his mind when I told him I loved him and allowed him to take a few liberties."

"How few? Never mind. I do not want to know. Well, then. Everything is all right."

"Everything is not all right. He is not the duke. We are not wed. He may change his mind again."

"I think not. Once he has the title, he will be bound to produce a worthy heir. He will need you for that."

"Yes. That is true. But he must become the duke soon. The masquerade ball—"

"—will be the perfect opportunity. Yes."

"Have you obtained the costume?"

"I have. It is identical to the one you described."

"Good. I must go now."

"Not quite yet. This is the first time you have visited my rooms in weeks."

"We decided we must be discreet. Now and for several months after I am wed. But then, after I have produced an heir and my position is secure, we will be together again."

Neville took her by the arms. She thought she was in charge, that she would not need him once she was a duchess. He decided it was time to prove her wrong. "We are together now. And you are seething with emotion. Anger. Jealousy. Greed. I can see the blood lust building in you. It excites me. You excite me. You want to be punished, Christabel. You know how soothing pain can be."

"No." She tried to jerk her arms free. "I must go. There is not time—"

He let her go. He could force her, but he wanted her to surrender to his will, not to his superior strength. "Make time. You want to keep me happy, Christabel. Otherwise, I might find I have another engagement the night of the Duke of Wolverton's ball."

Eyes flashing with resentment, Christabel removed her pelisse.

Neville smiled. Christabel would never escape from him. Once they had murdered together, she would always be his.

Twenty-three

He had not written so much as a thank-you note.

Men in the Regency were every bit as callous the morning after—several mornings after—as men in the twenty-first century with their insincere "I'll call you." She should have known. Evolution did not operate in reverse, after all. Arden flicked the brush through her hair one more time, then laid the silver-backed brush on her dressing table.

All right. She had burned her bridges. She had shot her wad. She had seduced and failed. At least she had tried. And she would have centuries to get over Lord Royce Warrick. Once she was back in her own time, his memory would fade like a forgettable episode of last year's sitcom.

One more day to get through and she would be out of here.

She had to go to the ball tonight, but like Cinderella, she would leave at midnight. The return trip to 2001 was scheduled to depart at two A.M. Everything was ready for her departure. She had packed the carpetbag. She had made arrangements with Mr. Mendlicott to set up a trust for her servants, so that they would be able to retire in comfort. She had written letters to Dora, William, and Giles saying good-bye. After crumpling countless half-written notes, she had given up trying to explain where or why she was going. The truth would not be believed, and she could not work up any enthusiasm for telling more lies.

She had not even attempted to write to Royce. What more could she say to him? She had told him she loved him. He had said "Thank you," polite gentleman that he was. Too bad she hadn't realized sooner that she was making love with the reformed version of Lord Royce Warrick, not the rogue.

"Are we having fun yet?" she asked her reflection mournfully.

Fun. What a stupid goal. She had wasted an unbelievable opportunity looking for a good time. She should have gone for knowledge, for broadening her horizons, for changing the course of world history. Instead, she had fallen in love with a man who refused to admit that he loved her back.

Being reckless and bold was not at all what it was cracked up to be. But she had not lied when she told Royce she had no regrets. She had known exactly what she was doing when she allowed her Freret side to take over. Risk taking was in her blood, and she had been itching to take a chance. She had risked her heart and lost, but she would not have had it any other way.

Once was more than enough, however. When she got home, she would be one hundred percent St. Clare, docile and demure. She would do everything Aunt Marie and Uncle Fred expected of her.

Except marry.

They could forget about her marrying the next CEO. She would never marry. She would devote her life to making St. Clare Spices the most successful company in the United States. The world. She would forget all about love and marriage and children. Who needed that old-fashioned life? She would be a shining example of the twenty-first-century woman, strong, independent, needing no one—

Enough.

She would get over this. She would.

Arden got up and went to the armoire, ready to get on with the evening. She had sent Jane away after her bath. She wanted to dress herself without having to explain the dress, pantyhose, or high-heeled sandals. She had taken the black dress out of its tissue paper wrapping earlier in the day and hung it in the armoire between her two riding habits. The silk and Lycra dress had not wrinkled at all.

She slipped the dress over her head. The dress was not completely black. Sprinkled with silver stars in a random pattern, it clung to every curve. The neckline was conservative, higher than the ball gowns favored by Regency misses, but the skirt ended three inches above her knees. Slipping her nylon-clad feet into black sandals with four-inch silver heels, she looked at herself in the cheval mirror. The tiny stars on the dress twinkled at her.

"This will do," she said, satisfied that Royce would have a memory of her that he would find hard to forget.

When she descended from her rented carriage, Wolverton House was ablaze with light. It shone from every window, and lanterns illuminated the gardens. Arden walked slowly up the steps, her dress hidden beneath a long black cape.

A buccaneer appeared in front of her as soon as the butler announced her arrival. She untied the cape and handed it to a waiting footman, watching the eyes behind the pirate's mask.

"That is your idea of a woman of the future?"

Royce sounded outraged. Delighted, Arden turned around slowly. "I suppose you do not approve."

"I do not." He snatched the cape from the footman, wrapped it around her, and began leading her to the small parlor. "You are not going into the ballroom dressed like that. One purpose of this ball is to restore you to respectability, or have you forgotten?"

"I don't care about being respectable. Or have you

forgotten?" Arden said haughtily, trying to pull free of his grasp. "And what I wear is none of your concern."

"It most certainly is—"

Lady Christabel de Courcy was announced.

Royce let Arden go. "Do not move. I must speak with Christabel."

"I'll move if I want to. You are not the boss of me." The words were spoken to his back.

"I will be," he threw back at her over his shoulder, closing the parlor door behind him.

Arden narrowed her eyes. What did that mean? Not much, considering that he had left her to go to Christabel's side. Arden could not resist peeking at her nemesis. Easing the door open, she looked. Lady Christabel was dressed in a filmy white gown. Gauze wings fluttered from her shoulders. She had come as an *angel?* Arden almost gagged. "Oh, please."

"Please, what, Arden?" Another pirate opened the door wide.

"Hello, Giles. Where did you come from? Where is Dora?"

"She and William are receiving guests in the ballroom upstairs. You are late."

"Not as late as Christabel."

"I am surprised she came."

"Why wouldn't she come?"

"Because . . . never mind. Royce will tell you later. Come, let me have your cape."

She handed it to him. He took one look, a long one, at her legs, and wrapped the cape around her again. "You cannot appear in public like that. What are you supposed to be?"

"A woman of the future. Don't you like it, either? I thought you were a leg man."

"A—a what?"

"I thought you liked looking at women's legs. Many men do, so it makes sense that in the future skirts will get shorter. Besides, short skirts are easier to walk in."

She shrugged out of the cape and let it fall to the floor. "I'm going to say hello to Dora and William." She sauntered off, leaving Giles staring after her with his mouth open.

Arden made her way to the ballroom, ignoring the stares and the gasps that followed her every step.

"Arden! What an unusual dress. And those shoes. How can you walk on such high heels?" Dora asked.

"Years of practice. To tell you the truth, my feet hurt already." She lowered her voice. "Has anything suspicious happened? Where are Dawkes and Murch?"

"Dawkes is that red devil lurking behind that pillar over there. He is keeping an eye on William. Murch is wearing a devil mask, as well, but his costume is black. I am not sure where he is at the moment. There are several Bow Street Runners, also dressed as some sort of devil. Nothing has happened yet, except Giles and Royce are—"

"Arden! You came!" William rushed up, followed by Dawkes. William was dressed in a toga, to complement his mother's Roman gown.

"Well, of course I came. I wouldn't have missed your very first ball."

"Will you dance with me?"

"Only if it's a waltz. I am afraid that is the only dance I know."

"There will be a waltz after I announce Mother's betrothal to Lord Stanton. Will you save that one for me?"

"Of course."

"Thank you. Now I must see to my other guests." With a quick bow, William hurried off, followed by his devilish shadow.

"My, William is the perfect host."

"Yes," Dora agreed, her eyes filling with tears. "He is growing up so fast."

"You were saying something about Royce and Giles," Arden prompted.

"Oh, yes. They are up to something. There have been several meetings the past few days, meetings from which I was excluded. I believe they know who is behind the attacks."

"They do? Who?"

"I do not know. They have not seen fit to confide in me. I swear, Arden, if I did not love Giles so much, I would refuse to announce our engagement tonight. He promised me a partnership, and here he is, on the evening of our betrothal, keeping secrets from me. Has Royce seen you in that costume?"

"Yes. He did not approve."

Another costumed guest made his bows to the duchess. "Your Grace, I believe this is our dance."

Dora was whirled away in the arms of a monk.

Arden strolled slowly around the perimeter of the ballroom, trying to keep William in sight. It was not easy. The crowd shifted and moved, blocking her view at times. She did not see Royce or Giles, but Christabel's white wings fluttered across Arden's line of sight several times, and there seemed to be devils everywhere.

At ten o'clock the music stopped and William appeared on a raised platform in front of the orchestra. He held up his hands, and the throng quieted. "Ladies and gentlemen. It is my pleasure to announce the betrothal of my mother, the Duchess of Wolverton, to Giles Fairfax, Viscount Stanton."

Cheers went up, Giles and Dora bowed, and the orchestra struck up a waltz. Most of the guests ignored the music, apparently preferring to congratulate the engaged couple. The crowd moved in a tight circle against the stage, making it almost impossible for Arden to get through.

She used her spike heels to advantage, and finally reached the spot where she had last seen William. He was not there. She looked for a devil in a red suit, but did not see one. Dawkes must be with William.

If Dawkes was with him, then he was all right.

But something didn't feel right. William would not have forgotten their waltz. A bit of fluttery white exiting the room caught her eye. Christabel? She hurried toward the French doors leading to the terrace overlooking the Wolverton House gardens. Stone steps led from the first-floor terrace to the ground floor.

Arden heard muffled footsteps on the stairs, and followed the sound. The Wolverton House garden boasted a small maze, with a fountain in the center. William had showed her the maze on one of her visits. Entering the maze, she paused and listened. Now she could hear nothing except the faint tinkling sound of the fountain. "William? Are you in here?"

A vision in white appeared at the first turn in the maze. "Christabel? Have you seen William?"

"No."

Arden took another step inside the maze. "I am sure I saw him come this way."

"No. He is not here. Go away, Miss St. Clare, unless you want to be embarrassed. Royce is meeting me here."

"Help!"

"That was William!" Shoving Christabel aside, Arden ran toward the sound. She reached a dead end, and wasted valuable time backtracking. "William? Where are you?"

Royce and Giles appeared in the maze. "Oh, thank God you're here. William yelled for help."

"We heard him. This way," said Royce. "Hurry."

They reached the center of the maze in a matter of seconds. A devil stood over a boy dressed as a Roman senator, holding his head under water. "Let him go!" Royce launched himself at the man, shoving him aside, then knocked him to the ground.

Giles and Arden pulled William from the pond.

"He is not breathing!" said Giles. "He is dead."

"No!" cried Arden. She knelt next to William and

egan CPR. After only a minute or two, William
hoked.

He sat up, turned his head, and vomited pond water.
"Who is the devil?" asked Arden, using an end of
he toga to wipe William's face. "Not Dawkes."

"No," said Giles. "We found Dawkes unconscious in
he butler's pantry. We were almost too late, Royce."

"I know. We did not anticipate the crush around the
lais after William made his announcement. *He* obvi-
usly did." Royce pointed to the man in the devil's
nask. "Take off your mask, de Courcy," ordered Royce,
olding a pistol aimed at his heart.

The man stripped off the mask, and bowed.

Arden gasped. "Lord Neville. But why? Why would
ou want to harm a little boy?"

"Not any little boy. A duke. And my darling wanted
o much to be a duchess. I did it for her, of course."

"Christabel. Where is she?" asked Royce, his voice
old.

"She was outside the maze when I got here," said
Arden.

"I will have the Runners look for her," said Giles,
eading for the exit.

Other people crowded into the maze, Dora among
hem.

In the confusion, Arden slipped away.

After Neville had been trussed up and handed over
o a magistrate, and after Dora had put William to bed,
he, Giles, and Royce returned to the ballroom. Most
f the guests remained, clustered in tight little circles,
iscussing the shocking events of the evening.

"Where is Arden?" asked Royce, searching the
rowd.

The footman Percy cleared his throat. "Miss St.
Clare left."

"Left? When? Where did she go?"

"A few minutes ago. She asked me for her cape, and
hen she left. I was to give you these notes later, but—"

Dora snatched the envelopes from his hand. "For me Giles, and William." She opened hers. "She is leaving."

"Leaving? When? Where is she going?" asked Royce.

"Home."

"Ah. Well, she is not leaving tonight," said Giles "No ship bound for America would set sail after dark."

"Give me my note," Royce demanded.

"There does not seem to be one for you," Dora said.

"Why not, may I ask?"

"I do not know. Could it be that you are not in her good graces?"

"No. Yes. I am going after her."

Royce did not bother with a carriage. He walked briskly to Arden's house and knocked on the door. After a wait, Jane opened the door, her eyes red-rimmed and swollen.

"Where is she?"

"Gone. Never to return."

"Have you been reading more novels? Where is her ship docked."

"She is not going by ship. Not one that sails the seas."

"Jane, do not force me to shake you. Where is Arden?"

"She has gone to a shop called Any Time, Any Place." Jane rattled off the direction.

"What sort of shop is open after midnight?"

"A time-travel shop. Miss St. Clare is returning to her own time in the future."

"Time-travel? Jane. Sit down and gather your wits."

"I am telling the truth. Miss St. Clare traveled here through time from February 27, 2001. If you love her, you must go after her and stop her, or you will never see her again."

"You really must stop reading those horrific novels."

Jane grabbed the ends of his cravat and tugged. "Listen to me. Arden is from the future. And she is going back because she thinks you do not love her. How else can you explain her pie-jamas? The dress she was wearing tonight? The way she appeared in the forest without a horse or carriage?"

"What was that address again?"

She repeated it. "She leaves at two A.M."

"I will stop her. Never fear." Now he sounded like the hero in a melodramatic novel. But if what Jane said was true, he did not have time to think, only time to act. Royce returned to Wolverton House and had his horse saddled. He rode as quickly as possible through the streets crowded with carriages, picking up speed once he left the fashionable part of town.

Arriving on a dark street, with light showing from only one shop window, he slowed his mount's gait to a walk. Noises behind him—the clop, clop of shod hooves and the creak of carriage wheels—made him turn. He could see nothing in the gloom.

Royce dismounted and tied his horse's reins to a post in front of the shop. He could just make out the name on the wooden sign above the door: *Any Time, Any Place. Tobias Thistlewaite, Prop.*

Thistlewaite. That was the name of the man Arden said abandoned her in the forest. A chill went down his spine. It could not be true. But it explained so much. Arden's strange way of speaking, her underclothes. The things she knew—how to throw a man over her shoulder, how to revive a drowned boy.

A shadow moved inside the shop. Royce knocked briskly on the door.

"Go away," said a gruff voice. "We are closed."

"Let me in this instant, my good man. I must see Miss St. Clare."

The door opened, and Arden stood in the doorway. She was dressed in trousers, unlike any he had ever seen before. A short, middle-aged man hovered behind her. "Be quick about it. Time waits for no man."

"Or woman. You said that before, Tobias. Hell
Royce. How did you know where to find me?"

"Jane told me."

"Oh. Well, I guess a woman has no secrets from h
maid. It was nice of you to come to say good-by
Good-bye." She held out her hand.

"You are not leaving." He took her hand and pulle
Thistlewaite grabbed her other hand and held o

"She is leaving. Time marches on."

"Stay, Arden."

"Wait one moment, please, Tobias. Why should I?
she asked Royce.

"No delays. No postponements. No refunds. It's no
or never," said the time-travel agent.

"I love you," said Royce, desperate to convince he
but with no time to do so. "Stay with me."

"The time has come," said Tobias. "Go or stay, bu
you must choose now."

"I can't. I need more time." This was too importan
a decision to make impulsively. "I don't know why—

"No time to spare. Choose." The shop gave
shimmy.

With sudden clarity, Arden realized that some im
pulses were rooted in reason and knowledge. She kne
that Royce was her heart's desire. That had to b
enough. "Stay. I choose to stay. Good-bye, Tobias." A
den stepped through the doorway onto the street.

Any Time, Any Place gave a shudder and disap
peared, leaving in its stead a shop with a dilapidate
facade. A To Let sign was propped against the dust
glass of the shop window.

Royce pulled her into his arms and hugged her unti
she thought her ribs would crack. "You stayed."

"Yes. I did. I'm not sure why I did. I ought to hav
learned not to act on impulse—"

"You stayed because you love me, and I love you
and because you know I cannot live without you."

"Now you say that—now that you know what kind of woman Christabel really is."

"I knew before that, but I could not—"

"Break your engagement. Honor. I know."

"—tell you until Christabel was exposed."

"You knew she was the killer?"

"I had strong suspicions after I went to her and asked to be released from the betrothal."

Arden's eyes shimmered with love and unshed tears. "You asked to be released? When?"

"The day you and I made love. I wanted to return to you that same day a free man. But something she said made me suspect her, and I decided to give her enough rope to hang herself. I thought there would be time to explain all this to you after William was safe. But you ran from me. And you did not write me a note."

"I'm sorry. I couldn't think what to say to you that I had not already said."

"I forgive you. You gave up the future for me. I am the most fortunate of men—"

A shot rang out.

Royce staggered and fell to the ground.

He awoke in his own bed. Dora, Giles, and Arden were hovering about him. He reached out, and Arden took his hand in both of hers. "What happened?"

"Christabel tried to kill you. Or me. We cannot be sure which of us she intended the bullet for."

"She must have followed me to the shop. I thought I heard a carriage . . . Has she been caught? Where is she?"

Giles, holding Dora close to him, answered. "Murch saw her leaving the ball. He followed her to Any Time, Any Place, but he did not realize what she intended until she fired the gun. Once that happened, he grabbed her. She has been turned over to the magistrate."

"I cannot believe she wanted to be a duchess enough to kill for it," said Dora, shuddering.

"It is over now. William is safe, and we can plan our wedding. Perhaps we should leave Arden and Royce alone."

"Alone? With him? What about my reputation?" asked Arden, grinning. "I do believe the rogue is back."

"You are a heroine. You saved William's life one more time. Your reputation is above reproach in this family," said Dora. "And Royce is too weak to cause too much trouble. Come, Giles. We have plans to make."

The couple left arm in arm.

As soon as the door closed behind them, Royce tugged on Arden's hand, tumbling her onto the bed beside him.

"Am I badly hurt?"

"No. The bullet only grazed your temple. The doctor says you will be good as new in a day or two."

"Did he by any chance prescribe massage as a treatment?"

"Of course not. Rubbing your head would not help the wound to heal."

"I had in mind other parts of my anatomy. I am on my back, in my bed, and I do not seem to be wearing any trousers."

"You want me to rub you . . . there?"

"Yes. Please."

"How roguish of you to ask me to massage that particular part of your anatomy. I am sure no proper English lady would do such a thing."

"Isn't it fortunate that you are not—"

"A lady?"

"—English."

Arden laughed out loud, and after a moment, her untamed rogue joined in.

Epilogue

Tobias Thistlewaite closed the door behind his latest customer. Another satisfactory trip—she had found her heart's desire as he had promised she would—and a very profitable one, besides. Arden St. Clare had paid for a round trip, and he had only had to use the magic in Merlin's Stone for a one-way voyage. His research had led him to believe that only a finite number of trips through time were possible. Unfortunately, he had not yet discovered what that number was.

A nagging worry was that when the last trip was taken, he would be stranded in some inhospitable time. For that reason, Tobias tended to return to times he liked, and to steer his customers toward those times, as well.

He sat at the Sheraton table and opened the *Wall Street Journal* dated April 10, 2002. When he began his business, Tobias had read several major dailies, among them the *London Times,* the *New York Times,* and the *Chicago Tribune,* from a variety of prosperous and peaceful eras. He had found the *Wall Street Journal* the most reliable source of potential clients, and with a minor but useful spell taught him by his mother, he had arranged for a continuing subscription through time.

A story from Seattle caught his eye. Dot.com millionaires were notoriously unreceptive to time-travel.

Dorks, nerds, and computer geeks apparently lacked the ability to believe in the possibility of magic, but he could always hope. They had so much disposable income, and so little to spend it on. Sooner or later one of them would take the plunge into the space-time continuum.

Perhaps sooner than he had anticipated. The subject of the story, H. Walter Harrington IV, was a descendant of one of the largest winners in the Gold Rush of '49. Not content to rest on his forefather's bankroll, H. Walter had tripled, some said quadrupled, his family's fortune by providing venture capital to the most daring of the e-commerce crowd. His personal fortune rivaled that of Bill Gates.

The story revealed an interesting fact about H. Walter, in addition to his net worth. He was the sponsor of the Seattle Medieval Fair, a tribute to knights and fair maidens complete with medieval food, costumes, and entertainment. Jousts, jesters, and troubadours would figure prominently in the affair.

It turned out that H. Walter was enamored of the Middle Ages. His dream, confessed to the *WSJ* reporter in a moment of camaraderie not usual between billionaires and the press, was to be a knight in shining armor. He longed for the days of old, when a man's home really was a castle, and when women lived to serve their lords and masters. He confided that he could not even count on his personal assistant, Victoria Desmond, to obey his every command. He paid her a fortune—a six-figure salary, stock options, 401K—gave her a company penthouse and a new Lexus every year, and she still said "no" to him more often than not.

The reporter, a female, speculated that H. Walter's attitude toward what he referred to as the weaker sex could explain his bachelor status, despite the sex appeal generated in large part by his great wealth—but he did have that dimple in his chin.

Tobias folded the newspaper and smiled. He had

found his next candidate for time-travel. Using a calculator, he figured the cost of the trip, taking into account the size of the Harrington fortune and the personality of the traveler—H. Walter was, according to the *WSJ* reporter, a combination of a hardheaded businessman and hopeless romantic. Ms. Desmond was quoted as saying her boss also exhibited a strong streak of male chauvinism which, thus far, she had been unable to correct.

H. Walter Harrington IV was the perfect candidate for travel to Medieval England. He and his twenty-first-century political incorrectness would fit right in with the pragmatic English barons who hid their ruthless and bloody quests for wealth and power behind a pretty code of chivalry.

Tobias was not a fan of the Middle Ages. People like H. Walter, who romanticized the era, tended to forget things like the plague, constant armed conflict, and no indoor plumbing. But for the big bucks Tobias could wheedle out of H. Walter Harrington IV, he would risk the trip.

Humming a ditty from 1284, Tobias consulted his spell book and muttered the words that would take him to Seattle, Washington on the opening day of the Medieval Fair.

ABOUT THE AUTHOR

Linda Kay lives in Louisiana. She is currently working on her next time-travel romance, TO CHARM A KNIGHT, which will be published in November 2001. Linda loves to hear from readers and you may write to her c/o Zebra Books. Please include a self-addressed stamped envelope if you wish a response.

Put a Little Romance in Your Life With
Constance O'Day-Flannery

Thrilling Romance from
Meryl Sawyer

__Half Moon Bay $6.50US/$8.00CAN
  0-8217-6144-7

__The Hideaway $5.99US/$7.50CAN
  0-8217-5780-6

__Tempting Fate $6.50US/$8.00CAN
  0-8217-5858-6

__Unforgettable $6.50US/$8.00CAN
  0-8217-5564-1

Call toll free **1-888-345-BOOK** to order by phone or use this coupon to order by mail.

Name _____

Address _____

City _____ State _____ Zip _____

Please send me the books I have checked above.

I am enclosing $_____
Plus postage and handling* $_____
Sales tax (in New York and Tennessee) $_____
Total amount enclosed $_____

*Add $2.50 for the first book and $.50 for each additional book.

Send check or money order (no cash or CODs) to:

Kensington Publishing Corp., 850 Third Avenue, New York, NY 10022

Prices and Numbers subject to change without notice.

All orders subject to availability.

Check out our website at **www.kensingtonbooks.com**

Merlin's Legacy

A Series From
Quinn Taylor Evans

Put a Little Romance in Your Life With

Stella Cameron

__The Best Revenge $6.50US/$8.00CAN
0-8217-5842-X

__French Quarter $6.99US/$8.50CAN
0-8217-6251-6

__Guilty Pleasures $5.99US/$7.50CAN
0-8217-5624-9

__Pure Delights $5.99US/$6.99CAN
0-8217-4798-3

__Sheer Pleasures $5.99US/$6.99CAN
0-8217-5093-3

__True Bliss $5.99US/$6.99CAN
0-8217-5369-X

Call toll free **1-888-345-BOOK** to order by phone, use this coupon
to order by mail, or order online at **www.kensingtonbooks.com.**

Name_____
Address_____
City _____ State _____ Zip_____
Please send me the books I have checked above.
I am enclosing $_____
Plus postage and handling* $_____
Sales tax (in New York and Tennessee only) $_____
Total amount enclosed $_____
*Add $2.50 for the first book and $.50 for each additional book.
Send check or money order (no cash or CODs) to:
Kensington Publishing Corp., Dept. C.O., 850 Third Avenue, New York, NY 1002
Prices and numbers subject to change without notice.
All orders subject to availability.
Visit our website at **www.kensingtonbooks.com.**